Praise for Victoria Aveyard

'A sizzling, imaginative thriller, where romance and revolution collide, where power and justice duel. It's exhilarating. Compelling. Action-packed. Unputdownable' *USA Today*

'Aveyard weaves a compelling new world of action-packed surprises . . . inventive, character-driven' *Kirkus*

'With world building to rival the likes of George R. R. Martin, a cast of fiery and powerful characters and betrayals which left many gaping, *Red Queen* is a victory worthy of its debut Crown' *Guardian*

'A whirlwind of betrayal and plot twists' *Sci-Fi Now*

'A clever blend of *The Hunger Games*, *The Selection*, *Graceling* and *Divergent*' *Starburst*

'The dystopian novel will please fans of *The Hunger Games* but uses a supernatural twist to explore the theme of social injustice'
We Love This Book

'If you're having hangovers over the *Divergent* series, or having withdrawal symptoms from *The Hunger Games*, then this is the book that will get you out of that funk' Dark Readers

'A wonderful mash up of Ancient Rome and Marie Antoinette with a dash of Catherine Fisher's *Incarceron* and Ridley Scott's *Gladiator*, not to mention some of Marvel Comic's box of tricks . . . Exciting and original' Sam Hawksmoor, author of the *The Repossession Trilogy*

Also by Victoria Aveyard

Novels

Red Queen

Glass Sword

King's Cage

War Storm

Novella Collection

Cruel Crown

BROKEN THRONE

A RED QUEEN COLLECTION

VICTORIA AVEYARD

An Orion paperback

First published in Great Britain in 2019
by Orion Fiction,
This paperback edition published in 2020
by Orion Fiction,
an imprint of The Orion Publishing Group Ltd.,
Carmelite House, 50 Victoria Embankment
London EC4Y 0DZ

An Hachette UK company

3 5 7 9 10 8 6 4

A CIP catalogue record for this book is available from the British Library.

ISBN (Paperback) 978 1 4091 7603 9

Printed and bound in Great Britain by Clays Ltd, Elcograf S.p.A.

www.orionbooks.co.uk

I can't believe you've been with me this long. Thank you.

Throughout my studies in Norta, I always found myself working around the edges of events known only as the Calamities. I have always been fascinated with the histories of our distant past, as well as the lessons therein. Unfortunately, the pre-Silverian time lines have always been riddled with holes and are difficult to verify, as primary sources were largely lost. Only relatively recent events (recent being within the last 1500 years) can be considered set in stone. Despite being already accepted points of record, they are still vital, like the first steps down a pathway.

Therefore, I must base all my research on this relevant time line, correlating with both the archives at Delphie and the vaults of Horn Mountain (note: dates are based on the Nortan calendar; my apologies to the Republic):

- OE = Old Era, before the formation of Norta
- NE = New Era, after the formation of Norta

Before 1500 OE: Civilization across the continent still in state of flux following the Calamities

1500 OE: Beginning of the Reformation Period—civilizations of the continent begin to stabilize and rebuild

950 OE: Trial of Barr Rambler—earliest verifiable record of Silver individuals (a strongarm displays his abilities while being tried for thievery)

~900 OE: Foundation of the Finix Dynasty, formation of the Kingdom of Ciron, the oldest Silver-led kingdom on the continent (according to Cironian lore)

202 OE: Following civil war, the Kingdom of Tiraxes restructures into the present-day triarchy

180 OE: Formation of the Kingdom of Tetonia in what will become present-day Montfort. Tetonia is one of many small kingdoms and lands to sprout up in the mountains

72 OE: Formation of the Kingdom of the Lakelands through the conquests of the Cygnet Line

0 NE: Formation of modern Norta under the dynasty of House Calore—the smaller kingdoms and city-states of the region are forged into one

2 NE: An alliance between Piedmont and Norta is established through marriage, forming the bedrock of a longstanding bond between both nations.

170–195 NE: The Border Wars between the Lakelands and various Prairie warlords

200 NE: The Lakelander War begins between Norta and the Lakelands

296 NE: Dane Davidson, future premier of the Free Republic of Montfort, flees Norta

321 NE: The Nortan Civil War—secession of the Rift, abdication of King Tiberias VII of Norta, fall of the Kingdom of Norta, abdication of King Ptolemus of the Rift, abdication of Queen Evangeline of the Rift, formation of the Nortan States

The above are selected highlights of historical fact, which can be found in most any passable text from Ascendant to Harbor Bay. I'm not terribly interested in what I've already learned, and neither are the scholars of Horn Mountain. After weeks of study, to Sara's chagrin, I've attempted to compile some kind of overview of the time before the Reformation. It must be noted, the information is hardly scientific and, at present, impossible to correlate. Much of what I've encountered directly contradicts other sources, therefore I have attempted to paint a picture of the overlap.

Most helpful has been a painstakingly preserved collection of paper annuals or pamphlets, kept in a climate-controlled and pressurized room deep in the vaults of Horn Mountain. Records indicate they were stored there before the existence of Montfort, more than a thousand years ago when the vaults were first sealed. I must assume that the vaults, originally built to survive the Calamities, were stocked with information meant to outlive their owners. Several of the documents appear to be of the same set, and feature what were once beautiful photographs. Translation has been difficult, but not impossible. One set was perhaps called Nation's Geography or the like, while the other is quite simply labeled Time.

First, we must work backward from a fixed point in history—this being, for us, the 1500 NE benchmark that begins the Reformation. Everything before and during the Calamities is shrouded in historical fog, with myth often overtaking fact.

We know for certain that the Calamities themselves effectively ended or severely crippled the

I was also extremely partial to some illustrated books detailing the exploits of a crime-fighting, angst-ridden bat person.

civilizations that came before our own, so much so that we are still, even now, piecing together a picture of that time.

According to the sources in Horn Mountain, the first of the so-called Calamities—the most destructive and longest lasting—was a catastrophic change in climate due to widespread pollution on a global scale. It worsened over decades, each year worse than the last. Drought rocked much of the world, including lands beyond the oceans bordering our continent, places I have not yet begun to fathom.

It's possible those places beyond our continent no longer exist, or are still in reformation periods of their own. For the Silver kingdoms, war and self-interest have kept us restricted to our own backyards, so to speak. Perhaps the same can be said of the rest.

Drought, in time, led to agricultural collapse, famine, migration, upheaval, and war in the affected areas, with many refugees attempting to flee into the regions still producing food. Resource wars sparked everywhere and often, over water, fuel, land, etc. These were largely seen in clashes between organizations, or between organizations and indigenous peoples. Very few larger governments were directly in conflict in the first years of the resource wars.

The changing climate fed into deadly storm systems, both on land and at sea, driving many people inland from the coasts, where they found themselves facing blizzards, ice storms, tornadoes, and drought-born, long-lasting dust storms. Rapidly changing temperature norms effectively pushed humans to the brink, while leading to the extinction of many plants and animals. Sea-level rise also contributed to the boxing-in effect, forcing populations into smaller and smaller areas of habitation. There was also extreme flooding, which transformed the mouth of the Great River and the surrounding region, submerging hundreds of miles of land to form the coastlines we know today.

In conjunction with flooding, widespread earthquakes changed the western coastline, forming a sea in what was once a massive valley. Long-dormant volcanoes erupted in the northwest, shooting millions of tons of ash into the air.

It is interesting to note that, while multiple earthquakes and natural disasters laid waste to the continent, the most feared cataclysm never came to pass. According to the preserved texts, scientists and civilians alike were incredibly concerned by the possible eruption of the caldera volcano beneath what is now the Paradise Valley.

Said eruption would have changed the world climate and destroyed most of the continent we now live on. At the time of the preserved texts, scientists postulated that the caldera basin was long overdue for eruption. By now, we are far beyond that. I will be petitioning the Premier and the People's Assembly to organize an analytical team to keep tabs on the Paradise Valley and the sleeping giant beneath it.

It's no surprise that, in the midst of such turmoil, disease sprang up in many regions, spreading outward even into "safe" groups. Many diseases were mutated versions of less-threatening illnesses or previously eradicated diseases finding new purchase in once-protected populations. Millions the world over succumbed to illnesses that had once been considered curable, and most civilizations began to fall apart.

All these, of course, were actions of nature or, some might argue, actions of the gods. Not so for the last of the Calamities, an act of choice and an act of men. We have military might today, bombs and missiles of varying size and quality, but nothing to compare to the monstrous weapons our ancestors created. Somehow, by splitting the tiniest pieces of existence, scientists of the old world discovered they could make the most destructive of weapons, called nuclear bombs. These were, throughout the various disasters above, used across the known world to varying degrees of destruction. Even before the advent of nuclear war, governments and citizens feared these weapons. Many planned accordingly. The vaults at Horn Mountain were themselves designed to survive such an attack, carved deep into the rock. According to the texts there, our own continent was largely spared the worst of these weapons. There are lands across the ocean that no longer exist, now either frozen over or sand swept, flattened by the wrath of a few and the ignorance of many. Far worse than the bombs themselves was, apparently, the aftermath. Radiation disease spread with the smoke and ash. Entire countries were destroyed, civilizations collapsing. Such is the case on our own continent, as demonstrated by the ruins of the Wash and the Cog. These lands are still too irradiated to reinhabit, poisoned by deeds thousands of years ago.

Despite what my research tells me, I find the vast destruction achieved by military technology to be inconceivable, and will do more to corroborate these findings. It simply cannot be possible. Even the strongest of Silvers cannot level a city, and even our bombs cannot cross an ocean to incinerate tens of thousands of people. Perhaps this is my own ignorance, but I cannot fathom the death of millions by the order of one.

There are few fixed markers of time during the Calamities, especially with long-lasting events such as climate change, which is still largely in play with our own world.

The scientists of Montfort have been attempting ice digs that I don't entirely understand, but their work in the north is reportedly invaluable to the time line before the Reformation and even during the Calamities themselves. I will record what I can of their findings when they become available, but so far, early reports seem to indicate that radiated ashfall landed in the far north sometime around two thousand years ago. This places at least one act of nuclear warfare (ANW) at approximately 2000 OE, five hundred years before the Reformation. We can then ascertain that true collapse, at least on our continent, lasted half a millennium before civilizations began re-forming.

Connecting the Reformation and the ANW to a pre-Silverian, pre-Calamities time line proves tricky, and again we must look for points of crossover. There are several mentions of catastrophic drought in the preserved texts utilizing the date 2015 CE (sometimes recorded as AD; could be an error in translation—must verify) onward. Other Calamitous events, such as earthquakes, sea-level rise, hurricanes, and the like are mentioned throughout fifty to sixty years' worth of the preserved texts, but rapidly grow in size and scope toward the end of the collection. They are, however, small in comparison to the earthquake that split the western coast and the flood that re-formed the Great River Delta.

Again, translation can be unreliable. Some texts vary in quality of preservation, and to my surprise and chagrin, many seem to disagree on the severity or magnitude of events, particularly those regarding climate. While one record might consider a warm winter to be the harbinger of a catastrophic climate shift, another downplays the same period of time or highlights a colder winter elsewhere. This pattern is very troubling, though I assume most consumers of these documents were able to identify the bias, as well as the lies or manipulations being presented.

I have managed to find mention of a small nuclear attack dated to the year 2022 CE. I could not discern the combatants involved, only that the attack occurred on a different continent, far from large population centers, in a cold climate. This leads me to think it was a show of strength rather than an act of war, if something so foolish can be believed. However, it does mean, when taken in conjunction with the radiated-ashfall dating, that at the very least the year 2000 OE

in our calendar may have been the equivalent of the year 2022 CE in the pre-Calamities calendar. But, if pressed, I would assume that some time separates the two, perhaps a decade or even a century. The research is slow going, but I very much feel that these steps are in the right direction, and the information I'm able to find will be vital to our future.

If anything were to happen to the vaults of Horn Mountain, our own civilization would lose any link to the past and what warnings it left us. Therefore, I will be spearheading an effort to translate, to the best of our ability, as much of the later volumes of the preserved texts as possible. If nothing else, world leaders should know what befell our ancestors, so they can avoid such disaster in the future. I am particularly concerned by man-made climate change, an easy trap to fall into, especially for advancing societies. I speculate that it has already begun in pieces, but I'm hopeful that our nations can avoid what our ancestors did not.

I have included a translation on the next page, albeit incomplete. It paints a stark picture of the sword hanging over all of us.

New studies <UNTRANSLATED> current drought in the Middle East (?) is the worst in the region <UNTRANSLATED> last 900 years <UNTRANSLATED> Exacerbated by global warming <UNTRANSLATED> Rainfall down 40% <UNTRANSLATED> Deep wells draining aquifers <UNTRANSLATED> crop failure <UNTRANSLATED> millions flee into already strained cities <UNTRANSLATED> political instability <UNTRANSLATED> civil war <UNTRANSLATED> refugee crisis across region <UNTRANSLATED> into bordering nations <UNTRANSLATED> political fallout worldwide

This is an integral piece of the puzzle we must finish if we can hope to understand the world that came before ours, and how we came to exist in the world now.

I am simply one curious man, but perhaps I can take at least a step forward into the fog surrounding us, so that others might follow. You have some of your mother in you, Cal, enough to delight in the knowledge of how things work. Hopefully these copies of my studies are of some interest to you. Hopefully you'll join me in clearing the fog.

—Uncle Julian

I'm aware you're well versed in the history of your house, having taught you some of it myself. But I thought you'd like to keep these for your own, instead of relying on the survival of the Nortan libraries, as well as your own flawed memory. Yes, I said flawed. I apologize that the record of my own house and your mother's family is not so extensive, but I was regrettably uninterested in my heritage in my youth. And my bloodline is not so well documented as a line of kings for some reason. So strange. —Uncle Julian

Caesar Calore
Zira Cerolan
CAESARION
m. RIANNON RHAMBOS
JULIANA
m. GARION SAVANNA
High Prince of Piedmont
FYRIAS
died in battle
JULIAS
m. ELLYN MACANTHOS
PIEDMONT
ROYALTY
JULIAS
died in battle
TIBERIAS I
m. ALISE GLIACON
m. PRINCESS IRANNE
of the Lakelands
CRISSAN
m. IRINA IRAL
TIBERIAS II
m. IRINA CALORE
FYRION
m. LADY CRESTINA TITANOS
CAESERA
m. LORD EVANDER SAMOS
CRISSAN
m. IRINA CALORE
CAESAR II
died young
JULIAS II
m. LADY SERENA SKONOS
CREST CALORE
exiled
EXILED
CALORE LINE
SAMOS
MAIN LINE
CALORE
MAIN LINE
JULIAS III
m. HELENA MERANDUS
MARCAS
m. PRINCESS ELISABETA
of the Tidewater
TIBERIA
m. LORD ERIK MERANDUS
IRINA
m. PRINCE CARLES
of the Lowcountry
SARIANE
m. PRINCE ORLEAN
of the River
JULIAS
died in battle
AERION
m. MIRA OSANOS
MERANDUS
MAIN LINE
PIEDMONT
ROYALTY
PIEDMONT
ROYALTY
ANDURA
m. BRANNON BLONOS
MARCAS

MARCAS
m. MORGANA RHAMBOS
m. WARLORD ROZIN
of the Mirrors
TIBALT
m. PRINCESS ARIELLE
of the River
AMBROSIN
KING TRIARCH
of the North
VARIOUS COMPANIONS
TIBERIAS III
m. TARIONNE OSANOS
CAESERA CALORE
m. LORD VOLTER SAMOS
PRAIRIE
MAIN LINE
JULIANA CALORE
m. LORD LAROS HAVEN
TIRAXIAN
ROYALTY
SAMOS
MAIN LINE
TIBERIAS IV
m. NIGHTINGALE WELLE
HAVEN
MAIN LINE
LEONORA
KING VOLO SAMOS
m. LARENTIA VIPER
AERIK
died in battle
TIBERIAS V
m. ANABEL LEROLAN
PTOLEMUS SAMOS
TIBERIANE
m. LORD CYRON TYROS
EVANGELINE SAMOS
TIBERIAS VI
m. CORIANE JACOS
m. ELARA MERANDUS
TYROS
MAIN LINE
AERIN
m. PRINCE ANNOS
of the Tidewater
TEREZA
m. PRINCE AUGUST
of the Floridians
PIEDMONT
ROYALTY
LEONORA CALORE
m. PRINCE HELION
of the River
Tiberias VII
MAVEN
PIEDMONT
ROYALTY

Jacos Family Tree

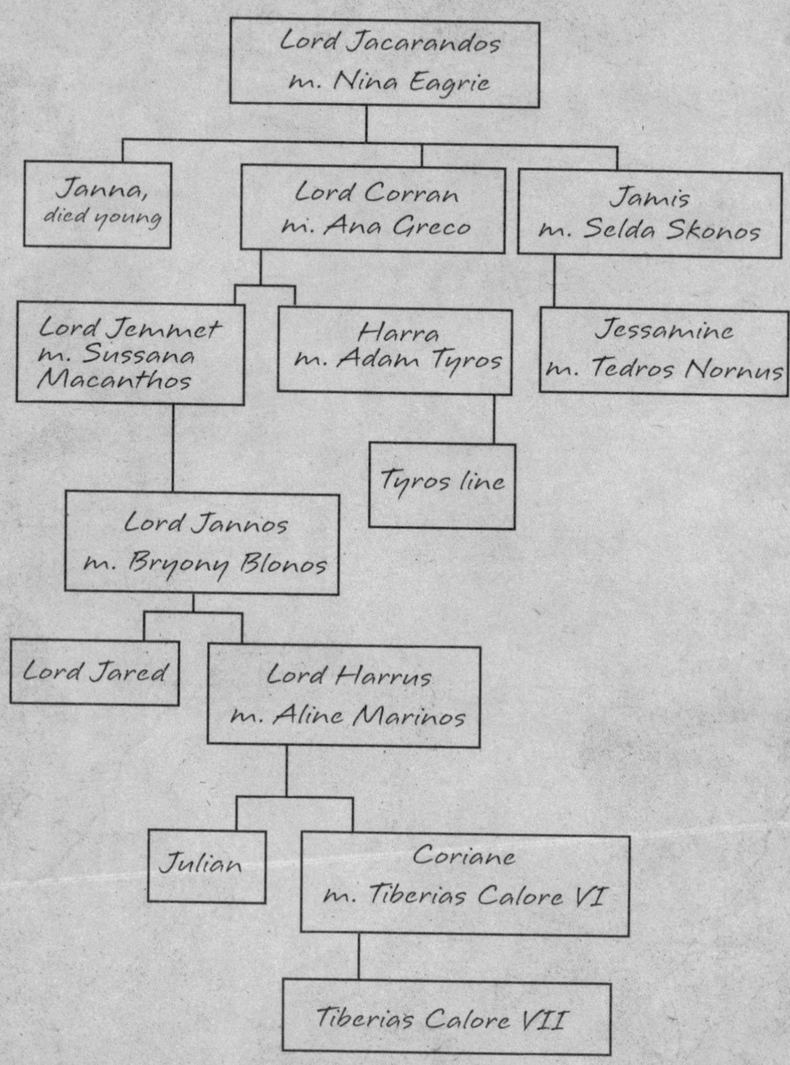

Lord Jacarandos
m. Nina Eagrie
Janna,
died young
Lord Corran
m. Ana Greco
Jamis
m. Selda Skonos
Lord Jemmet
m. Sussana
Macanthos
Harra
m. Adam Tyros
Jessamine
m. Tedros Nornus
Tyros line
Lord Jannos
m. Bryony Blonos
Lord Jared
Lord Harrus
m. Aline Marinos
Julian
Coriane
m. Tiberias Calore VI
Tiberias Calore VII

The history books haven't quite caught up to you, though I doubt you mind.
—JJ

MONARCHS *of* HOUSE CALORE

CAESAR I

JANUARY 1, 0–OCTOBER 3, 37 NE

So dedicated to his new dynasty, nation, and image was Alexandrus Caesar Calore that he waited a full two months after conquering Norta to coronate himself at the stroke of midnight on the turn of the year. He declared a new age with the beginning of his reign. Therefore, the Nortan calendar starts at the exact moment the crown touched a Calore's head. Though a warrior first, King Caesar was a skilled diplomat. He married his daughter Juliana to the High Prince of Piedmont, cementing a long-standing alliance to protect Norta's southern border. King Caesar also created the rite of Queenstrial. Except under extraordinary circumstances or when marrying outside the kingdom, any Calore heir to the throne would wed the strongest suitor who presented him- or herself. King Caesar also founded the new capital at Archeon, building Whitefire Palace and the Nortan seat of government. The king died in a dueling "accident," struck through the heart. The blunted training sword of his opponent had been replaced with a sharpened blade. Legend says the last word King Caesar ever spoke was "Fyrias," the name of his youngest son, who had died in a skirmish along the border of the Disputed Lands. Following an investigation, his dueling partner was executed, but historians postulate that Caesar's own son arranged his father's murder.

CAESARION

October 3, 37–July 20, 44 NE

Filling the footsteps of a great father proved difficult for Caesarion, who grew up with little knowledge of war and less military skill than his father. He was more preoccupied with the luxuries of the monarchy, and began building the summer palace: the Hall of the Sun. Before its completion, he died at sea when his pleasure yacht sank off the Bahrn Islands. Witnesses say the king drowned due to the weight of his jewels and crown, though there are reports of sharks feeding on him as well. It's possible the sinking of his ship was orchestrated by those loyal to his father, the murdered king.

JULIAS I

July 20, 44–August 1, 60 NE

In stark contrast to his father, Julias was a warrior to the bone, and sometimes to a fault. He regularly fought with the lords to the north in the Kingdom of the Lakelands. His firstborn son and heir, Julias, died in one such skirmish at the age of seventeen. His death plunged his father into deep mourning, and he died quietly, after refusing skinhealer treatment for illness.

TIBERIAS THE GREAT

August 1, 60–November 10, 105 NE

The great-grandson of Caesar Calore is considered his true successor, and remains the longest-reigning monarch of the Calore dynasty. Over the course of his forty-five-year reign, Tiberias I finished the Hall of the Sun, bolstered relations with the Lakelands to the north, and extended Nortan borders to include the entirety of the Rift. Pieces of the Samos lands still resisted Calore rule, and Tiberias himself led an army himself into the Rift hills. The remaining Samos rebels were brought to heel, and, against the urging of his council, Tiberias did not eradicate the Samos dynasty, instead granting them clemency in exchange for their loyalty and lands. The governance of the Rift was given to House Laris, though House Samos remained one of the strongest families in the kingdom.

King Tiberias also pioneered the use of Red tech towns, establishing several throughout Norta. The Silver kingdom would reap the benefits of his rule for many centuries, growing in economic and technological might. After many years without producing an heir, Tiberias I divorced his Nortan wife to marry a Lakelander princess, who bore him three children. He died peacefully in his sleep.

TIBERIAS II

August 1, 105–May 30, 107 NE

Tiberias II succeeded his father as an older man and ruled for less than two years. He died suddenly of an ailment cited only as "bad nerves." Even over such a brief period of time, it became clear that he was unfit for the throne and would most likely have been easily manipulated by his council and lords had he lived.

CAESAR II

May 30, 107–December 9, 118 NE

Because King Caesar was not yet of age when he came to the throne, his grandmother, the Lakelander princess Iranne, and his mother, Irina Calore, ruled as his regents. His uncle, Prince Fyrion Calore, objected to a foreign ruler and claimed that he was better suited to the throne. Fyrion and his wife, backed by her Titanos family, led a civil war against Caesar

II. They were eventually put down by the forces of the Queen Regent and Princess Caesera. Caesera, the daughter of Tiberias the Great, had married into House Samos, and their support was integral to keeping Caesar II in power. Prince Fyrion was executed for his attempt to usurp the throne, and his infant son, Prince Crest Calore, was exiled from Norta. He fathered a cadet branch of House Calore in the west, but records of such a dynasty have been lost or destroyed. Fyrion's line, if still in existence, would be the only other branch of the Calore tree left.

Caesar II himself was a sickly boy, constantly watched by Skonos guards, and he required blood healing regularly. He is described as having "rotted away," dying at age twenty-five. He had no children, and it is rumored that his illness was due to his parents, Tiberias II and Queen Irina, being first cousins.

JULIAS II

December 9, 118–March 22, 140 NE

Because Caesar II had no children, the crown passed to his younger brother. Julias II married Serena Skonos, one of his brother's constant guardians, and showed none of his brother's genetic illnesses. For this reason, it is believed by some historians that his father was not Tiberias II and that his mother, Queen Irina, had had an affair with someone at the Nortan court. Julias II was largely unbothered by such whisperings, as his mother was a Calore by birth herself, and he was still a direct descendant of Caesar I. Most importantly, Julias II was a burner like all the Calore kings before him. If his mother had been unfaithful, it would have been extremely rare for him to have inherited her ability and not his true father's. His reign was otherwise quiet, as the kingdoms of Norta, Piedmont, and the Lakelands were at peace. During his thirty-two-year rule, Julias II undertook a campaign of arena building, expanding the practice of First Friday throughout the kingdom. He wed two of his daughters to Piedmont princes, deepening the bonds between the two kingdoms.

JULIAS III

MARCH 22, 140–DECEMBER 28, 151 NE

Despite his father's urging, Julias III bypassed the rite of Queenstrial for a love match, and married Helena of House Merandus. Historians openly wonder if the young prince was swayed by her ability rather than a romance. After Julias III was coronated, his son and heir embarked on a tour of Norta. While visiting the border at Maiden Falls, the convoy was set upon by Red bandits, and Prince Julias was killed. In retaliation, Julias III decreed that the Red towns around the border would be razed and cleared to make way for a fortress city. He commanded the Reds to build Corvium and then conscripted most of them into the Nortan military. The rest were deported to tech cities throughout the kingdom to bolster worker population. No Calore ever named a child Julias again, as it was considered a bad-luck name.

MARCAS

December 28, 151–December 12, 159 NE

Like his father, King Marcas forwent the rite of Queenstrial, albeit for a stronger alliance with Piedmont. He married Elisabeta, a princess of the Tidewater. Though he only reigned for eight years, his rule was considered a fruitful age in Norta, due mostly to his Merandus mother and his wife. The king was largely ineffectual and unintelligent, delegating his duties to the two queens, who undertook a campaign to improve the Nortan infrastructure and economy. Queen Elisabeta, originally of Piedmont, pioneered the Greenway, a road system connecting Norta and her native country. Dowager Queen Helena turned her attentions toward expanding the Nortan electrical grid from border to border, reaching even remote Red communities. When King Marcas died in a drunken fall, the two queens continued their work in conjunction with his heir and only child, Aerion.

AERION

December 12, 159–February 2, 188 NE

King Aerion shared his mother's passion for architecture, and together they built the now-iconic Bridge of Archeon. During this period, Nortan spies led by House Merandus and House Iral aided Prairie warlords in their border war with the Lakelands. Backed with money from the Nortan treasury and the king himself, Prairie armies won valuable farmland in the Minnowan region and pushed the Lakelander border back across the Great River. King Aerion used this tactic to weaken Norta's closest neighbor, knowing that their two kingdoms would inevitably clash in the future. Influenced by his mother and grandmother, King Aerion decreed that his line of succession would depend on ability, not gender. Therefore his firstborn child, a daughter named Andura, was heir to the throne, followed by her younger brother.

ANDURA

February 2, 188–September 27, 199 NE

As the first ruling queen of Norta, Andura faced considerable opposition from the nobility and her government. She married through the first Princestrial, wedding a son of House Blonos, who became her prince consort. Queen Andura was a famed warrior and diplomat, able to hide Nortan involvement in the Prairie wars with the Lakelands. She maintained a shaky peace with the north while secretly building up her nation's armies, expanding Red conscription to include females as well as opening the military to any Silver woman who wished to enlist. Andura's only child did not inherit her burner abilities, and to maintain peace in the kingdom, she upheld her father's decree of succession. Her brother remained her heir until his death during a Red uprising in Harbor Bay. Similar uprisings were gaining strength in Norta, the Lakelands, and Piedmont, where Silver overlords struggled to maintain control of a larger Red population. Andura's son, Ambrosin, left Norta following his mother's death to seek his fortune in the west. He is a highly skilled blood healer, nearly immortal because of his ability, and still lives as King Triarch in Tiraxes. He is over one hundred years old.

TIBERIAS III

September 27, 199–March 30, 222 NE

As the firstborn son of Queen Andura's brother, Tiberias became heir to the throne after his father's death. He ascended during a chaotic time of Red rebellion and worsening relations with the Lakelands. One of his first acts as king was to call a summit with the monarchy of the Lakelands, but negotiations broke down quickly, and the Lakelander War was declared. It would last more than a century and claim millions of lives, both Red and Silver. It has been suggested that the war was indeed a war of anger, but of necessity as well, serving to curtail Red populations in both Norta and the Lakelands.

LEONORA

March 30, 222–January 3, 237 NE

Like her grandmother, Leonora was the firstborn child of a Calore monarch, and so inherited the throne over her younger brother. She refused the rite of Princestrial and never married, but Mariane Nolle was her consort until death, and given the rank of princess. Leonora was the first ruling

Calore to leave Norta during her reign, embarking on a tour of Piedmont to visit cousins and various dignitaries. She also visited Corvium many times to survey the Choke, a rapidly expanding wasteland serving as the war border between the Lakelander and Nortan trenches. By her decree, her nieces and nephews were partially raised at the war front to learn military matters firsthand.

TIBERIAS IV

January 3, 237–September 2, 270 NE

Continuing the military tradition set by his ancestors, Tiberias IV was a general in the Nortan armies before succeeding his older sister. He oversaw more than thirty years of war as king, and toward the end of his reign began a more clandestine campaign against the Lakelands. He utilized a vast spy network, headed by House Iral, to infiltrate Lakelander strongholds, track troop moments, sabotage supply chains, and assassinate key figures within their government and military. The king's second son, Aerik, died in retaliation for one such assassination. While reviewing troops on the Lakelander border, Aerik was ambushed and killed by Lakelanders disguised as Reds. After his son's death, Tiberias IV spent most of his time at the front, leaving his heir to rule from the capital in his place and learn statecraft firsthand.

TIBERIAS V

September 2, 270–August 1, 296 NE

After observing the rite of Queenstrial, Tiberias married Anabel of House Lerolan, the traditional governors of Delphie. Tiberias V also kept a male consort, Robert Iral, whom he crowned as a prince. Queen Anabel and Prince Robert were both great patrons of the arts during their king's reign. Though less inclined to the military than his father, Tiberias V partially raised his son at the front to prepare him to lead a nation at war. Despite conflict with the Lakelands, his reign was considered peaceful and prosperous for the Silvers of Norta. Tiberias V died of a cancerous wasting disease, despite the best efforts of his personal skin healers.

TIBERIAS VI

August 1, 296 NE–present

Before he ascended the throne, Tiberias VI refused the rite of Queenstrial and shocked the court when he married Coriane Jacos, a lady of a relatively low and poor Silver house.

QUEEN SONG

As usual, Julian gave her a book.

Just like the year before, and the year before, and every holiday or occasion he could find in between his sister's birthdays. She had shelves of his so-called gifts. Some given in truth, and some to simply clear space in the library he called a bedroom, where books were stacked so high and so precariously that even the cats had trouble navigating the labyrinthine piles. The subjects varied, from adventure tales of Prairie raiders to stuffy poetry collections about the insipid Royal Court they both strived to avoid. *Better for kindling,* Coriane would say every time he left her another dull volume. Once, for her twelfth birthday, Julian gave her an ancient text written in a language she could not read. And one she assumed he only pretended to understand.

Despite her dislike for the majority of his stories, she kept her own growing collection on neat shelves, strictly alphabetized, their spines facing forward to display titles on leather bindings. Most would go untouched, unopened, unread, a tragedy even Julian could not find the words to bemoan. There is nothing so terrible as a story untold. But Coriane kept them all the same, well dusted, polished, their gold-stamped letters gleaming in the hazy light of summer or winter's gray castings. *From Julian* was scrawled in each one, and those words she treasured above almost all. Only his true gifts were loved more: the manuals and guides sheathed in plastic, tucked between the pages of a genealogy or encyclopedia. A few held court at her bedside, snug beneath her mattress, to be pulled out at night when she could devour technical schematics and machine studies. How to build, break down, and maintain transport engines, airjets, telegraphy equipment, even lightbulbs and kitchen stoves.

Her father did not approve, as was the usual way. A Silver daughter of a noble High House should not have fingers stained in motor oil, nails chipped by "borrowed" tools, or bloodshot eyes from too many nights spent straining over unsuitable literature. But Harrus Jacos forgot his misgivings every time the video screen in the estate parlor shorted out, hissing sparks and blurred transmissions. *Fix it, Cori, fix it.* She did as he commanded, hoping each time would be the one to convince him. Only to have her tinkerings sneered at a few days later, and all her good work forgotten.

She was glad he was gone, away in the capital aiding their uncle, the lord of House Jacos. This way she could spend her birthday with the people she loved. Namely, her brother, Julian, and Sara Skonos, who had come specifically for the occasion. *Growing prettier by the day,* Coriane thought, noting her dearest friend. It had been months since their last meeting, when Sara turned fifteen and moved permanently to the Royal Court. Not so long really, but already the girl seemed different, sharper. Her cheekbones cut cruelly beneath skin somehow paler than before, as if drained. And her gray eyes, once bright stars, seemed dark, full of shadows. But her smile came easily, as it always did around the Jacos children. *Around Julian, truly,* Coriane knew. And her brother was just the same, grinning broadly, keeping a distance no uninterested boy would think to keep. He was surgically aware of his movements, and Coriane was surgically aware of her brother. At seventeen, he was not too young for proposals, and she suspected there would be one in the coming months.

Julian had not bothered to wrap her gift. It was already beautiful on its own. Leatherbound, striped in the dusty yellow-golds of House Jacos, with the Burning Crown of Norta embossed into the cover. There was no title on the face or spine, and Coriane could tell there was no hidden guidebook in its pages. She scowled a little.

"Open it, Cori," Julian said, stopping her before she could toss the book onto the meager pile of other presents. All of them veiled insults: gloves to hide "common" hands, impractical dresses for a court she refused to visit, and an already opened box of sweets her father didn't want her to eat. They would be gone by dinnertime.

Coriane did as instructed and opened the book to find it empty. Its cream pages were blank. She wrinkled her nose, not bothering to put on the show of a grateful sister. Julian required no such lies, and would see through them anyway. What's more, there was no one here to scold her for such behavior. *Mother is dead, Father gone, and Cousin Jessamine is blessfully still asleep.* Only Julian, Coriane, and Sara sat alone in the garden parlor, three beads rattling around the dusty jar of the Jacos estate. It was a yawning room that matched the ever-present, hollow ache in Coriane's chest. Arched windows overlooked a tangled grove of once-orderly roses that had not seen the hands of a greenwarden in a decade. The floor needed a good sweeping and the gold draperies were gray with dust, and most likely spiderwebs as well. Even the painting over the soot-stained marble fireplace was missing its gilt frame, sold off long ago. The man who stared out from the naked canvas was Coriane and Julian's own grandfather, Janus Jacos, who would certainly despair of his family's state. Poor nobles, trading on an old name and traditions, making do with little and less every year.

Julian laughed, making the usual sound. *Fond exasperation*, Coriane knew. It was the best way to describe his attitude toward his younger sister. Two years his junior, and always quick to remind her of his superior age and intellect. Gently, of course. As if that made any difference.

"It's for you to write in," he pressed on, sliding long, thin fingers over the pages. "Your thoughts, what you do with your days."

"I know what a diary is," she replied, snapping the book shut. He didn't mind, not bothering to be offended. Julian knew her better than anyone. *Even when I get the words wrong.* "And my days don't warrant much of a record."

"Nonsense, you're quite interesting when you try."

Coriane grinned. "Julian, your jokes are improving. Have you finally found a book to teach you humor?" Her eyes flickered to Sara. "Or someone?"

While Julian flushed, his cheeks bluing with silverblood, Sara took it in stride. "I'm a healer, not a miracle worker," she said, her voice a melody.

Their joined laughter echoed, filling the emptiness of the estate house for one kind moment. In the corner, the old clock chimed, tolling the hour of Coriane's doom. Namely, Cousin Jessamine, who would arrive at any moment.

Julian was quick to stand, stretching a lanky form transitioning into manhood. He still had growing to do, both up and out. Coriane, on the other hand, had been the same height for years and showed no sign of changing. She was ordinary in everything, from almost colorless blue eyes to limp chestnut hair that stubbornly refused to grow much farther than her shoulders.

"You didn't want these, did you?" he said as he reached across his sister. He snatched a few sugar-glassed candies from the box, earning a swat in reply. *Etiquette be damned. Those are mine.* "Careful," he warned, "I'll tell Jessamine."

"No need," came their elderly cousin's reedy whistle of a voice, echoing from the columned entrance to the parlor. With a hiss of annoyance, Coriane shut her eyes, trying to will Jessamine Jacos out of existence. *No use in that, of course. I'm not a whisper. Just a singer.* And though she could have tried to use her meager abilities on Jessamine, it would only end poorly. Old as Jessamine was, her voice and ability were still whip-sharp, far quicker than her own. *I'll end up scrubbing floors with a smile if I try her.*

Coriane pasted on a polite expression and turned to find her cousin leaning upon a bejeweled cane, one of the last beautiful things in their house. Of course, it belonged to the foulest. Jessamine had long ago stopped frequenting Silver skin healers, to "age gracefully" as she put it. Though, in truth, the family could no longer afford such treatments from the most talented of House Skonos, or even the skin healer apprentices of common, lesser birth. Her skin sagged now, gray in pallor, with purple age spots across her wrinkled hands and neck. Today she wore a lemon silk wrap around her head, to hide thinning white hair that barely covered her scalp, and a flowing dress to match. The moth-eaten edges were well hidden, though. Jessamine excelled at illusion.

"Be a dear and take those to the kitchen, Julian, won't you?" she said, jabbing a long-nailed finger at the candies. "The staff will be so grateful."

It took all Coriane's strength not to scoff. "The staff" was little more than a Red butler more ancient than Jessamine, who didn't even have *teeth*, as well as the cook and two young maids, who were somehow expected to maintain the entire estate. They might enjoy the candies, but of course Jessamine had no true intention of letting them. *They'll end up at the bottom of the trash, or tucked away in her own room more like.*

Julian felt quite the same, judging by his twisted expression. But arguing with Jessamine was as fruitless as the trees in the corrupted old orchard.

"Of course, Cousin," he said with a voice better suited to a funeral. His eyes were apologetic, while Coriane's were resentful. She watched with a thinly veiled sneer as Julian offered one arm to Sara, the other scooping up her unsuitable gift. Both were eager to escape Jessamine's domain, but loath to leave Coriane behind. Still, they did it, sweeping away from the parlor.

That's right, leave me here. You always do. Abandoned to Jessamine, who had taken it upon herself to turn Coriane into a proper daughter of House Jacos. Put simply: *silent.*

And always left to their father, when he returned from court, from long days waiting for Uncle Jared to die. The head of House Jacos, governor of the Aderonack region, had no children of his own, and so his titles would pass to his brother, and then Julian after him. At least, he had no children anymore. The twins, Jenna and Caspian, were killed in the Lakelander War, leaving their father without an heir of his flesh, not to mention the will to live. It was only a matter of time before Coriane's father took up the ancestral seat, and he wanted to waste no time doing so. Coriane found the behavior perverse at best. She couldn't imagine doing such a thing to Julian, no matter how angry he made her. To stand by and watch him waste away with grief. It was an ugly, loveless act, and the thought of it turned her stomach. *But I have no desire to lead our family, and Father is a man of ambition, if not tact.*

What he planned to do with his eventual rise, she did not know. House Jacos was small, unimportant, governors of a backwater with little more than the blood of a High House to keep them warm at night. And of course, Jessamine, to make sure everyone pretended like they weren't drowning.

She took a seat with the grace of one half her age, knocking her cane against the dirty floor. "Preposterous," she muttered, striking at a haze of dust motes swirling in a beam of sunlight. "So hard to find good help these days."

Especially when you can't pay them, Coriane sneered in her head. "Indeed, Cousin. So difficult."

"Well, hand them over. Let's see what Jared sent along," she said. One clawed hand reached out, flapping open and closed in a gesture that made Coriane's skin crawl. She bit her lip between her teeth, chewing it to keep from saying the wrong thing. Instead, she lifted the two dresses that were her uncle's gifts and laid them upon the sofa where Jessamine perched.

Sniffing, Jessamine examined them as Julian did his ancient texts. She squinted at the stitching and lacework, rubbing the fabric, pulling at invisible stray threads in both golden dresses. "Suitable," she said after a long moment. "If not outdated. None of these are the latest fashions."

"What a surprise," Coriane could not help but drawl.

Thwack. The cane hit the floor. "No sarcasm, it's unbecoming of a lady."

Well, every lady I've met seems well versed in it, yourself included. If I can even call you a lady. In truth, Jessamine had not been to the Royal Court in at least a decade. She had no idea what the latest fashions were, and, when she was deep in the gin, could not even remember which king was on the throne. "Tiberias the Sixth? Fifth? No, it's the Fourth still, certainly, the old flame just won't *die.*" And Coriane would gently remind her that they were ruled by Tiberias the *Fifth.*

His son, the crown prince, would be Tiberias the Sixth when his father died. Though with his reputed taste for warfare, Coriane wondered if the prince would live long enough to wear a crown. The history of Norta was fraught with Calore firebrands dying in battle, mostly second princes and cousins. She quietly wished the prince dead, if only to see what would happen. He had no siblings that she knew of, and the Calore cousins were few, not to mention weak, if Jessamine's lessons could be trusted. Norta had fought Lakelanders for a century, but another war within was certainly on the horizon. Between the High Houses, to put another family on the throne. Not that House Jacos would be involved at all. Their insignificance was a constant, just like Cousin Jessamine.

"Well, if your father's communications are to be believed, these dresses should be of use soon enough," Jessamine carried on as she set the presents down. Unconcerned with the hour or Coriane's presence, she drew a glass bottle of gin from her gown and took a hearty sip. The scent of juniper bit the air.

Frowning, Coriane looked up from her hands, now busy wringing the new gloves. "Is Uncle unwell?"

Thwack. "What a stupid question. He's been unwell for years, as you know."

Her face burned silver with a florid blush. "I mean, worse. Is he *worse?*"

"Harrus thinks so. Jared has taken to his chambers at court, and rarely attends social banquets, let alone his administrative meetings or the governors' council. Your father stands in for him more and more these days. Not to mention the fact that your uncle seems determined to drink away the coffers of House Jacos." Another swig of gin. Coriane almost laughed at the irony. "How selfish."

"Yes, selfish," the young girl muttered. *You haven't wished me a happy birthday, Cousin.* But she did not press on that subject. It hurts to be called ungrateful, even by a leech.

"Another book from Julian, I see, oh, and gloves. Wonderful, Harrus took my suggestion. And Skonos, what did she bring you?"

"Nothing." *Yet.* Sara had told her to wait, that her gift wasn't something to be piled with the others.

"No gift? Yet she sits here, eating our food, taking up space—"

Coriane did her best to let Jessamine's words float over her and away, like clouds in a windblown sky. Instead, she focused on the manual she read last night. *Batteries. Cathodes and anodes, primary use are discarded, secondary can be recharged—*

Thwack.

"Yes, Jessamine?"

A very bug-eyed old woman stared back at Coriane, her annoyance written in every wrinkle. "I don't do this for my benefit, Coriane."

"Well, it certainly isn't for mine," she couldn't help but hiss.

Jessamine crowed in response, her laugh so brittle she might spit dust. "You'd like that, wouldn't you? To think that I sit here with you, suffering your scowls and bitterness for fun? Think less of yourself, Coriane. I do this for no one but House Jacos, for all of us. I know what we are better than you do. And I remember what we were before, when we lived at court, negotiated treaties, were as indispensable to the Calore kings as their own flame. *I remember.* There is no greater pain or punishment than memory." She turned her cane over in her hand, one finger counting the jewels she polished every night. Sapphires, rubies, emeralds, and a single diamond. Given by suitors or friends or family, Coriane did not know. But they were Jessamine's treasure, and her eyes glittered like the gems. "Your father will be lord of House Jacos, and your brother after him. That leaves you in need of a lord of your own. Lest you wish to stay here forever?"

Like you. The implication was clear, and somehow Coriane found she could not speak around the sudden lump in her throat. She could only shake her head. *No, Jessamine, I do not want to stay here. I don't want to be you.*

"Very good," Jessamine said. Her cane thwacked once more. "Let's begin for the day."

Later that evening, Coriane sat down to write. Her pen flew across the pages of Julian's gift, spilling ink as a knife would blood. She wrote of everything. Jessamine, her father, Julian. The sinking feeling that her brother would abandon her to navigate the coming hurricane alone. He had Sara now. She'd caught them kissing before dinner, and while she smiled, pretending to laugh, pretending to be pleased by their flushes and stuttered explanations, Coriane quietly despaired. *Sara was my best friend. Sara was the only thing that belonged to me.* But no longer. Just like Julian, Sara would drift away, until Coriane was left with only the dust of a forgotten home and a forgotten life.

Because no matter what Jessamine said, how she preened and lied about Coriane's so-called prospects, there was nothing to be done. *No one will marry me, at least no one I want to marry.* She despaired of it and accepted it in the same turn. *I will never leave this place,* she wrote. *These golden walls will be my tomb.*

Jared Jacos received two funerals.

The first was at court in Archeon, on a spring day hazy with rain. The second would be a week after, at the estate in Aderonack. His body would join the family tomb and rest in a marble sepulcher paid for with one of the jewels from Jessamine's cane. The emerald had been sold off to a gem merchant in East Archeon while Coriane, Julian, and their aged cousin looked on. Jessamine seemed detached, not bothering to watch as the green stone passed from the new Lord Jacos's hand to the Silver jeweler. *A common man*, Coriane knew. He wore no house colors to speak of, but he was richer than they were, with fine clothes and a good amount of jewelry all over. *We might be noble, but this man could buy us all if he wanted.*

The family wore black, as was custom. Coriane had to borrow a gown for the occasion, one of Jessamine's many horrid mourning frocks, for Jessamine had attended and overseen more than a dozen funerals of House Jacos. The young girl itched in the getup but kept still as they left the merchant quarter, heading for the great bridge that spanned the Capital River, connecting both sides of the city. *Jessamine would scold or hit me if I started scratching.*

It was not Coriane's first visit to the capital, or even her tenth. She'd been there many times, usually at her uncle's bidding, to show the so-called strength of House Jacos. A foolish notion. Not only were they poor, but their family was small, wasting, especially with the twins gone. No match to the sprawling family trees of Houses Iral, Samos, Rhambos, and more. Rich bloodlines that could support the immense weight of their many relations. Their place as High Houses was firmly cemented in the hierarchy of both nobility and government. Not so with Jacos, if Coriane's father, Harrus, could not find a way to prove his worth to his peers and his king. For her part, Coriane saw no way through it. Aderonack was on the Lakelander border, a land of few people and deep forest no one needed to log. They could not claim mines or mills or even fertile farmland. There was nothing of use in their corner of the world.

She had tied a golden sash around her waist, cinching in the ill-fitting, high-collared dress in an attempt to look a bit more presentable, if not in fashion. Coriane told herself she didn't mind the whispers of court, the sneers from the other young ladies who watched her like she was a bug, or worse, a *Red.* They were all cruel girls, silly girls, waiting with bated breath for any news of Queenstrial. But of course that wasn't true. Sara was one of them, wasn't she? A daughter of Lord Skonos, training to be a healer, showing great promise in her abilities. Enough to service the royal family if she kept to the path.

I desire no such thing, Sara said once, confiding in Coriane months before, during a visit. *It will be a waste if I spend my life healing paper cuts and crow's-feet. My skills would be of better use in trenches of the Choke or the hospitals of Corvium. Soldiers die there every day, you know. Reds and Silvers both, killed by Lakelander bombs and bullets, bleeding to death because people like me stay here.*

She would never say so to anyone else, least of all her lord father. Such words were better suited to midnight, when two girls could whisper their dreams without fear of consequence.

"I want to build things," Coriane told her best friend on such an occasion.

"Build what, Coriane?"

"Airjets, airships, transports, video screens—ovens! I don't know, Sara, I don't know. I just want to—to make something."

Sara smiled then, her teeth glinting in a slim beam of moonlight. "Make something of yourself, you mean. Don't you, Cori?"

"I didn't say that."

"You didn't have to."

"I can see why Julian likes you so much."

That quieted Sara right away, and she was asleep soon after. But Coriane kept her eyes open, watching shadows on the walls, wondering.

Now, on the bridge, in the middle of brightly colored chaos, she did the same. Nobles, citizens, merchants seemed to float before her, their skin cold, pace slow, eyes hard and dark no matter their color. They drank in the morning with greed, a quenched man still gulping at water while others died of thirst. The others were the Reds, of course, wearing the bands that marked them. The servants among them wore uniforms, some striped with the colors of the High House they served. Their movements were determined, their eyes forward, hurrying along on their errands and orders. *They have purpose at least,* Coriane thought. *Not like me.*

She suddenly felt the urge to grab on to the nearby lamppost, to wrap her arms around it lest she be carried away like a leaf on the wind, or a stone dropping through water. Flying or drowning or both. Going where some other force willed. Beyond her own control.

Julian's hand closed around her wrist, forcing her to take his arm. *He'll do*, she thought, and a cord of tension relaxed in her. *Julian will keep me here.*

Later on, she recorded little of the official funeral in her diary, long spattered with ink splotches and cross outs. Her spelling was improving though, as was her penmanship. She wrote nothing of Uncle Jared's body, his skin whiter than the moon, drained of blood by the embalming process. She did not record how her father's lip quivered, betraying the pain he truly felt for his brother's death. Her writings were not of the way the rain stopped, just long enough for the ceremony, or the crowd of lords who came to pay their respects. She did not even bother to mention the king's presence, or that of his son, Tiberias, who brooded with dark brows and an even darker expression.

Uncle is gone, she wrote instead of all this. *And somehow, in some way, I envy him.*

As always, she tucked the diary away when she was finished, hiding it beneath the mattress of her bedchamber with the rest of her treasures. Namely, a little pallet of tools. Jealously guarded, taken from the abandoned gardener's shed back home. Two screwdrivers, a delicate hammer, one set of needle-nose pliers, and a wrench rusted almost beyond use. *Almost.* There was a coil of spindly wire as well, carefully drawn from an ancient lamp in the corner that no one would miss. Like the estate, the Jacos town house in West Archeon was a decaying place. And damp, too, in the middle of the rainstorm, giving the old walls the feel of a dripping cave.

She was still wearing her black dress and gold sash, with what she told herself were raindrops clinging to her lashes, when Jessamine burst through the door. To fuss, of course. There was no such thing as a banquet without a twittering Jessamine, let alone one at court. She did her best to make Coriane as presentable as possible with the meager time and means available, as if her life depended upon it. *Perhaps it does. Whatever life she holds dear. Perhaps the court is in need of another etiquette instructor for the noble children, and she thinks performing miracles with me will win her the position.*

Even Jessamine wants to leave.

"There now, none of this," Jessamine muttered, swiping at Coriane's tears with a tissue. Another swipe, this time with a chalky black pencil, to make her eyes stand out. Purple-blue rouge along her cheeks, giving her the illusion of bone structure. Nothing on the lips, for Coriane had never mastered the art of not getting lipstick on her teeth or water glass. "I suppose it will do."

"Yes, Jessamine."

As much as the old woman delighted in obedience, Coriane's manner gave her pause. The girl was sad, clearly, in the wake of the funeral. "What's the matter, child? Is it the dress?"

I don't care about faded black silks or banquets or this vile court. I don't care about any of it. "Nothing at all, Cousin. Just hungry, I suppose." Coriane reached for the easy escape, throwing one flaw to Jessamine to hide another.

"Mercy upon your appetite," she replied, rolling her eyes. "Remember, you must eat daintily, like a bird. There should always be food on your plate. Pick, pick, *pick*—"

Pick pick pick. The words felt like sharp nails drumming on Coriane's skull. But she forced a smile all the same. It bit at the corners of her mouth, hurting just as much as the words and the rain and the falling sensation that had followed her since the bridge.

Downstairs, Julian and their father were already waiting, huddled close to a smoky fire in the hearth. Their suits were identical, black with pale golden sashes across their chests from shoulder to hip. Lord Jacos tentatively touched the newly acquired pin stuck in his sash—a beaten gold square as old as his house. Nothing compared to the gems, medallions, and badges of the other governors, but enough for this moment.

Julian caught Coriane's eye, beginning to wink for her benefit, but her downcast air stopped him cold. He kept close to her all the way to the banquet, holding her hand in the rented transport, and then her arm as they crossed through the great gates of Caesar's Square. Whitefire Palace, their destination, sprawled to their left, dominating the south side of the tiled Square now busy with nobles.

Jessamine buzzed with excitement, despite her age, and made sure to smile and nod at everyone who passed. She even waved, letting the flowing sleeves of her black and gold gown glide through the air.

Communicating with clothes, Coriane knew. *How utterly stupid. Just like the rest of this dance that will end with the further disgrace and downfall of House Jacos. Why delay the inevitable? Why play at a game we can't hope to compete in?* She could not fathom it. Her brain knew circuitry better than high society, and despaired at ever understanding the latter. There was no reason to the court of Norta, or even her own family. Even Julian.

"I know what you asked of Father," she muttered, careful to keep her chin tucked against his shoulder. His jacket muffled her voice, but not enough for him to claim he couldn't hear her.

His muscles tightened beneath her. "Cori—"

"I must admit, I don't quite understand. I thought—" Her voice caught. "I thought you would want to be with Sara, now that we'll have to move to court."

You asked to go to Delphie, to work with the scholars and excavate ruins rather than learn lordship at Father's right hand. Why would you do that? Why, Julian? And the worst question of all, the one she didn't have the strength to ask—*how could you leave me too?*

Her brother heaved a long sigh and tightened his grip. "I did—I *do.* But—"

"But? Has something happened?"

"No, nothing at all. Good or bad," he added, and she could hear the hint of a smile in his voice. "I just know she won't leave court if I'm here with Father. I can't do that to her. This place—I won't trap her here in this pit of snakes."

Coriane felt a pang of sorrow for her brother and his noble, selfless, stupid heart. "You'd let her go to the front, then."

"There's no *let* where I'm concerned. She should be able to make her own decisions."

"And if her father, Lord Skonos, disagrees?" *As he surely will.*

"Then I'll marry her as planned and bring her to Delphie with me."

"Always a plan with you."

"I certainly try."

Despite the swell of happiness—her brother and best friend *married*—the familiar ache tugged at Coriane's insides. *They'll be together, and you left alone.*

Julian's fingers squeezed her own suddenly, warm despite the misting rain. "And of course, I'll send for you as well. You think I'd leave you to face the Royal Court with no one but Father and Jessamine?" Then he kissed her cheek and winked. "Think a bit better of me, Cori."

For his sake, she forced a wide, white grin that flashed in the lights of the palace. She felt none of its gleam. *How can Julian be so smart and so stupid at the same time?* It puzzled and saddened her in succession. Even if their father agreed to let Julian go to study in Delphie, Coriane would never be allowed to do the same. She was no great intellect, charmer, beauty, or warrior. Her usefulness lay in marriage, in alliance, and there were none to be found in her brother's books or protection.

Whitefire was done up in the colors of House Calore, black and red and royal silver from every alabaster column. The windows winked with inner light, and sounds of a roaring party filtered from the grand entrance, manned by the king's own Sentinel guards in their flaming robes and masks. As she passed them, still clutching Julian's hand, Coriane felt less like a lady, and more like a prisoner being led into her cell.

Coriane did her best to *pick pick pick* at her meal.

She also debated pocketing a few gold-inlaid forks. If only House Merandus did not face them across the table. They were whispers, all of them, mind readers who probably knew Coriane's intentions as well as she did. Sara told her she should be able to feel it, to notice if one of them poked into her head, and she kept rigid, on edge, trying to be mindful of her own brain. It made her silent and white-faced, staring intensely at her plate of pulled-apart and uneaten food.

Julian tried to distract, as did Jessamine, though she did so unintentionally. All but falling over herself to compliment Lord and Lady Merandus on everything from their matching outfits (a suit for the lord and gown for the lady, both shimmering like a blue-black sky of stars) to the profits of their ancestral lands (mostly in Haven, including the techie slum of Merry Town, a place Coriane knew was hardly merry). The Merandus brood seemed intent on ignoring House Jacos as best they could, keeping their attentions on themselves and the raised banquet table where the royals ate. Coriane could not help but steal a glance at them as well.

Tiberias the Fifth, King of Norta, was in the center naturally, sitting tall and lean in his ornate chair. His black dress uniform was slashed with crimson silk and silver braid, all meticulously perfect and in place. He was a beautiful man, more than handsome, with eyes of liquid gold and cheekbones to make poets weep. Even his beard, regally speckled with gray, was neatly razored to an edged perfection. According to Jessamine, his Queenstrial was a bloodbath of warring ladies vying to be his queen. None seemed to mind that the king would never love them. They only wanted to mother his children, keep his confidence, and earn a crown of their own. Queen Anabel, an oblivion of House Lerolan, did just that. She sat on the king's left, her smile curling, eyes on her only son. Her military uniform was open at the neck, revealing a firestorm of jewels at her throat, red and orange and yellow as the explosive ability she possessed. Her crown was small but difficult to ignore—black gems that winked every time she moved, set into a thick band of rose gold.

The king's paramour wore a similar band on his head, though the gemstones were absent from this crown. He didn't seem to mind, his smile fiercely bright while his fingers intertwined with the king's. Prince Robert of House Iral. He had not a drop of royal blood, but held the title for decades at the king's orders. Like the queen, he wore a riot of gems, blue and red in his house colors, made more striking by his black dress uniform, long ebony hair, and flawless bronze skin. His laugh was musical, and it carried over the many voices echoing through the banquet hall. Coriane thought he had a kind look—a strange thing for one so long at court. It comforted her a little, until she noticed his own house seated next to him, all of them sharp and stern, with darting eyes and feral smiles. She tried to remember their names, but knew only one—his sister, Lady Ara, the head of House Iral, seeming it in every inch. As if she sensed her gaze, Ara's dark eyes flashed to Coriane's, and she had to look elsewhere.

To the prince. Tiberias the Sixth one day, but only Tiberias now. A teenager, Julian's age, with the shadow of his father's beard splotched unevenly across his jaw. He favored wine, judging by the empty glass hastily being refilled and the silver blush blooming across his cheeks. She remembered him at her uncle's funeral, a dutiful son standing stoic by a grave. Now he grinned easily, trading jokes with his mother.

His eyes caught hers for a moment, glancing over Queen Anabel's shoulder to lock on to the Jacos girl in an old dress. He nodded quickly, acknowledging her stare, before returning to his antics and his wine.

"I can't believe she allows it," said a voice across the table.

Coriane turned to find Elara Merandus also staring at the royals, her keen and angled eyes narrowed in distaste. Like her parents', Elara's outfit sparkled, dark blue silk and studded white gems, though she wore a wrapped blouse with slashed, cape sleeves instead of a gown. Her hair was long, violently straight, falling in an ash curtain of blond over one shoulder, revealing an ear studded with crystal brilliance. The rest of her was just as meticulously perfect. Long dark lashes, skin more pale and flawless than porcelain, with the grace of something polished and pruned into court perfection. Already self-conscious, Coriane tugged at the golden sash around her waist. She wished nothing more than to walk out of the hall and all the way back to the town house.

"I'm speaking to you, Jacos."

"Forgive me if I'm surprised," Coriane replied, doing her best to keep her voice even. Elara was not known for her kindness, or much else for that matter. Despite being the daughter of a ruling lord, Coriane realized she knew little of the whisper girl. "What are you talking about?"

Elara rolled bright blue eyes with the grace of a swan. "The queen, of course. I don't know how she stands to share a table with her husband's whore, much less his family. It's an insult, plain as day."

Again, Coriane glanced at Prince Robert. His presence seemed to soothe the king, and if the queen truly minded, she didn't show it. As she watched, all three crowned royals were whispering together in gentle conversation. But the crown prince and his wineglass were gone.

"*I* wouldn't allow it," Elara continued, pushing her plate away. It was empty, eaten clean. *At least she has spine enough to eat her food.* "And it would be my house sitting up there, not his. It's the queen's right and no one else's."

So she'll be competing in Queenstrial, then.

"Of course I will."

Fear snapped through Coriane, chilling her. *Did she—?*

"Yes." A wicked smile spread across Elara's face.

It burned something in Coriane and she nearly fell back in shock. She felt nothing, not even a brush inside her head, no indication that Elara was listening to her thoughts. "I—" she sputtered. "Excuse me." Her legs felt foreign as she stood, wobbly from sitting through thirteen courses. But still under her own power, thankfully. *Blank blank blank blank,* she thought, picturing white walls and white paper and white nothing in her head. Elara only watched, giggling into her hand.

"Cori—?" she heard Julian say, but he didn't stop her. Neither did Jessamine, who would not want to cause a scene. And her father didn't notice at all, more engrossed in something Lord Provos was saying.

Blank blank blank blank.

Her footsteps were even, not too fast or too slow. *How far away must I be?*

Farther, said Elara's sneering purr in her head. She nearly tripped over at the sensation. The voice echoed in everything around and in her, windows to bone, from the chandeliers overhead to the blood pounding in her ears. *Farther, Jacos.*

Blank blank blank blank.

She did not realize she was whispering the words to herself, fervent as a prayer, until she was out of the banquet hall, down a passage, and through an etched glass door. A tiny courtyard rose around her, smelling of rain and sweet flowers.

"Blank blank blank blank," she mumbled once more, moving deeper into the garden. Magnolia trees twisted in an arch, forming a crown of white blossoms and rich green leaves. It was barely raining anymore, and she moved closer to the trees for shelter from the final drippings of the storm. It was chillier than she expected, but Coriane welcomed it. Elara echoed no longer.

Sighing, she sank down onto a stone bench beneath the grove. Its touch was colder still and she wrapped her arms around herself.

"I can help with that," said a deep voice, the words slow and plodding.

Coriane whirled, wide-eyed. She expected Elara haunting her, or Julian, or Jessamine to scold her abrupt exit. The figure standing a few feet away was clearly not any of them.

"Your Highness," Coriane said, jumping to her feet so she could bow properly.

The crown prince Tiberias stood over her, pleasant in the darkness, a glass in one hand and a half-empty bottle in the other. He let her go through the motions and kindly said nothing of her poor form. "That'll do," he finally said, motioning for her to stand.

She did as commanded with all haste, straightening up to face him. "Yes, Your Highness."

"Would you care for a glass, my lady?" he said, though he was already filling the cup. No one was foolish enough to refuse an offer from a prince of Norta. "It's not a coat, but it will warm you well enough. Pity there's no whiskey at these functions."

Coriane forced a nod. "Pity, yes," she echoed, never having tasted the bite of brown liquor. With shaking hands, she took the full glass, her fingers brushing his for a moment. His skin was warm as a stone in the sun, and she was struck by the need to hold his hand. Instead, she drank deep of the red wine.

He matched her, albeit sipping straight from the bottle. *How crude,* she thought, watching his throat bob as he swallowed. *Jessamine would skin me if I did that.*

The prince did not sit next to her, but maintained his distance, so that she could only feel the ghost of his warmth. Enough to know his blood ran hot even in the damp. She wondered how he managed to wear a trim suit without sweating right through it. Part of her wished he would sit, only so she could enjoy the secondhand heat of his abilities. But that would be improper, on both their parts.

"You're the niece of Jarred Jacos, yes?" His tone was polite, well trained. An etiquette coach probably followed him since birth. Again, he did not wait for an answer to his question. "My condolences, of course."

"Thank you. My name is Coriane," she offered, realizing he would not ask. *He only asks what he already knows the answer to.*

He dipped his head in acknowledgment. "Yes. And I won't make fools of both of us by introducing myself."

In spite of propriety, Coriane felt herself smile. She sipped at the wine again, not knowing what else to do. Jessamine had not given her much instruction on conversing with royals of House Calore, let alone the future king. *Speak when spoken to* was all she could recall, so she kept her lips pressed together so tightly they formed a thin line.

Tiberias laughed openly at the sight. He was maybe a little drunk, and entirely amused. "Do you know how annoying it is to have to lead *every single conversation*?" He chuckled. "I talk to Robert and my parents more than anyone else, simply because it's easier than extracting words from other people."

How wretched for you, she snapped in her head. "That sounds awful," she said as demurely as she could. "Perhaps when you're king, you can make some changes to the etiquette of court?"

"Sounds exhausting," he muttered back around swigs of wine. "And unimportant, in the scheme of things. There's a war on, in case you haven't noticed."

He was right. The wine did warm her a bit. "A war?" she said. "Where? When? I've heard nothing of this."

The prince whipped to face her quickly, only to find Coriane smirking a little at his reaction. He laughed again, and tipped the bottle at her. "You had me for a second there, Lady Jacos."

Still grinning, he moved to the bench, sitting next to her. Not close enough to touch, but Coriane still went stock-still, her playful edge forgotten. He pretended not to notice. She tried her best to remain calm and poised.

"So I'm out here drinking in the rain because my parents frown upon being intoxicated in front of the court." The heat of him flared, pulsing with his inner annoyance. Coriane reveled in the sensation as the cold was chased from her bones. "What's your excuse? No, wait, let me guess—you were seated with House Merandus, yes?"

Gritting her teeth, she nodded. "Whoever arranged the tables must hate me."

"The party planners don't hate anyone but my mother. She's not one for decorations or flowers or seating charts, and they think she's neglecting her queenly duties. Of course, that's nonsense," he added quickly. Another drink. "She sits on more war councils than Father and trains enough for the both of them."

Coriane remembered the queen in her uniform, a splendor of medals on her chest. "She's an impressive woman," she said, not knowing what else to say. Her mind flitted back to Elara Merandus, glaring at the royals, disgusted by the queen's so-called surrender.

"Indeed." His eyes roved, landing on her now empty glass. "Care for the rest?" he asked, and this time he truly was waiting for an answer.

"I shouldn't," she said, putting the wineglass down on the bench. "In fact, I should go back inside. Jessamine—my cousin—will be furious with me as it is." *I hope she doesn't lecture me all night.*

Overhead, the sky had deepened to black, and the clouds were rolling away, clearing the rain to reveal bright stars. The prince's bodily warmth, fed by his burner ability, created a pleasant pocket around them, one Coriane was loath to leave. She heaved a steady breath, drawing in one last gasp of the magnolia trees, and forced herself to her feet.

Tiberias jumped up with her, still deliberate in his manners. "Shall I accompany you?" he asked as any gentleman would. But Coriane read the reluctance in his eyes and waved him off.

"No, I won't punish both of us."

His eyes flashed at that. "Speaking of punishment—if Elara whispers to you ever again, you show her the same courtesy."

"How—how did you know it was her?"

A storm cloud of emotions crossed his face, most of them unknown to Coriane. But she certainly recognized anger.

"She knows, as everyone else knows, that my father will call for Queenstrial soon. I don't doubt she's wriggled into every maiden's head, to learn her enemies and her prey." With almost vicious speed, he drank the last of the wine, emptying the bottle. But it was not empty for long. Something on his wrist sparked, a starburst of yellow and white. It ignited into flame inside the glass, burning the last drops of alcohol in its green cage. "I'm told her technique is precise, almost perfect. You won't feel her if she doesn't want you to."

Coriane tasted bile at the back of her mouth. She focused on the flame in the bottle, if only to avoid Tiberias's gaze. As she watched, the heat cracked the glass, but it did not shatter. "Yes," she said hoarsely. "It feels like nothing."

"Well, you're a singer, aren't you?" His voice was suddenly harsh as his flame, a sharp, sickly yellow behind green glass. "Give her a taste of her own medicine."

"I couldn't possibly. I don't have the skill. And besides, there are laws. We don't use ability against our own, outside the proper channels—"

This time, his laugh was hollow. "And is Elara Merandus following that law? She hits you, you hit her back, Coriane. That's the way of my kingdom."

"It isn't your kingdom yet," she heard herself mutter.

But Tiberias didn't mind. In fact, he grinned darkly.

"I suspected you had a spine, Coriane Jacos. Somewhere in there."

No spine. Anger hissed inside her, but she could never give it voice. He was the prince, the future king. And she was no one at all, a limp excuse for a Silver daughter of a High House. Instead of standing up straight, as she wished to do, she bent into one more curtsy.

"Your Highness," she said, dropping her eyes to his booted feet.

He did not move, did not close the distance between them as a hero in her books would. Tiberias Calore stood back and let her go alone, returning to a den of wolves with no shield but her own heart.

After some distance, she heard the bottle shatter, spitting glass across the magnolia trees.

A strange prince, an even stranger night, she wrote later. *I don't know if I ever want to see him again. But he seemed lonely too. Should we not be lonely together?*

At least Jessamine was too drunk to scold me for running off.

Life at court was neither better nor worse than life on the estate.

The governorship came with greater incomes, but not nearly enough to elevate House Jacos beyond much more than the basic amenities. Coriane still did not have her own maid, nor did she want one, though Jessamine continued to crow about needing help of her own. At least the Archeon town house was easier to maintain, rather than the Aderonack estate now shuttered in the wake of the family's transplant to the capital.

I miss it, somehow, Coriane wrote. *The dust, the tangled gardens, the emptiness and the silence. So many corners that were my own, far from Father and Jessamine and even Julian.* Most of all she mourned the loss of the garage and outbuildings. The family had not owned a working transport in years, let alone employed a driver, but the remnants remained. There was the hulking skeleton of the private transport, a six-seater, its engine transplanted to the floor like an organ. Busted water heaters, old furnaces cannibalized for parts, not to mention odds and ends from their long-gone gardening staff, littered the various sheds and holdings. *I leave behind unfinished puzzles, pieces never put back together. It feels wasteful. Not of the objects, but myself. So much time spent stripping wire or counting screws. For what? For knowledge I will never use? Knowledge that is* cursed, inferior, stupid, *to everyone else? What have I done with myself for fifteen years? A great construct of nothing. I suppose I miss the old house because it was with me in my emptiness, in my silence. I thought I hated the estate, but I think I hate the capital more.*

Lord Jacos refused his son's request, of course. His heir would not go to Delphie to translate crumbling records and archive petty artifacts. "No point in it," he said. Just as he saw no point in most of what Coriane did, and regularly voiced that opinion.

Both children were gutted, feeling their escape snatched away. Even Jessamine noticed their downturn in emotion, though she said nothing to either. But Coriane knew their old cousin went easy on her in their first months at court, or rather, she was hard on the drink. For as much as Jessamine talked of Archeon and Summerton, she didn't seem to like either very much, if her gin consumption was any indication.

More often than not, Coriane could slip away during Jessamine's daily "nap." She walked the city many times in hopes of finding a place she enjoyed, somewhere to anchor her in the newly tossing sea of her life.

She found no such place—instead she found a person.

He asked her to call him Tibe after a few weeks. A family nickname, used among the royals and a precious few friends. "All right, then," Coriane said, agreeing to his request. "Saying 'Your Highness' was getting to be a bit of a pain."

They first met by chance, on the massive bridge that spanned the Capital River, connecting both sides of Archeon. A marvelous structure of twisted steel and trussed iron, supporting three levels of roadway, plazas, and commercial squares. Coriane was not so dazzled by silk shops or the stylish eateries jutting out over the water, but more interested in the bridge itself, its construction. She tried to fathom how many tons of metal were beneath her feet, her mind a flurry of equations. At first, she didn't notice the Sentinels walking toward her, nor the prince they followed. He was clearheaded this time, without a bottle in hand, and she thought he would pass her by.

Instead, he stopped at her side, his warmth a gentle ebb like the touch of a summer sun. "Lady Jacos," he said, following her gaze to the steel of the bridge. "Something interesting?"

She inclined her head in a bow, but didn't want to embarrass herself with another poor curtsy. "I think so," she replied. "I was just wondering how many tons of metal we're standing on, hoping it will keep us up."

The prince let out a puff of laughter tinged with nerves. He shifted his feet, as if suddenly realizing exactly how high above the water they were. "I'll do my best to keep that thought out of my head," he mumbled. "Any other frightening notions to share?"

"How much time do you have?" she said with half a grin. Half only, because something tugged at the rest, weighing it down. The cage of the capital was not a happy place for Coriane.

Nor Tiberias Calore. "Would you favor me with a walk?" he asked, extending an arm. This time, Coriane saw no hesitation in him, or even the pensive wonderings of a question. He knew her answer already.

"Of course." And she slipped her arm in his.

This will be the last time I hold the arm of a prince, she thought as they walked the bridge. She thought that every time, and she was always wrong.

In early June, a week before the court would flee Archeon for the smaller but just as grand summer palace, Tibe brought someone to meet her. They were to rendezvous in East Archeon, in the sculpture garden outside the Hexaprin Theater. Coriane was early, for Jessamine started drinking during breakfast, and she was eager to get away. For once, her relative poverty was an advantage. Her clothes were ordinary, clearly Silver, as they were striped in her house colors of gold and yellow, but nothing remarkable. No gems to denote her as a lady of a High House, as someone worth noticing. Not even a servant in uniform to stand a few paces behind. The other Silvers floating through the collection of carved marble barely saw her, and for once, she liked it that way.

The green dome of Hexaprin rose above, shading her from the still rising sun. A black swan of smooth, flawless granite perched at the top, its long neck arched and wings spread wide, every feather meticulously sculpted. A beautiful monument to Silver excess. *And probably Red made,* she knew, glancing around. There were no Reds nearby, but they bustled on the street. A few stopped to glance at the theater, their eyes raised to a place they could never inhabit. *Perhaps I'll bring Eliza and Melanie someday.* She wondered if the maids would like that, or be embarrassed by such charity.

She never found out. Tibe's arrival erased all thoughts of her Red servants, and most other things along with them.

He had none of his father's beauty, but was handsome in his own way. Tibe had a strong jaw, still stubbornly trying to grow a beard, with expressive golden eyes and a mischievous smile. His cheeks flushed when he drank and his laughter intensified, as did his rippling heat, but at the moment he was sober as a judge and twitchy. *Nervous,* Coriane realized as she moved to meet him and his entourage.

Today he was dressed plainly—*but not as poorly as me.* No uniform, medals, nothing official to denote this a royal event. He wore a simple coat, charcoal-gray, over a white shirt, dark red trousers, and black boots polished to a mirror shine. The Sentinels were not so informal. Their masks and flaming robes were mark enough of his birthright.

"Good morning," he said, and she noticed his fingers drumming rapidly at his side. "I thought we could see *Fall of Winter.* It's new, from Piedmont."

Her heart leapt at the prospect. The theater was an extravagance her family could hardly afford and, judging by the glint in Tibe's eye, he knew that. "Of course, that sounds wonderful."

"Good," he replied, hooking her arm in his own. It was second nature to both of them now, but still Coriane's arm buzzed with the feel of him. She had long decided theirs was only a friendship—*he's a prince, bound to Queenstrial*—though she could still enjoy his presence.

They left the garden, heading for the tiled steps of the theater and the fountained plaza before the entrance. Most stopped to give them room, watching as their prince and a noble lady crossed to the theater. A few snapped photographs, the bright lights blinding Coriane, but Tibe smiled through it. He was used to this sort of thing. She didn't mind it either, not truly. In fact, she wondered whether or not there was a way to dim the camera bulbs, and prevent them from stunning anyone who came near. The thought of bulbs and wire and shaded glass occupied her until Tibe spoke.

"Robert will be joining us, by the way," he blurted as they crossed the threshold, stepping over a mosaic of black swans taking flight. At first, Coriane barely heard him, stunned as she was by the beauty of Hexaprin, with its marbled walls, soaring staircases, explosions of flowers, and mirrored ceiling hung with a dozen gilded chandeliers.

But after a second, she clamped her jaw shut and turned back to Tibe to find him blushing furiously, worse than she had ever seen.

She blinked at him, concerned. In her mind's eye she saw the king's paramour, the prince who was not royal. "That's quite all right with me," she said, careful to keep her voice low. There was a crowd forming, eager to enter the matinee performance. "Unless it isn't all right with you?"

"No, no, I'm very happy he came. I—I asked him to come." Somehow, the prince was tripping over his words, and Coriane could not understand why. "I wanted him to meet you."

"Oh," she said, not knowing what else to say. Then she glanced down at her dress—ordinary, out of style—and frowned. "I wish I wore something else. It's not every day you meet a prince," she added with the shadow of a wink.

He barked a laugh of humor and relief. "Clever, Coriane, very clever."

They bypassed the ticket booths, as well as the public entrance to the theater. Tibe led her up one of the winding staircases, offering her a better view of the massive foyer. As on the bridge, she wondered who made this place, but deep down, she knew. Red labor, Red craftsmen, with perhaps a few magnetrons to aid the process. There was the usual twinge of disbelief. *How could servants create such beauty and still be considered inferior? They are capable of wonders different from our own.*

They gained skill through handiwork and practice, rather than birth. *Is that not equal to Silver strength, if not greater than it?* But she did not dwell on such thoughts long. She never did. *This is the way of the world.*

The royal box was at the end of a long, carpeted hall decorated by paintings. Many were of Prince Robert and Queen Anabel, both great patrons of the arts in the capital. Tibe pointed them out with pride, lingering by a portrait of Robert and his mother in full regalia.

"Anabel *hates* that painting," a voice said from the end of the hall. Like his laugh, Prince Robert's voice had a melody to it, and Coriane wondered if he had singer blood in his family.

The prince approached, gliding silently across the carpet with long, elegant strides. *A silk*, Coriane knew, remembering he was of House Iral. His ability was agility, balance, lending him swift movement and acrobat-like skill. His long hair fell over one shoulder, gleaming in dark waves of blue-black. As he closed the distance between them, Coriane noticed gray at his temples, as well as laugh lines around his mouth and eyes.

"She doesn't think it a true likeness of us—too pretty, you know your mother," Robert continued, coming to stop in front of the painting. He gestured to Anabel's face and then his own. Both seemed to glow with youth and vitality, their features beautiful and eyes bright. "But I think it's just fine. After all, who doesn't need a little help now and then?" he added with a kind wink. "You'll find that soon enough, Tibe."

"Not if I can help it," Tibe replied. "Sitting for paintings might be the most boring act in the kingdom."

Coriane angled a glance at him. "A small price to pay, though. For a crown."

"Well said, Lady Jacos, well said." Robert laughed, tossing back his hair. "Step lightly around this one, my boy. Though it seems you've already forgotten your manners?"

"Of course, of course," Tibe said, and waved his hand, gesturing for Coriane to come closer. "Uncle Robert, this is Coriane of House Jacos, daughter of Lord Harrus, Governor of Aderonack. And Coriane, this is Prince Robert of House Iral, Sworn Consort of His Royal Majesty,

King Tiberias the Fifth."

Her curtsy had improved in the past months, but not by much. Still, she attempted, only to have Robert pull her into an embrace. He smelled of lavender and—*baked bread*? "A pleasure to finally meet you," he said, holding her at arm's length. For once, Coriane did not feel as if she was being examined. There didn't seem to be an unkind bone in Robert's body, and he smiled warmly at her. "Come now, they should be starting momentarily."

As Tibe did before, Robert took her arm, patting her hand like a doting grandfather.

"You must sit by me, of course."

Something tightened in Coriane's chest, an unfamiliar sensation. Was it . . . happiness? She thought so.

Grinning as widely as she could, she looked over her shoulder to see Tibe following, his eyes on hers, his smile both joyous and relieved.

The next day, Tibe left with his father to review troops at a fort in Delphie, leaving Coriane free to visit Sara. House Skonos had an opulent town house on the slopes of West Archeon, but they also enjoyed apartments in Whitefire Palace itself, should the royal family have need of a skilled skin healer at any moment. Sara met her at the gates unaccompanied, her smile perfect for the guards, but a warning to Coriane.

"What's wrong? What is it?" she whispered as soon as they reached the gardens outside the Skonos chambers.

Sara drew them farther into the trees, until they were inches from an ivy-draped garden wall, with immense rosebushes on either side, obstructing them both from view. A thrum of panic went through Coriane. *Has something happened? To Sara's parents? Was Julian wrong—would Sara leave them for the war?* Coriane selfishly hoped that was not the case. She loved Sara as well as Julian did, but was not so willing to see her go, even for her own aspirations. Already the thought filled her with dread, and she felt tears prick her eyes.

"Sara, are you—are you going to—?" she began, stammering, but Sara waved her off.

"Oh, Cori, this has nothing to do with me. Don't you dare cry," she added, forcing a small laugh while she hugged Coriane. "Oh, I'm sorry, I didn't meant to upset you. I just didn't want to be overheard."

Relief flooded through Coriane. "Thank my colors," she mumbled. "So what requires such secrecy? Is your grandmother asking you to lift her eyebrows again?"

"I certainly hope not."

"Then what?"

"You met Prince Robert."

Coriane scoffed. "And? This is court, everyone's met Robert—"

"Everyone *knows* him, but they don't have private audiences with the king's paramour. In fact, he is not at all well liked."

"Can't imagine why. He's probably the kindest person here."

"Jealousy mostly, and a few of the more traditional houses think it's wrong to elevate him so high. 'Crowned prostitute' is the term most used, I think."

Coriane flushed, both with anger and embarrassment on Robert's behalf. "Well, if it's a scandal to meet him and like him, I don't mind in the least. Neither did Jessamine, actually, she was quite excited when I explained—"

"Because Robert isn't the scandal, Coriane." Sara took her hands, and Coriane felt a bit of her friend's ability seep into her skin. A cool touch that meant her paper cut from yesterday would be gone in a blink. "It's you and the crown prince, your closeness. Everyone knows how tightly knit the royal family is, particularly where Robert is concerned. They value him and protect him above everything. If Tiberias wanted you two to meet then—"

Despite the pleasant sensation, Coriane dropped Sara's hands. "We're friends. That's all this ever can be." She forced a giggle that was quite unlike herself. "You can't seriously think Tibe sees me as anything more, that he *wants* or even *can want* anything more from me?"

She expected her friend to laugh with her, to wave it all off as a joke. Instead, Sara had never looked so grave. "All signs point to yes, Coriane."

"Well, you're wrong. I'm not—he wouldn't—and besides, there's Queenstrial to think of. It must be soon, he's of age, and no one would ever choose me."

Again, Sara took Coriane's hands and gave them a gentle squeeze. "I think he would."

"Don't say that to me," Coriane whispered. She looked to the roses, but it was Tibe's face she saw. It was familiar now, after months of friendship. She knew his nose, his lips, his jaw, his eyes most of all. They stirred something in her, a connection she did not know she could make with another person. She saw herself in them, her own pain, her own joy. *We are the same*, she thought. *Searching for something to keep us anchored, both alone in a crowded room.* "It's impossible. And telling me this, giving me any kind of hope where he is concerned . . ." She sighed and bit her lip. "I don't need that heartache along with everything else. He's my friend, and I'm his. Nothing more."

Sara was not one for fancies or daydreaming. She cared more for mending broken bones than broken hearts. So Coriane could not help but believe her when she spoke, even against her own misgivings.

"Friend or not, Tibe favors you. And for that alone, you must be careful. He's just painted a target on your back, and every girl at court knows it."

"Every girl at court hardly knows who I am, Sara."

But still, she returned home vigilant.

And that night, she dreamed of knives in silk, cutting her apart.

There would be no Queenstrial.

Two months passed at the Hall of the Sun, and with every dawn the court waited for some announcement. Lords and ladies pestered the king, asking when his son would choose a bride from their daughters. He was not moved by anyone's petition, meeting all with his beautiful, stoic eyes. Queen Anabel was quite the same, giving no indication as to when her son would undertake his most important duty. Only Prince Robert had the boldness to smile, knowing precisely what storm gathered on the horizon. The whispers rose as days passed. They wondered if Tiberias was like his father, preferring men to women—but even then, he was bound to choose a queen to bear him sons of his own. Others were more astute, picking up the trail of carefully laid bread crumbs Robert had left for them. They were meant to be gentle, helpful signposts. *The prince has made his choice clear, and no arena will change his mind.*

Coriane Jacos dined with Robert regularly, as well as Queen Anabel. Both were quick to praise the young girl, so much so that the gossips wondered if House Jacos was as weak as they appeared. "A trick?" they said. "A poor mask to hide a powerful face?" The cynics among them found other explanations. "She's a singer, a manipulator. She looked into the prince's eyes and made him love her. It would not be the first time someone broke our laws for a crown."

Lord Harrus reveled in the newfound attention. He used it as leverage, to trade on his daughter's future for tetrarch coins and credit. But he was a poor player in a large, complicated game. He lost as much as he borrowed, betting on cards as well as Treasury stocks or undertaking ill-thought, costly ventures to "improve" his governed region. He founded two mines at the behest of Lord Samos, who assured him of rich iron veins in the Aderonack hills. Both failed within weeks, turning up nothing but dirt.

Only Julian was privy to such failures, and he was careful to keep them from his sister. Tibe, Robert, and Anabel did the same, shielding her from the worst gossip, working in conjunction with Julian and Sara to keep Coriane blissful in her ignorance. But of course, Coriane heard all things even through their protections. And to keep her family and friends from worry, to keep *them* happy, she pretended to be the same. Only her diary knew the cost of such lies.

Father will bury us with both hands. He boasts of me to his so-called friends, telling them I'm the next queen of this kingdom. I don't think he's ever paid so much attention to me before, and even now, it is minuscule, not for my own benefit. He pretends to love me now because of another, because of Tibe. Only when someone else sees worth in me does he condescend to do the same.

Because of her father, she dreamed of a Queenstrial she did not win, of being cast aside and returned to the old estate. Once there, she was made to sleep in the family tomb, beside the still, bare body of her uncle. When the corpse twitched, hands reaching for her throat, she would wake, drenched in sweat, unable to sleep for the rest of the night.

Julian and Sara think me weak, fragile, a porcelain doll who will shatter if touched, she wrote. *Worst of all, I'm beginning to believe them. Am I really so frail? So useless? Surely I can be of some help somehow, if Julian would only ask? Are Jessamine's lessons the best I can do? What am I becoming in this place? I doubt I even remember how to replace a lightbulb. I am not someone I recognize. Is this what growing up means?*

Because of Julian, she dreamed of being in a beautiful room. But every door was locked, every window shut, with nothing and no one to keep her company. Not even books. Nothing to upset her. And always, the room would become a birdcage with gilded bars. It would shrink and shrink until it cut her skin, waking her up.

I am not the monster the gossips think me to be. I've done nothing, manipulated no one. I haven't even attempted to use my ability in months, since Julian has no more time to teach me. But they don't believe that. I see how they look at me, even the whispers of House Merandus. Even Elara. I have not heard her in my head since the banquet, when her sneers drove me to Tibe. Perhaps that taught her better than to meddle. Or maybe she is afraid of looking into my eyes and hearing my voice, as if I'm some kind of match for her razored whispers. I am not, of course. I am hopelessly undefended against people like her. Perhaps I should thank whoever started the rumor. It keeps predators like her from making me prey.

Because of Elara, she dreamed of ice-blue eyes following her every move, watching as she donned a crown. People bowed under her gaze and sneered when she turned away, plotting against their newly made queen. They feared her and hated her in equal measure, each one a wolf waiting for her to be revealed as a lamb. She sang in the dream, a wordless song that did nothing but double their bloodlust. Sometimes they killed her, sometimes they ignored her, sometimes they put her in a cell. All three wrenched her from sleep.

Today Tibe said he loves me, that he wants to marry me. I do not believe him. Why would he want such a thing? I am no one of consequence. No great beauty or intellect, no strength or power to aid his reign. I bring nothing to him but worry and weight. He needs someone strong at his side, a person who laughs at the gossips and overcomes her own doubts. Tibe is as weak as I am, a lonely boy without a path of his own. I will only make things worse. I will only bring him pain. How can I do that?

Because of Tibe, she dreamed of leaving court for good. Like Julian wanted to do, to keep Sara from staying behind. The locations varied with the changing nights. She ran to Delphie or Harbor Bay or Piedmont or even the Lakelands, each one painted in shades of black and gray. Shadow cities to swallow her up and hide her from the prince and the crown he offered. But they frightened her too. And they were always empty, even of ghosts. In these dreams, she ended up alone. From these dreams, she woke quietly, in the morning, with dried tears and an aching heart.

Still, she did not have the strength to tell him no.

When Tiberias Calore, heir to the throne of Norta, sank to a knee with a ring in hand, she took it. She smiled. She kissed him. She said yes.

"You have made me happier than I ever thought I could be," Tibe told her.

"I know the feeling," she replied, meaning every word. She was happy, yes, in her own way, as best she knew.

But there is a difference between a single candle in darkness, and a sunrise.

* * *

There was opposition among the High Houses. Queenstrial was their right, after all. To wed the most noble son to the most talented daughter. House Merandus, Samos, Osanos were once the front-runners, their girls groomed to be queens only to have even the chance of a crown snatched away by some nobody. But the king stood firm. And there was precedent. At least two Calore kings before had wed outside the bonds of Queenstrial. Tibe would be the third.

As if to apologize for the Queenstrial slight, the rest of the wedding was rigidly traditional. They waited until Coriane turned sixteen the following spring, drawing out the engagement, allowing the royal family to convince, threaten, and buy their way to the acceptance of the High Houses. Eventually all agreed to the terms. Coriane Jacos would be queen but her children, all of them, would be subject to political weddings. A bargain she did not want to make, but Tibe was willing, and she could not tell him no.

Of course, Jessamine took credit for everything. Even as Coriane was laced into her wedding gown, an hour from marrying a prince, the old cousin crowed across a brimful glass. "Look at your bearing, those are Jacos bones. Slender, graceful, like a bird."

Coriane felt nothing of the sort. *If I was a bird, then I could fly away with Tibe.* The tiara on her head, the first of many, poked into her scalp. Not a good omen.

"It gets easier," Queen Anabel whispered into her ear. Coriane wanted to believe her.

With no mother of her own, Coriane had willingly accepted Anabel and Robert as substitute parents. In a perfect world, Robert would even walk her down the aisle instead of her father, who was still wretched. As a wedding gift, Harrus had asked for five thousand tetrarchs in allowance. He didn't seem to understand that presents were usually *given* to the bride, not requested of her. Despite her soon-to-be royal position, he had lost his governorship to poor management. Already on thin ice due to Tibe's unorthodox engagement, the royals could do nothing to help and House Provos gleefully took up the governance of Aderonack.

After the ceremony, the banquet, and even after Tibe had fallen asleep in their new bedchamber, Coriane scrawled in her diary. The penmanship was hasty, slurred, with sloping letters and blots of ink that bled through the pages. She did not write often anymore.

I am married to a prince who will one day be a king. Usually this is where the fairy tale ends. Stories don't go much further than this moment, and I fear there's a good reason for it. A sense of dread hung over today, a black cloud I still can't be rid of. It is an unease deep in the heart of me, feeding off my strength. Or perhaps I am coming down with sickness. It's entirely possible. Sara will know.

I keep dreaming of her eyes. Elara's. Is it possible—could she be sending me these nightmares? Can whispers do such a thing? I must know. I must. I must. I MUST.

For her first act as a princess of Norta, Coriane employed a proper tutor, as well as taking Julian into her household. Both to hone her ability, and help her defend against what she called "annoyances." A carefully chosen word. Once more, she elected to keep her problems to herself, to stop her brother from worry, as well as her new husband.

Both were distracted. Julian by Sara, and Tibe by another well-guarded secret.

The king was sick.

It took two long years before the court knew anything was amiss.

"It's been like this for some time now," Robert said, one hand in Coriane's. She stood on a balcony with him, her face the picture of sorrow. The prince was still handsome, still smiling, but his vigor was gone, his skin gray and dark, leached of life. He seemed to be dying with the king. But Robert's was an ailment of the heart, not the bones and blood, as the healers said of the king's ills. A cancer, a gnawing, riddling Tiberias with rot and tumors.

He shivered, despite the sun above, not to mention the hot summer air. Coriane felt sweat on the back of her neck, but like Robert, she was cold inside.

"The skin healers can only do so much. If only he'd broken his spine, that'd be no trouble at all." Robert's laugh sounded hollow, a song without notes. The king was not yet dead, and already his consort was a shell of himself. And while she feared for her father-in-law, knowing that a painful, diseased death waited for him, she was terrified of losing Robert as well. *He cannot succumb to this. I won't let him.*

"It's fine, no need to explain," Coriane muttered. She did her best not to cry, though every inch of her hoped to. *How can this be happening? Are we not Silvers? Are we not gods?* "Does he need anything? Do you?"

Robert smiled an empty smile. His eyes flashed to her stomach, not yet rounded by the life inside. A prince or princess, she did not know yet. "He would have liked to have seen that one."

House Skonos tried everything, even cycling the king's blood. But whatever sickness he had never disappeared. It wasted at him faster than they could heal. Usually Robert stayed by him in his chamber, but today he left Tiberias alone with his son, and Coriane knew why. The end was near. The crown would pass, and there were things only Tibe could know.

The day the king died, Coriane marked the date and colored the entire diary page in black ink. She did the same a few months later, for Robert. His will was gone, his heart refusing to beat. Something ate at him too, and in the end, it swallowed him whole. Nothing could be done. No one could hold him back from taking shadowed flight. Coriane wept bitterly as she inked the day of his ending in her diary.

She carried on the tradition. Black pages for black deaths. One for Jessamine, her body simply too old to continue. One for her father, who found his end in the bottom of a glass.

And three for the miscarriages she suffered over the years. Each one came at night, on the heels of a violent nightmare.

Coriane was twenty-one, and pregnant for a fourth time.

She told no one, not even Tibe. She did not want the heartache for him. Most of all, she wanted no one to know. If Elara Merandus was truly still plaguing her, turning her own body against her unborn children, she didn't want any kind of announcement regarding another royal child.

The fears of a fragile queen were no basis for banishing a High House, let alone one as powerful as Merandus. So Elara was still at court, the last of the three Queenstrial favorites still unmarried. She made no overtures to Tibe. On the contrary, she regularly petitioned to join Coriane's ladies, and was regularly denied her request.

It will be a surprise when I seek her out, Coriane thought, reviewing her meager but necessary plan. *She'll be off guard, startled enough for me to work.* She had practiced on Julian, Sara, even Tibe. Her abilities were better than ever. *I will succeed.*

The Parting Ball signaling the end of the season at the summer palace was the perfect cover. So many guests, so many minds. Elara would be easy to get close to. She would not expect Queen Coriane to speak to her, let alone *sing* to her. But Coriane would do both.

She made sure to dress for the occasion. Even now, with the wealth of the crown behind her, she felt out of place in her crimson and gold silks, a girl playing dress-up against the lords and ladies around her. Tibe whistled as he always did, calling her beautiful, assuring her she was the only woman for him—in this world or any other. Normally it calmed her, but now she was only nervous, focused on the task at hand.

Everything moved both too slowly and too quickly for her taste. The meal, the dancing, greeting so many curled smiles and narrowed eyes. She was still the Singer Queen to so many, a woman who bewitched her way to the throne. *If only that were true. If only I was what they thought me to be, then Elara would be of no consequence, I would not spend every night awake, afraid to sleep, afraid to dream.*

Her opportunity came deep into the night, when the wine was running low and Tibe was in his precious whiskey. She swept away from his side, leaving Julian to attend to her drunken king. Even Sara did not notice her queen steal away, to cross the path of Elara Merandus as she idled by the balcony doors.

"Come outside with me, won't you, Lady Elara?" Coriane said, her eyes wide and laser-focused on Elara's own. To anyone who might pass by, her voice sounded like music and a choir both, elegant, heartbreaking, dangerous. A weapon as devastating as her husband's flame.

Elara's eyes did not waver, locked upon Coriane's, and the queen felt her heart flutter. *Focus,* she told herself. *Focus, damn you.* If the Merandus woman could not be charmed, then Coriane would be in for something worse than her nightmares.

But slowly, sluggishly, Elara took a step back, never breaking eye contact. "Yes," she said dully, pushing the balcony door open with one hand.

They stepped out together, Coriane holding Elara by the shoulder, keeping her from wavering. Outside, the night was sticky hot, the last gasps of summer in the upper river valley. Coriane felt none of it. Elara's eyes were the only things in her mind.

"Have you been playing with my mind?" she asked, cutting directly to her intentions.

"Not for a while," Elara replied, her eyes faraway.

"When was the last time?"

"Your wedding day."

Coriane blinked, startled. *So long ago.* "What? What did you do?"

"I made you trip." A dreamy smile crossed Elara's features. "I made you trip on your dress."

"That—that's it?"

"Yes."

"And the dreams? The nightmares?"

Elara said nothing. *Because there's nothing for her to say,* Coriane knew. She sucked in a breath, fighting the urge to cry. *These fears are my own. They always have been. They always will be. I was wrong before I came to court, and I'm still wrong long after.*

"Go back inside," she finally hissed. "Remember none of this." Then she turned away, breaking the eye contact she so desperately needed to keep Elara under her control.

Like a person waking up, Elara blinked rapidly. She cast a single confused glance at the queen before hurrying away, back into the party.

Coriane moved in the opposite direction, toward the stone bannister ringing the balcony. She leaned over it, trying to catch her breath, trying not to scream. Greenery stretched below her, a garden of fountains and stone more than forty feet down. For a single, paralyzing second, she fought the urge to jump.

The next day, she took a guard into her service, to defend her from any Silver ability someone might use against her. If not Elara, than surely someone else of House Merandus. Coriane simply could not believe how her mind seemed to spin out of control, happy one second and then distraught the next, bouncing between emotions like a kite in a gale.

The guard was of House Arven, the silent house. His name was Rane, a savior clad in white, and he swore to defend his queen against all forces.

They named the baby Tiberias, as was custom. Coriane didn't care for the name, but acquiesced at Tibe's request, and his assurance that they would name the next after Julian. He was a fat baby, smiling early, laughing often, growing bigger by leaps and bounds. She nicknamed him Cal to distinguish him from his father and grandfather. It stuck.

The boy was the sun in Coriane's sky. On hard days, he split the darkness. On good days, he lit the world. When Tibe went away to the front, for weeks at a time now that the war ran hot again, Cal kept her safe. Only a few months old and better than any shield in the kingdom.

Julian doted on the boy, bringing him toys, reading to him. Cal was apt to break things apart and jam them back together incorrectly, to Coriane's delight. She spent long hours piecing his smashed gifts back together, amusing him as well as herself.

"He'll be bigger than his father," Sara said. Not only was she Coriane's chief lady-in-waiting, she was also her physician. "He's a strong boy."

While any mother would revel in those words, Coriane feared them. *Bigger than his father, a strong boy.* She knew what that meant for a Calore prince, an heir to the Burning Crown.

He will not be a soldier, she wrote in her newest diary. *I owe him that much. Too long the sons and daughters of House Calore have been fighting, too long has this country had a warrior king. Too long have we been at war, on the front and—and also within. It might be a crime to write such things, but I am a queen. I am* the *queen. I can say and write what I think.*

As the months passed, Coriane thought more and more of her childhood home. The estate was gone, demolished by the Provos governors, emptied of her memories and ghosts. It was too close to the Lakelander border for proper Silvers to live, even though the fighting was contained to the bombed-out territories of the Choke. Even though few Silvers died, despite the Reds dying by the thousands. Conscripted from every corner of the kingdom, forced to serve and fight. *My kingdom,* Coriane knew. *My husband signs every conscription renewal, never stopping the cycle, only complaining about the cramp in his hand.*

She watched her son on the floor, smiling with a single tooth, bashing a pair of wooden blocks together. *He will not be the same,* she told herself.

The nightmares returned in earnest. This time they were of her baby grown, wearing armor, leading soldiers, sending them into a curtain of smoke. He followed and never returned.

With dark circles beneath her eyes, she wrote what would become the second-to-last entry into her diary. The words seemed to be carved into the page. She had not slept in three days, unable to face another dream of her son dying.

The Calores are children of fire, as strong and destructive as their flame, but Cal will not be like the others before. Fire can destroy, fire can kill, but it can also create. Forest burned in the summer will be green by spring, better and stronger than before. Cal's flame will build and bring roots from the ashes of war. The guns will quiet, the smoke will clear, and the soldiers, Red and Silver both, will come home. One hundred years of war, and my son will bring peace. He will not die fighting. He will not. HE WILL NOT.

Tibe was gone, at Fort Patriot in Harbor Bay. But Arven stood just outside her door, his presence forming a bubble of relief. *Nothing can touch me while he is here,* she thought, smoothing the downy hair on Cal's head. *The only person in my head is me.*

The nurse who came to collect the baby noticed the queen's agitated manner, her twitching hands, the glazed eyes, but said nothing. It was not her place.

Another night came and went. No sleep, but one last entry in Coriane's diary. She had drawn flowers around each word—magnolia blossoms.

The only person in my head is me.

Tibe is not the same. The crown has changed him, as you feared it would. The fire is in him, the fire that will burn all the world. And it is in your son, in the prince who will never change his blood and will never sit a throne.

The only person in my head is me.

The only person who has not changed is you. You are still the little girl in a dusty room, forgotten, unwanted, out of place. You are queen of everything, mother to a beautiful son, wife to a king who loves you, and still you cannot find it in yourself to smile.

Still you make nothing.

Still you are empty.

The only person in your head is you.

And she is no one of any importance.

She is nothing.

The next morning, a maid found her bridal crown broken on the floor, an explosion of pearls and twisted gold. There was silver on it, blood dark from the passing hours.

And her bathwater was black with it.

The diary ended unfinished, unseen by any who deserved to read it.

Only Elara saw its pages, and the slow unraveling of the woman inside.

She destroyed the book like she destroyed Coriane.

And she dreamed of nothing.

While the Delphie archives and libraries of Norta are all but brimming with the Silver side of our recent history, a Red perspective is far more difficult to find. Naturally, such records were neither scientifically made nor well maintained, and I've done what I can to begin piecing together some form of a Red point of view. The vaults of Horn Mountain have been supplemental to my research, and, while helpful, their records are lacking as well. Most useful have been my contacts within the Scarlet Guard, who have connected me as best they can. Unlike Silvers, many Red communities have relied on oral tradition to pass down their histories. Unfortunately, this can sometimes be unreliable, and I've done what I can to corroborate this evidence with other, more concrete historical records. Despite the difficulty of such an endeavor, I find it more than necessary to do what we can to preserve some other angle on our history, lest we forget what came before and what befell the Reds of this world. As such, I've compiled what I have so far from Red-specific sources, in a combination of documents and interview transcripts.

Though I am as guilty as any Silver for the abhorrent treatment of Reds throughout my lifetime and deserve no penance, I hope this is helpful to the future.

—JJ

(MR. ELLDON turns over a small but brilliant RUBY)

ELLDON: Been in my family near 300 years. We used to serve kings, the first kings of this land. The old Calores, Caesar and his heirs. He was good to his servants, so they say. Son wasn't. That's how my grandfather's grandfather's grandfather or whoever ended up with this. Used to be more. A whole necklace full of them. But they disappeared over the years, sold or traded or just lost. This is all that's left.

JACOS: He stole it?

ELLDON: He took it. The king's pleasure boat was sinking. The king was shouting orders, shoving Reds into the water trying to save himself. Old Grandfather didn't like that. And in the confusion, he ripped the rubies right off Caesarion's neck and pushed him into the sea.

JACOS: I see.

ELLDON: King wasn't a relative of yours, was he?

JACOS: Most likely yes.

(Mr. Elldon holds out the ruby.)

ELLDON: You want it back?

JACOS: Not in the slightest.

Mr. Tem Elldon of the Archeon Red sector claims his ancestor was responsible for the death of King Caesarion, who drowned in a boating incident in 44 NE.

removed from the outskirts of Archeon to make way for the barrier-tree forest. By King Tiberias I's decree, Reds were given the option to relocate to the newly built tech community Grand Town. They were promised full employment and exemption from conscription. Most leapt at the opportunity to live in the new
city, wit
abundant
tion. The
communit
such as
Town nea
Town was
to suit t
Within a
ated earn
Gray Town
rapidly,
ring rare
Burgeonin
ers, and
of life i
ties had
productio
were not
towns or

NEW HOUSING • RUNNING WATER • ELECTRICITY • RATIONS
NO NO NO NO

RELOCATE
TODAY

GRAND TOWN
GRAY
NEW TOWN
MERRY TOWN

~ by ROYAL DECREE of KING TIBERIAS ~

ALL REDS who migrate to a technological town will be given jobs at **FAIR WAGES** and made **EXEMPT** from **MILITARY SERVICE**, their families included.
NO

Master a skill, live well, serve the kingdom.

BECOME A SLAVE

While overseen by Silvers, the center itself was staffed by Reds—either those favored by the overseers or those who bribed their way into the less-grueling position. Their daily notes were stored and ignored with other official documentation.

From the Records of the New Town Administrative Center:

June 1, 144 NE: Still snowed under by the deported from up north. Staffing otherwise untrained individuals is more dangerous than difficult. Two got chewed up in the gear works yesterday, and another nearly ignited a depot in the weapons sector. We've sent requests up to the overseers to approve accelerated training for the Maiden Falls Reds, just to give them enough so they don't kill themselves or anyone else on the manufacturing floors, but every single one has been denied. Any training is to be done outside shift hours, at our own discretion. The center is currently organizing volunteers to get the surviving two hundred or so ready to work. Most are under eighteen and separated from their families, as they're too young to be conscripted with the rest of their communities up north. Still attempting to improve housing, especially for the young children.

The above corresponds with Julias III's crackdown on the Red communities around Maiden Falls following the death of his son at the hands of Red bandits. He forced them to destroy their villages and build the fortress city Corvium at the border. Thousands of Reds were either conscripted into the Nortan military or deported to tech slums in punishment.

From the Records of the Red Watch in Harbor Bay:

. . . what we can to hide our people across the city, now that the Silvers are on the hunt. They don't know who killed the queen's brother, just that it was a Red with the Allegiance. As far as we know, the Allegiance is being rounded up. Some whisper got a hold of one of them and cracked the poor man right open. All the safe houses and escape routes. Tore it out like a bad tooth. We're trying to coöperate, or look like we're cooperating at least. Keep our own safe. Not much we can do for the Allegiance. They weren't smart about this. Weren't smart at all, and we're going to suffer for it. . . .

The Red Watch officer's account refers to the assassination of Queen Andura's brother and heir, Prince Marcas, in 197 NE. He was killed by a Red uprising in Harbor Bay. I assume the "Allegiance" referred to above was a predecessor to the Scarlet Guard.

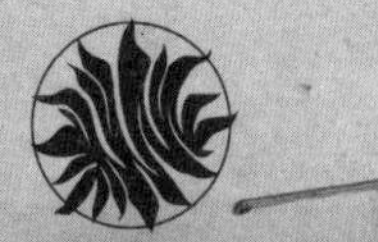

Increased movement out of the Lakelands along the River, look to be Red soldiers. Odd, they don't head south, but turn east and head upriver at the Fork. All pay in full up front. Have ferried the same group twice this year. Other ferriers say they're done the same. ~~I've got a strange feeling about this lot.~~ I've got a strange feeling about this lot. They aren't running, that's for sure. And they aren't acting on Silver orders. They pay too well for our ~~descretion~~ discretion.

The Red soldiers gave me enough coin to buy my boat twice over to move them now and move them quick. Paid again at the border. Couldn't resist. Took them up the Ohius, along the Nortan border. Dangerous ground. Won't risk that again. Still haven't gotten their names, but they're heading north, judging by their gear. Far, far north.

The Lakelander smugglers tipped off the ferriers at the Fork. Silvers will be cracking down on the border checks, and have orders to destroy our boats if we land on their banks. There's been some trouble with Reds on the Lakes. Enough to keep an eye on the border. They're hunting.

COL. FARLEY: Started slow, started small. Enough not to be noticed. A bridge collapse backs up transports and convoys for a few days. A citadel doesn't get a weapons shipment on time. A troop march can't go out. They have to double-time to keep a schedule, and the officers are frustrated, frazzled. Maybe one takes a bad step and cracks his head open. Maybe his children come to visit, and end up lost in the woods. That sort of thing.

JACOS: That sort of thing.

COL. FARLEY: You look a bit green, Jacos. I thought you studied this? Thought you've seen worse?

JACOS: Words on the page are very different from hearing it firsthand, sir. So you say this began in the army?

COL. FARLEY: That's right. My unit wasn't assigned to a Citadel or specific legion. We floated. We were good at war, good at killing. The Silvers sent us where we were needed. To the front—or somewhere else.

JACOS: Within the Lakelands?

COL. FARLEY: The border, mostly, but yes. We were dispatched all over.

JACOS: I believe it's your turn to look a little green, Colonel.

COL. FARLEY: That's what did it, in the end. Sending us after our own. Making us stop a riot any way we could. Pull a mother away from her child as the kid's taken away to conscript. It didn't sit well.

JACOS: I can imagine it didn't.

COL. FARLEY: We had a Silver officer keeping us in check, but he liked to drink. Liked to eat. Liked life with the higher-ups at the Citadels. And so long as we showed up where we had to be, he didn't mind what we did in the meantime.

JACOS: Blowing up bridges and killing officers.

COL. FARLEY: Right. We kept the circle small. Just my unit at first. We were all from the Hud, the north, a cold and barren place. You learn to hunt when you learn to walk up there. Sentry was with me from the beginning, and so was Crimson. He was our best contact with the Rivermen.

JACOS: The Rivermen?

COL. FARLEY: That's what we call the ferriers

and smugglers of the Disputed Lands. No one better at getting you over the border or moving along the river. We weren't allowed to travel with weaponry, but they were good at keeping us armed when we needed to be.

JACOS: So the Command Generals code-named Sentry and Crimson were part of your unit. How did you meet the others?

COL. FARLEY: Crossed paths over the years. Most of them were doing the same thing we were. Sabotaging the Silvers without much plan beyond a week or two. It was Palace and Swan who really brought us together, gave us an objective. They knew the Silvers better than we did. Knew how they thought, how they acted. And they knew that, if we really wanted to make a difference, this had to be bigger than us.

JACOS: And it certainly is. Would you like to talk about the incident at the Hud? It's referred to as the Drowning of the Northlands.

(Colonel Farley stares for a long time)

COL. FARLEY: No I fucking would not.

While the Disputed Lands keep a different calendar from Nortans, and the river ferrier is hardly a scholar, I can triangulate his entries to sometime after 300 NE. Based on my conversation with Colonel Farley, I suspect these Red soldiers moving along the border included himself, General Sentry, General Crimson, and the beginnings of the Scarlet Guard.

JACOS: Before Huntress, what was your code name within the Scarlet Guard?

GEN. FARLEY: I was Lamb. And my father is Ram.

JACOS: You were quite young when you joined.

GEN. FARLEY: Yes.

JACOS: And you aided your father with his missions throughout the Lakelands. Planting operatives in key positions, sabotaging Silver trade and transport, smuggling, intelligence gathering, assassinations, et cetera.

GEN. FARLEY: They were my missions as well.

JACOS: Of course. And you were hand-selected for the Nortan infiltration.

GEN. FARLEY: Yes.

JACOS: How old were you when your mother and sister died?

(General Farley does not respond)

JACOS: Would you like to talk about the incident at the Hud?

GEN. FARLEY: No I fucking would not.

FROM MILITARY RECORDS OF HORN MOUNTAIN AND THE MONTFORT DEFENSE CENTER:

Our spies in the Lakelands have reported a major event in the north, on the shores of the Bay of Hud. Based on our intelligence, several attacks and acts of sabotage throughout the kingdom have been traced to a small group based out of a remote village. The King of the Lakelands retaliated with force, and moved the waters of the bay to quite literally extinguish the first embers of rebellion. We're still waiting on casualty counts, but preliminary reports place it in the hundreds. I've put in a request to send an operative to investigate properly and report back. I'm most interested in this so-called group, their organization, and their size. They seem to be well coordinated and able to move. Not to mention smart. Several have been captured but have given nothing under interrogation. It seems they operate on a need-to-know basis, very militaristic. No one knows the whole picture. Will see how they respond.

Drowning of the Northlands most likely early spring, 315 NE.

Jacos: I understand you played no small part in recent events, particularly those surrounding Mare Barrow.

Mr. Whistle: Wasn't much of anything. Girl's a good thief. I used to sell off what she lifted, take a little for my troubles.

Jacos: You also introduced her to General Diana Farley and the Scarlet Guard.

(Mr. Whistle narrows his eyes and shrugs.)

Jacos: It's all right to tell me as much or as little as you like, sir. I'm simply here to get every angle.

Whistle: You know Whistle isn't actually my last name, right? It's a code. Guard's not the only people around with code names, eh.

Jacos: I see.

Whistle: It's part of a bigger operation. The Whistle network. Fences and smugglers all over the country, relaying with each other. Someone down south can move sugar, up north we got batteries, and so on. Necessary, you know, with your type running everything. How else were we supposed to survive in the cracks?

Jacos: I certainly agree with you. And the Scarlet Guard infiltrated the Whistle network early on, didn't they?

Whistle: Infiltrated? No, they partnered with us. We helped them move, carried information, smuggled supplies and people. But we were in charge of ourselves. No one took a job they didn't want. That was the agreement, and the Guard kept it.

Jacos: How long were you working with the Guard?

Whistle: Oh, me? Not long. Less than two years, I suppose. They move pretty quickly, that Guard. Once they set to moving.

Jacos: And before the Guard? What was life like then? I assume you've seen a great deal of it.

Whistle: Is that your way of saying I look old?

(Mr. Whistle laughs)

Whistle: Yes, I've seen my share. The good, the bad. The Stilts is better than most places. We're no tech town, and I never had to pass through one of those, thankfully.

But you still have to watch kids ripped out of their homes and marched off. Still have to see the letters come in and send a parent to their knees. I'm lucky. No kids. No family. And I had good cover. Swept the streets to keep myself employed in the eyes of any Silver who cared to look. At least no one has to do that anymore. They don't have to worry about the army, even if they're worrying about their next meal or the next angry Silver to come blasting through their town. Not that I'm complaining. Things were worse before the Guard, before the war. We didn't know they could be better. We didn't hope for it. We knew what happened to Reds who stood up. Uprisings that failed. Firebrands killed for a speech or a secret letter. There was no use in trying to change the world. It was just too big, too strong, the Silvers always better than us. No more.

Jacos: No more.

Whistle: Rise, Red as the dawn.

STEEL SCARS

THE FOLLOWING MESSAGE HAS BEEN DECODED
CONFIDENTIAL, COMMAND CLEARANCE REQUIRED

Day 61 of Operation LAKER, Stage 3.
Operative: Colonel REDACTED.
Designation: RAM.
Origin: Solmary, LL.
Destination: COMMAND at REDACTED.

-Operation LAKER completed ahead of schedule, deemed successful. Canals and lock points of LAKES PERIUS, MISKIN, and NERON under control of the Scarlet Guard.
-Operatives WHIPPER and OPTIC will control LAKER moving forward, maintain close contact,

open channels to MOBILE BASE and COMMAND. Stand-and-report protocol, awaiting action orders.
-Returning to TRIAL with LAMB at present.
-LAKER overview: Killed in action: D. FERRON, T. MILLS, M. PERCHER (3).
Wounded: SWIFTY, WISHBONE (2).
Silver casualty count (3): Greenwarden (1), Strongarm (1), Skin healer? (1).
Civilian casualty count: Unknown.

RISE, RED AS THE DAWN.

"Storms ahead."

The Colonel speaks to fill the silence. His one good eye presses to a crack in the compartment wall, fixing on the horizon. The other eye stares, though it can hardly see through a film of scarlet blood. Nothing new. His left eye has been like that for years.

I follow his gaze, peering through slats in the rattling wood. Dark clouds gather a few miles off, trying to hide behind the forested hills. In the distance, thunder rolls. I pay it no mind. I only hope the storms don't slow the train down, forcing us to spend one second longer hidden here, beneath the false floor of a cargo car.

We don't have time for thunderstorms or pointless conversation. I haven't slept in two days and I have the face to prove it. I want nothing more than quiet and a few hours of rest before we make it back to the base in Trial. Luckily there's not much to do here but lie down. I'm too tall to stand in such a space, as is the Colonel. We both have to sprawl, leaning as best we can in the dim partition. It'll be night soon, with only darkness to keep us company.

I can't complain about the mode of transportation. On the trip out to Solmary, we spent half the journey on a barge shipping fruit. It stalled out on Lake Neron, and most of the cargo rotted. Spent the first week of operations washing the stink from my clothes. And I'll never forget the mess before we started Laker, in Detraon. Three days in a cattle car, only to find the Lakelander capital utterly beyond reach. Too close to the Choke and the warfront to have shoddy defenses, a truth I willingly overlooked. But I wasn't an officer then, and it wasn't my decision to try to infiltrate a Silver capital without adequate intelligence or support. That was the Colonel. Back then he was only a captain with the code name Ram and too much to prove, too much to fight for. I only tagged along, barely more than an oathed soldier. I had things to prove too.

He continues to squint at the landscape. Not to look outside, but to avoid looking at me. *Fine.* I don't like looking at him either.

Bad blood or not, we make a good team. Command knows it, we know it, and that's why we keep getting sent out together. Detraon was our only misstep in an endless march for the cause. And for them, for the Scarlet Guard, we put aside our differences each and every time.

"Any idea where we go next?" Like the Colonel, I won't abide the heavy silence.

He pulls back from the wall, frowning, still not looking my way. "You know that's not how it works."

I've spent two years as an officer, two more as an oathed soldier of the Guard, and a lifetime living in its shadow. *Of course I know how it works,* I want to spit.

No one knows more than they must. No one is told anything beyond their operation, their squadron, their immediate superiors. Information is more dangerous than any weapon we possess. We learned that early, after decades of failed uprisings, all laid low by one captured Red in the hands of a Silver whisper. Even the best-trained soldier cannot resist an assault of the mind. They are always unraveled, their secrets always discovered. So my operatives and my soldiers answer to me, their captain. I answer to the Colonel, and he answers to Command, whoever they might be. We know only what we must to move forward. It's the only reason the Guard has lasted this long, surviving where no other underground organization has before.

But no system is perfect.

"Just because you haven't received new orders doesn't mean you don't have an *idea* as to what they might be," I say.

A muscle in his cheek twitches. To pull a frown or a smile, I don't know. But I doubt it's the latter. The Colonel doesn't smile, not truly. Not for many years.

"I have my suspicions," he replies after a long moment.

"And they are . . . ?"

"My own."

I hiss through my teeth. *Typical.* And probably for the best, if I'm being honest with myself. I've had enough close shaves of my own with Silver hunting dogs to know exactly how vital the Guard's secrecy is. My mind alone contains names, dates, operations, enough information to cripple the last two years of work in the Lakelands.

"Captain Farley."

We don't use our titles or names in official correspondence. I'm Lamb, according to anything that could be intercepted. Another defense. If any of our messages fall into the wrong hands, if the Silvers crack our cyphers, they'll have a hard time tracking us down and unraveling our vast, dedicated network.

"Colonel," I respond, and he finally looks at me.

Regret flashes in his one good eye, still a familiar shade of blue. The rest of him has changed over the years. He's noticeably harder, a wiry mass of old muscle, coiled like a snake beneath threadbare clothes. His blond hair, lighter than mine, has begun to thin. There's white at the temples. I can't believe I never noticed it before. He's getting old. But not slow. Not stupid. The Colonel is just as sharp and dangerous as ever.

I keep still under his quiet, quick observation. Everything is a test with him. When he opens his mouth, I know I've passed.

"What do you know about Norta?"

I grin harshly. "So they've finally decided to expand out."

"I asked you a question, Little Lamb."

The nickname is laughable. I'm almost six feet tall.

"Another monarchy like the Lakelands," I spit out. "Reds must work or conscript. They center on the coast, their capital is Archeon. At war with the Lakelands for nearly a century. They have an alliance with Piedmont. Their king is Tiberias—Tiberias the—"

"The Sixth," he offers. Chiding as a schoolteacher, not that I spent much time in school. His fault. "Of the House Calore."

Stupid. They don't even have brains enough to give their children different names.

"Burners," I add. "They lay claim to the so-called Burning Crown. Fitting opposite to the nymph kings of the Lakelands." A monarchy I know all too well, from a lifetime living beneath their rule. They are as unending and unyielding as the waters of their kingdom.

"Indeed. Opposite but also horribly alike."

"Then they should be just as easy to infiltrate."

He raises an eyebrow, gesturing to the cramped space around us. He almost looks amused. "You call this easy?"

"I haven't been shot at today, so, yes, I'd say so," I reply. "Besides, Norta is what, half the size of the Lakelands?"

"With comparable populations. Dense cities, a more advanced basis of infrastructure—"

"All the better for us. Crowds are easy to hide in."

He grits his teeth, annoyed. "Do you have an answer to everything?"

"I'm good at what I do."

Outside, the thunder rumbles again, closer than before.

"So we go to Norta next. Do what we've done here," I press on. Already, my body buzzes with anticipation. This is what I've been waiting for. The Lakelands are only one spoke of the wheel, one nation in a continent of many. A rebellion contained to its borders would eventually fail, stamped out by the other nations of the continent. But something bigger, a wave across two kingdoms, another foundation to explode beneath the Silvers' cursed feet—that has a chance. And a chance is all I require to do what I must.

The illegal gun at my hip has never felt so comforting.

"You must not forget, Captain." Now he's staring. I wish he wouldn't. *He looks so much like her.* "Where our skills truly lie. What we started as, what we came from."

Without warning, I slam my heel against the boards below us. He doesn't flinch. My anger is not a surprise.

"How could I forget?" I sneer. I resist the urge to tug at the long blond braid over my shoulder. "My mirror reminds me every day."

I never win arguments with the Colonel. But this feels like a draw at least.

He looks away, back to the wall. The last bit of sunlight glints through, illuminating the blood of his wounded eye. It glows red in the dying light.

His sigh is heavy with memory. "So does mine."

THE FOLLOWING MESSAGE HAS BEEN DECODED
CONFIDENTIAL, COMMAND CLEARANCE REQUIRED

Operative: Colonel REDACTED.
Designation: RAM.
Origin: Trial, LL.
Destination: COMMAND at REDACTED.

-Returned to TRIAL with LAMB.
-Reports of LL Silver pushback in ADELA verified.
-Request permission to dispatch HOLIDAY and her team to observe/respond.
-Request permission to begin assessment of contact viability in NRT.

RISE, RED AS THE DAWN.

THE FOLLOWING MESSAGE HAS BEEN DECODED
CONFIDENTIAL, SENIOR CLEARANCE REQUIRED

Operative: General REDACTED.
Designation: DRUMMER.
Origin: REDACTED.
Destination: RAM at Trial, LL.

-Permission to dispatch HOLIDAY granted. Observe

only, EYES ON Operation.
-Permission to assess contact viability in NRT granted.
-LAMB will take point on Operation RED WEB, making contact with smuggling and underground networks in NRT, emphasis on the WHISTLE black market ring. Orders enclosed, her eyes only. Must dispatch to NRT within week.
-RAM will take point on Operation SHIELDWALL. Orders enclosed, your eyes only. Must dispatch to Ronto within week.

RISE, RED AS THE DAWN.

Trial is the single largest city on the Lakelander border, its intricately carved walls and towers looking across Lake Redbone and deep into the heart of the Nortan backcountry. The lake hides a flooded city, all raided and stripped by nymph divers. Meanwhile, the slave workers of the Lakelands built Trial on the shores, in mockery of the drowned ruins and the Nortan wilderness.

I used to wonder what kinds of idiots are fighting this Silver war, if they insist on containing the battlegrounds to the forsaken Choke. The northern border is long and winding, cutting along the river, mostly forested on both sides, always defended but never attacked. Of course, in the winter, it's a brutal land of cold and snow, but what about the late spring and summer? *Now?* If Norta and the Lakelands hadn't been fighting for a century, I would expect an assault on the city at any moment. But there's nothing at all, and never will be.

Because the war is not a war at all.

It is an extermination.

Red soldiers conscript, fight, and die in the thousands, year after year. They're told to fight for their kings, to defend their country, their families, who would surely be overrun and overthrown if not for their forced bravery. And the Silvers sit back, moving their toy legions to and fro, trading blows that never seem to do much of anything. Reds are too small, too restricted, too uneducated to notice. It's sickening.

Only one of a thousand reasons I believe in the cause and in the Scarlet Guard. But belief doesn't make it easy to take a bullet. Not like the last time I returned to Irabelle, bleeding from the abdomen, unable to walk without the damned Colonel's aid. At least then I got a week to rest and heal. Now I doubt I'll be here much longer than a few days before they send us back out again.

Irabelle is the only proper Guard base in the region, to my limited knowledge at least. Safe houses scatter along the river and deeper into the woods, but Irabelle is certainly the beating heart of our organization. Partly underground and entirely overlooked, most of us would call Irabelle home if we had to. But most of us have no true home to speak of, none but the Guard and the Reds alongside us.

The structure is much larger than we need, easy for an outsider—or an invader—to get lost in. Perfect for seeking quiet. Not to mention most of the entrances and halls are rigged with floodgates. One order from the Colonel and the whole place goes under, drowned like the old world before it. It makes the place damp and cool in summer, frigid in winter, with walls like sheets of ice. No matter the season, I like to walk the tunnels, taking a lonely patrol through dim concrete passages forgotten by anyone but me. After my time on the train, avoiding the Colonel's accusing, crimson gaze, the cool air and open tunnel before me feels like the closet brush of freedom I'll ever know.

My gun spins idly on my finger, a careful balance I'm good at keeping. It's not loaded. I'm not stupid. But the lethal weight of it is still pleasing. *Norta.* The pistol keeps spinning. *Their arms laws are stricter than the Lakelands. Only registered hunters are allowed to carry. And those are few.* Just another obstacle I'm eager to overcome. I've never been to Norta, but I assume it's the same as the Lakelands. Just as Silver, just as dangerous, just as *ignorant.* A thousand executioners, a million to the noose.

I've long stopped questioning *why* this is allowed to continue. I was not raised to accept a master's cage, not like so, so many are. What I see as a maddening surrender is the only survival to so many others. I suppose I have the Colonel to thank for my stubborn belief in freedom. He never let me think otherwise. He never let me accept what we came from. Not that I'll ever tell him that. He's done too much to ever earn my thanks.

But so have I. That's fair, I suppose. And don't I believe in fairness?

Footsteps turn my head, and I slip the gun to my side, careful to keep it hidden. A fellow Guardsman would not mind the weapon, but a Silver officer certainly would. Not that I expect one to find us down here. They never do.

Indy doesn't bother with a greeting. She halts a few feet away, her tattoos evident against her tan skin even in the meager light. Thorns up one side, from her wrist to the crown of her shaved head, with roses winding down the other arm. Her code name is Holiday, but Garden would've been more fitting. She's a fellow captain, another one of us who answers to the Colonel. There's ten in all under his command, each with a larger detachment of oathed soldiers sworn to their captains.

"The Colonel wants you in his office. New orders," she says. Then her voice lowers, even though no one can hear us this deep into Irabelle. "He isn't happy."

I grin and push past her. She's shorter than me, like most people, and has to work to keep up. "Is he ever?"

"You know what I mean. This is different."

Her dark eyes flash, betraying a rare fear. I saw it last in the infirmary, as she stood over the body of another captain. Saraline, code named Mercy, who ended up losing a kidney during a routine arms raid. She's still recovering. The surgeon was shaky at best. *Not your fault. Not your job,* I remind myself. But I did what I could. I'm no stranger to blood and I was the best medic we had at the moment. Still, it was the first time I held a human organ in my hand. *At least she's alive.*

"She's walking," Indy offers, reading the guilt on my face. "Slow, but she's doing it."

"That's good," I say, neglecting to add that she should've been walking weeks ago. *Not your fault* echoes again.

When we make it back to the central hub, Indy breaks off, heading to the infirmary. She hasn't left Saraline's side for anything but assignments and, apparently, the Colonel's errands. They came to the Guard at the same time, close as sisters. And then, quite obviously, *not* sisters anymore. No one minds. There's no rules against fraternizing within the organization, so long as the job gets done and everyone comes back alive. So far, no one at Irabelle has been foolish or sentimental enough to let something so petty as a feeling jeopardize our cause.

I leave Indy to her worries and head in the opposite direction, to where I know the Colonel waits.

His office would make a marvelous tomb. No windows, concrete walls, and a lamp that always seems to burn out at precisely the wrong moment. There are far better places in Irabelle for him to conduct business, but he likes the quiet and the closed space. He's tall enough, and the low ceiling makes him seem like a giant. Probably why he likes the room so much.

His head scrapes the ceiling when he stands to greet my entrance.

"New orders?" I ask, already knowing the answer. We've been here two days. I know better than to expect any kind of vacation, even after the grand success of Operation Laker. The central passages of three lakes, each one key to the inner Lakelands, now belong to us, and no one is the wiser. For what higher purpose, I don't know. That's for Command to worry about, not me.

The Colonel slides a folded paper across the table to me. Sealed edges. I have to snap it open with a finger. *Strange.* I've never received sealed orders before.

My eyes scan the page, widening with every passing word. Command orders. Straight from the top, past the Colonel, directly to me.

"These are—"

He holds up a hand, stopping me short. "Command says your eyes only." His voice is controlled, but I hear the anger anyway. "It's your operation."

I have to clench a fist to keep calm. *My own operation.* Blood pounds in my ears, pressed on by a rising heartbeat. My jaw clenches, grinding my teeth together so I don't smile. I look back at the orders again to make sure they're real. *Operation Red Web.*

After a moment, I realize something is missing.

"There's no mention of you, sir."

He raises the eyebrow of his bad eye. "Do you expect there to be? I'm not your *nanny*, Captain." He bristles. The mask of control threatens to slip and he busies himself with an already pristine desk, flicking away a piece of dust that doesn't exist.

I shrug off the insult. "Very well. I assume you have orders of your own."

"I do," he says quickly.

"Then a bit of a celebration is in order."

The Colonel all but sneers. "You want to celebrate being a poster girl? Or would you rather cheer a suicide mission?"

Now I really do smile. "I don't see it that way." Slowly, I fold the orders again and slip them into my jacket pocket. "Tonight, I drink to my first independent assignment. And tomorrow, I head to Norta."

"*Your eyes only*, Captain."

When I reach the door, I glare at him over my shoulder. "As if you didn't already know."

His silence is admission enough.

"Besides, I'll still be reporting to you, so you can pass on my relays to Command," I add. I can't help but goad him a little. He deserves it for the nanny comment. "What's that called? Oh yes. The middleman."

"Careful, Captain."

I nod my head, smiling as I wrench open the office door. "Always, sir."

Thankfully, he doesn't let another uncomfortable silence linger. "Your broadcast crew is waiting in your barracks. Best get on."

"I do hope I'm camera ready." I giggle falsely, pretending to preen.

He waves a hand, officially dismissing me from his sight. I go willingly, weaving through the halls of Irabelle with enthusiasm.

To my surprise, the excitement pulsing through me doesn't last long. I started out sprinting to the barracks, intending to hunt down my team of oathed soldiers and tell them the good news. But my pace soon slows, my delight giving way to reluctance. And fear.

There's a reason they call us Ram and Lamb, other than the obvious.

I've never been sent anywhere without the Colonel to follow. He's always been there, a safety net I've never wanted, but one I've become far too familiar with. He's saved my life too many times to count. And he's certainly why I'm here instead of a frozen village, losing fingers to every winter and friends to every round of conscription. We don't see eye to eye on much, but we always get the job done, and we always stay alive. We succeed where others can't. We survive. Now I must do the same alone. Now I have to protect others, taking their lives—and deaths—onto my shoulders.

My pace halts, allowing me a few more moments to collect myself. The cool shadows are calming, inviting. I press up against the slick concrete wall, letting the cold seep through me. *I must be like the Colonel when I assemble my team. I am their captain, their commander, and I must be perfect. No room for mistakes and no hesitation. Forward at all costs. Rise, Red as the dawn.*

The Colonel may not be a good person, but he's a brilliant leader. That's always been enough. And now I'll do my best to be the same.

I think better of my plan. Let the rest idle a few minutes longer.

I enter my barracks on my own, chin raised. I don't know why I was chosen for this, why Command wants me to be the one to shout our words. But I'm sure there's a good reason. A young woman holding a flag is quite a striking figure—but also a puzzling one. Silvers might send men and women to die on the lines in equal measure, but a rebel group led by a woman is easier to underestimate. Just what Command wants. Or they simply prefer I'm the one eventually identified and executed, rather than one of their own.

The first crewman, a slumtown escapee judging by his tattooed neck, waves me to the camera already waiting. Another hands me a red scarf and a typed message, one that will not be heard for many months.

But when it is, when it rings out across Norta and the Lakelands, it will land with the strength of a hammer's fall.

I face the cameras alone, my face hidden, my words steel.

"Rise, Red as the dawn."

THE FOLLOWING MESSAGE HAS BEEN DECODED
CONFIDENTIAL, COMMAND CLEARANCE REQUIRED

Operative: Colonel REDACTED.
Designation: RAM.
Origin: Trial, LL.
Destination: COMMAND at REDACTED.

-EYES ON team led by HOLIDAY met opposition in ADELA.
-ADELA safe house destroyed.
-EYES ON overview: Killed in action: R. INDY, N. CAWRALL, T. TREALLER, E. KEYNE (4).
Silver casualty count: Zero (0).
Civilian casualty count: Unknown.

RISE, RED AS THE DAWN.

THE FOLLOWING MESSAGE HAS BEEN DECODED
CONFIDENTIAL, SENIOR CLEARANCE REQUIRED

Day 4 of Operation RED WEB, Stage 1.
Operative: Captain REDACTED.
Designation: LAMB.
Origin: Harbor Bay, NRT.

Destination: RAM at REDACTED.

-Transit smooth through ADERONACK, GREATWOODS, MARSH COAST regions.
-BEACON region transit difficult, heavy NRT military presence.
-Made contact with MARINERS. Entered HARBOR BAY with their aid.
-Meeting with EGAN, head of the MARINERS. Will assess.

RISE, RED AS THE DAWN.

As any good cook can tell you, there are always rats in the kitchen.

The Kingdom of Norta is no different. Its cracks and crevices crawl with what the Silver elite would call vermin. Red thieves, smugglers, army deserters, teenagers fleeing conscription, or feeble elders trying to escape punishment for the idle "crime" of growing old. In the backcountry, farther north toward the Lakeland border, they keep to the woods and small villages, finding safety in the places no self-respecting Silver would condescend to live. But in cities like Harbor Bay, where Silvers keep fine houses and ugly laws, Reds turn to more desperate measures. And so must I.

Boss Egan is not easy to get to. His so-called associates take me and my lieutenant, Tristan, through a maze of tunnels under the walls of the coastal city. We double back more than once, to confuse me as well as anyone who might try to follow. I all but expect Melody, the soft-voiced and sharped-eyed thief leading the way, to blindfold us. Instead, she lets the darkness do its work, and by the time we emerge, I can barely find true north, let alone my way out of the city.

Tristan is not a trusting man, having learned well at the hands of the Scarlet Guard. He hovers at my side, one hand inside his jacket, always gripping the long knife he keeps close. Melody and her men laugh off the obvious threat, pulling back coats and shawls to reveal edged weapons of their own.

"Not to worry, Stretch," she says, raising an eyebrow at Tristan's scraping height. "You're well protected."

He flushes, angry, but doesn't loosen his grasp. And I'm still keenly aware of the knife in my boot, not to mention the pistol tucked into the back of my pants.

Melody keeps walking, leading us through a market trembling with noise and the sharp smell of fish. Her thick body cuts through the crowd, which parts to let her pass. The tattoo on her upper arm, a blue anchor surrounded by red, coiling rope, is warning enough. She's a Mariner, a member of the smuggling operation Command assigned me to feel out. And judging by the way she orders her own detachment, three of them following her lead, she's highly ranked and well respected.

I feel her assessing me, even though her eyes are forward. For this reason, I decided not to take the rest of my team into the city to meet with her boss. Tristan and I are enough to evaluate his operation, judge his motives, and report back.

Egan, it seems, takes the opposite approach.

I expect a subterranean stronghold much like ours at Irabelle, but Melody leads us to an ancient lighthouse, its walls weathered by age and the salty air. Once a beacon used to guide ships into port; now it's too far from the water, as the city expanded out into the harbor. From the outside, it looks abandoned, its windows shuttered and doors barred. The Mariners pay it no mind. They don't even bother to hide their approach, though every instinct in me screams for discretion. Instead, Melody leads us across the open market, head high.

The crowd moves with us like a school of fish. Providing camouflage. Escorting us all the way to the lighthouse and a battered, locked door. I blink at the action, noting how well organized the Mariners seem to be. They command respect, that's obvious, not to mention loyalty. Both valuable prizes to the Scarlet Guard, things that cannot truly be bought with money or intimidation. My heart leaps in my chest. The Mariners look to be viable allies indeed.

Once safely inside the lighthouse, at the foot of an endless, spiraling stair, I feel a cord of tension release in my chest. I'm no stranger to infiltrating Silver cities, prowling the streets with poor intent, but I certainly don't enjoy it. Especially without the Colonel at my side, a gruff but effective shield against anything that might befall us.

"You're not afraid of officers?" I wonder aloud, watching as one of the Mariners locks the door behind us. "They don't know you're here?"

Again, Melody chuckles. She's already a dozen steps up, and still climbing. "Oh, they know we're here."

Tristan's eyes almost bug out of his head. "What?" He blanches, mirroring my thoughts.

"I said, Security knows we're here," she repeats. Her voice echoes.

When I put a foot on the first step, Tristan grabs my wrist. "We shouldn't be here, Cap—" he murmurs, forgetting himself. I don't give him the chance to say my name, to go against the rules and protocols that have protected us for so long. Instead I jam my forearm into his windpipe, pushing him back against stairs with all my strength. He sprawls, falling, his weedy length stretched across several steps.

My face flushes with heat. This isn't something I want to do, in front of outsiders or not. Tristan is a good lieutenant, if overprotective. I don't know what's more damaging—showing the Mariners dissension in our ranks or showing them fear. I hope it's the latter. With a calculated shrug, I step back and offer my hand to Tristan but no apology. He knows why.

And without another word, he follows me up the stairs.

Melody lets us pass and I feel her eyes with every step. She is certainly watching me now. And I let her, my face and manner impassive. I do my best to be like the Colonel, unreadable and unflinching.

At the crown of the lighthouse, the boarded-up windows give way to a wide view of Harbor Bay. Literally built on top of another ancient city, the Bay is an old knot. The narrow lanes and twists are better suited to horses rather than transports, and we had to duck into alleys to avoid being run over. From this vantage point, I can see everything centers around the famous harbor, with too many alleys, tunnels, and forgotten corners to fully patrol. Paired with a high concentration of Reds, Harbor Bay is a perfect place for the Scarlet Guard to start. Our intelligence identified the city as the most viable root of Red rebellion in Norta, when an uprising comes. Unlike the capital, Archeon, where the seat of government demands absolute command, Harbor Bay is not so controlled.

But it is not undefended. There's a military base built out on the water, dividing the perfect semicircle of land and waves in two. *Fort Patriot*. A hub for the Nortan army, navy, and air force, the only one of its kind to serve all three branches of the Silver military. Like the rest of the city, its walls and buildings are painted white, tipped with blue roofs and tall silver spires. I try to memorize it from this vantage point. Who knows when the knowledge might come in handy? And thanks to the useless war currently being fought in the north, Fort Patriot is entirely blind to the city around it. The soldiers keep to their walls, while Security keep the city in line. According to reports, they protect their own, the Silver citizens, but the Reds of the Bay largely govern themselves, with separate groups and bands keeping their own sort of order. Three in particular.

The Red Watch forms a police force of sorts, upholding what Red justice they can, protecting and enforcing laws Silver Security won't bother with. They settle Red disputes and crimes committed against our own, to prevent any more abuse by merciless, Silver-blooded hands. Their work is acknowledged, tolerated even by the officers of the city, and for this reason, I will not go to them. Noble as their cause might be, they run too close to Silvers for my taste.

But the Seaskulls, a glorified gang, make me just as wary. They are violent by all accounts, a trait I would normally admire. Their business is blood, and they have the feel of a rabid dog. Vicious, relentless, and stupid, their members are often executed and quickly replaced. They maintain control of their sector of the city through murder and blackmail, and often find themselves at odds with their rival operation, the Mariners.

Who I must assess for myself.

"You're Lamb, I presume."

I turn on my heel, away from the horizon stretching in all directions.

The man I assume to be Egan leans against the opposite windows, either unaware or unafraid of the fact that nothing but aged glass stands between him and a long fall. Like me, he's putting on a charade, showing the cards he wants while hiding the rest.

I came here with only Tristan to present a certain image. Egan, flanked by Melody and a troop of Mariners, elects to show his strength. To impress me. *Good.*

He crosses his arms, displaying two muscled and scarred forearms marked with twin anchor tattoos. I'm reminded of the Colonel, though they look nothing alike. Egan is short, squat, barrel-chested, with sun-damaged skin and long, salt-worn hair in a tangled plait. I don't doubt he's spent half his life on a boat.

"Or at least, that's whatever code name you've been saddled with," Egan continues, grinning. He's missing a good amount of teeth. "Am I right?"

I shrug, noncommittal. "Does my name matter?"

"Not at all. Only your intentions. And those are?"

Matching his grin, I cross to the center of the room, careful to avoid the sunken circle where the lighthouse lantern used to live. "I believe you know that already." My orders stated contact was made, but not to what extent. A necessary omission, to make sure outsiders cannot use our correspondence against us.

"Yes, well, I know well enough the goals and tactics of your people, but I'm talking to you. What are *you* here for?"

Your people. The words twinge, tugging at my brain. I'll decipher them later. I wish very much for a fistfight, instead of this nauseating game of back-and-forth. I'd rather a black eye than a puzzle.

"My goal is to establish open lines of communication. You're a smuggling operation, and having friends across the border is beneficial to us both." With another winning smile, I run my fingers through my braided hair. "I'm just a messenger, sir."

"Oh, I don't think I'd ever call a captain of the Scarlet Guard *just* a messenger."

This time, Tristan keeps still. It's my turn to react, despite my training. Egan doesn't miss my eyes widen or my cheeks flush. His deputies, Melody especially, have the audacity to smirk among themselves.

Your people. The Scarlet Guard. He's met us before.

"I'm not the first, then."

Another manic grin. "Not by a long shot. We've been running goods for yours since . . ." He glances at Melody, pausing for effect. "Two years ago, was it?"

"September 300, Boss," she replies.

"Ah, yes. I take it you don't know anything about that, Sheep."

I fight the urge to grit my teeth and growl. *Discretion*, the orders said. I doubt tossing one up-jumped criminal from his decaying tower is considered discreet. "It's not our way." And that's the only explanation I offer. Because while Egan thinks himself above me, far more informed than I am, he's wrong. He has no idea what we are, what we've done, and how much more we plan to do. He can't even fathom it.

"Well, your comrades pay well, that's for certain." He jingles a bracelet, nicely crafted silver, braided like rope. "I expect you'll do the same."

"If you do what's asked, yes."

"Then I'll do what's asked."

One nod at Tristan sets his wheels spinning. He tromps to my side in two long steps, so fast and gangly Egan laughs.

"Stars, you're a twiggy one," Egan says. "What do they call you? Beanpole?"

A corner of my mouth twitches, but I don't smile. For Tristan's sake. No matter how much he eats or trains, he can't seem to gain any sort of muscle. Not that it makes much difference where he's concerned. Tristan is a gunman, a sniper, not a brawler. He's most valuable a hundred yards away with a good rifle. I won't mention to Egan that his code name is Bones.

"We require overview and introduction to the so-called Whistle network," Tristan says, making my demands for me. Another tactic of the Colonel's that I've adopted. "We're looking for viable contacts in these key areas."

He passes over a marked map, plain but for the red dots on important cities and crossroads throughout the country. I know it without looking. The industrial slums of Gray Town and New Town; the capital, Archeon; Delphie; the military city Corvium; and many smaller towns and villages in between. Egan doesn't glance at the paper, but nods all the same, a picture of confidence.

"Anything else?" he gravels out.

Tristan glances my way, giving me one last chance to refuse this final order from Command. But I won't.

"We will require use of your smuggling network soon."

"Easy enough. With the Whistles, the whole country's open to you. You can send lightbulbs from here to Corvium and back if you want."

I can't help but smile, showing my teeth.

But Egan's grin fades a little. He knows there's more. "What's the cargo?"

With quick hands, I drop a tiny bag of tetrarch coins at his feet. All silver. Enough to convince him.

"The right people."

THE FOLLOWING MESSAGE HAS BEEN DECODED
CONFIDENTIAL, SENIOR CLEARANCE REQUIRED

Day 6 of Operation RED WEB, Stage 1.
Operative: Captain REDACTED.
Designation: LAMB.
Origin: Harbor Bay, NRT.

Destination: RAM at REDACTED.

-MARINERS led by EGAN agree to terms. Will run BEACON region transport upon undertaking of RED WEB Stage 2.
-Be advised, MARINERS aware of SG organization. Other cells active in NRT. Request clarification?

RISE, RED AS THE DAWN.

THE FOLLOWING MESSAGE HAS BEEN DECODED
CONFIDENTIAL, SENIOR CLEARANCE REQUIRED

Operative: Colonel REDACTED.
Designation: RAM.
Origin: REDACTED.
Destination: LAMB at Harbor Bay, NRT.

-Disregard. Focus on RED WEB.

RISE, RED AS THE DAWN.

THE FOLLOWING MESSAGE HAS BEEN DECODED
CONFIDENTIAL, SENIOR CLEARANCE REQUIRED

Day 10 of Operation RED WEB, Stage 1.
Operative: Captain REDACTED.
Designation: LAMB.
Origin: Albanus, NRT.

Destination: RAM at REDACTED.

-Made contacts in WHISTLE network across BEACON region/into CAPITAL VALLEY, all Stage 2 willing.
-Working way up the CAPITAL RIVER.
-Town of ALBANUS closest Red center to SUMMERTON (seasonal home of King Tiberias + his govt).
-Valuable? Will assess.

RISE, RED AS THE DAWN.

The locals call it the Stilts. I can see why. The river is still high, flooded by the spring melts, and much of the town would be underwater if not for the high pylons its structures are built on. An arena frowns over it all from the crest of a hill. A firm reminder of who owns this place and who rules this kingdom.

Unlike the larger cities of Harbor Bay or Haven, there are no walls, no gates, and no blood checks. My soldiers and I enter in the morning with the rest of the merchants moving along the Royal Road. A Silver officer checks our false identification cards with a disinterested flicker of a glance before waving us on, letting a pack of wolves into his village of sheep. If not for the location and Albanus's proximity to the king's summer palace, I wouldn't give this place another glance. There's nothing here of use. Just overworked woodcutters and their families, barely alive enough to eat, let alone rebel against a Silver regime. But Summerton is a few miles upriver, making Albanus worthy of my attention.

Tristan memorized the town before we entered, or at least he tried to. It would not do to consult our maps openly and let everyone know we do not belong. He turns left quickly. The rest of us follow, tracking off the paved Royal Road to the muddy, rutted avenue that runs along the swollen riverbank. Our boots sink, but no one slips.

The stilt houses rise on the left, dotting what I think is Marcher Road. A few dirty children watch us pass, idly throwing stones in the lapping river. Farther out, fishermen on their boats haul glistening nets, filling their little boats with the day's catch. They laugh among themselves, happy to work. Happy to have jobs that keep them from conscription and pointless war.

The Whistle in Orienpratis, a quarry city on the edge of the Beacon, is the reason we're here. She assured us that another one of her kind operated in Albanus, serving as a fence for the town's thieves and not-so-legal dealings. But she told us only that a Whistle existed, not where to find him or her. Not because she didn't trust me but because she didn't know who operated in Albanus. Like in the Scarlet Guard, the Whistles use their own secrets as a shield. So I keep my eyes open and searching.

The Stilts market throbs with activity. It's going to rain soon, and everyone wants to finish their errands before the downpour. I brush my braid over my left shoulder. A signal. Without looking, I know my Guardsmen split off, moving in the usual pairs. Their orders are clear. Case the market. Feel out potential leads. Find the Whistle if you can. With their packs of harmless contraband—glass beads, batteries, stale ground coffee—they'll attempt to trade or sell their way to the fence. *So will I.* My own pouch dangles at my hip, heavy but small, hidden by the untucked hem of a rough cotton shirt. Inside are bullets. Mismatched, of different calibers, seemingly stolen. In fact, they came from our own cache at our new Nortan safe house, a glorified cave tucked away in the Greatwoods region. But no one in the town can know that.

As always, Tristan keeps close. But he's more relaxed here. Smaller towns and villages are not dangerous, not by our standards. Even though Silver Security officers patrol the market, they are few, and uninterested. They don't care much if Reds steal from each other. Their punishments are reserved for the bold, the ones who dare look a Silver in the eye, or make enough trouble they have to get off their asses and involve.

"I'm hungry," I say, turning to a stall selling coarse bread. The prices are astronomical compared to what we're used to in the Lakelands, but then, Norta is no good at growing grain. Their soil is too rocky for much success in farming. How this man supports himself selling bread no one can buy is a mystery. Or it would be, to someone else.

The bread baker, a man too slim for his occupation, barely glances at us. We don't look like promising customers. I jingle the coins in my pocket to get his attention.

He finally looks up, eyes watery and wide. The sound of coinage this far from the cities surprises him. "What you see is what I have."

No nonsense. I like him already. "These two," I reply, pointing to the finest baked loaves he has. Not a very high bar.

Still, his eyebrows raise. He snaps up the bread, wrapping the loaves in old paper with practiced efficiency. When I produce the copper coins without haggling for a lower price, his surprise deepens. As does his suspicion.

"I don't know you," he mutters. He glances away, far to the right, where an officer busies himself berating several underfed children.

"We're traders," Tristan offers. He leans forward, bracing himself on the rickety frame of the bread stall. One sleeve lifts, showing something on his wrist. A red band circling all the way around, the mark of the Whistles as we've come to find. It's a tattoo, and a false one. *But the baker doesn't know that.*

The man's eyes linger on Tristan for only a moment, before trailing back to me. Not so foolish as he looks, then. "And what are you looking to trade?" he says, pushing one of the loaves into my hands. The other he keeps. Waiting.

"This and that," I reply. And then I whistle, soft and low, but unmistakable. The two-note tune the last Whistle taught me. Harmless to those who know nothing.

The baker does not smile or nod. His face betrays nothing. "You'll find better business in the dark."

"I always do."

"Down Mill Road, around the bend. A wagon," the baker adds. "After sunset, but before midnight."

Tristan nods. He knows the place.

I dip my head as well, in a tiny gesture of thanks. The baker doesn't offer his own. Instead, his fingers curl around my other loaf of bread, which he puts back down on the stall counter. In a single motion, he tears off its paper wrappings and takes a taunting bite. Crumbs flake into his meager beard, each one a message. My coin has been traded for something more valuable than bread.

Mill Road, around the bend.

Fighting a smile, I pull my braid over my right shoulder.

All over the market, my soldiers abandon their pursuits. They move as one, a school of fish following their leader. As we make our way back out of the market, I try to ignore the grumblings of two Guardsmen. Apparently, someone picked their pockets.

"All those batteries, gone in a second. Didn't even notice," Cara grumbles, pawing through her satchel.

I glance at her. "Your comm?" If her broadcaster, a tiny radio that passes our messages in beeps and clicks, is gone, we'll be in serious trouble.

Thankfully, she shakes her head and pats a bump in her shirt. "Still here," she says. I force a simple nod, swallowing my sigh of relief.

"Hey, I'm missing some coin!" another Guardsman, the muscle-bound Tye, mutters. She shoves her scarred hands into her pockets.

This time, I almost laugh. We entered the market looking for a master thief, and my soldiers fell prey to a pickpocket instead. On another day, I might be angry, but the tiny hiccup rolls right off my shoulders. A few lost coins are of no matter in the scheme of things. After all, the Colonel called our endeavor a suicide mission only a few weeks ago.

But we are succeeding. And we are still very much alive.

THE FOLLOWING MESSAGE HAS BEEN DECODED
CONFIDENTIAL, SENIOR CLEARANCE REQUIRED

Day 11 of Operation RED WEB, Stage 1.
Operative: Captain REDACTED.
Designation: LAMB.
Origin: Albanus, NRT.
Destination: RAM at REDACTED.

-ALBANUS/STILTS WHISTLE willing to collaborate w/ Stage 2.
-Has eyes inside SUMMERTON/King's seasonal palace.
-Also mentioned contacts within the Red Army at CORVIUM. Will pursue.

RISE, RED AS THE DAWN.

THE FOLLOWING MESSAGE HAS BEEN DECODED
CONFIDENTIAL, SENIOR CLEARANCE REQUIRED

Operative: Colonel REDACTED.
Designation: RAM.
Origin: REDACTED.
Destination: LAMB at Albanus.

-Not orders, too dangerous. Continue with RED WEB.

RISE, RED AS THE DAWN.

THE FOLLOWING MESSAGE HAS BEEN DECODED
CONFIDENTIAL, SENIOR CLEARANCE REQUIRED

Day 12 of Operation RED WEB, Stage 1.
Operative: Captain REDACTED.
Designation: LAMB.
Origin: Siracas, NRT.
Destination: RAM at REDACTED.

-Intent of RED WEB Stage 1 is to introduce SG into NRT via existing networks. Army within orders.
-Red Army contacts invaluable. Will pursue. Pass up message to COMMAND.

-En route to CORVIUM.

RISE, RED AS THE DAWN.

THE FOLLOWING MESSAGE HAS BEEN DECODED

CONFIDENTIAL, SENIOR CLEARANCE REQUIRED

Operative: Colonel REDACTED.

Designation: RAM.

Origin: REDACTED.

Destination: LAMB at Siracas.

-Stand down. Do not proceed to CORVIUM.

RISE, RED AS THE DAWN.

THE FOLLOWING MESSAGE HAS BEEN DECODED

CONFIDENTIAL, SENIOR CLEARANCE REQUIRED

Operative: General REDACTED.

Designation: DRUMMER.

Origin: REDACTED.

Destination: LAMB at Siracas, RAM at REDACTED.

-Proceed to CORVIUM. Assess Red Army contacts for information and Stage 2/Asset Removal.

RISE, RED AS THE DAWN.

THE FOLLOWING MESSAGE HAS BEEN DECODED

CONFIDENTIAL, COMMAND CLEARANCE REQUIRED

Day 12 of Operation RED WEB.
Operative: Captain REDACTED.
Designation: LAMB.
Origin: Corvium, NRT.
Destination: COMMAND at REDACTED, RAM at REDACTED.

-Acknowledged.
-Clearly not too dangerous.

RISE, RED AS THE DAWN.

THE FOLLOWING MESSAGE HAS BEEN DECODED
CONFIDENTIAL, COMMAND CLEARANCE REQUIRED

Operative: Colonel REDACTED.
Designation: RAM.
Origin: REDACTED.
Destination: COMMAND at REDACTED.

-Please note my strong opposition to developments in RED WEB. LAMB needs a short leash.

RISE, RED AS THE DAWN.

THE FOLLOWING MESSAGE HAS BEEN DECODED
CONFIDENTIAL, SENIOR CLEARANCE REQUIRED

Operative: General REDACTED.
Designation: DRUMMER.
Origin: REDACTED.
Destination: RAM at REDACTED.

-Noted.

RISE, RED AS THE DAWN.

I can smell the Choke from here. Ash, smoke, corpses.

"It's a slow day. No bombs yet." Tye fixes her eyes on the northwest horizon, and the dark haze in the distance that can only be the front of this pointless war. She served on the lines herself, albeit on the opposite side we are now. She fought for Lakelander masters and lost an ear to a frostbitten winter in trenches. She doesn't hide the deformity. Her blond hair is pulled back tightly, letting everyone see the ruined stump her so-called loyalty bought her.

Tristan scans the landscape for the third time, squinting through the scope of his long rifle. He lies on his belly, half-hidden by the ropy spring grass. His motions are slow and methodical, practiced in the gun range at Irabelle, as well as the deep forests of the Lakelands. The notches on the barrel, tiny scratches in the metal, stand out brightly in the daylight. Twenty-two in all, one for every Silver killed with that very weapon. For all his itchy paranoia, Tristan has a surprisingly steady trigger finger.

From our place on the rise, we have a commanding view of the surrounding woods. The Choke some miles to the northwest, clouded even under the morning sun, and Corvium another mile to the east. There are no more towns here, or even animals. Too close to the trench lines for anything but soldiers. But they keep to the Iron Road, the main thoroughfare that passes through Corvium and ends at the front lines. Over the last few days, we've learned much about the Red legions constantly moving, replacing defeated soldiers on the lines, only to march back with their own dead and wounded a week later. They march in at dawn and late evening. We keep our distance from the Road, but we can still hear them when they go. Five thousand in each legion, five thousand of our Red brothers and sisters resigned to living targets. Supply convoys are harder to predict, moving when required, and not on any schedule. They too are manned by Red soldiers and Silver officers, albeit officers of the useless kind. There's no honor in commanding a transport full of stale food and worn bandages. The supply convoys are a punishment for Silvers, and a reprieve for Reds. And best of all, they are poorly guarded. After all, the Lakelander enemy is firmly on the other side of the Choke, separated by miles of wasteland, trenches, and popping artillery. No one looks to the trees as they pass. No one suspects another enemy already inside their diamondglass walls.

I can't see the Iron Road from this ridge—the trees are in full leaf, obscuring the paved avenue—but we're not watching the Road today. We aren't gathering intelligence from troop movements. We're going to talk to the troops themselves.

My internal clock tells me they are late.

"Could be a trap," Tristan mutters, always eager to voice his panicked opinion. He keeps his eye firmly pressed to the scope in warning. He's been expecting a trap since the moment Will Whistle told us about his army contacts. And now that we're going to meet them, he's been on edge more than usual, if that's possible. Not a bad instinct to have, but not a helpful one at the moment. Risk is part of the game. We won't get anywhere if we think only of our own skins.

But there is a reason only three of us are waiting.

"If it's a trap, we'll get out of it," I reply. "We've beaten worse."

It's not a lie. We all have scars and ghosts of our own. Some drove us to the Scarlet Guard, and some were because of it. I know the sting of both.

My words are for Tye more than Tristan. Like all who escaped the trenches, she's not at all happy to be back, even if she isn't wearing a Lakelander's blue uniform. Not that she would ever complain about this out loud. But I can tell.

"Movement."

Tye and I crouch lower, whipping in the direction of Tristan's gaze. The rifle nose tracks at a snail's pace, following something in the trees. Four shadows. *Outnumbered.*

They emerge with their palms out, showing empty hands. Unlike the soldiers on the Road, these four have their uniforms turned inside out, favoring stained brown and black lining over their usual rust colors. Better camouflage for the woods. Not to mention their names and ranks. I can't see any insignia or badges of any kind. I have no idea who they are.

A calm breeze rustles the grass. It ripples like a pond disturbed by a single stone, its green waves breaking against the four as they approach in single file. I narrow my eyes at their feet. They're careful to step in the leader's footprints. Any tracker would think only one person came this way, not four. *Smart.*

A woman leads, her jaw like an anvil. She's missing both her trigger fingers. Unable to shoot, but still a soldier, judging by the crags of weariness on her face. Like the willowy, copper-skinned girl on her heels, her head is shaved to the scalp.

Two men bring up the rear. They are young, both probably within their first year of conscription. Neither is scarred or visibly injured, so they can't be masquerading as wounded back in Corvium. Supply soldiers, most likely. Lucky to haul crates of ammunition and food. Although the second, the one at the very back, seems too slight for manual labor.

The bald woman stops ten feet away, her palms still raised. Too close for both our liking. I force myself to stand from the grass and close the distance between us. Tye and Tristan keep still, not hidden, but not moving either.

"We're the ones," she says.

I keep my hands on my hips, fingers inches from the gun belted across my waist. A naked threat. "Who sent us?" I ask her in testing. Behind me, Tristan tightens like a snake. The woman has the bravery to keep her eyes from his rifle, but the others behind her don't.

"Will Whistle of the Stilts," she replies. She doesn't stop there, though it's enough for the moment. "Children taken from their mothers, soldiers sent to slaughter, countless generations of slavery. Each and every one of them sent you."

My fingers drum quietly. Rage is a double-edged sword, and this woman has been bled by both edges. "The Whistle will do. And you are?"

"Corporal Eastree, of the Tower Legion, like the rest." She gestures behind, to the other three still watching Tristan. I nod at him, and his trigger finger relaxes a little. But not much. "We're support troops, conscripted to Corvium."

"Will told me as such," I lie quickly. "And what did he tell you of me?"

"Enough to get us out here. Enough to risk our necks for." The voice comes from the lean young man at the back of the line. He angles forward, around his comrade, his smile crooked, teasing, and cold. His eyes flash. "You know it's execution if we're caught out here, right?"

Another breeze, sharper than the last. I force my own empty grin. "Oh, is that all?"

"We best make this quick," Eastree says. "Your lot might protect your names, but we have no use for such things. They have our blood, our faces. This is Private Florins, Private Reese, and—"

The one with the crooked smile steps out of line before she can say his name. He crosses the gap between us, though he doesn't extend a hand to shake. "I'm Barrow. Shade Barrow. And you better not get me killed."

My eyes narrow at him. "No promises."

THE FOLLOWING MESSAGE HAS BEEN DECODED
CONFIDENTIAL, SENIOR CLEARANCE REQUIRED

Day 23 of Operation RED WEB, Stage 1.
Operative: Captain REDACTED.
Designation: LAMB.
Origin: Corvium, NRT.
Destination: RAM at REDACTED.

-CORVIUM intelligence enclosed: fort statistics, city map, tunnel overlay, army schedules/timetables.
-Early assessment: Most promising are Corp E (eager, angry, a gamble) and Aide B (connected, officer's aide recently stationed to CORVIUM). Possible for recruitment or Stage 2.
-Both seem willing to pledge but are otherwise ignorant to SG presence in NRT, LL. Invaluable to have two operatives inside CORVIUM. Will continue

progress, request to fast-track recruitment?

RISE, RED AS THE DAWN.

THE FOLLOWING MESSAGE HAS BEEN DECODED
CONFIDENTIAL, SENIOR CLEARANCE REQUIRED

Operative: Colonel REDACTED.
Designation: RAM.
Origin: REDACTED.
Destination: LAMB at Corvium.

-Request denied. Corp E and Aide B nonessential.
-Move on from CORVIUM. Continue assessing WHISTLE contacts/RED WEB Stage 2 assets.

RISE, RED AS THE DAWN.

THE FOLLOWING MESSAGE HAS BEEN DECODED
CONFIDENTIAL, SENIOR CLEARANCE REQUIRED

Operative: Captain REDACTED.
Designation: LAMB.
Origin: Corvium, NRT.
Destination: RAM at REDACTED.

-CORVIUM intelligence vital to SG cause at large. Request more time at location. Pass up to COMMAND.

-Firmly believe Corp E and Aide B are strong candidates.

RISE, RED AS THE DAWN.

THE FOLLOWING MESSAGE HAS BEEN DECODED
CONFIDENTIAL, SENIOR CLEARANCE REQUIRED

Operative: General REDACTED.
Designation: DRUMMER.
Origin: REDACTED.
Destination: LAMB at Corvium, RAM at REDACTED.

-Request denied. Orders are to continue Stage 1 assessment for Stage 2/Asset Removal.

RISE, RED AS THE DAWN.

THE FOLLOWING MESSAGE HAS BEEN DECODED
CONFIDENTIAL, COMMAND CLEARANCE REQUIRED

Operative: Captain REDACTED.
Designation: LAMB.
Origin: Corvium, NRT.
Destination: DRUMMER at REDACTED.

-Strong opposition. Many military assets present at CORVIUM, must be assessed for Stage 2 removal.
-Request more time at location.

RISE, RED AS THE DAWN.

THE FOLLOWING MESSAGE HAS BEEN DECODED
CONFIDENTIAL, SENIOR CLEARANCE REQUIRED

Operative: General REDACTED.
Designation: DRUMMER.
Origin: REDACTED.
Destination: LAMB at Corvium.

-Request denied. Move out.

RISE, RED AS THE DAWN.

Following protocol, I light the thin strip of correspondence paper on fire. The dots and dashes detailing Command orders char away to nothing, consumed by flame. I know the feeling. Hot anger licks at my insides. But I keep my face still, for Cara's sake.

She looks on, thick glasses perched on her nose. Her fingers itch, ready to click out my response to orders she cannot read.

"No need," I say, waving her off. The lie sits in my mouth for a moment. "Command bent. We stay."

I bet the Colonel's damned red eye is rolling in his skull right now. But his orders are stupid, narrow-minded, and now Command thinks the same. They must be disobeyed, for the cause, for the Scarlet Guard. Corporal Eastree and Barrow would be invaluable to us, not to mention they're both risking their lives to get me the information I need. The Guard owes them an oath, if not evacuation in Stage 2.

They're aren't here, in the thick of things, I tell myself. It helps ease the sting of disobedience. The Colonel and Command don't understand what Corvium means to the Nortan military, or how important our information will become. The tunnel system alone is worth my time—it connects every piece of the fortress city, allowing not only clandestine troop movements but easy infiltration of Corvium itself. And thanks to Barrow's position as aide to a high-ranking Silver, we know less-savory intelligence as well. Which officers prefer the unwilling company of Red soldiers. That Lord General Osanos, the nymph governor of the Westlakes region and commander of the city, continues a family feud with Lord General Laris, commander of the entire Nortan Air Fleet. Who is essential to the military and who wears rank for show. The list goes on. Petty rivalries and weaknesses to be exploited. There are places of rot for us to poke at.

If Command doesn't see this, then they must be blind.

But I am not.

And today is the day I set foot inside the walls myself and see the worst of what Norta has to offer tomorrow's revolution.

Cara folds up her broadcaster and reattaches it to the cord around her neck. It stays with her always, nestled next to her heart. "Not even to the Colonel?" she asks. "To gloat?"

"Not today." I force my best smirk. It placates her.

And it convinces me. The last two weeks have been a goldmine of information. The next two will certainly be the same.

I force my way out of the stuffy, shuttered closet we use for transmissions, the only part of the abandoned house with four walls and an intact roof. The rest of the structure does its job well, serving as the safe house for our dealings in Corvium. The main room, as long as it is wide, has brick walls, though one side is collapsed along with the rusted tin roof. And the smaller chamber, probably a bedroom, has no roof at all. Not that we mind. The Scarlet Guard has suffered worse, and the nights have been unseasonably warm, albeit humid. Summer is coming to Norta. Our plastic tents keep out the rain, but not the moist air. *It's nothing*, I tell myself. *A mild discomfort.* But sweat drips down my neck anyway. *And it's not even midday yet.*

Trying to ignore the sticky sensation that comes with the rising humidity, I pile my braid on top of my head, wrapping it like a crown. If this weather keeps up, I might just cut it all off.

"He's late," Tristan says from his lookout at a glassless window. His eyes never still, always darting, searching.

"I'd be worried if he wasn't." Barrow hasn't been on time once in the past two weeks, not for any of our meetings.

Cara joins Tye in the corner, dropping down with a merry flop. She sets to cleaning her glasses as intently as Tye cleans pistols. Both of them share the same look, fair-haired Lakelanders. Like me, they're not used to the May heat, and they cluster together in the shade.

Tristan is not so affected. He's a Piedmont boy originally, a son of mild winter and swampy summer. The heat doesn't bother him. In fact the only indicator of the changing season are his freckles, which seem to breed. They dot his arms and face, more every day. And his hair is longer too, a dark red mop that curls in the humidity.

"I told him as much," Rasha says from the opposite corner. She busies herself braiding her hair out of her dark face, taking care to divide her curling black locks into even pieces. Her own rifle, not so long as Tristan's but just as well used, props against the wall next to her. "Starting to think they don't sleep down in Piedmont."

"If you want to know more about my sleeping habits, all you have to do is ask, Rasha," Tristan replies. This time he turns over his shoulder, just for a second, to meet her black eyes. They share a knowing look.

I fight the urge to scoff. "Keep it to the woods, you two," I mutter. *Hard enough sleeping on the ground without listening to rustling tents.* "Scouts still out?"

"Tarry and Shore are taking the ridge, they won't be back until dusk, same as Big Coop and Martenson." Tristan ticks off the rest of our team on his fingers. "Cristobel and Little Coop are about a mile out, in the trees. Waiting on your Barrow boy, and looking to wait awhile."

I nod. All in order then.

"Command happy so far?"

"Happy as they can be," I lie as smoothly as I can. Thankfully, Tristan doesn't turn from his watch. He doesn't notice the flush I feel creeping up my neck. "We're feeding good intelligence. Worth our time for sure."

"They looking to oath Eastree or Barrow?"

"What makes you say that?"

He shrugs. "Seems like a long time to put into a pair we don't mean to recruit. Or are you suggesting them for Stage Two?"

Tristan doesn't mean to pry. He's a good lieutenant, the best I've ever seen, loyal to his bones. He doesn't know what he's picking at, but it stings all the same.

"Still working that out," I mumble, doing my best to walk slow as I run from his questions. "I'm going to do a turn around the property. Grab me if Barrow shows his face."

"Will do, boss," echoes from the room.

Keeping my steps even is a battle, and it seems like an eternity before I'm safely into the green trees. I heave a single collecting breath, forcing myself to calm down. *It's for the best. Lying to them, disobeying the orders, it's for the best. It's not your fault the Colonel doesn't understand. It's not your fault.* The old refrain levels me out, as comforting as a stiff drink. Everything I've done and everything I will do is for the cause. No one can say otherwise. No one will ever question my loyalty, not once I give them Norta on a silver platter.

A smile slowly replaces my usual scowl. My team doesn't know what's coming. Not even Tristan. They don't know what Command has planned for this kingdom in the coming weeks, or what we've done to put things in motion. Grinning, I remember the whirring video camera. The words I said in front of it. Soon, the world will hear them.

I don't like the woods here. They're too still, too quiet, with the smell of ash still clinging to the air. Despite the living trees, this is a dead place.

"Nice time for a walk."

My pistol jams against his temple before I have time to think. Somehow, Barrow doesn't flinch. He only raises his palms in mock surrender.

"You're a special kind of stupid," I say.

He chuckles. "Must be, since I keep wandering back to your ragtag rebel club."

"*And* you're late."

"I prefer *chronologically challenged.*"

With a humorless scoff, I holster the gun, but keep my hand on it. I narrow my eyes at him. Usually his uniform is turned inside out for camouflage, but this time he hasn't bothered. His jacket is red as blood, dark and worn. He sticks out against the greenery.

"I've got two spotters waiting on you."

"They must not be very good." Again, that smile. Another would think Shade Barrow was warm, open, always laughing. But there's a chill beneath all that. An iron cold. "I came the usual way."

Sneering, I pat his jacket. "Did you now?"

There. His eyes flash, chips of frozen amber. Shade Barrow has secrets of his own. Just like everyone else.

"Let me tell my crew you're here," I press on, taking a step back from Barrow's lean form. His eyes follow my movements, quietly assessing. He's only nineteen, little more than a year into his military service, but his training certainly stuck.

"You mean tell your watchdog."

A corner of my mouth lifts. "His name is Tristan."

"Tristan, right. Ginger hair, permanently glued to his rifle." Barrow gives me my space, but follows all the same as I pick back toward the farmhouse. "Funny, I never expected to find a Southie embedded with you."

"Southie?" My voice doesn't quaver, despite Barrow's not-so-vague probing.

His pace quickens, until he's almost stepping on my heels. I fight the urge to kick back into his knee. "He's from Piedmont. Has to be, with his drawl. Not that it's much of a secret. Just like the rest of your bunch. All Lakelanders, yeah?"

I glance over my shoulder. "What gave you that idea?"

"And you're from the deep north, I suppose. Farther than our maps go," he presses on. I get the feeling he enjoys this, like a puzzle. "You're in for some fun come true summer, when the days run long and thick with heat. Nothing like a week of storm clouds that never break, and air that threatens to drown."

"No wonder you're not a trench soldier," I say as we reach the door. "There's no need for a poet on the front lines."

The bastard actually *winks* at me. "Well, we can't all be brutes."

In spite of Tristan's many warnings, I follow Barrow unarmed. If I'm caught in Corvium, I can plead as a simple Red Nortan in the wrong place at the wrong time. But not if I'm carrying my Lakelander pistol or a well-worn hunting knife. Then it'll be execution on the spot, not only for bearing arms without permission, but for being a Lakelander to boot. They'd probably slap me in front of a whisper for good measure, and that is the worst fate of all.

While most cities sprawl, with smaller towns and neighborhoods ringing round their walls and boundaries, Corvium stands alone. Barrow stops just before the end of the tree line, looking north at the cleared landscape around a hill. My eyes scan over the fortress city, noting anything of use. I've pored over the stolen maps of Corvium, but seeing it with my own eyes is something else entirely.

Black granite walls, spiked with gleaming iron, as well as other "weapons" to be harnessed by Silver abilities. Green vines thick as columns coil up the dozen or so watchtowers, a moat of dark water fed by piping rings the entire city, and strange mirrors dot between the metal prongs fanging the parapets. For Silver shadows, I assume, to concentrate their ability to harness light. And of course, there are more traditional weapons to take stock of. The oil-dark watchtowers bristle with grounded heavy guns, artillery ready to fire on any- and everything in the vicinity. And behind the walls, the buildings rise high, made tall by the cramped space. They too are black, tipped in gold and silver, a shadow beneath brightest sunlight. According to the maps, the city itself is organized like a wheel, with roads like spokes, all branching from the central square used to muster armies and stage executions.

The Iron Road marches straight through the city, from east to west. The western Road is quiet. No marching this late in the afternoon. But the eastern Road bustles with transports, most of them Silver-issue, carrying blue-blushing nobles and officers away from the fortress. The last, the slowest, is a Red delivery convoy returning to the markets of Rocasta, the nearest supply city. It consists of servants in wheeled transports, in horse-drawn carts, even on foot, all making the twenty-five-mile journey only to return again in a few days. I fish the spyglass from my jacket and hold it to my eye, following the ragged train.

A dozen transports, as many carts, maybe thirty Reds walking. All slow, keeping pace with each other. It'll take them at least nine hours to get where they're going. A waste of manpower, but I doubt they mind. Delivering uniforms is safer than wearing them. As I watch, the last of the convoy leaves the eastern gate.

"The Prayer Gate," Barrow mutters.

"Hmm?"

He taps my glass, then points. "We call it the Prayer Gate. As you enter, you pray to leave. As you leave, you pray never to return."

I can't help but scoff. "I didn't know Norta found religion." He only shakes his head. "Then who do you pray to?"

"No one, I guess. Just words, at the end of it all."

Somehow, in the shadow of Corvium, Shade Barrow's eyes find a bit of warmth.

"You get me in that gate, I'll teach you a prayer of my own." *Rise, Red as the Dawn.* Annoying as Barrow might be, I have a sneaking feeling he'll be Scarlet soon enough.

He tips his head, watching me as keenly as I watch him. "Deal."

"Although I don't see how you plan to do it. Our best chance was that convoy, but unfortunately you're—what did you say? Chronologically challenged?"

"No one's perfect, not even me," he replies with a shit-eating grin. "But I said I'd get you inside today, and I mean what I say. Eventually."

I look him up and down, gauging his manner. I do not trust Barrow.

It's not in me to truly trust anyone. *But risk is part of the game.* "Are you going to get me shot?"

His grin widens. "I guess you'll have to find out."

"Well then, how do we do this?"

To my surprise, he extends a long-fingered hand. I stare at it, confused. *Does he mean to skip up to the gates like a pair of giggling children?* Frowning, I cross my arms and turn my back.

"Well, let's get moving—"

A curtain of black blots my vision as Barrow slips a scarf over my eyes.

I would scream if I could, signaling to Tristan following us from a quarter mile away. But the air is suddenly crushed from my lungs and everything seems to shrink. I feel nothing but the tightening world and the warm bulk of Barrow's chest against my back. Time spins, everything falls. The ground tips beneath my feet.

I hit concrete hard, enough to rattle an already rattling brain. The blindfold slips off, not that it does me much good. My vision spots, black against something darker, all of it still spinning. I have to shut my eyes again to convince myself I'm not spinning with it.

My hands scrabble against something slick and cold—hopefully water—as I try to push myself back up. Instead, I fall backward, and force my eyes open to find blue, dank darkness. The spots recede, slow at first, then all at once.

"What the f—!"

I turn onto my knees, throwing up everything in my belly.

Barrow's hand finds my back, rubbing what he assumes are soothing circles. But his touch makes my skin crawl. I spit, finished retching, and force myself to uneasy feet, if only to get away from him.

He puts out a hand to steady me but I smack it away, wishing I'd kept my knife.

"Don't touch me," I snarl. "What was that? What happened? *Where am I?*"

"Careful, you're turning into a philosopher."

I spit acidic bile at his feet. "Barrow!" I hiss.

He sighs, annoyed as a schoolteacher. "I took you through the pipe tunnels. There's a few in the tree line. Had to keep you blinded, of course. Can't let all my secrets go for free."

"Pipes my ass. We were standing outside a minute ago. Nothing moves that fast."

Barrow tries his best to smother a grin. "You hit your head," he says after a long moment. "Passed out on the slide down."

That would explain the vomiting. *Concussion.* Yet I've never felt so alert. All the pain and nausea of the last few seconds are suddenly gone. Gingerly, I feel along my skull, searching for a bump or a tender spot. But there's nothing at all.

He watches my examination with strangely focused attention. "Or do you think you ended up a half mile away, beneath the fortress of Corvium, some other way?"

"No, I suppose not."

As my eyes adjust to the gloom, I realize we're in a supply cellar. Abandoned or forgotten, judging by the dust on the empty shelves and the inch of standing water on the floor. I avoid looking at the fresh pile of sick.

"Here, put these on." He fishes a grimy bundle of cloth from somewhere in the dark, carefully hidden but easy to find. It sails my way, colliding with my chest in a puff of dust and odor.

"Wonderful," I mutter, unfolding it to find a regulation uniform. It's well worn, patched and stained with who-knows-what. The insignia is simple, a single white bar outlined in black. An infantry soldier, enlisted. *A walking corpse.* "Whose body did you swipe this off?"

The shock of cold sparks in him again, only for a moment. "It'll fit. That's all you need to worry about."

"Very well."

I shrug out of my jacket without much fanfare, then peel off my battered pants and shirt in succession. My undergarments are nothing special, mismatched and thankfully clean, but Barrow stares anyway, his mouth open a little.

"Catching flies, Barrow?" I taunt as I pull on the uniform trousers. In the dim light, they look red and battered as rusted pipes.

"Sorry," he mutters, turning his head, then his body. As if I care about privacy. I smirk at the blush spreading up his neck.

"I didn't think soldiers were so embarrassed by the female form," I press on as I zip myself into the uniform top. It's snug but fits well enough. Obviously meant for someone shorter, with narrower shoulders.

He whips back around. The flush has reached his cheeks. It makes him seem younger. *No,* I realize. *It makes him seem his age.* "I didn't know Lakelanders were so free with them."

I flash him a smile as cold as his eyes. "I'm Scarlet Guard, boy. We have worse things to worry about than naked flesh."

Something trembles between us. A current of air maybe, or perhaps the ache of my head injury finally coming back. *That must be it.*

Then Barrow laughs.

"What?"

"You remind me of my sister."

It's my turn to grin. "You spy on her a lot, do you?"

He doesn't flinch at the jab, letting it glance past. "In your manner, Farley. Your ways. You think the same."

"She must be a bright girl."

"She certainly thinks so."

"Very funny."

"I think you two would be great friends." Then he tips his head, pausing a second. "Or you might kill each other."

For the second time in as many minutes, I reluctantly touch Barrow. This is not so gentle as his hands on my back. Instead, I punch him lightly on the arm. "Let's get moving," I tell him. "I don't fancy standing around in a dead woman's clothes."

THE FOLLOWING MESSAGE HAS BEEN DECODED
CONFIDENTIAL, SENIOR CLEARANCE REQUIRED

—Captain, return to orders. COMMAND won't stand for this. —RAM—

THE FOLLOWING MESSAGE HAS BEEN DECODED
CONFIDENTIAL, COMMAND CLEARANCE REQUIRED

Day 29 of Operation SHIELDWALL, Stage 2.
Operative: Colonel REDACTED.
Designation: RAM.
Origin: REDACTED.
Destination: DRUMMER at REDACTED.

-No contact from LAMB in 2 days.
-Request permission to intercept.
-SHIELDWALL ahead of schedule. Island #3 operational but transit problematic. More boats needed than previously thought.

RISE, RED AS THE DAWN.

THE FOLLOWING MESSAGE HAS BEEN DECODED
CONFIDENTIAL, SENIOR CLEARANCE REQUIRED

Operative: General REDACTED.
Designation: DRUMMER.
Origin: COMMAND at REDACTED.
Destination: RAM at REDACTED.

-Permission to intercept granted, will relay further info re. her location.
-Use force if necessary. She was your suggestion and your mistake if things continue.
-Get RED WEB to Stage 2. Collab with other teams to begin removal.
-Will explore other transit options for #3.

RISE, RED AS THE DAWN.

THE FOLLOWING MESSAGE HAS BEEN DECODED
CONFIDENTIAL, SENIOR CLEARANCE REQUIRED

—LAMB get your ass in line, or it's your head.
—RAM—

Another message to the fire.

"Charming," I mutter, watching the Colonel's words burn up.

This time, Cara doesn't bother to ask. But her lips purse into a thin line, holding back a torrent of questions. Five days now since I've responded to any messages, official or otherwise. She obviously knows something is afoot.

"Cara—," I begin, but she holds up a hand.

"I don't have clearance," she replies. Her eyes meet mine with startling ferocity. "And I don't care to know what path you're leading us down, so long as you think it's the right one."

A warmth fills my insides. I do my best to keep it from showing, but a bit of a smile bleeds out anyways. My hand finds her shoulder, offering her the smallest touch of thanks.

"Don't get sappy on me now, Captain." She chuckles, tucking away the broadcaster.

"Will do." I straighten, turning around to face the rest of my team. They cluster at the edge of the steaming alley, a respectful distance away to allow for my private correspondences. To hide our presence, Tristan and Rasha sit on the alley curb, facing the street beyond. They keep their hands out and their hoods up, begging for food or money. Everyone slides past, looking elsewhere.

"Tye, Big Coop." The pair in question steps forward. Tye tips her head, pointing her good ear at me, while Big Coop lives up to the nickname. With a chest like a barrel and almost seven feet of heavy muscle, he's nearly twice the size of his brother, Little Coop. "Stay with Cara, keep the second radio ready."

She extends a hand, all but itching to get hold of our newest prize. One of three top-of-the-line, techie-made, long-range secure radios, all swiped from the Corvium stores by Barrow's light fingers. I pass along the radio, though I keep the second tucked close. Barrow kept the third. Should he need to get in touch. Not that he's used it yet. Not that I'm keeping tally of his communications. Usually Barrow just shows up when he wants to trade information, always without warning, slipping past every spotter I put around the farmhouse. But today we're beyond even his sly reach. Twenty-five miles east, in the middle of Rocasta.

"As for the rest. Cristobel, Little Coop, you're on over watch. Get high, get hidden. Usual signals."

Cris grins, showing a mouth of missing teeth. Punishment for "smirking" at her Silver master, back when she was a twelve-year-old serving girl in a Trial mansion. Little Coop is just as eager. His size and mousy demeanor, not to mention his brick wall of a brother, hide a skilled operative with a steel spine. Needing nothing more, they set to their work. Little Coop picks a drain pipe, scrabbling up the brick walls of the alley, while Cris scrambles to a fence, using it to boost herself onto a narrow window ledge. Both disappear in moments, to follow us from the Rocastan rooftops.

"The rest of you, track your marks. Keep your ears open. Memorize movements. I want to know everything from birthdays to shoe sizes. Gather whatever you can in the time we can." The words are familiar. Everyone knows why I called for this scout. But it serves as a rallying cry, one last thread drawing us together. *Tying them to your disobedience, you mean.*

My fist curls, nails digging into my palm where no one can see. The sting erases the thought quite nicely. As does the breeze sweeping through the alley. It stinks of garbage, but it's cool at least, blowing off Lake Eris to the north.

"The more we know about the Corvium supply convoy, the easier it'll be to infiltrate." *As good a reason as any to be here, to stay when all the Colonel does is tell me to leave.* "Gates close at sundown. Return to rally point within the hour. Understood?"

Their heads bob in taut unison, their eyes alive, bright, and eager.

A few blocks away, a clock tower chimes nine times. I move without thought, stepping through my Guardsmen as they fall in line behind me. Tristan and Rasha are the last to stand. My lieutenant looks bare without his rifle, but I know there's a pistol on him somewhere, probably collecting sweat at the base of his back.

We head into the street, a main avenue through the Red sector of the city. Safe for now, surrounded by nothing more than Red homes and businesses, with few if any Silver officers to watch us pass. As in Harbor Bay, Rocasta maintains its own Red Watch, to protect what Silvers won't. Though we're heading for the same place, my team splits into their pairs, putting space between us. Can't exactly rove into the city center looking like a jumped-up assault squad, let alone a gang. Tristan keeps close again, letting me lead us to our destination—the Iron Road. As in Corvium, the Road bisects Rocasta, driving right through its heart like river through valley. As we get closer to the main thoroughfare, traffic picks up. Late servants hurrying to the homes of their masters, volunteer watchmen returning from their night posts, parents hustling their children to ramshackle schools.

And of course, more officers with every passing street. Their uniforms, black with silver trim, are severe in the harsh sun of late spring, as are the gleaming guns and clubs at their waists. Funny, they feel the need to wear uniforms, as if they're at risk of being mistaken for Red. One of us. *Not a chance.* Their skin, undershot with blue and gray, leached of everything alive, is distinguishing enough. There is no Red on earth so cold as a Silver.

Ten yards ahead of us, Rasha stops so quickly her partner, Martenson, almost trips over her. No mean feat, considering she has about six inches on the graying Little Papa. Next to me, Tristan tenses, but doesn't break formation. He knows the rules. Nothing is above the Guard, not even affection.

The Silver legionnaires drag a boy by the arms. His feet kick at open air. He's small, looking young for eighteen. I doubt he needs to shave. I do my best to block out the sound of his begging, but his mother's wail cannot be ignored. She follows, two more children on her heels, with a solemn father trailing behind. Her hands clutch at her son's shirt, offering one last bout of resistance to his conscription.

The street seems to hold its breath as one, watching the familiar tragedy.

A crack echoes and she falls backward, clutching a bruising cheek. The legionnaire didn't even lift a finger or even look up from his grim work. He must be a telkie and used his abilities to swat the woman away.

"You want worse?" he snaps when she moves to stand.

"Don't!" the boy says, using his last free words to beg.

This will not last. This will not continue. This is why I'm here.

Even so, it makes me sick to know I cannot do anything for this boy and his mother. Our plans are falling into place, but not fast enough for him. *Perhaps he will survive,* I tell myself. But one look at his thin arms and the eyeglasses trampled beneath a legionnaire's foot says otherwise. The boy will die like so many others. In a trench or in a wasteland, alone at the very end.

"I can't watch this," I mutter, and turn down another alley.

After a long moment of strange hesitation, Tristan follows.

I can only hope Rasha stays the course as well as he does. But I understand. She lost two sisters to Lakelander conscriptions, and fled her home before meeting the same fate.

* * *

Rocasta is not a walled city, and has no gates to choke the ends of the Iron Road. An easy place to enter, but it makes our task a bit more difficult. The main body of the returning supply convoy comes along the Road, but a few of the walking escorts peel off, taking different shortcuts to the same destination. On another day, my team would spend hours tracking them all to their homes, only to watch them sleep off the long journey. Not so now. Because it's First Friday. Today is the Feat of July.

A ridiculous Nortan tradition, albeit an effective one, if the intelligence is to be believed. Arenas in almost every town and city, casting long shadows and spitting blood once a month. Reds are required to attend, to sit and watch Silver champions exchange blows and abilities with the glee of stage performers. We have no such thing in the Lakelands. Silvers don't feel the need to show off against us, and the storied threat of Norta is enough to keep everyone terrified.

"They do it in Piedmont too," Tristan mutters. He leans against the poured concrete fence edging the promenade around the arena's entrance. Our gazes flick in unison, one of us always watching our marks, another always watching the band of officers directing people into the gaping maw of Arena Rocasta.

"Call them Acts, not Feats. And we didn't just have to watch. Sometimes, they made Reds fight too." I hear the tremor of rage in his voice, even above the organized chaos of today's spectacle.

I nudge his shoulder as gently as I can. "Fight each other?" *Kill Reds, or be killed by Silvers?* I don't know which is worse.

"Targets are moving," he simply growls.

One more glance at the officers, now occupied with a band of mangy kids halting foot traffic. "Let's go." *And let that wound fester with the rest.*

I push off the wall next to him and slip into the crowd, eyes trained on the four red uniforms up ahead. It isn't easy. This close to Corvium, there's a lot of Red military, either marching through to take their places in the Choke or attached to different convoys like the one we're tailing. But the four men, three bronze, one dark skinned, all bone tired, keep close to each other. We haunt their footsteps. They manned a horse cart for the convoy, carrying what, I'm not sure. It was empty when they returned with the rest. But judging by the lack of Security and Silvers, I know their supply train isn't for weaponry or ammunition. The three bronze men are brothers, I assume, judging by their similar faces and mannerisms. It's almost comical to watch them spit and scratch their behinds in staggered unison. The fourth, a burly fellow with vividly blue eyes, is subdued in his itching, though he smiles more than the rest put together. Crance, I think his name is, based on my eavesdropping.

We enter the arches of the arena entrance like prowling cats, close enough to hear our marks but not be noticed. Overhead, harsh electric lights flicker, illuminating the high-ceilinged chamber connecting the outer promenade to the interior. The crowd thickens to our left, where a variety of Reds wait to place their bets on the ensuing match. Above it, the boards announce the Silvers to fight, and their odds of victory.

FLORA LEROLAN, OBLIVION, 3/1

MADDUX THANY, STONESKIN, 10/1

"Hang on a second," Crance says, halting the rest by the betting boards. With a grin, one of the bronze men joins him. The pair dig in their pockets for something to gamble.

Under the pretense of doing the same, Tristan and I stop no more than a few feet away, hidden in the swelling crowd. The betting boards are popular among the Reds of Rocasta, where a thriving military economy keeps most from going hungry. There are several well-to-do among the crowd—merchants and business owners in proudly clean clothes. They make their bets and hand over dull coppers, even a few silver tetrarchs. I bet the till of Arena Rocasta is nothing to sneer at, and make a note to pass on such information to Command. *If they'll still listen to me.*

"Come on, look at the odds—it's easy money!" Still smiling infectiously, Crance points between the boards and the betting windows. The other two tailing along don't look so convinced.

"You know something about stoneskins we don't?" the tallest says. "He'll get blown to pebbles by the oblivion."

"Suit yourself, Horner. But I didn't trudge all the way from Corvium to sit bored in the stands." Bills in hand, Crance slips away with his friend on his heels, leaving Horner and the other man to wait. Somehow, despite Crance's size, he's surprisingly good at cutting through a crowd. Too good.

"Watch them," I murmur with a touch to Tristan's elbow. And then I'm weaving too, careful to keep my head angled at the ground. There are cameras here, enough to be wary of. Should the next few weeks go as planned, I might want to start hiding my face.

I see it as Crance passes his paper through the window. His sleeve lifts as it scrapes the betting ledge, pulling back to reveal a tattoo. It almost blends into his umber skin, but the shape is unmistakable. I've seen it before. Blue anchor. Red rope.

We're not the only crew working this convoy. The Mariners already have a man inside.

This is good. We can work with this. My mind fires as I fight my way back. *Pay for their information. Less Guard involvement, but the same outcome. And odds are the Mariner is alone, working the job solo. We could try to turn him, get our own eyes inside the Mariners. Start pulling strings, absorb the gang into the Guard.*

Tristan stands a head above the crowd, still watching the other two marks. I fight the urge to sprint to his side and divulge everything.

But an obstacle sprouts between us. A bald man and a familiar sheen of sweat across his brow. *Lakelander.* Before I can run or shout, a hand closes around my throat from behind. Tight enough to keep me quiet, loose enough to let me breathe, and certainly enough to drag me through the crowd with Baldy keeping close.

Another might thrash or fight, but I know better. Silver officers are everywhere here, and their "help" is not anything I want to risk. Instead I put my trust in myself, and in Tristan. He must keep watch, and I must get free.

The crowd takes us in its current, and still I cannot see who it is marching me through. Baldy's bulk hides most of me, as does the scarf my captor tosses around my neck. Funny, it's scarlet. And then we climb. Up the steps, high above the arena floor, to long slab seats that are mostly abandoned.

Only then am I released, pushed to sit.

I whirl in a fury, fists clenched and ready, only to find the Colonel staring back, very much prepared for my rage.

"You want to add striking your commanding officer to your list of offenses?" he says. It's almost a purr.

No, I don't. Glumly, I drop my fists. Even if I could fight my way past Baldy, I don't want to try myself at the Colonel and his wiry strength. I raise a hand to my neck instead, massaging the now tender skin beneath the red scarf.

"It won't bruise," he continues.

"Your mistake. I thought you wanted to send a message. Nothing says 'get your ass back in line' like a blue neck."

His red eye flashes. "You stop responding and think I'll let that go? Not a chance, Captain. Now tell me what's going on here. What of your team? Have you all gone rogue, or did some run off?"

"No one's run off," I force through gritted teeth. "Not one of them. No one's rogue either. They're still following orders."

"At least someone is."

"I am still under operation, whether you choose to see it or not. Everything I'm doing here is for the cause, for the Guard. Like you said, this isn't the Lakelands. And while getting the Whistle network online is priority, so is Corvium." I have to hiss to be heard over the crowding arena. "We can't rely on the slow creep here. Things are too centralized. People will notice, and they'll root us out before we're ready. We have to hit hard, hit big, hit where the Silvers can't hide us."

I'm gaining ground, but not much. Still, it's enough for him to keep his voice from shaking. He's angry, but not livid. He can still be reasoned with.

"That's precisely what you recorded for," he says. "You remember, I assume."

A camera and a red scarf across half my face. A gun in one hand, a newly made flag in the other, reciting words memorized like a prayer. *And we will rise up, Red as the dawn.*

"Farley, this is how we operate. No one holds all the cards. No one knows the hand. It's the only way we stay ahead and alive," he presses on. From another, it might sound like pleading. But not the Colonel. He doesn't ask things. He just orders. "But believe me when I say, we have plans for Norta. And they aren't so far from what you want."

Below us, the champions of the Feat march out onto the strange gray sand. One, the Thany stoneskin, has a boulder belly, and is nearly as wide as he is tall. He has no need for armor, and is naked to the waist. For her part, the oblivion looks every inch her ability. Dressed in interlocking plates of red and orange, she dances like a nimble flame.

"And do those plans include Corvium?" I whisper, turning back to the Colonel. I must make him understand. "Do you think me so blind that I wouldn't notice if there was another operation in this city? Because there isn't. There's no one here but me. No one else seems to care about that fortress where every single Red doomed to die passes through. *Every single one.* And you think that place isn't important?"

Corporal Eastree flashes in my head. Her gray face and gray eyes, her stern resolve. She spoke of slavery, because that's what this world is. No one dares say it, but that's what Reds are. *Slaves and graves.*

For once, the Colonel holds his tongue. *Good, or else I might cut it out.*

"You go back to Command and you tell someone else to continue with Red Web. Oh, and let them know the Mariners are here too. They're not so shortsighted as the rest of us."

Part of me expects to be slapped for insubordination. In all our years, I've never spoken to him like this. Not even—not even in the north. At the frozen place we all used to call home. But I was a child then. A little girl pretending to be a hunter, gutting rabbits and setting bad snares to feel important. I am not her anymore. I am twenty-two years old, a captain of the Scarlet Guard, and no one, not even the Colonel, can tell me I am wrong now.

"Well?"

After a long, trembling moment, he opens his mouth. "No."

An explosion below matches my rage. The crowd gasps in time with the fight, watching as the wispy oblivion tries to live up to her odds.

But the Mariner was right. The stoneskin will win. He is a mountain against her fire, and he will endure.

"My team will stand with me," I warn. "You'll lose ten good soldiers and one captain to your pride, Colonel."

"No, Captain, someone else is not going to take over Red Web from you," he says. "But I will petition Command for a Corvium operation, and when they've secured a team, it will take your place."

When. Not if. I can barely believe what he's saying.

"Until such time, you will remain in Corvium and continue work with your contacts. Relay all pertinent information through the usual channels."

"But Command—"

"Command is more open-minded than you know. And for whatever reason, they think the world of you."

"I can't tell if you're lying."

He merely raises one shoulder, shrugging. His eyes rove back to the arena floor, to watch as the stoneskin rips the young oblivion apart.

Somehow, his reason grates on me more than anything else. It's hard to hate him in a time like this, when I remember who he used to be. And then of course, I remember the rest. What he did to us, to our family. To my mother and sister, who were not so horrible as we were, who could not survive in the monster he made.

I wish he wasn't my father. I've wished it so many times.

"How goes Shieldwall?" I murmur to keep my thoughts at bay.

"Ahead of schedule." Not a hint of pride, just sober fact. "But transit could be an issue, once we set in on removal."

Supposedly the second stage of my operation. The removal and transport of *assets* deemed useful to the Scarlet Guard. Not just Reds who would pledge to the cause but ones who can fire a gun, drive a transport, read, fight.

"I shouldn't know—," I begin, but he cuts me off. I get the feeling he doesn't have anyone to talk to, if Baldy is any indication. *Now that I'm gone.*

"Command gave me three boats. *Three.* They think three boats can help get an entire island populated and working."

Somewhere in my brain, a bell rings. And on the floor, the stoneskin raises his rocky arms, victorious. Skin healers tend to the oblivion girl, fixing up her broken jaw and crushed shoulders with quick touches. *Crance will be happy.*

"Does Command ever mention pilots?" I wonder aloud.

The Colonel turns, one eyebrow raised. "Pilots? For what?"

"I think my man inside Corvium can get us something better than boats, or at least, a way to steal something better than boats."

Another man would smile, but the Colonel simply nods.

"Do it."

THE FOLLOWING MESSAGE HAS BEEN DECODED
CONFIDENTIAL, COMMAND CLEARANCE REQUIRED

Operative: Colonel REDACTED.
Designation: RAM.
Origin: Rocasta, NRT.
Destination: COMMAND at REDACTED

-Contact made with LAMB. Her team still online, no losses.
-Assessment: CORVIUM worth an operation team. Suggest MERCY. Suggest a rush. LAMB will hand off and return to RED WEB.
-LAMB passing intelligence vital to SHIELDWALL and removal/transit.

-Returning to post.

RISE, RED AS THE DAWN.

THE FOLLOWING MESSAGE HAS BEEN DECODED
CONFIDENTIAL, SENIOR CLEARANCE REQUIRED

Operative: General REDACTED.
Designation: DRUMMER.
Origin: COMMAND at REDACTED.
Destination: RAM at REDACTED, LAMB at Corvium, NRT.

-CORVIUM suggestion under advisement.
-Captain Farley will return to RED WEB in two days.
-COMMAND split on punishment as is.
-Awaiting intelligence.

RISE, RED AS THE DAWN.

THE FOLLOWING MESSAGE HAS BEEN DECODED
CONFIDENTIAL, SENIOR CLEARANCE REQUIRED

Operative: Captain REDACTED.
Designation: LAMB.
Origin: Corvium, NRT.
Destination: RAM at REDACTED, COMMAND at REDACTED.

-Request a week.

RISE, RED AS THE DAWN.

—You're a special kind of stupid, kid. —RAM—

THE FOLLOWING MESSAGE HAS BEEN DECODED
CONFIDENTIAL, SENIOR CLEARANCE REQUIRED

Operative: General REDACTED.
Designation: DRUMMER.
Origin: COMMAND at REDACTED.
Destination: RAM at REDACTED, LAMB at Corvium, NRT.

-Five days. No more negotiation.

RISE, RED AS THE DAWN.

Somehow the farmhouse has begun to feel like a home.

Even with the collapsed roof, the tents wicked with humidity, and the silence of the woods. It's the longest I've been anywhere since Irabelle, but that was always base. And while the soldiers there are the closest thing I have to family, I never could see the cold concrete and mazelike passages as anything more than a way station. A place to train and wait for the next assignment.

Not so with the ruin on the doorstep of the killing grounds, in the shadow of a grave city.

"That's it," I tell Cara, and lean back against the closet wall.

She nods and folds away the broadcaster. "Nice to see you all chatting again."

Before I can laugh, Tristan's neat knock jars the shuttered excuse for a door. "Got company."

Barrow.

"Duty calls," I grumble as I scoot past Cara, bumping her in the closed space. Wrenching open the door, I'm surprised to find Tristan standing so close, his usual nervous energy on overdrive.

"Spotters got him this time, finally," he says. On another day, he might be proud, but something about this sets him off. I know why. We never see Barrow coming. *So why today?* "Signaled it's important—"

Behind him, the farmhouse door bangs open, revealing a red-faced Barrow flanked by Cris and Little Coop.

One look at his terrified face is enough.

"Scatter," I snap.

They know what it means. They know where to go.

A hurricane moves through the farmhouse, taking home with it. The guns, the provisions, our gear disappears in a practiced heartbeat, shoved into bags and packs. Cris and Little Coop are already gone, into the trees, to get as high as they can. Their mirrors and birdcalls will carry the message to the others in the woods. Tristan supervises the rest, all while loading his long rifle.

"There isn't *time*, they're coming now!" Barrow hisses, suddenly at my side. He takes my elbow and not gently. "You have to go!"

Two snaps of my fingers. The team obeys, dropping whatever isn't packed away. I guess we'll have to steal some more tents down the line, but it's the least of my worries. Another snap, and they fly like bullets from a gun. Cara, Tye, Rasha, and the rest going through the door and the collapsed wall, in all directions with all speed. The woods swallow them whole.

Tristan waits for me because it's his job. Barrow waits because—because I don't know.

"*Farley*," he hisses. Another tug at my arm.

I cast one last glance, making sure we have everything, before making my own escape into the tree line. The men follow, keeping pace with my sprint through tangled roots and brush. My heart pounds in my ears, beating a harried drum. *We've had worse. We've had worse.*

Then I hear the dogs.

Animos-controlled hounds. They'll smell us, they'll follow, and the swifts will run us down. If we're lucky they'll think we're deserters and kill us in the forest. If not—I don't want to think about what horrors the black city of Corvium holds.

"Get to water," I force out. "They'll lose the scent!"

But the river is a half mile on.

I only hope they take the time to search the farmhouse, giving us the window we need to escape. At least the others are farther on, spread wide. No pack can follow us all. But me, us, the freshest, closest scent? Easy prey.

Despite the protest in my muscles, I push harder and run faster than I ever have before. But after only a minute, *only a minute*, I start to tire. If only I could run as fast as my thundering heart.

Tristan slows with me, though he doesn't need to. "There's a creek," he hisses, pointing south. "Shoots off the river, closer. You head for it."

"What are you talking about?"

"I can make it to the river. You can't. And they can't follow us both."

My eyes widen. I almost trip in my confusion, but Barrow catches me before I can, sternly helping me over a gnarled root. "Tristan—"

My lieutenant only smiles and pats the gun slung across his back. Then he points. "That way, Boss."

Before I can stop him, before I can order him not to, he leaps through the trees, using his long legs and the lower branches to vault over worsening ground. I can't shout after him. Somehow I don't even get a good look at his face. Only a mop of red hair, gleaming through the green.

Barrow all but shoves me. I think he looks relieved, but that can't be right. Especially when a dog howls not a hundred yards away. And the trees above us seem to bow, their branches reaching like cloying fingers. *Greenwardens. Animosi. Swifts. The Silvers will catch us both.*

"Farley." Suddenly both his hands are on my jaw, forcing me to look at a shockingly calm face. There's fear, of course, flickering in his golden eyes. But not nearly enough for the situation. Not like me. I am terrified. "You have to promise not to scream."

"Wha—?"

"Promise."

I see the first dog. A hound the size of a pony, its jowls dripping. And next to it, a gray blur like the wind made flesh. *Swift.*

Again, I feel the squeeze of Shade's body against mine, and then something less pleasant. The tightening of the world, the spin, the tipping forward through empty air. All of it compounds and contracts, and I think I see green stars. Or maybe trees. I feel a familiar wave of nausea first. This time I land in a streambed instead of on concrete.

I sputter, spitting water and bile, fighting the urge to scream or be sick or both.

Barrow crouches over me, one hand raised.

"Ah, don't scream."

Sick it is.

"I suppose that's preferable at the moment," he mutters, kindly looking anywhere but my green face. "Sorry, I guess I need more practice. Or maybe you're just sensitive."

The gurgling stream cleans up what I can't, and the cold water does more for me than a mug of black coffee. I snap to attention, looking around at the trees bowing over us. Willows, not oaks like where we were just seconds ago. *They're not moving,* I realized with a swell of relief. *No greenwardens here. No dogs either.* But then—*where are we?*

"How?" I whisper, my voice ragged. "Don't say pipes."

The practiced shield of Shade Barrow drops a little. He takes a few steps back from me so he can sit on a stone above the stream, perching like a gargoyle. "I don't quite have an explanation," he says as if he's admitting a crime. "The best—the best I can do is show you. And, again, you have to promise not to scream."

Dully, I nod. My head swims, still off balance. I can barely sit up in the stream, let alone shout.

He heaves a breath, his fingers gripping the stone until his knuckles turn white. "Okay."

And then he's gone. Not—not from running away or hiding or even falling off the rock. He just simply *isn't.* I blink, not believing what I see.

"Here."

My head turns so quickly I'm almost sick again.

There he is, standing on the opposite bank. Then he does it again, returning to the stone, taking a slow seat once more. He forces a tentative smile without any joy behind it. And his eyes are wide, so wide. If I was afraid a few minutes ago, he is completely petrified. And he should be.

Because Shade Barrow is Silver.

Muscle memory lets me draw my gun and cock the hammer without blinking.

"I might not be able to scream, but I can shoot you."

He flushes, somehow his face and neck turning red. *An illusion, a trick. His blood is not that color.*

"There's a few reasons why that won't work," he says, daring to look away from my pistol. "For one thing, your barrel's full of water. Two, in case you haven't noticed—"

Suddenly he's by my ear, crouching next to me in the stream. The shock of it raises a shriek, or at least it would if he didn't clamp a hand over my mouth. "—I'm pretty fast."

I'm dreaming. This isn't real.

He hauls my dazed body up, forcing me to stand. I try to shove him off but even that makes me dizzy.

"And three, the dogs might not be able to smell us anymore, but they can certainly hear a gunshot." His hands don't leave my shoulders, gripping each tightly. "So, are you going to rethink your little strategy, Captain?"

"You're Silver?" I breathe, turning in his grasp. This time I right myself before I fall. As in Corvium, the nausea is wearing off quickly. *A side effect of his ability. His Silver ability. He's done this to me before and I didn't even know it.* The thought burns through my brain. "All this time?"

"No, no. I'm Red as that dawn thing you keep going on about."

"Don't lie to me." I still have the gun in hand. "This has all been a trick so you could catch us. I bet you led those hunters right to my team—!"

"I *said* no screaming." His mouth hangs open, drawing ragged breath past his teeth. He's so close I can see the blood vessels spindling through the whites of his eyes. They're red. *An illusion, a trick*, rings again. But memories of him come with the warning. How many times did he meet me alone? How many weeks has he worked with us, passing information, relaying with the blood-Red Corporal Eastree? How many times did he have the opportunity to spring a trap?

I can't. I can't make sense of this.

"And no one followed me. *Obviously* no one can follow me. They found out about you on their own. Something about spies in Rocasta, didn't quite catch it all."

"So you're still safe in Corvium, still *working* for them? As *one of them*?"

His patience snaps like a twig. "I told you, I'm not Silver!" he growls, an animal in that quaking second. I want to take a step backward, but force myself to stand firm, unmoving, unafraid of him. *Though I have every right to be.*

Then he shoves his arm out, drawing back the sleeve with shaking fingers. "Cut me." He nods, answering my question before I can ask. "Cut. Me."

To my surprise, my fingers shake just as badly as his when I draw the knife from my boot. He flinches when I press it to his skin. *At least he feels pain.*

My heart skips a beat when blood swells beneath the blade. *Red as the dawn.*

"How is this possible?"

I look up to find him staring at my face, looking for something. By the way his eyes flash, I think he finds it.

"I honestly don't know. I don't know what this is or what I am. I only know I'm not one of them. I'm one of *yours*."

For a blistering moment, I forget my team, the woods, my mission, and even Shade standing in front of me. Again, the world tips, but not from anything he can do. This is something more. A shifting. A change. And a *weapon* to be used. *No, a weapon I've already wielded many times. To get information, to infiltrate Corvium. With Shade Barrow, the Scarlet Guard can go anywhere. Everywhere.*

You'd think, with all my breaches in protocol, I'd try to steer away from breaking any more rules. But at the same time, *what's one more going to do?*

Slowly, I close my fingers around his wrist. He still bleeds, but I don't mind. *It's fitting.*

"Will you oath yourself to the Scarlet Guard?"

I expect him to smile. Instead his face turns to stone.

"On one condition."

My eyebrows raise so high they might disappear into my hairline. "The Guard does not bargain."

"This isn't a request to the Guard, but to you," he replies. For a man who can move faster than the blink of an eye, somehow he manages to take the world's slowest step forward. We stand eye to eye, blue meeting gold.

Curiosity gets the better of me. "And that is?"

"What's your name?"

My name. The others don't mind using their own, but for me, there is no such thing. My name holds no importance. Only rank and designation truly matter. What my mother called me is of no consequence to anyone, least of all me. It is a burden more than anything, a stinging reminder of her voice and the life we lived in early days. When the Colonel was called Papa, and the Scarlet Guard was the pipe dream of hunters and farmers and empty soldiers. My name is my mother, my sister Madeline, and their graves dug in the frozen ground of a village no one lives in anymore.

Shade looks on, expectant. I realize he's holding my hand, not minding the blood coagulating beneath my fingers.

"My name is Diana."

For once, his smile is real. No jokes, no mask.

"Are you with us, Shade Barrow?"

"I'm with you, Diana."

"Then we will rise."

His voice joins mine.

"Red as the dawn."

THE FOLLOWING MESSAGE HAS BEEN DECODED
CONFIDENTIAL, SENIOR CLEARANCE REQUIRED

Day 34 of Operation RED WEB, Stage 1.
Operative: Captain REDACTED.
Designation: LAMB.
Origin: On the move.
Destination: RAM at REDACTED, COMMAND at REDACTED.

-Leaving CORVIUM, heading to DELPHIE. Stopping at WHISTLE points along route.
-Plan to be in Stage 2 within a week.
-Advise CORVIUM operation that CORVIUM officials believe there are "bandits and deserters" in the woods.
-Enclosed is detailed information about Air Fleet grounded in DELPHIE, procured by newly oathed

operative Aide B (designation: SHADOW) still in CORVIUM.

-Suggest Corp E be oathed as well.

-I am and will remain SHADOW's SG contact.

-SHADOW will be removed from CORVIUM at my discretion.

-CORVIUM overview: Killed in action: G. TYE, W. TARRY, R. SHORE, C. ELSON, H. "Big" COOPER (5). Missing in action: T. BOREEVE, R. BINLI (2). Silver casualty count: Zero (0).

THE FOLLOWING MESSAGE HAS BEEN DECODED
CONFIDENTIAL, SENIOR CLEARANCE REQUIRED

Operative: General REDACTED.

Designation: DRUMMER.

Origin: COMMAND at REDACTED.

Destination: RAM at REDACTED.

-Air intel good. DELPHIE Operation in motion.

-Train transit online between ARCHEON and City #1.

-Begin 3 week countdown for Operation DAYBREAK.

RISE, RED AS THE DAWN.

—Your girl has balls. —DRUMMER—

—The girl gets our people killed. —RAM—

—Worth it for her results. But her attitude leaves something to be desired. —DRUMMER—

THE FOLLOWING MESSAGE HAS BEEN DECODED
CONFIDENTIAL, SENIOR CLEARANCE REQUIRED

Day 54 of Operation RED WEB, Stage 2.
Operative: Captain REDACTED.
Designation: LAMB.
Origin: Albanus, NRT.
Destination: RAM at REDACTED.

-CAPITAL VALLEY WHISTLES coming online. In ALBANUS to open removal with oathed WHISTLE operative WILL.
-30 assets removed in 2 weeks.
-SHADOW still operating out of CORVIUM. Intel: legions are being rotated off the trench lines, leaves gaps.

RISE, RED AS THE DAWN

I hate this stinking wagon.

The fencer, old Will, burns a candle, as if it can do anything for the smell. It only makes it hotter in here, more stifling if that's even possible. Besides the stench, though, I feel at ease.

The Stilts is a sleepy village, without much cause for concern. In fact, this happens to be Shade's own birthplace. Not that he talks about home much, other than his sister. I know he writes to them, though. I "mailed" his latest letter myself, leaving it at the post only this morning. Faster than relying on the army to get a letter through, he said, and he was right. Only two or so weeks since he wrote it, rather than the usual month it takes for any kind of Red mail to get anywhere.

"So does this have anything to do with the *new cargo* you've been having my compatriots ferry downriver and overland? To Harbor Bay, yes?" Will glares at me, eyes so bright for someone his age. But his beard looks thinner than it did last month, as is his body. Still, he pours himself a cup of tea with the still hands of a surgeon.

I politely decline the offer of hot tea in an even hotter wagon. *How is he wearing long sleeves?* "What have you heard?"

"This and that."

Wily to the end, these Whistles. "It's true. We're beginning to move people, and the Whistle network has been integral to that operation. I'm hoping you'll agree to join the same."

"Now why would I be stupid enough to do that?"

"Well, you were stupid enough to oath yourself to the Scarlet Guard. But if you need more convincing . . ." With a grin, I pull five silver tetrarchs from my pocket. They barely touch the small table before he snaps them up. They disappear between his fingers. "More for every item."

Still, he does not agree. Putting on a show like the other Whistles did before I eventually won their agreements.

"You would be the first to refuse," I tell him with a slick smile. "And our partnership would cease."

He waves a hand, dismissive. "I do fine without your sort, anyways."

"Is that so?" My smile widens. *Will is no good at bluffing.* "Very well then, I'll go and never darken your . . . wagon again."

Before I can even get up, he stands to stop me. "Who are you planning to move?"

Got you.

"Assets. People who will be valuable to our cause."

As I watch, his bright eyes darken. *A trick of the light.*

"And who makes that decision?"

Despite the heat, a finger of cold runs down my spine. Here comes the usual sticking point. "There are operations all over the country seeking out such people, myself included. We assess, propose our candidates, and wait for approval."

"I assume the old, the sick, and the children set to conscript do not make any of your proposals. No use saving the ones who truly need it."

"If they have valuable skills—"

"Pah!" Will spits, his cheeks going red. He gulps at his tea with angry gasps, draining the cup. The liquid seems to calm him though. When he sets down the empty cup, he rests his chin on his hand thoughtfully. "I suppose that's the best we can hope for."

Another channel opened. "For now."

"Very well."

"Oh, and this most likely won't be a problem here, but I'd stay away from any Silvers you see tomorrow. They won't be happy."

Tomorrow. The thought of it singes my blood. I don't know what the Colonel and Command have planned, only that it includes my broadcast, and something worth waving our flag for.

"Do I want to know?" Will wonders with a pointed smirk. "Do *you* even know?"

I have to laugh openly. "Do you have anything stronger than tea?"

He doesn't get a chance to answer, as someone starts pounding on the wagon door. He jumps, nearly smashing the cup. I catch it deftly, but my eyes are on him. An old tremor of fear shivers through me and we sit still, waiting. Then I remember. *Officers do not knock.*

"Will Whistle!" a girl's voice says. Will all but collapses in relief, and the cord of tension in me releases as well. With one hand, he gestures for me to get behind the curtain dividing his wagon.

I do as asked, hiding myself seconds before she wrenches open the door.

"Miss Barrow!" I hear him say.

A thousand crowns. I curse under my breath as I walk back to the roadside tavern. *Each.* Why I picked such an outrageous number, I can't say. Why I even agreed to see the girl—*Shade's sister, that must have been her*—is less puzzling. But telling her I would help? Save her friend, save *her* from conscription? Two teenagers I don't know, thieves who would most likely get their ferriers killed? But deep down, I know why. I remember the boy in Rocasta, dragged away from his mother. The same happened to Shade and his two older brothers in front of that girl who begged me tonight. *Mare, her name is Mare.* She begged for herself and another, her boyfriend most likely. In her voice, I heard and saw so many people. The Rocastan mother. Rasha, stopping to watch. Tye, dying so close to the place she wanted to escape. Cara, Tarry, Shore, Big Coop. All gone, risking their lives and paying the price the Scarlet Guard always seems to collect.

Not that Mare will come up with the money. It was an impossible task. Still, I owe Shade much and more for his service. I suppose getting his sister away from conscription will be a small price to pay for his intelligence. And whatever she does bring me will go straight to the cause.

Tristan joins me midway between the Stilts and the road tavern. I half expected him to be all the way there, waiting with Rasha, Little Coop, and Cristobel, the only remaining members of our ill-fated team.

"Successful?" he asks, carefully adjusting his coat to hide the pistol at his hip.

"Very," I respond. The word is surprisingly hard to force out.

Tristan knows me well enough not to pry. Instead, he changes the subject and hands over the Corvium radio. "Barrow's been clicking for the last hour."

Bored again. I don't know how many times I've told Shade the radio is for official business and emergencies, not to annoy me. Still, I can't help but grin. I do my best to keep my lips still, at least in front of Tristan, and start fumbling with the radio.

I click the receiver, sending a pulse of seemingly random dots. *I'm here*, they say.

His response comes so quickly I almost drop the radio.

"Farley, I need out." His voice crackles, tinny through the small speaker. "Farley? I have to get away from Corvium."

Panic spikes down my spine. "Okay," I respond, my mind flying at top speed. "You—you can't get out yourself?" If not for Tristan, I would ask him outright. Why can't he jump himself away from that nightmare fortress?

"Meet me in Rocasta."

"Done."

THE FOLLOWING MESSAGE HAS BEEN DECODED
CONFIDENTIAL, SENIOR CLEARANCE REQUIRED

Day 56 of Operation RED WEB, Stage 2.
Operative: Captain REDACTED.

Designation: LAMB.
Origin: Rocasta, NRT.
Destination: RAM at REDACTED.

-Congratulations on ARCHEON bombing.
-In ROCASTA to remove SHADOW.

RISE, RED AS THE DAWN

THE FOLLOWING MESSAGE HAS BEEN DECODED
CONFIDENTIAL, SENIOR CLEARANCE REQUIRED

Day 60 of Operation SHIELDWALL, Stage 2.
Operative: Colonel REDACTED.
Designation: RAM.
Origin: REDACTED.
Destination: LAMB at Rocasta.

-Proceed. Send him to TRIAL. Return to RED WEB ASAP.

RISE, RED AS THE DAWN.

It took longer to get here than I anticipated. Not to mention the fact that I came alone.

After the bombing in Archeon, travel is difficult, even through our usual channels. Whistle cargo boats and transports are harder to come by. And getting into cities, even Rocasta, is no mean feat. Reds must present identity cards or even their blood at different checkpoints entering the city, checkpoints I must avoid at all cost. Even though my face was masked, hidden in the video during which I announced the presence of the Scarlet Guard to the entire country, I can't take any chances.

I even shaved my head, parting with the long blond braid clearly visible in that broadcast.

Crance, the Mariner working the supply convoy, had to smuggle me in, and it took a great amount of back channeling to get him to agree. Even so, I managed to get into the city proper in one piece, my radio firmly tucked into my waistband.

Red sector. Marketgrove.

That's where Shade wanted to meet, and that's where I must get to. I don't dare cover or hood my face, which would give anyone a better clue as to my identity. Instead, I wear shaded glasses, hiding the one part of my face anyone saw in the video. Still, I feel risk in every step. *Risk is part of the game.* But somehow, my fear isn't for myself. I've done my part, more than my part, for the Scarlet Guard. I could die now and be considered a successful operative. My name would go into someone's correspondence, Tristan's probably, clicked out in dots for the Colonel to read.

I wonder if he would mourn.

It's cloudy today and the mood of the city reflects the weather. And the bombing is on everyone's lips, in everyone's eyes. The Reds are a strange mix of hopeful and downcast, some openly whispering about this so-called Scarlet Guard. But many, the old especially, scowl at their children, scolding them for believing our nonsense, telling them it will bring more trouble to their people. I'm not stupid enough to stop and argue.

Marketgrove is deep in the Red sector, but still crawling with Silver

Security officers. Today they look like wolves on the prowl, their guns in hand rather than holster. I heard news of riots in the major cities, Silver citizens going after any Reds they could get their hands on, blaming everyone they could for the Scarlet Guard's deeds. But something tells me these officers aren't here to protect my people. They only want to instill fear and keep us quiet.

But even they can't stop the whispers.

"Who are they?"

"The Scarlet Guard."

"Never heard of the like."

"Did you see? West Archeon in flames—"

"—but no one was hurt—"

"—they'll bring more trouble—"

"—worse and worse times—"

"—blaming us for it—"

"I want to find them."

"Farley."

The last is a warm breath against the shell of my ear, his voice familiar as my own face. I turn instinctually and pull Shade into a hug, surprising both of us.

"Good to see you too," he mutters.

"Let's get you out of here," I murmur as I pull back. When I look at him properly, I realize the last few weeks have not been kind. His face is pale, his expression drawn, and dark circles ring his eyes. "What happened?"

He tucks my arm in his and I let him lead us through the crowd dutifully walking the market. We look like anyone. "A transfer, to the Storm Legion, to the front."

"Punishment?"

But Shade shakes his head. "Not for passing information. They still don't know I'm the leak or that I'm bleeding everything to the Guard. No, this order is strange."

"Strange how?"

"A general's request. High up. For *me*, an aide. It makes no sense. Just like *something else* doesn't make any sense." His eyes narrow pointedly, and I nod. "I think they know, and I think they're going to get rid of me."

I swallow hard and hope he doesn't notice. My fear for him cannot be construed as anything but professional. "Then we'll execute you first, say you ran off and got shot for deserting. Eastree can falsify the documents like she does with other assets. And besides, it's high time we moved you anyways."

"Do you have any idea where that might be?"

"You'll be going to Trial, across the border. That shouldn't be too difficult for someone with your skills."

"I'm not invincible. I can't jump hundreds of miles, or even, well, *navigate* myself that far. Can you?" he mumbles.

I have to smile. *Crance should work.* "I think I can secure you a map and a guide."

"You're not coming?" I tell myself I'm imagining the disappointment in his voice.

"I have other business to handle first. Careful," I add, noting a cluster of officers up ahead. Shade's arm tightens on mine, pulling me closer. *He'll jump if he has to, and I'll get sick all over my boots again.*

"Try not to make me sick this time," I grumble, drawing his crooked grin.

But there's no need for his trepidation. The officers are focused elsewhere, on a cracked video screen, likely the only one in the Red market.

Used for official broadcasts, but there isn't anything official about what they're watching.

"Forgot Queenstrial was today," one of them says, leaning forward to squint at the picture. It blurs occasionally. "Couldn't get a better set for us, eh, Marcos?"

Marcos flushes gray, annoyed. "This is Red sector, what did you expect? You're welcome to go back to rounds if this doesn't satisfy!"

Queenstrial. I remember something about the word. In the briefing on Norta, the packet of cobbled-together information the Colonel made me read before I was sent here. Something about princes—choosing brides, maybe. I wrinkle my nose at the idea, but somehow I can't tear my eyes away from the screen as we get closer and closer.

On it, a girl in black leather demonstrates her storied abilities. *Magnetron,* I realize as she manipulates the metal of whatever arena she's been dropped into.

Then a flash of red drops across the screen, landing hard against the electric shield separating the magnetron girl from the rest of the Silver elite watching her display.

The officers gasp in unison. One of them even turns away. "I don't want to see this," he groans, as if he's about to be sick.

Shade is rooted to the spot, his eyes hard on the screen, watching the red blotch. His grip tightens on me, forcing me to look. *The blotch has a face. His sister.*

Mare Barrow.

He goes cold against me as the lightning swallows her whole.

"It should have killed her."

Shade's hands are shaking and he has to crouch in the alley to keep the rest from following suit. I drop to my knees next to him, one hand on his shivering arm.

"It should have killed her," he says again, his eyes wide and hollow.

I don't need to ask to know he's replaying the scene in his head, over and over again. His young sister falling into the Queenstrial arena. To her death under all circumstances. But Mare didn't die. She was electrocuted on camera, but she didn't die.

"She's alive, Shade," I tell him, turning his face to mine. "You saw yourself, she got up and ran."

"How is that possible?"

Now is not the time to appreciate the joke. "I asked you the same thing once."

"Then she's different too." His eyes darken, sliding away from my face. "And she's with *them*. I have to help her."

He tries to scramble to his feet, but the shock has not worn off. I help him back down as gently as I can, letting him lean on me.

"They'll kill her, Diana," he whispers. His voice breaks my heart. "They could be doing it right now."

"Somehow, I don't think they will. They can't. Not after everyone saw her, a Red girl surviving lightning." *They'll need to explain first. Come up with a story. Just like the stories they used to cover us until we made sure they couldn't anymore.* "She planted a flag of her own today."

Suddenly the alley feels too small. Shade levels a glare, one only a soldier could muster. "I won't leave my sister there alone."

"She won't be. I will make sure of it."

His eyes harden, mirroring the resolve I feel inside.

"So will I."

THE FOLLOWING MESSAGE HAS BEEN DECODED
CONFIDENTIAL, COMMAND CLEARANCE REQUIRED

Day 2 of Operation LIGHTNING.

Operative: Captain REDACTED.
Designation: LAMB.
Origin: Summerton, LL.
Destination: COMMAND at REDACTED.

-Op under way. MARE BARROW made contact with WHISTLE WILL and BONES in ALBANUS, oathed to SG. SHADOW leverage successful.
-Operative MAIDEN will act as her contact within HALL OF THE SUN.
-Operative STEWARD made contact regarding new asset for recruitment inside HALL OF THE SUN, will explore further.

RISE, RED AS THE DAWN.

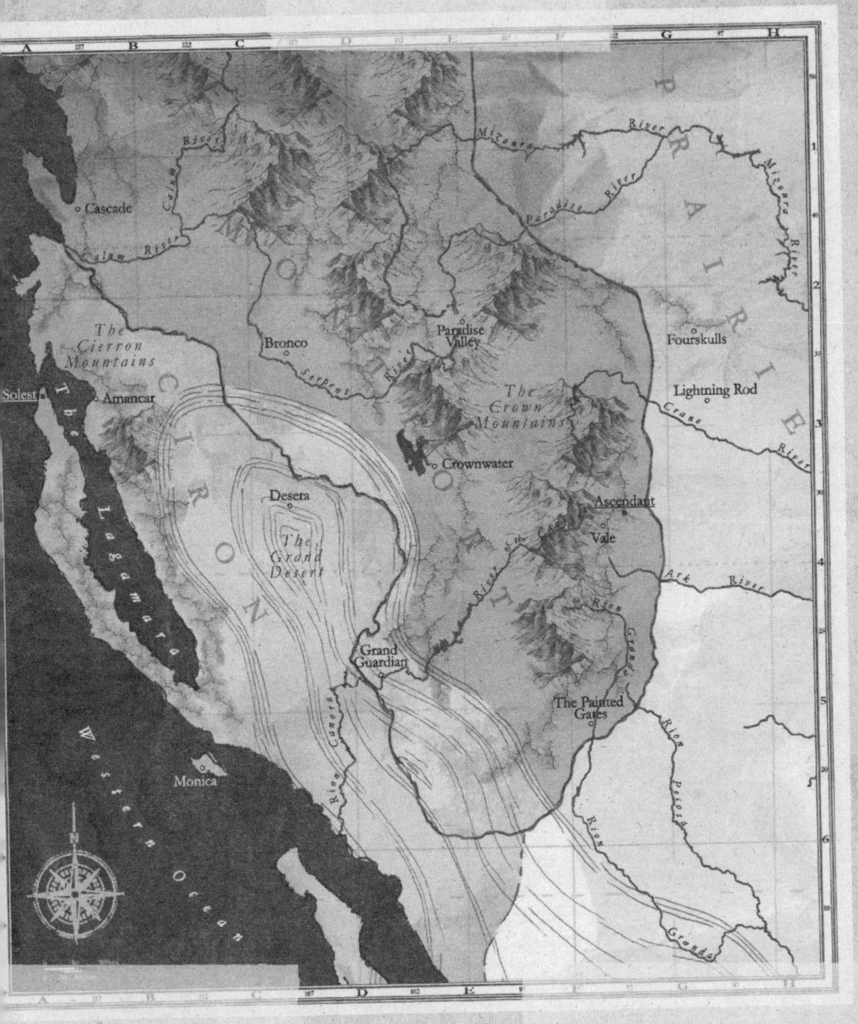

Cascade
Calum River
The Cierron Mountains
Solest
Amancar
The Lagamara
Western Ocean
Monica
Bronco
Serpent River
Paradise Valley
Mizoura River
Paradise River
PRAIRIE
Fourskulls
Lightning Rod
Crane River
The Crown Mountains
Crownwater
Desera
The Grand Desert
CIERRON
Ascendant
Vale
Ark River
Rion Granda
Grand Guardian
Rion Canora
The Painted Gates
Rion Pecosa
Rion Granda

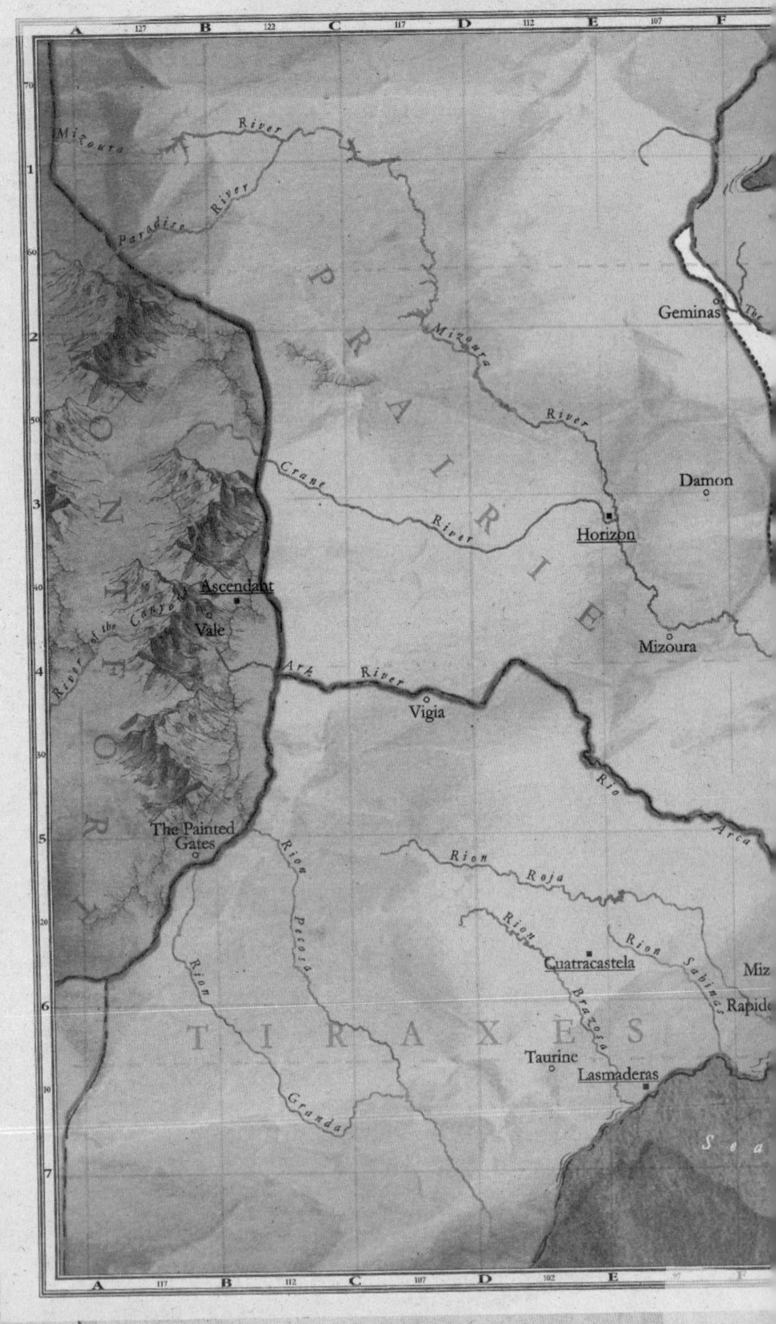

Mizoura River
Paradise River
PRAIRIE
Mizoura River
Geminas
Damon
Crane River
Horizon
Ascendant
Vale
River of the Canyon
Mizoura
Ark River
Vigia
Rio Arca
The Painted Gates
Rion Pecosa
Rion Roja
Rion Brazosa
Cuatracastela
Rion Sabinas
Rapide
Rion Granda
TIRAXES
Taurine
Lasmaderas
Sea

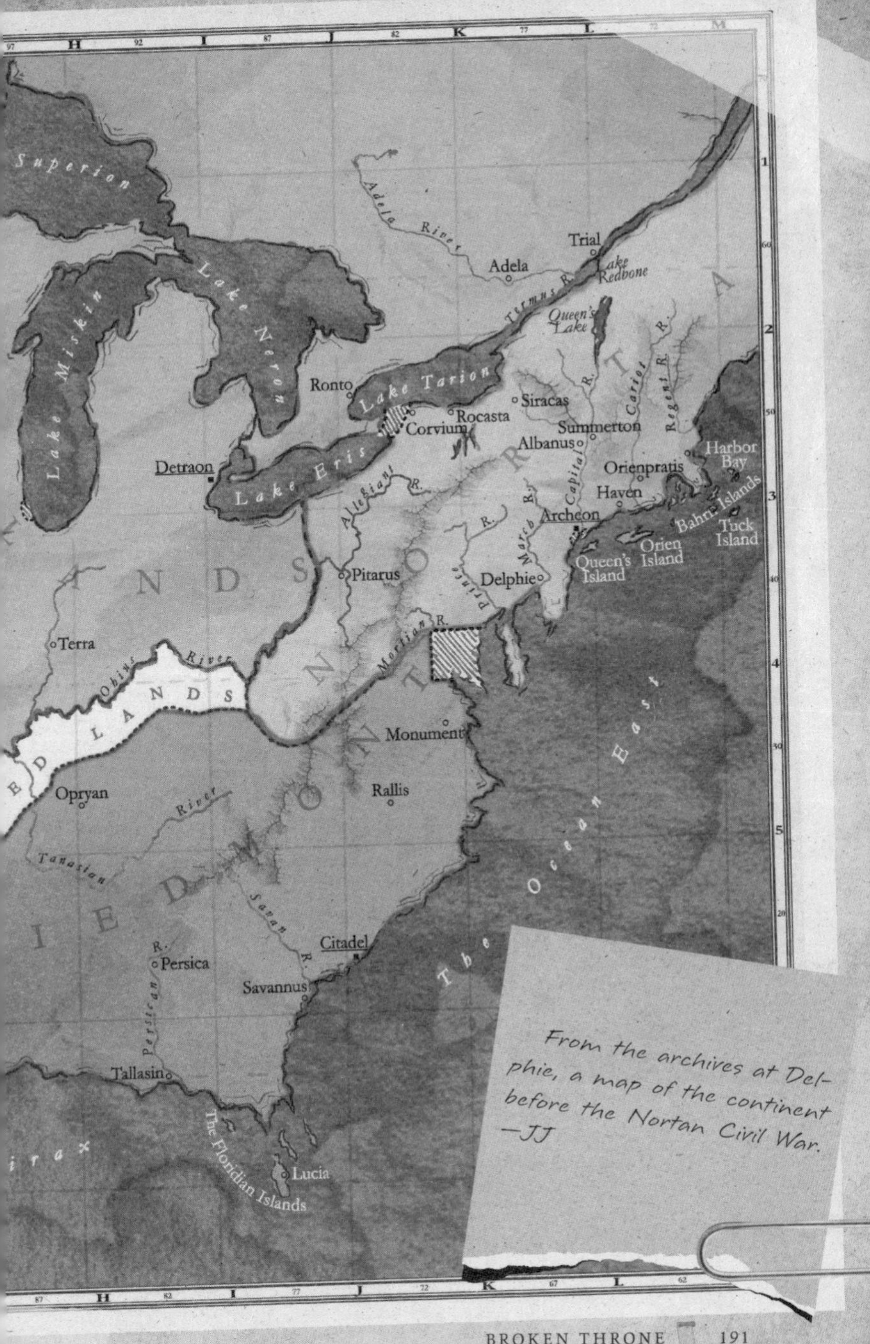
Superior
Lake Miskin
Lake Neron
Lake Tarion
Lake Eris
Adela River
Adela
Trial
Lake Redbone
Termus R.
Queen's Lake
Ronto
Rocasta
Corvium
Siracas
Summerton
Albanus
Capital R.
Cariot
Regent R.
R.
Harbor Bay
Orienpratis
Haven
Bahri Islands
Tuck Island
Archeon
Orien Island
Queen's Island
Detraon
Allegiant R.
Marsh R.
R.
Pitarus
Delphie
Prince
Mortian R.
Terra
Obius River
BADLANDS
Monument
Rallis
Opryan
River
Tanasian
Savan R.
Citadel
R.
Persica
Persican
Savannus
Tallasin
The Floridian Islands
Lucia
The Ocean East
NORTA
LANDS
PIEDMONT
From the archives at Delphie, a map of the continent before the Nortan Civil War.
—JJ

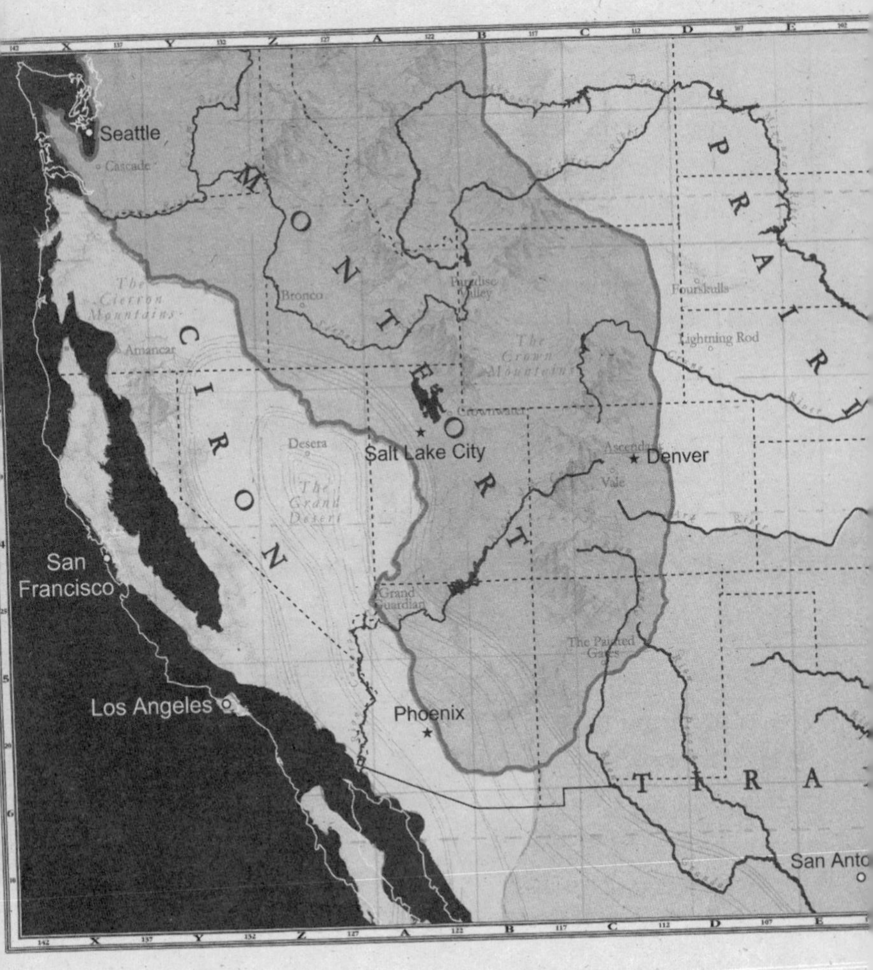
Seattle
Cascade
MONTFORT
PRAIRIE
The Cierron Mountains
Amancar
CIRON
Bronco
Paradise Valley
The Crown Mountains
Fourskulls
Lightning Rod
Desera
Salt Lake City
Denver
Ascendant
Vale
The Grand Desert
San Francisco
Grand Guardian
The Painted Gates
Los Angeles
Phoenix
TIRA
San Anto

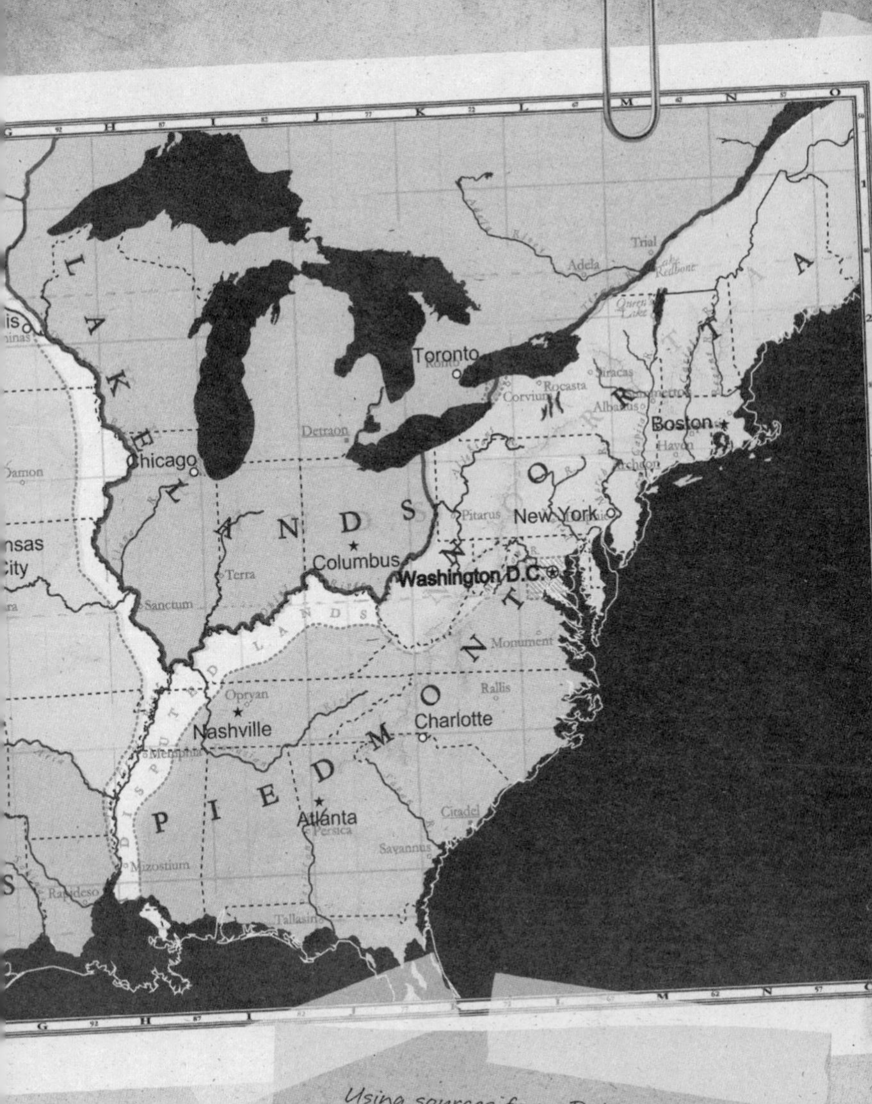

Using sources from Delphie, Horn Mountain, and my own collection, I've done what I can to reconstruct a map of the old world beneath our own. This is only a first attempt and more research must be done to accurately include borders and cities long since lost to us.
—JJ

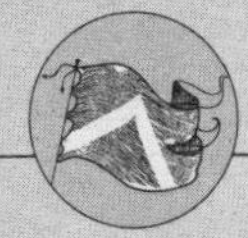

CONTINENTAL GOVERNMENTS OVERVIEW

Compiled and assessed by JULIAN JACOS

NOTES:

Collection of the continental governments, sourced from both the Nortan historical archives in Delphie and the Republic's vaults in Horn Mountain. Recent information on the governments of Ciron, parts of Prairie, and Tiraxes can only be verified to early 321 NE, before the Secession of the Rift. Therefore I have summarized this overview for all nations up to said year.—J. Jacos

THE KINGDOM OF NORTA is an absolute monarchy, wherein supreme authority is retained by a single ruler. The Silver burners of House Calore have controlled the crown for more than three hundred years. Theirs is the only dynasty to have ruled Norta since her formation as a modern state.

At present, KING MAVEN CALORE is the eighteen-year-old ruler of Norta, having inherited his throne when his father, KING TIBERIAS VI, was murdered. *To put it lightly.* His older brother, TIBERIAS VII, was framed for the killing and fled Norta after escaping execution. In some circles of Norta, Tiberias VII is seen as the legitimate king, adding to the instability of King Maven's young reign.

King Maven signed a peace treaty with the Lakelands, ending the decades-long war that raged between the neighbor countries. He will marry Princess Iris Cygnet, the second daughter of Queen Cenra and King Orrec of the Lakelands.

Participation in national government is restricted to members of the High Houses, the nobility of Norta. Regional governances are inherited within families, and it is very rare for a region to change hands from one house to another. Governors from the eight regions of the kingdom regularly convene with the monarch, and are given great control over their territories. However, greater command is given to the superior Lords and Ladies of each High House, currently numbering twenty-three individuals. All advise the king in council, with certain houses holding greater sway dependent on the strength of their families, territories, and resources.

Only House Jacos has accomplished such a magnificent feat in the last fifty years.

Society is structured and subsequently organized along the blood divide, separating Silvers from Reds. Silvers are further separated into the nobility and common class, though this stratification can become blurred, as intermarriage between noble and common Silvers is not outlawed. Upward mobility is possible for common Silvers, either through skill, accrual of wealth, or marriage.

Possible but not advised.

Red society is entirely restricted, with no representation in government. Red citizens of Norta are subject to conscription laws that require all Reds over the age of eighteen to be employed or drafted into the Nortan military. Job scarcity is an issue in most Red communities outside tech towns, where techie Reds are forbidden to be conscripted, leave their city of birth, or change their profession. Conscription lasts several decades, with intervals of leave before discharge, or until a Red is no longer physically able to serve due to injury.

Education is usually poor among Reds, who tend to focus on their professions or on preparing for conscription. Red travel in Norta is outwardly restricted, but impossible to fully enforce. It is not unheard of for Reds along the southern border to make their way into the Disputed Lands, the only bordering country without a Silver-dominated government.

Or any government at all.

Black markets, crime syndicates, and underground trade thrive in Red-majority communities. In cities such as Harbor Bay, Red communities organize themselves, maintaining their own laws and enforcement where Silvers will not.

Blood intermarriages are outlawed, and intermingling is frowned upon on both sides of the blood divide. Upon birth, Reds are subject to blood registration. Their blood samples are given to the Nortan government for the stated purpose of tracking and control. However, it has been suggested that the blood registration began several decades ago when it became clear to Nortan officials that a shift had begun in the Red population, giving rise to the newblood phenomenon.

THE KINGDOM OF THE LAKELANDS is an absolute monarchy, wherein supreme authority is retained by a single ruler. The Silver nymphs of House Cygnet currently hold the throne of the Lakelands. The dynasty is quite large, with both QUEEN CENRA and KING ORREC hailing from different branches of the Cygnet tree. Queen Cenra is the ruling monarch, and, as is custom in the Lakelands, her heir, PRINCESS TIORA, is not permitted to leave the borders of the Lakelands, to ensure the survival of the bloodline. Queen Cenra herself is also confined within her country except in times of great need.

The Silvers of the Lakelands are deeply religious, with their faith based in a pantheon of dozens of faceless, nameless, all-powerful gods. People worship in shrines, often built around water or fountains. The Lakelander religion is strongly rooted in balance, as well as the afterlife. Silver Lakelanders bury their dead in their abilities, and those who live evil lives are said to meet punishment in the afterlife. Red Lakelanders do not follow this faith, and very little is known about their religion. Not because they do not believe, but because their faiths are numerous and carefully guarded within their communities.

The long-lasting war between the Lakelands and Norta was ended by a peace treaty proposed by King Maven. He then married Princess Iris Cygnet to cement a new bond between nations in alliance against the Red rebellion that was brewing across both countries. The Scarlet Guard, a Red rebel organization, had begun in the Lakelands and trickled across the Nortan border to fight both nations.

by their definition

Despite their tumultuous history, Norta and the Lakelands have similar societies, with noble Silvers serving in government, common Silvers possessing little but still-existent upward mobility, and severely restricted Red citizens. The Lakelands have fewer tech towns than Norta, and mostly keep their Red workers in agricultural work. There is food in abundance in the Lakelands, though electricity is scarce in Red communities.

THE PRINCIPALITY OF PIEDMONT is an oligarchic aristocracy. The government of the nation is shared by ruling princes and princesses, each with their own territories, families, and resources at their disposal.

Ultimately, rule of Piedmont is ceded to the most powerful prince or princess in the country. The oligarchy can elect this position through popular vote, though sometimes it is taken through military strength. At present, that title belongs to PRINCE BRACKEN of the Lowcountry, the largest holding in Piedmont, with valuable access to the coast and fertile farmland. Other ranking Silver nobles within Piedmont include PRINCE DENNIARDE, PRINCESS ANA, and PRINCESS MARRION. One of Bracken's strongest supporters, PRINCE ALEXANDRET, was killed while visiting the court of Norta, putting undue strain on the once-strong alliance between Norta and Piedmont.

Unbeknownst to the monarchs of the north, Prince Bracken is currently under the control of the Scarlet Guard, aided by the Republic of Montfort. His extensive resources are at the disposal of the Scarlet Guard and Montfort. His military base in the Lowcountry is the first solid foothold for either in the east.

As in Norta and the Lakelands, the lives of Reds in Piedmont are severely restricted, and the population largely works in agriculture or industrial production. Piedmont also utilizes conscription, both to bolster its armies and to control the size of the Red population.

THE PRAIRIE LANDS are strange in comparison to their neighbors to the east, due in large part to their sprawling geography and lack of centralized population. Their government can only be described as a feudal kraterocracy. The will of the strong rules across the endless plains. Warlords and warladies control their varying fiefdoms through power and cunning, and land often passes between Silver bloodlines from generation to generation. The son of a warlord is just as likely to lose rule of his father's territory as he is to gain it. For this reason, bloodlines and dynasties are not so important to the Silvers of the Prairie lands. Sometimes the Prairie rulers will even adopt or choose successors from outside their own bloodline.

There are four major territories within Prairie, controlled by their respective rulers. Warlady HENGE, a windweaver, rules from the Ark River to the plains north of the Crane River, known as the SANDHILLS. Her fiefdom regularly contends with the Silver raiders driven out of Montfort, both in conflict and peace. She maintains a small city at LIGHTNING ROD, a rock formation in the midst of the plain.

Based on Montfort intelligence. Still unclear

Farther north, the stoneskin Warlord CARHDON rules the vast territory known as FOURSKULLS, centered upon a sacred and strange mountain into which are carved the gigantic heads of four men. Erosion has weathered them into cracked and disintegrating specters, their names and faces lost to time.

Is that a challenge?

The swift Warlord RIONO controls some of the most valuable farmland in Prairie, and rules from the city of Mizoura. His territory, THE HEART, shares a tumultuous border with the Disputed Lands, and he is known to execute Reds who attempt to flee his fiefdom. The Heart sits at the convergence of the

Prairie lands, Tiraxes, Piedmont, the Lakelands, and the Disputed Lands, making it a chaotic place.

Finally, Warlady NEEDA, a nymph, rules the territory THE MIRRORS from the city Geminas, sharing a thin border along the Great River with the Disputed Lands and the Lakelands. Needa is rumored to be a distant cousin of House Cygnet, the rulers of the Lakelands, and she openly encourages Reds to flee across the border and work her fiefdom.

Reds in the Prairie lands are generally bound to the land they are born on, and belong to the Silvers who rule that piece of field or plain. The Silvers then in turn owe fealty to their lords, up to the Warlords and Warladies in feudal hierarchy. Therefore, most Reds in Prairie are bound in servitude, with little education. Their life spans are shorter than their counterparts in neighboring nations, and most of the Reds in the Disputed Lands are refugees from Prairie.

THE FREE REPUBLIC OF MONTFORT was formed from the collapse of several smaller mountain kingdoms ruled by Silver overlords and monarchs. The new government relies on people's representation, from both sides of the blood divide. Representatives are elected from communities within the Republic to serve in the People's Assembly, where an even split of Red and Silvers is maintained. The head of state is known as a premier, and while the first premier was elected directly by the People's Assembly, the system has expanded to utilize a national vote.

Currently, PREMIER DANE DAVIDSON is several years into his term as leader of the Free Republic. He is a newblood shield who was born in Norta and fled to Montfort after escaping the Nortan military, which was attempting to exterminate newbloods.

Montfort is uniquely situated as the only nation on the continent with blood equality, which was only achieved after total civil war. Following the collapse of the mountain kingdoms and the formation of Montfort, the Silvers who chose to remain in the Republic swore an oath to uphold the new status quo. They were granted amnesty for any crimes committed before or during the wars. This approach was championed by LEONIDE RADIS, a Silver prince of the former kingdom of TETONIA, who abdicated his throne in favor of the Republic. He now serves as a representative in the Assembly.

And will be running for premier in the future if my instincts are correct.

Due to still-chaotic volcanic activity in the northwest, as well as the barren Grand Desert on the Cironian border, the majority of Montfort's population is clustered in the east. The capital of ASCENDANT is the largest city, followed by CROWNWATER, BRONCO, and THE PAINTED GATES. The port city of CASCADE is the only Montfortan holding on the Western Ocean.

Because of both geography and national borders, the crossing to Montfort is very difficult for any hoping to reach the Free Republic. However, large

Must ask the premier to arrange a visit.

migrant populations exist, mostly from neighboring Prairie. Montfort maintains a policy of open borders to any willing to accept a blood-equal society. Migrating Silvers are subject to greater scrutiny than Reds, but welcome in the Free Republic. They must swear to uphold the blood laws, dictating the equality of all humans, as well as restricting speech or actions seeking to diminish the value of red-blooded humans. Punishments for Silvers attempting to undermine blood equality are harsh deterrents, ranging from exile to execution.

Montfort reportedly has the highest population of newblood citizens, though this number is impossible to ascertain as Silver-led nations either do not recognize the existence of newbloods or have not begun recording them. Many newbloods are refugees and are most likely to join the Montfortan military to defend their adopted home.

The Montfortan military, due in large part to the information kept in the vaults of Horn Mountain, is very technologically advanced. The Free Republic also champions military recruitment, and most citizens serve or served in the military in some capacity. The wars to form Montfort are fresh in most minds, and most citizens are eager to spread their way of life to their oppressed Red brethren. Montfortans share a pride in their country and its duty to free the world.

Like the Lakelands, **CIRON** is strongly rooted in religion, and the kingdom is both a monarchy and a theocracy. The monarch and the religious head, known as the Sun's Voice, rule together. Before coronation, a prospective monarch of Ciron must be blessed and accepted by the Voice, which has resulted in several succession crises over the centuries. Ciron has the longest-standing monarchy on the continent, its dynasty stretching back more than a thousand years, when Silvers were fewer and were worshipped as gods in their lands.

The current king of Ciron is the burner ILFONSO FINIX, of the long-standing Finix Dynasty. The Sun's Voice is the Silver woman SERANNA, a talented shadow of no noble bloodline. Both the crown and the religious post must pass to a burner and a shadow, respectively, for fire and light are the closest mankind comes to the sun upon the earth.

As in Montfort, the northwest coast of Ciron is subject to a large amount of volcanic activity. The large inland sea, known as the Lagamara, is sacred to Cironian religion as well as central to their economy. Its shores are incredibly fertile for agriculture, while a maritime fishing industry flourishes throughout the sea.

Reds work both farms and the sea, with their populations centered in the coastal fishing communities as well as on the city outskirts. While Reds are currently not forcibly conscripted into military service,

Ciron has been known to do so in times of war. Because of the harsh climate of the Grand Desert, many Reds never attempt the crossing to Montfort, or they die trying.

Both the Sun's Voice and the monarchy are based in the city of Solest, a holy place at the tip of the massive peninsula bordering the Lagamara. From there, residents can see both sunrise and sunset, and worship the sun at these holy times.

Due to both distance and the Grand Desert, Ciron is largely removed from the wars of the eastern countries. They treat mostly with Tiraxes along their southern border, and maintain a shaky neutrality with Montfort.

So no decisions are ever made, then.

THE KINGDOM OF TIRAXES is a triarchy, with power vested in three scions of three Silver dynasties, who rule the kingdom together. Each King or Queen Triarch maintains his or her own lands, while decisions for the kingdom at large, such as whether or not to go to war, must be made unanimously. Because the kingdom is so vast, with varying weather and landscape, Reds outside the major settlements are often left alone by their Silver overlords. There are rumors of Red-only enclaves along the western border and deep in the southern desert.

The Queen Triarch of the West, MAILUNA TORMAS, rules the desert, mountains, and grasslands west of the Rion Pecosa to the southwestern border with

Ciron. She is a storm, like the rest of her line, an ability that allows her otherwise-barren territory to flourish beneath revitalizing rainstorms and floods. The Tormas line has transformed pieces of the Tiraxean desert over the last century, making them suitable for agriculture.

The King Triarch of the North is the blood healer AMBROSIN, who is well over one hundred years old but so skilled in ability that he has been rendered ageless and nearly immortal. Ambrosin is the son of Queen ANDURA CALORE, one of two women to have ruled Norta in their own right. Though he is the son of the queen, he inherited his father's blood-healer abilities and was thus excluded from Calore succession. To acknowledge the house that denied him, he recognizes no last name and sought his destiny elsewhere. He rules from the Prairie border to the Rion Roja, and his capital, VIGIA, is often subject to attack from the Sandhills, raiders, or sometimes both working together.

BELLEZ ALLIRION, the Queen Triarch of the Midland, is the strongest of the three triarchs, ruling the majority of the Tiraxean population from her capital at Cuatracastela. Her territory stretches from the Tiraxean coast to the interior between the Rion Roja and the Rion Pecosa. Not only is she a talented eye, able to see the immediate future, but the Queen Triarch is famed throughout the southern territories for her beauty.

Tiraxes is the only nation to openly trade with the criminal syndicates of the Disputed Lands. King Triarch Ambrosin even has a treaty allowing his ships full movement along the Great River in tandem with the river smugglers.

THE DISPUTED LANDS are anarchy.

Tempting

WORLD BEHIND

ONE
Ashe

I'm only twenty years old, but I've seen countless rat days, as crew and as captain. They're always the same.

This one starts like any other. Busy, stinking, noisy. A sea of faces and waving hands stretches across the ragged docks on the Lakelander side of the river, hundreds of mouths open in plea, fingers clutching full purses or useless stacks of paper currency. They beg in many voices, all asking the same thing. *Take us away. Bring us downriver. Carry me west or south or north, in any direction but the one I have come from.* Like rats on a burning raft, trying to scamper up the ropes.

Used to be only Reds who looked downriver, eager to leave the Silver rule of the Crownlands. Willing to brave the Freelands and the infamous Rivermen, seeking a better life than the one they left behind. Not anymore. There's a war on, spreading like disease up and down the eastern kingdoms. Even Silvers are not immune to it. Fewer of them run, but the ones who do run the same as the rest of us. I find that comforting, somehow.

Most Rivermen are Reds. The few Silvers among us live farther south, on the Tiraxean border or in the few established cities on the Great River. They don't bother this far north. Not worth their time or the risk of facing their kin. They're self-obsessed cowards no matter who they pledge allegiance to, only willing to fight what they know they can defeat.

And many Red Rivermen won't take Silvers on the boats. Most of us hate them, hate their abilities, hate who they are. They aren't worth the trouble or the headache, no matter how well they pay.

Not me. There are no colors on a rat day. No Red or Silver. All that matters on my boat is coin.

I count quickly in my head, scanning the docks. I could book passage for six—they would fit even with the cargo I took on upriver at the border. Better if a few were small—young children. A family is best. One destination, more likely to work together, keep one another in check. Less chance of trouble. *Easy job, easy river.* My father's old words rise like a Lakelander prayer, floating above the shouts across the water.

I lean against the rigging of my keelboat, eyes narrowed against the dawn slanting through the trees on the Lakelander bank. I venture at least two hundred souls hope for passage, ratting on the docks. With only three boats waiting, my own included, most will find their hopes unanswered.

This isn't even one of the busy points of crossing, like the Geminas city port, the Memphia islands, the Gates of Mizostium, or the major confluences along the Great River. But this part of the Ohius has the closest public docks to the Rift border, a region now in open revolt against Norta. Red refugees and Silver deserters have flooded downriver over the last few months, like leaves on the current. Things must be going poorly in the east—because my business has never been better.

I prefer honest smuggling to passenger work if given the choice. Cargo doesn't talk back. Right now half my shallow boat is packed with crates, some stamped with the Nortan crown, others the blue flower of the Lakelander king and queen. I don't ask what I transport, but I can guess. Grain from the Lakelands, slum-made batteries fresh from the Nortan factories. Oil fuel, bottles of alcohol. All stolen, to be handed off downriver south or upriver west. I wager I'll replace them with crates stamped with the Montfort mountain for the return journey. Guns and ammunition come down the Ark River to the Great on seemingly every boat, bound for the rebels fighting in the northeast. The gun runs pay best, but they carry the most risk. Most Crownland patrols will let Rivermen pass for a bribe, but not if you're carrying weaponry. That'll earn you a bullet if you're lucky, or Silver torture if the patrols are feeling bored.

No guns on my boat today, except for the ones my small crew and I carry. The Freelands are no place to travel unarmed.

The other two keelboats, shallow as my own, built to ride strong currents and ford the changing depths of rivers and streams, wait off the starboard side. I know their captains, and they know me. Old Toby waves from the prow of her boat, a red patchwork scarf tied around her neck despite the humidity of early summer. She's taken up with the Scarlet Guard and works almost exclusively for them now. She must have an arrangement waiting to board her boat. Guard operatives or the like, catching transport to river knows where.

I shake my head. Not worth the trouble, those Guard folk. They'll get you killed quicker than a gun run.

"You want to pick your rats first, Ashe?" the other captain, Hallow, calls to me from his deck. He's my age and lanky as a scarecrow, taller than I am, but I don't mind. I prefer muscle to height. Hallow is fair where I am dark, brown all over from my hair to my eyes to the river-worn, scarred, tanned hands in my pockets. Our fathers worked together downriver at the Gates. They died together too.

I shake my head. "It's your turn," I reply, grinning at him. I always give Hallow first pick, ever since we both earned our own boats two years ago.

He nods to me, then to his crew. They jump to action, a pair of them using the long poles to direct the keel into the center of the river, where the water is deepest and the current flows true. The third, his scurrier, hops into the scurry, the smaller boat lashed to the side of the keel. With sure hands, she unties the scurry and paddles her way to the docks, careful to stop a few yards out of reach.

While the Lakelander regulations don't impede our work, they don't make it easy for us. No Riverman is permitted to set foot on their side of the river, where the border is starkly drawn. We must do our business on the water, or on our side of the bank. There isn't a patrol at this dock, or even an outpost, but it's best to take all precautions. Times nowadays are as unpredictable as the spring melts.

The scurrier shouts at the jostling horde of rats on the shore, beginning the back and forth of bargains. She keeps her gun ready, in plain sight of the crowd. Fingers are held up, coins brandished, paper notes from all over the Crownlands flutter on the breeze. She signals to Hallow with her hands, using signs we all know well, and he signals back. After a moment, three Reds jump into the shallows, laden with packs. They look like siblings, reedy teenagers. Probably outrunning conscription in Norta. Merchant class, with parents who love them and enough money to bribe their way to the border and onto a keelboat. *Lucky bastards*, I think. Usually conscription runners have little to offer, and sometimes they have a Silver patrol hunting them down for good measure. I hate taking on runners and deserters. *Hard job, hard river.*

Soon Hallow has his passengers, hustled back in the scurry. He must be smuggling a good amount of cargo today, to only take three on board. Our keels are the same size, and I wonder what he's got in his hold. Hallow isn't as careful as I am. He lets the river take him where it wills.

He smiles at me with a flourish, showing the golden tooth where a canine incisor should be. I have the same, the other half of a matching set. "Got them all thirsty for you, Captain," he calls over the constant rush of the river.

I nod to my crew, and the keel moves beneath me, taking Hallow's place.

My scurrier, Big Ean, is already in his little boat, his broad frame taking up nearly half the scurry.

"Six," I mutter down to him, leaning over the side. "You know what I prefer."

He just waves a hand and grunts, pushing off the keel with his paddle. With a few powerful strokes, he maneuvers the scurry to the opposite end of the docks from where Hallow drew his rats.

I stare after him, shading my eyes with a hand. From the center of the river, I can hunt the faces myself, looking for good jobs. *Easy river.*

A group of four stands out on one end of the dock, wrapped in matching blue cloaks hemmed in mud. I glimpse uniforms on the two women clutching each other and two children. The adults clearly maids from a fine Silver household. They'll have money certainly, if not something more valuable to trade. Stolen jewels from their master, adorned knives from a mistress.

I signal to Big Ean, gesturing for him to approach them, but he's already focused on another rat planted in the shallows. Though dozens of the rats beg, bending toward him to plead their case or bargain, he gestures to one figure in the crowd. I squint, trying to assess the rat as best I can from my place at the prow.

Tall, hooded in a filthy coat too big for her frame. It nearly trails on the ragged docks. Nearly.

The coat doesn't quite hide the polished leather boots, well fitted and well made.

My jaw tightens as a real gold coin flashes between her fingers, catching the dawn light.

Someone bumps her shoulder hard, fighting for Big Ean's attention, but she doesn't budge, unmoved. She says something to Big Ean that I can't hear.

Big Ean looks back to me. *She'll pay ten times the rate, in gold,* he signals.

Take her, I signal back with ease.

With a wave of his hand, he passes on the message and she leaps from the dock, landing hip deep in the water without hesitation. In an instant she climbs onto Big Ean's boat, settling into her coat despite the rising heat. I catch a glimpse of straight, gleaming black hair beneath the hood before she tucks it back.

My stomach twists, a familiar dread settling in me. I suspect already—but I won't know for certain until I can look her in the eye.

As with all fat rats, the kind who pay more than they should for what we offer, Big Ean ferries her back alone, without filling the rest of the scurry. I need to assess her, figure out why she's throwing so much gold away on a few days' journey. And if she's worth the risk of transport. If not, I'll toss her back in the river and leave her to ratting on the shore.

She climbs from the scurry to the keel deck without aid, dripping water everywhere. The coat stinks close up, like sewage. I wrinkle my nose as I approach her, gesturing for Big Ean and my polers, Gill and Riette, to stand aside. She doesn't drop her hood, so I yank it back for her.

Silver veins her eyes, and her skin is cold bronze. I try not to flinch.

"Half the gold now, half at the Gates" is all she says, her voice softened and slowed by a butter-rich Piedmont accent. Freckles dust her cheeks, a spread of stars beneath her angled, black eyes. "Is that suitable?"

She's educated, rich, and noble, even with the disgusting coat. And she wants to go all the way to the end of the line, to the Gates of Mizostium, the place where the Great River meets the sea.

I clench my jaw. "What's your name and what's your business on the rivers?"

"I'm paying you for transport, not questions," she responds without hesitation.

Sneering, I wave a hand back to the scurry. "You can find another keel if my terms don't agree with you."

Her reply is whipcrack fast. Again no hesitation. No second-guessing herself. I wonder if she even knows how to do so.

"My name is Lyrisa," she says, chin still high. Her eyes rake over me. I get the feeling she's looked down on men like me all her life. "I am a blood princess of the Lowcountry, and I need to be at the Gates of Mizostium as soon as possible."

I almost toss her back into the river then and there. Only the danger of her ability, trained and lethal whatever it may be, stills my hand. Behind her, Gill tightens a grip on his pole. As if he could simply strike her and be done with it. Riette is more intelligent. Her hand goes to the pistol on her hip, unfastening the button keeping it holstered. Even Silvers aren't immune to bullets. *Most of them, anyway.*

I wish I could touch my own gun, but she'll see me do it. "Who, and more importantly how many, of your father's Silver hunters are following you?"

Finally she wavers, if only for a moment. Her eyes drop to the deck, then blaze back to mine. "My father is dead."

A corner of my mouth lifts in a cold smirk. "Your father is the ruling prince of Piedmont, currently at war with the Rift. We Rivermen aren't as stupid as you think we are."

"Bracken is my uncle, my mother's brother," she snaps. Her eyes narrow, and I wonder what her ability could be. How many ways she could kill me or my crew. How someone like her could possibly need *us* to get downriver—or why. "My father is dead, for six years now. I did not lie and I resent the implication, Red."

Despite her blood, her Silver-born tendency to lie, cheat, and abuse us, I can't see a lie in her eyes or hear it in her voice. She doesn't flinch under my inspection. "How many hunters?" I ask again, leaning toward her, though all my Red instincts cry out in protest.

Lyrisa doesn't move, neither retreating nor meeting my challenge.

"None. I was journeying north into the Lakelands with a convoy when we were attacked by rebels." She jabs a thumb over her shoulder at the bank. A breeze stirs her hair, blowing a gleaming, thick curtain of black over one shoulder. "I am the only survivor."

Ah. It clicks in my head. "I suppose you want your uncle to think you died with the rest?"

She nods, her face betraying no emotion. "I do."

A Silver princess abandoning her kingdom, dead to all who knew her. And wanting to stay that way. I'm intrigued, to say the very least.

Perhaps not all rat days are the same.

The choice is already made in me. The offered gold, ten times the usual rate, will go far on the river and among my crew. I can't speak for the others, but most of my share will go back to my mother, for safekeeping. I angle my shoulders away from the princess, opening the deck to her. I trail a hand, waving her toward the shallow benches backed by the stocked cargo hold.

"Find a seat and stay out of the way," I tell her, shifting my focus back to my scurrier still in the river. "Ean, the family in blue cloaks. See what they're offering."

Lyrisa doesn't move, her manner calm. She's used to getting what she asks for, or demands. "Captain, I'm paying you to take me and me alone downriver. I have need of speed."

"Very well, Silver," I reply, turning to lean over the side of the keel. Below me, Ean has one hand on the rope ladder, ready to climb back aboard. I wave him off as Lyrisa takes a seat, arms crossed.

I speak louder than I must.

"Ean, the blue cloaks."

There is only one captain aboard my keel.

TWO
Ashe

She tosses her rancid coat into the river once we're moving, not bothering to watch as it floats in the current and tangles in the roots along the bank. It stains the water as it goes, swirling with dirt and worse. I suppose it must be blood or excrement or both. Not that I'll bother asking. I've ferried Silvers before, and the river runs easy when we keep our distance from them.

The Red family we took on knows that too. They're a pair of mothers, one dark-skinned and one light, who keep their two children angled away from the Piedmont princess, all avoiding her eye line. She doesn't seem to mind and leans back on her elbows, enjoying the ample room their absence affords her.

Gill throws a glare at her from his place at the side, long pole in hand. He pushes methodically, navigating us around rocks and high riverbed. He has more reason to hate Silvers than most, but he keeps his temper in check. I pass by him on my way to the prow of the keel, giving his shoulder a squeeze.

"Just to the Gates," I mutter, reminding him of our goal. Two weeks only, if we're lucky in the current and the patrols. I've run the Gates in less time, but I'd rather not push the keel or the crew. Besides, it looks to be an easy river. No use making things more complicated than they need be.

"To the Gates," he echoes. It isn't difficult to hear the words unspoken. *And not one second longer.*

I nod to him. The Piedmont princess will be gone soon enough.

We know the path to the Gates like the back of our scarred hands, like the deck of the keel. Down the Ohius to the confluence, that's the worst stretch. To our right, north, is the Lakelander bank, the borderline of the Crownlands drawn right up to the water's edge. To the left, south, stretches the Freelands. This far northeast, it's woodland and fields, mostly overgrown. Should a Lakelander patrol decide to try us here, we'd have no choice but to flee overland. Keels are fast but not faster than vehicle transports, and are little use if a powerful nymph decides to turn the river against us. I've only felt the water push back once, and that was enough. I don't intend to face it again.

I check our progress against the other keels and captains. Old Toby is already gone from view, lagging behind. Her Scarlet Guard business must require slow movement, or many stops along the border. I certainly don't envy her such a job. Nor do I have any desire to throw my lot in with those rebels, no matter how sweet their words may sound. They certainly don't make for an easy job or an easy river.

Hallow is about a hundred yards ahead, his keel riding low in the water. He'll probably stay in sight until we reach the confluence, where the Ohius and Great River meet. Then he'll spend a day or so dumping cargo to go upriver north. I won't see him again until the Gates.

At the prow I can see far, the Lakelands stretching in clear-cut fields of wheat and corn. Half-height. Summer is coming on, and by fall these fields will be stripped bare for winter. Every year I pass the workers, watching the Reds sweat and toil for their distant overlords. Sometimes they run to the bank when they see us, begging for passage. We never take them. Patrols are too close and farmworkers have too little coin. A few make the journey on their own, though, building boats on the bank through the summer. We help those along if we can, out of Silver sight.

Quick, light footsteps on the deck shake me out of my thoughts as one of the passenger children scuttles up next to me, her eyes wide in a golden face framed by curly brown hair. She looks afraid. I grin at her, if only to keep the kid settled. The last thing I need is a screaming child. She immediately grins, pointing at my mouth, then to her own tooth.

"You like that?" I murmur, running a tongue over my gold incisor. It replaced a tooth knocked out in a fight in Memphia. A fight I won.

"Your tooth is shiny," she exclaims giddily. She can't be more than eight.

I glance back up the deck, at her mothers pressed together on the bench. They look on, apprehensive. I wonder if the child is adopted, or born of one of the women. Probably the latter. She has the same look as the paler one, the same spark in her eyes.

Gently, I nudge her back toward her family. Cute as the kid is, I don't want to interact with her any more than I must. It's easier that way. "You should go sit down. I've got work to do up here."

She doesn't move, still staring. "You're the captain," she says, persistent.

I blink at her. Even though keelboat crews don't have any kind of insignia or markings to denote officers, it's clear where I stand on my deck. "Yes."

"Captain what?"

Nodding, I nudge her again, this time moving with the child so she has to follow. "Ashe," I offer, if only to get her going.

"I'm Melly." Then her voice drops to a whisper, one hand suddenly clutching mine. "There's a Silver on the boat."

"I'm very aware of that," I mutter, prying my fingers from hers.

At the benches, I catch the Piedmont princess watching despite her lazing appearance. She glances at us beneath her lashes, pretending not to look. A good tactic. A smart one.

"Why did you let her on?" The little girl continues without any concern for the rest of the ship—or those who might overhear.

From her position at the side, Riette shoots me a smirk as she poles the river. I grimace in reply. Somehow the rat kids always gravitate to me, and somehow I keep letting them.

"Same reason I let you on," I tell her, sounding short and gruff. *Just let me work, kid.*

"They're dangerous," she whispers back. "I don't like them."

I don't bother to drop my voice. Let the Silver princess hear me. "Neither do I."

One of the Red mothers, the pale one, gratefully reaches for her daughter when I push her over. She has short-cropped hair the color of wheat. "Apologies for Melly, sir," she says, pulling the child close. Not out of fear, but out of respect. "You sit still now."

I nod curtly. It isn't in me to scold passengers, especially those fleeing a civil war. "Just keep out of the hold and out of the way."

The other Red mother, holding tight to their young boy, smiles warmly. "Of course, sir."

Sir seems to bounce off my skin. Though this is my keel and my crew, my river hard-earned, I never get used to it. Two grown women calling me such a thing still feels odd. Even if it's true. Even if I deserve it.

As I leave the couple, I pass by the princess. She's still stretched out, taking more room than she should. The Silver angles her chin to survey me. All thoughts of inadequacy or unworthiness vanish. If there's anyone who doesn't deserve my respect, it's a Silver.

I harden under her attention, losing any warmth.

"When do we eat, Ashe?" she asks, one hand idly tapping the bench. Overhead, the strengthening summer sun forces her to shade her eyes with the other hand.

Ashe.

The Red child bristles before I can, leaning around one of her mothers.

"He's a captain, miss," she says, her voice wavering. I can't fathom the bravery it must take for her to speak to a Silver at all, let alone correct one. She'd make a fine keel captain herself one day.

Her mother hushes her quickly, pulling her back into place.

I shift if only a little, putting more of myself between the child and the Silver, in case the latter takes offense.

But she doesn't move, her focus entirely fixed on me.

"We eat at sundown," I tell her evenly.

Her lip curls. "No lunch?"

On the bench, one of the Red mothers shifts a foot slowly, pushing her pack farther out of sight. I almost smirk. Of course they had the common sense to bring provisions for the journey.

"When I said *we*, I meant my crew," I tell the Silver, each word sharp as a knife. "You didn't bring any food for yourself?"

The tapping hand ceases movement but doesn't clench. The gun at my hip hangs heavy. I don't expect a desperate Silver fleeing her homeland to attack us over a meal, but it doesn't hurt to stay vigilant. Silvers aren't used to being denied anything, and they don't react well to hardship.

She grimaces, showing white, even teeth. Too perfect to be natural. She must have had them knocked out and regrown by a skin healer. "Certainly my rate covers board."

"That wasn't part of our original deal. But you can pay for food if you'd like," I say. Her coin already given is for speed and silence and no questions. Not meals. And despite the money she's already paid out, I'm the one in position to bargain. Not her. "That's *certainly* an option."

Her eyes don't leave mine, but one of her hands brushes over the coin purse hooked to her belt. Weighing the gold left, listening to the subtle clink of metal. It's not an insubstantial amount. But still she hesitates to pay, even to feed herself.

The princess is saving her money. For more. *For worse.* For a longer journey than the river. I'd wager all the cargo in my hold she doesn't plan to stop at the Gates. Like before when she first landed on my deck, I'm intrigued.

Her expression changes, wiping clean. She sniffs and I get the sense of being dismissed like a courtier or a servant. One of her fingers twitches, as if remembering the urge to wave off a worthless Red.

"Do you dock anywhere along this stretch of the Ohius?" she asks, turning her head to survey the Freeland side of the river, where the Lakelands and a Silver crown hold no sway. The woodlands tangle into darkness, even in the morning sun. Her question and interest puzzle me only for a second.

Princess Lyrisa plans to hunt for her supper.

I survey her again, now that she's lost the coat. Her clothes are as fine as her boots, a dark blue uniform. No jewelry, no adornment. She has no weapons that I can see either, so her ability must allow her to bring down game. I know noble Silvers are trained to war as much as soldiers are, trained to fight one another for sport and pride. And the thought of one so powerful on my keel unsettles me deeply.

But not enough to turn away her money. Or stop antagonizing her.

I take a step back, grinning sharply. Her eyes narrow. "We don't dock until the confluence the day after tomorrow," I say.

One of her hands darts, and the coin sails end over end, a flash of gold in the sun. I catch it deftly, enjoying my own triumph and her poorly disguised disdain.

"A pleasure having you on board, Princess," I call over my shoulder as I walk away.

The sunset turns the river bloodred, lengthening every shadow until we seem to swim through darkness. At the prow, Gill keeps watch for errant logs or drifting sandbars. Crickets on the bank and frogs in the shallows sing. It's a quiet night on the Ohius, an easy current drawing us farther southeast. I hope, when it's my time, I die on a night like this.

When Big Ean doles out supper, I expect the Silver to balk at the quality of our food. It's not terrible, but our provisions certainly aren't up to the standards a princess would be used to. Instead she takes what she's given without a word, then eats quietly by herself on her bench. Salt jerky and hard biscuits seem to go down as easily as the finest desserts in Piedmont.

The rest of us gather on the deck, circled up on crates or the deck itself to eat. The pair of kids, Melly and her older brother, whose name I've learned is Simon, are already asleep against their mothers, their bellies full. The parents, named Daria and Jem, split their provisions evenly before offering some to us.

Riette waves them off before anyone else can, her gap-toothed grin wide. In the soft electric light of the keel, she looks worn, her scars of the river more pronounced. She's ten years my elder, but new to the keel life. Barely a year on my deck. She's Freeland born, raised without allegiance or obedience to any crown. Same as me, same as Hallow. We have a different way about us, the Freeland Reds.

"Long road?" Riette says kindly to the mothers, pointing with a biscuit at the kids.

The darker woman, Jem, her hair and eyes black as gunpowder, nods. "Yes," she says. One hand absentmindedly strokes Melly's curls. "But Melly and Simon have been warriors through it. It's taken a long while to reach the Disputed Lands." *Disputed.* That's what Crownlanders call us. As if we are something for the Silvers to fight over, and not a country unto ourselves, free of their rule. "We've come all the way from Archeon."

In my mind's eye, a map unfurls. Archeon is hundreds of miles away. I speak around a bite of jerky. "Servants."

"We were," Jem replies. "When the rebels attacked the king's wedding, it was easy to slip away in the confusion, escape the palace, flee the city."

News travels well along the river, and we heard about the Nortan king and his ill-fated wedding a month ago. The king lived, but the Silvers certainly felt the sting of the Scarlet Guard and the Montfort troops. Things have only deteriorated since, we hear—civil war in Norta, a Scarlet Guard insurgency, Montfort moving steadily east. And news of it all finds its way downriver eventually, carried on the war current.

From outside our circle, a voice sounds.

"You served Maven?" the princess asks. She stares at Jem, her face inscrutable in the weak light of the keel.

Jem doesn't quail under her gaze. She tightens her jaw. "Daria worked in the kitchens. I was a lady's maid. We had little to do with the king."

The Silver is undeterred, her supper forgotten. "Then his wife. The Lakelander princess."

"She had her own servants from her country to serve her directly." Jem shrugs. "I was a queen's servant, though, and in the absence of a queen, I served the prisoner. Not directly, of course—no Red was allowed near her—but I carried her linens, her food, that sort of thing."

Big Ean brushes biscuit crumbs from his short beard, dusting his crossed legs. "The prisoner?" he says, eyes narrowed in confusion.

The princess's voice is stern. "You're talking about Mare Barrow."

This only deepens Big Ean's bewilderment. He glances at Riette for an explanation. "Who's she?"

She sighs loudly, rolling her eyes at him. "The Scarlet Guard girl."

"Oh right," Big Ean replies. "The one who ran off with that prince."

Another cluck of annoyance escapes Riette. She swats him. "No, idiot, the one with an ability. Lightning. Like a Silver but not. How could you forget her?"

Big Ean just shrugs his massive shoulders. "Dunno. Red running off with a prince sounded more interesting."

"They're the same person," I grumble, shutting them both up.

Just because we get news doesn't mean we get it properly, in order, or entirely true. Some Rivermen and Freelanders spend their days sorting out what's going on outside our borders, in the chaos that rules the Crownlands. Personally, I don't bother with the rumors and just wait to see what solidifies into truth. Hallow cares more about any of it than I do, and tells me what I need to know.

"And Barrow isn't a prisoner," I add. I saw one of her broadcasts myself when I was far upriver, when the Red girl decried the Scarlet Guard and their agenda. She wore jewels and silk and spoke of the king's kindness and mercy. "She joined up with the Nortan king willingly."

On her bench, the Piedmont princess laughs sharply into her cup of water.

I cut a glance at her, only to find her already sneering. "Something funny about that?"

To my surprise, it's Jem who answers. "The girl certainly was a prisoner, sir. No doubt about that." Next to her, Daria bobs her head solemnly. "She spent most days locked in a room, guarded and chained, brought out only when that conniving little boy wanted to toy with her or use her voice to sow dissent."

The rebuke is soft, but my stomach churns uncomfortably. If that's true, then that's a punishment I can't imagine. I try to picture more of the lightning girl in my head. I remember the broadcast, her voice, but her face is obscure. I've seen it before, I know it. Brown hair, sharp eyes. But that's all that comes. I can say the same of the monarchs ruling the Crownlands. A teenage boy rules Norta, the bejeweled Prince Bracken holds sway in Piedmont, a nymph king and queen control the Lakelands.

Jem's gaze is still sharp on me, and I feel scolded in the lightning girl's name. It's my own fault. I try to stay out of things, try to keep my focus on what's right in front of me. I don't bother with great and terrible people of the world. I only know what I must of them to stay alive, stay ahead, and nothing more. And even that, it seems, is flawed.

I return to my meal in silence.

"Did you know any of them?" Jem asks, bold enough to address the princess with such a question.

I don't expect her to answer. There are many Silvers in this world, but not all are so highborn or important. Especially those in the Freelands. They don't know the distant names shaping the world behind us. But she continues to surprise me.

One corner of her mouth lifts in a grim smile. "I've met Maven, and his exiled brother. Long ago, when we were children of allied kingdoms. I can't say I know Iris of the Lakelands." Something in her voice sharpens. "But I know her family well enough."

As with her coat, she tosses the rest of her water into the river, watching it splash overboard, swallowed into darkness. And she speaks no more.

THREE
Lyrisa

I've slept in better places, but I've also slept in worse.

The meager cushion of the keel bench has become my kingdom, the only domain that is mine. It's more than I could say before, in my uncle's household, where everything was given with the threat of being taken away.

A few hours into the night, I wish I hadn't tossed away the guard's coat, and instead had washed it or bleached it or taken scraps from it or *something*. The air cools over the river, and I'm left to shiver myself to sleep. True, a man died in that coat. But that doesn't mean it didn't still have a use.

Maybe some Red will find it and fix it up.

Or maybe Orrian will. And he'll know where to follow.

The thought chills me more than the night air.

No, I tell myself. *Orrian thinks you are dead a hundred miles away. With the rest of his guards, with sweet Magida, another corpse charred in a pit. Killed by an ambush, Scarlet Guard or Montfort or both. Silvers slaughtered, more casualties of however many wars we're fighting now. He'll never find you if you keep running. You're safe on this river.*

I almost believe it.

When I wake up before dawn, there's a blanket tucked around my shoulders and feet, cocooning me in unfamiliar warmth. I can almost pretend I'm home, truly home, before Father died and we left the Tidewater for good. But that was six years ago, a far-gone memory, an impossibility.

I blink and I remember.

I'm on a Red Riverman's keelboat, outnumbered and hated by everyone around me, with nowhere to go but forward. A dead girl on the run.

Though I feel it in every breath, fear will not serve me here. And these Reds must not know I'm terrified of what lies behind, of what might still be coming.

So I sit up, raising my chin, pretending to sneer at the threadbare, soft blanket drawn over my lap. As if it is the most offensive thing in the world, and not a kindness I do not deserve.

Before surveying the deck, I look behind us, at the stretching ribbon of the Ohius. It looks much the same as it did yesterday. Muddy water, green banks, the Lakelands stretching to the north, the Disputed Lands to the south. Both are empty, without a person or town in sight. Neither side of the river likes to be this close together, and they keep their distance beyond the few dock points along the miles.

"Looking for something?"

That self-important captain leans against the rail two yards away, arms crossed and legs angled, his entire body facing toward me. The gun at his hip is visible, even in the dim light before dawn. He has the audacity to grin, his idiotic gold tooth winking like a taunting star.

"Just trying to assess how far we've gone," I reply swiftly, my voice cold. "Your boat is slow."

He doesn't flinch. Yesterday his hair shone almost dark red in the sun. Now in the early morning light it is black, pulled into a neat tail. I take in the rest of him, brown skin freckled and darkened from years on the water. Scarred hands, rope welts. I bet his fingers are rough.

"My boat does the job fine," he says. "Between the poles and the motor, we make the time we need to make."

The dwindling coins in my purse weigh heavy on my mind. *I could've paid him far less than I offered. Stupid. Idiot.* "I'm paying you to make better."

"And why is that?" He tips his head, pushing off the rail in a fluid motion. The man has a prowl to him. A predator, though he is little more than prey. "What's a Silver like you doing on my rivers?"

My jaw locks and I raise my chin. I settle into the imperious mask I've relied upon in many a Silver court, in front of my uncle, my mother, and any other noble Silver who might try my patience. It doesn't work on the captain.

He stands before me, his stance broad. He's taller than most, and muscular from work. Behind him, the rest of the meager crew have begun to busy themselves at their posts. It makes me wonder if the captain does anything of use at all. Indeed, I haven't seen him pick up a pole or touch the boat's wheel since we boarded. All he seems to do is keep too close an eye on his passengers and his cargo.

"Let me guess," he says. "You're not paying me to ask questions."

I'm seized by the urge to snap this annoyance in half. "No, I am not."

He knows I'm Silver. Knows I'm his best-paying passenger. Knows I'm a threat in more ways than one. And he still takes another step, looming over me, his form blocking out the rest of the boat.

"If you're putting this keel and this crew in danger, I need to know about it."

I regard him coolly. The man doesn't move back, but his eyes falter, just a little, as his mind catches up with his mouth. He doesn't know my ability. Doesn't know what I'm capable of. Doesn't know how I could kill him, or his passengers, or his crew.

I shove the blanket into his arms. "The only thing in danger here is you."

He turns without a second thought, bundling the blanket under one arm. As he passes his pet bear, he jabs a thumb at me. "Ean, feed her last."

The hulking monster of a Red man does as ordered. When food is passed out to the crew, he comes to me last, presenting me with the same thing we ate for dinner, accompanied by a mug of steaming black coffee. At least it smells good, and I take my time savoring the aroma. It makes me shudder, down to my toes.

Halfway through my meal, I notice the little Red girl watching me closely, peering around her waking mothers. Her brother, older by a year or so, still sleeps beneath their bench, curled up in blankets. I meet the girl's eye and she quickly turns away, terrified by my attention.

Good. At least someone is.

As the sun rises, I pace the boat slowly.

Yesterday, I woke up in the woods long before dawn, making my way down to the ramshackle docks to plead for passage with so many others. I was scared; I was hungry. I didn't know if I'd find a boat or be turned away. I should feel relief. The river moving steadily beneath us should bring me some peace.

It does not.

I try to shake the unease as I move, working my way up and down the empty walks of the keel to get my bearings. I didn't leave the bench yesterday, and my legs need stretching. Not that there's much room for it on a keelboat. The craft is long but thin, perhaps twenty feet across at its widest point, and less than a hundred long from end to end. The cargo hold takes up everything below deck, along with the captain's quarters. Even though he doesn't seem to do anything else, I've seen Ashe dart in there from time to time, then emerge with charts or the like. The river must always be changing, wearing new paths through the waterbed. Downed logs, new outposts, Silver checkpoints. Ashe and the crew know them all, and keep watch.

But they aren't looking behind. Only I know to do that.

My clothes aren't my own, and they fit poorly on my frame. Chest tight, sleeves short. I'm taller than the Lakelander guard I took them from, but she was the closest to my size. Every time I move, I'm afraid I might split a seam. Once I was vain about the curves of my body. Not anymore. I have more important things to think about. I make a note to try and buy something better suited when we dock next, wherever that may be.

I know the geography of the river well enough. The Disputed Lands are on our maps, albeit in far less detail than my own kingdom. I know the cities Memphia and Mizostium, both farther downriver. I admit, I'm eager to see them, if only from the river. I've known cities built by Silver crowns, beautiful but walled, ruled by one kind of blood. Of course I've seen Red slums, certainly, though not by choice. I wonder which the Disputed cities will be more like.

I wish I could see them under better circumstances. Without this horrible choice I've already made hanging over my head. Without running.

No, I'm not *running. Cowards run, and I'm not a coward. A coward would have stayed behind. A coward would have waited for Orrian, accepted him and the fate already chosen.*

A cool breeze plays off the water, balancing out the heat of the sun approaching high noon. It runs over me, light as a kiss, and I let my eyes flutter shut.

Then the deck creaks as someone stops beside me, and I grit my teeth, preparing myself for more of the needling captain.

Instead it's one of the Red servants. I think her name is Jem. Her son stands at her side, less fearful of me than his sister. He stares at me brazenly, eyes black and round. I stare back.

"Hello," I mutter after a moment, puzzled as to what else to do.

He nods curtly. Strange for a child.

Next to him, his mother looks on, warmly regarding her son. She ruffles his hair, golden as his sister's. True to her training as a palace servant, she doesn't speak to me and won't unless I speak first.

"We're in the Disputed Lands now," I tell her. "You don't have to stand on ceremony. You can talk if you want to talk."

She rests her hand on her son's shoulder and looks out at the river, regarding the far bank, where the Lakelands begin. "Who says I want to talk to you, Silver?"

I almost laugh. "Fair enough."

It must be strange to see someone like me and someone like her standing side by side. A Silver princess and a Red servant, her child between us. Both of us fleeing. Both of us at the mercy of this river and this crew. The same, in most ways.

Strange, how this world is shifting. The wars in the east may not be over, won or lost, but they've certainly brought change already.

I have no taste for war. I want no part of the world behind me.

Impossible lightning girls, murdered kings. Reds in rebellion, Silvers in exile. And I have no idea what kind of place that chaos will become.

But I don't have the time to wonder about the future. I have to look back. I have to keep watch.

I leave the Red servant where she stands and spend the next few hours at the back of the boat, feet planted firmly, my eyes on the river as the bends turn and twist. The keel is quiet, mostly. The Red captain speaks softly to his crew, directing them once or twice an hour. The crew, a scarred woman and a reedy man with poles, do their job well. The breathing mountain puffs in and out of the cargo hold, doing who knows what below. The Nortan servants speak together at the far end of the keel, mostly focused on keeping their daughter in hand. The son is far more manageable. He stands at the front of the boat as I stand at the back, his eyes forward. He never speaks at all.

He also doesn't make a sound when the river, elegant and lethal, reaches up over the rail and pulls him under.

Daria turns in time to see his legs go over the side, little feet flailing. She screams but I don't hear it, already moving, already knowing what took the boy.

It wasn't a wave. Rivers don't have them.

It wasn't some twist of the current or bad rapid.

This was designed, driven, *made.*

This was Orrian.

This was me.

A hand grips my arm, trying to stop me as I move down the keel, but I break the hold without thought. Out of the corner of my eye I see the captain blanch, his face nearly a blur. Ahead, the polers are working double time, turning the boat, slowing our course. I want to yell at them not to stop. To speed up. To do anything but slow down.

But then the boy will drown.

I have enough dead bodies on my conscience, Red and Silver.

The big oaf jumps into the water first, or certainly tries to. The river simply tosses him, sputtering and spitting, back onto the deck. His crew looks on in horror, the blood draining from their faces. They know what I know.

"Lyrisa, *don't—*" the captain's voice says somewhere as I plunge over the side.

The river doesn't toss me back. I'm doing what it wants.

We're in shallower water than I anticipated, and the current laps around my shoulders. It surges against me, trying to push me deeper, into the faster water and stronger course. I lock my muscles, letting my ability surge. Nothing can make me move if I don't want to, and the river breaks on me like stone.

Shouting echoes back on the keel. I don't hear a word.

The boy is a few yards off, visible beneath the surface, his eyes open, bubbles streaming from his mouth. Still alive, still fighting. I force my way to him, hands reaching for thin arms and legs. He's bait. I know that.

Orrian is sick in the head, a twisted sort. I'd rip him in two if I could.

My hands close around the boy's shoulders, and I can already feel the unnatural pressure of the water holding him down. I try to calculate in my mind, remembering my training with my father and his family. If I pull too hard, I'll break the boy. Crush him between my hands. Not enough pull, though, and the water will keep him.

There simply isn't time.

Another pair of hands joins mine, making me jump.

The captain stands over us, face flushed, the water rushing all around him. The river doesn't throw him back into the boat, and he stands firm, tugging on the boy. Still, the boy doesn't budge.

The captain curses like only a Riverman can.

I grit my teeth and pull.

The boy breaks the surface with a sick pop, spewing river water as he coughs and sputters. He clings to me, little arms surprisingly strong. And the water crashes over us, intending to catch us off guard. With one hand I reach out, grabbing onto the captain's shoulder. He falters beneath my grip, nearly losing his balance to the raging current. But I keep him steady.

Then gunfire echoes from the keel, cracking with precision into the Lakelander banks.

The river relaxes around us, releasing its hold.

"Move," I snarl, shoving the captain toward his boat.

I waste no time, the boy still cradled in one arm. He's featherlight. I barely notice his weight. I'm a strongarm, after all. Carrying around an underfed ten-year-old is nothing.

The captain pushes me ahead of him, toward the boat rail, as if I'm useless. I scoff at him, seize him by the collar, and toss him bodily over the side.

I go next, one hand more than enough to lift both me and the boy back up and into the keel.

The boy sputters still, spitting water as his mothers descend, wrapping him in dry blankets.

At the rail, the keel crew keeps up the volley of gunfire, and the captain sprints to the helm behind the cargo hold. He spins the wheel of the boat and guns the motor, letting it roar beneath us. We pick up speed, but not much.

Without a word, one of the polers hands a rifle to me.

I'm no grand shot, but I know how to lay down cover, and that's exactly what I do.

Orrian's hunters must be clustered in the single growth of trees and rushes on the bank, hidden from sight. *They were waiting.* I keep up my fire, round after round, in rhythm with the keel crew. When someone reloads, another takes over for them, giving the keel enough time to maneuver around the next bend.

The Lakelanders are not without guns of their own, but we have better cover, using the thick plank rails as shielding. I expect a swift to dart across the river and drag me screaming back into the Lakelands. Or perhaps a magnetron to shred the motor of the keel. A greenwarden to turn the riverbank plants against us. But so far, it seems, only a nymph lies in wait. *Has Orrian come to retrieve me alone? Is he only traveling with Red guards to aid him, because he knows he needs little more than that to bring me back? Or are he and his Silver friends taking sport in this, hunting me slowly?*

My teeth rattle with every round, the rifle pressed tightly in the crook of my shoulder.

At first I think the silhouette is a trick of the light. The sun on the rushes and the leaves, casting an odd shadow. But then it's unmistakable. Orrian parts the plants with a hand, his wicked smile visible even fifty yards away. I take aim and miss, the bullet plunking into the water. His grin only deepens. He doesn't need words to threaten me. The smile is enough.

When the keel rounds the bend, the captain shouts something I can't hear, but I feel relief all the same. His friend, the other keelboat captain, has stopped his craft in the middle of the river, waiting for us.

And standing on the cargo bed, loaded and waiting, is a fixed and ready heavy machine gun, perched like a black iron spider. The ammunition coils next to it, a snake of bullets.

With the grove of trees out of our sight, now hidden behind the river bend, everything falls quiet. No gunfire, just my thundering heartbeat and the gasping breaths of every person aboard the keel.

I keep my eyes behind, waiting for another strike, as the captain maneuvers the keel up to his friend's boat. Both crews are quick to lash the crafts together, working as diligently as ants in a colony.

Softly, Melly starts to cry.

My focus is still on the river, on the stand of trees just out of view, when the planks of the deck shudder beneath heavy footsteps. The captain's voice growls in my ear, his breath hot against me.

"You lied, strongarm."

FOUR
Lyrisa

Lied about not being a danger. Lied about no one pursuing me. Lied, lied, lied.

"A smuggler taking offense to dishonesty? There's a sight," I snap, stepping back to put some distance between me and the captain. The rifle is still under my arm, and his eyes trail along the barrel. He's gauging if he's fast enough to take it back.

I make the decision for him, and press the gun into his chest. "They're done with us for now."

Jem stands over her son, still crumpled on the deck. She glares at me with a leveling fury. "You care to explain who *they* are, Silver? The ones who tried to murder my boy?"

I'm suddenly aware of the dozen eyes watching me, both on this keel and the one tied up alongside ours. The other captain stands behind his machine gun, thumbs hooked in his belt loops. He looks like a skeleton leering down at me. I detest such an audience, and my insides crawl.

"Not hard to figure it out," one of our polers—the woman, Riette—drawls. "The princess got sick of the palace, and now her uncle's sent soldiers to bring her back. Without regard for anyone who might get in the way."

Captain Ashe narrows his eyes. "They were on the Lakeland side of the river. And you're far from Prince Bracken's Lowcountry." He steps back into my space, crowding me against the rail. "Seems like an awful long way for them to follow. You didn't outrun those Silvers all the way from Citadel."

No, just the border.

Scowling, the captain surveys me again. This time his eyes snag on my clothing, the dark blue of the Lakelander uniform soaked through with river water. He grabs my collar, rubbing the fabric between two rough fingers. I slap him away, working hard to keep my strength in check.

His eyes are livid; he's angry with me, and with himself. "You weren't traveling with a convoy, Princess, and you weren't attacked by rebels."

I don't expect a Red to understand. They don't know what it's like for us, what it's like to be sold the day you are born.

"Keep the payment," I hiss, stepping around the young captain. "I'll make my own way from here."

He grabs me by the collar again, daring to stop me. I could break his grip if I wanted. Shatter his hand without blinking. And Ashe knows it. But it doesn't stop him. That infernal gold tooth winks at me, gleaming and terrible.

"You tell me who that was and what you've dragged my crew into."

"Or what, Red?" I nearly spit. "I'll get out of your hair. I've paid your price. What does it matter?" I almost expect him to hit me, and I would welcome the glancing sting. Anything to combat this unfamiliar twist of wretchedness in my stomach. I do what I can to keep my eyes on the captain and not the sodden little boy who nearly died for my foolishness. Still, I can't help but look.

Big Ean shakes his head and answers for the captain. "You think they won't track the boat, miss? Even if you're gone?" He scratches his beard. "I think they will."

He isn't wrong. Orrian is nothing if not vengeful, petty, and altogether dismissive of Red life. The Lakelander prince has so much anger in him, and the rest is hatred.

"I'll make it clear I'm gone," I tell them weakly, the words already dying on my lips. It is a poor excuse, one we all see through.

The captain doesn't let go of my collar, even as his grip slackens. "Who are we dealing with?" he growls, though his voice is tinged with need.

"His name is Orrian Cygnet. He is a prince of the Lakelands, a cousin to the nymph queen, and a nymph himself." I focus on my boots. Looking down helps me speak. If I don't have to see their pity or their anger, I can manage to tell the truth. "He is a terrible person—violent, vengeful, a monster of a man—and I've been betrothed to him since I drew my first breath."

I look to the Red servants first, hoping for their derision. It was their son who almost died. They should hate me. But they soften before any of the rest, and it makes me want to vomit. They know firsthand what Silver monsters look like.

I don't deserve their compassion. I don't want it either.

"You slipped a Lakelander escort," the poler Gill guesses. "When you crossed the border."

Jaw tight, I turn to face the aging Riverman. "I killed a Lakelander escort. When I crossed the border."

The captain pulls his hand away as if burned. "How many guards?"

"Six. Seven, if you count my companion from home." I taste bile when I think of her, Magida, my oldest friend. Her blood silver between my fingers, her mouth trying to form words she would never speak. "She died helping me escape. But I suppose you could say I killed her too."

A murmur goes through the crew on the other keel, rippling in a line right up to their captain. He twitches, uncertain, nervous to the bone. "Ashe, you should let her go," he calls. "Shout up and down the river that she's off the water."

The captain doesn't respond, his teeth gritted. He knows as well as I do what a risk that would be. He watches me, looking for an answer I cannot give.

"Ashe, I've got hot cargo here. I'm with you easy river or hard, but if I'm caught with what I'm carrying . . . ," the other captain continues, pleading now. He expects Orrian and his gang to jump out of the river at any minute. It's not a bad instinct.

Orrian is nowhere near as powerful as the Lakelander queen or her daughters, but he is still formidable. And while he can't turn the entire river against us, he'll certainly try.

A muscle jumps in Ashe's cheek as he thinks, running a hand through his dark hair. Without knowing it, I do the same, twisting my hair away from my face.

"I'd be gone already if I thought he wouldn't follow you," I admit quietly, and it's the truth. I knew that by stepping onto this keel, I would be marking every other person on it. "There's a reason I told you not to take on anyone else," I add, hissing through my teeth. If only to jab at the captain, to ease the sting of my own shame.

He rounds on me again. I expect him to shout. His whispered snarl is somehow more horrible. "You lied from the start, Lyrisa. Don't put that on me. You'd still be ratting on the docks if I'd known what you were running from."

"Well, you know now," I reply, trying to look bolder than I feel. If he tosses me from the keel, I'm done for. Orrian will track me down in a few hours and march me all the way to the Lakelander capital at gunpoint. "You're the captain on this keel. It's your decision."

Rifle still in hand, Riette takes a step toward us. Her two tight braids have come undone in the skirmish, and her hair frizzes around her face in a brown cloud. "We could tie her up. Leave her on a rock on the Lakelander side. And be on our way."

The threat is so ludicrous I have to laugh. "Tie me up with *what*? I'm a strongarm."

She immediately retreats, flushing. "Just a suggestion."

"We should keep her," Gill argues. "If that Silver strikes again, I'd rather have one on our side to trade. Or to help."

"Help bury you, more like," Riette grumbles under her breath.

The captain lets it all pass like the current, standing firm as the crew chatters around him. Suddenly he shouts over their words, quieting them all. "Hallow, you got room for four more on your keel?"

On his deck, the other captain hesitates. He surveys his boat, already crowded with cargo, crew, and his own passengers. "Yeah, I suppose," he says after a long moment.

Ashe wastes no time and turns around with a snap. He waves Daria, Jem, and their children across the deck, gesturing to Hallow's ship.

"Get your things. He's your captain now," he says, his words trembling with the weight of a command. Then he looks to his crew with the same fervor. "We make for the confluence. Lose him on the Great River. He'll be beyond his own borders. Let him fight through the

Freelands if he wants his princess so badly."

His princess. I feel sick at the words, their implication. And their truth. Ashe is right: I belong to that foul person; I've belonged to him as long as I can remember. No matter what I have to say about it.

And still I feel the need to warn these Reds. "Orrian won't be deterred by borders," I say, pacing after Ashe.

He glares at me for a second. "Do I look stupid to you?" Leaning against the rail, he shouts to Hallow's crew and his own. "Put out the word to every boat and raft you pass: there's a Lakelander prince in our lands. That should set the bounty hunters foaming."

Confusion steals over me. I narrow my eyes. "Bounty hunters?"

"You think smugglers are the only lawless kind in the Freelands?" he says, throwing me a dark smirk. "If the right bounty crew gets word of your prince, they'll hunt him down before he can hunt you."

I blink, trying to imagine what kind of bounty crew would be required to stop Orrian. *But far from the Lakelands, with only his guards, without any kind of aid from his kingdom . . .* It's certainly a start.

I bite my lip, then nod. With one hand, I gesture for the rifle.

Ashe is quick to give it back.

"At least it's a plan."

The two keels move downriver at speed, putting a safe distance between us and Orrian's assault point. He'll be on the move again by now, but farther inland, away from the river's edge. There's no more cover on this stretch, and he'll certainly be moving by transport. The roads are some miles north, giving us time to make up ground. We pause every fifteen minutes, giving Hallow time to get ahead of us. Hour by hour, the distance between the boats spreads, until he's out of view even on the longest stretches of river. Our speed picks up too, between the motor and the strengthening current. I assume we must be getting close to the confluence, where the Ohius meets the Great River. Where no land, on either side of the water, answers to a Silver crown.

Every second ticks like a clock, grating inside my skull. I clench my teeth against the sensation. Two hours since the attack. Three. Four. I have the sneaking suspicion that Orrian is enjoying this. He always did like to play with his food. Hope is not something I'm used to, and while the captain seems to have faith in his river and his people, I cannot.

I'm glad the children are off the boat, and their mothers too. At the very least I won't have them dragging at the back of my mind. They're on a dangerous enough journey without adding a fugitive Silver to the equation.

I'm thinking of them when the captain eases up to me, this time with less of an attitude. He leans over the stern at my side, elbows planted on the rail. His sleeves are rolled up, showing more scars and fading bruises. River life is not easy for these people, not by a long shot.

"So, Orrian Cygnet." There's such disdain in his voice, even more than he expresses for me.

I sigh, looking at my hands. My fingers are crooked, broken so many times in my ability training that even skin healers couldn't fix them properly. "He's part of the royal line, close to the throne but not close enough for his own tastes."

A shadow crosses Ashe's face, even in the bright light of afternoon. "You know him well."

"I know him well enough." I shrug, remembering our few bitter encounters. He was quick to reveal himself as a terrible man. "We met a few times, and I found his character lacking."

"I take it your uncle didn't agree."

Scoffing, I shake my head. "Oh, he knows Orrian's nature. He just doesn't care." Next to me, Ashe flushes and I'm surprised. Reds are so strange, so emotional. "Just because you get secondhand news about Silvers doesn't mean you know how we live."

He smarts under the jibe, lashing out. "So you murdered six people and ran."

"Tell me you wouldn't have done the same?" I hiss at him, knowing the truth. My response is swift and cutting. As my words hang between us, I square to him, raising my chin so I can look him in the eye. Instead of the Red captain, I see six corpses laid out, their faces burned beyond recognition. Magida with them, her body in ashes.

He doesn't hesitate. Ashe is not one to second-guess himself or his intentions. "I would have done the same." Then he leans toward me, brave enough to put a finger in my face. As if scolding a child. *We're nearly the same age.* "But I wouldn't drag innocents into it."

"Really?" I sneer, my voice rising. "And your friend? He's running guns right now, isn't he? With passengers on board. You telling me you've never done that?" His flush darkens, and I know I've scored a point in whatever silly game we're playing. I keep pressing. "Odd, for a Red to be running guns this direction. The civil war and the Scarlet Guard are behind us."

The captain doesn't have a slick or smart response for that. His bravado falters, if only for a second. He probably didn't even know his friend was running guns west—and therefore running guns for Silvers. Tiraxeans, Prairie lords, maybe even raiders farther west. Selling gunmetal to those who would kill him without blinking.

Perhaps I understand the Red river folk as little as they understand me.

"There's a difference between us and you," Ashe finally snaps. "We do what we have to in order to survive, to carve out a life. Not because we don't agree with which palace we end up living in."

The words land like a blow from a hammer. I feel them deep in my chest, cracking my heart.

As a child, the first thing my father taught me was restraint. Even young strongarms can kill without control, so I learned early to keep my temper in check. If not for that stern tutelage, I suspect I might slap Ashe across his face and separate his head from his shoulders, or at least his teeth from his jaw.

I manage to hide my sudden rage behind my court mask.

"There's a difference between us and you," I force out, repeating his words. "I don't expect you to understand it, or me." Then I shutter my feelings, drawing a single, steadying breath. I'll tell him what he needs to know, to keep us both alive and this keel afloat. "Orrian hunts with his court friends. They're drunks, fools, noble idiots who take delight in the pain of others. I suspect that's who he's with. Their delight in the hunt and their taste for drink is why we aren't all dead on the river."

Ashe frowns. "Yet."

"Yet," I concede. I drag another hand through my hair, then tie it back into a quick tail. Better to keep it out of my way. Ashe watches me as I move, assessing me like the threat I am. I match his stare. "You really think you can lose him?"

I haven't been on the keel long, but I doubt its top speed can outrun a prince. And we are on a *boat*, after all. It severely limits our path.

Despite my misgivings, Ashe seems to inflate. This is his domain, and he knows it well. "I think men like him are cowards deep down, and he won't chase you beyond the safety of his own kingdom."

"Normally, I'd agree," I say. "But Orrian is proud. And losing me wounds his pride. That, he will not allow."

Something pulls at Ashe's face again, some tick of annoyance. He grumbles under his breath. "Easy job, easy river."

I cock my head. It sounded like a prayer, something a foolish Lakelander might mumble before battle. "What's that?"

He shrugs. "Just the code I like to live by."

"Oops," I say weakly, if only to lessen the tension a little. It doesn't work and he remains next to me, tight as a coiled wire, ready to spring. I turn a little, putting my back to the keel again.

He mirrors me, blocking out the crew diligently at work behind us.

"Why save the boy?" he says suddenly, and he sounds as young as he looks. Not a captain, but a young man barely older than a teenager. Unsure, confused. Unrooted for the first time in his life. Without anchor or path.

I chew on my lip. *Why save the boy?* Part of me smarts again. Would he ask that question of a Red? Does he think us Silvers so beyond heart and compassion? *Have we given him any reason not to think so?*

"You jumped in too," I finally reply. "Why save the boy?"

He blushes, red rising high on his cheeks.

"You know," I breathe, "you really could have left me. I'm sure he wouldn't have followed a Red keel out of spite."

I don't know why, but he relaxes, the great tension in his lean shoulders dropping away.

"Probably not," he agrees. Then, to my shock, he nudges my shoulder with his own. "Luckily, I have a better moral compass than you."

FIVE
Ashe

Idiot. Idiot. Idiot. Idiot.

I should throw her in the river and be done with it. Leave her to splash around until her prince fishes her out. Get her away from my keel and my crew. And somehow I just *can't damn do it.* Riette and Gill keep watching me like I'm insane. Big Ean has a stupid grin wider than he is. All three of them are probably thinking the same thing. That I'm smitten with the infernal Silver nuisance, and willing to risk all our lives to get her where she needs to go.

Just the accusation, even unspoken, makes me itch.

Easy job, easy river.

Well, this is a difficult fucking job on a suddenly difficult fucking river.

I decide to put as much distance between us as I can, leaving her to watch the stern while I patrol the bow. I point out rocks and errant obstacles on the current far more than I should, especially for Riette and Gill. They're good enough to ignore my nerves, letting me nanny them through the next few bends.

The sun dips ahead of us, approaching the western horizon. The trees thicken on the Freeland bank, and the Lakeland fields, open and empty, stretch to the north. The current quickens beneath us. Every second feels stolen and each breath is a gasp.

We should be at the confluence by morning, and that's where I'll leave her for good. There's no way I'm taking her to the Gates like this, not with a Lakelander prince lurking river knows where, hunting our ship. He could dry up the riverbed for all I know, leave us stranded in the mud to pick off as he likes. Silvers have done worse. I know it. I've seen it firsthand. We aren't human to them. We're just things to be used and discarded.

That's how she sees us. That's why she's here, to use us to get downriver.

So why save the kid?

She jumped into the river knowing a nymph was waiting for her, ready to drown her or drag her away. All for some quiet Red kid she didn't know from a stump. A Red servant's son, nothing and no one. And a Silver princess jumped into that water to save him, knowing what it could do to her. Knowing the danger. I can't shake it from my brain, what a risk she took, and for who.

I almost wish she hadn't. Then I wouldn't care what happens to her.

I shake my head. *Ludicrous.*

I'll dump her at the confluence docks when the borders open up. I'll give her a chance.

The chance she never gave us.

At the stern, she keeps her back to the keel, vigilant as a watchtower. If only I'd left her ratting on the Ohius docks, begging for passage with the rest. She'd be someone else's problem instead of mine.

Or she'd be as good as dead, chained to a cruel man, with no life but a cage.

Idiot. Idiot. Idiot. Idiot.

When I was young, my mother read me stories from her old collection of books. Before he died, my father used to bring them to her when he got them on the river or by trading on the docks. Most were reprinted a dozen times over, handed down through generations, translated and copied. Stories of warriors, kings, impossible creatures, bravery, and adventure. Stories of Red men and women defeating impossible odds. I wish I'd never known those stories. They are for fools.

And I'm certainly acting like a fool now.

As a Riverman, I've always felt safest on the water, but for the first time in my life, that isn't true. We don't dare keep the lights running, and instead make do by the moon. Thank the river, it's full tonight, bright enough to move by. I get Riette and Gill sleeping in shifts, one of them always ready should the current change. Big Ean sleeps in his scurry, ready to paddle off if we need to abandon the keel all together. I don't plan to sleep at all, my mind abuzz with half-formed battle plans. The princess doesn't sleep either.

Lyrisa said her Lakelander prince liked to hunt. I suppose he enjoys the sport of it, watching prey flee, terrified for its life. I wonder if he's watching us now, in shadows and silhouettes across the water, moving without making a sound. I've passed Silver patrols this way before. I'm good at what I do. But those could always be paid off or tricked. Those weren't noble Silvers, bred and trained to their abilities. Those weren't Silvers with revenge in their blood, hungry for something far more valuable than grain or alcohol or illicit guns.

Once or twice, I think I hear a distant chorus of laughter beyond the bank. It could be the wind in the fields or the splash of a fish. Or nothing at all. Every noise sets me further on edge, pushing my nerves beyond reason. By midnight I feel like my teeth may shatter in my clenched jaw.

When the moon is high above us, Lyrisa abandons her post at the stern. Her steps are quiet and steady, but she doesn't know which planks to avoid. Which ones creak and groan. I hear her move despite her best efforts, and so does the river.

Half asleep at his post, Gill shoots her a glare only I can see.

I move silently, joining her halfway down the deck. She leans over the rail, squinting into the darkness on the far bank. The moon glints off half-high cornfields, the perfect cover for anyone watching the river.

"You can sleep if you want," I whisper, my voice barely audible. *You should sleep. I'm abandoning you tomorrow. You need the rest.* Guilt claws at my stomach.

Lyrisa shakes her head. "Absolutely not." Then she sighs, resting her head on one hand. She stares into the dark without seeing. "He's enjoying this. Orrian."

Like all Reds, I carry a bone-deep hatred for Silvers. But this one inspires another layer of disgust I've not felt long these days. "You'd think a Silver would have far better and more interesting things to do. There's a war on, last I checked."

I expect her to smile. Instead she seems to shrink. I can almost forget her ability, looking at her now. How she could break me and this keel in half with a twist of her fingers.

"There's war everywhere these days," she says. "North, south, east."

"Not west?" That's hardly true. I say it just to speak, to give me a reason to keep my eyes open. Even we know of the raiders up and down the Prairie borders, Silver outcasts with no flag and no allegiance. The Prairie warlords are in constant flux. The Tiraxean triarchs are always chafing one another. Nowhere is quiet, not in the world ahead or the world behind.

"Not west," Lyrisa murmurs. "Have you heard of Montfort here on the rivers?"

Ah.

"The Free Republic."

"That's what they call it." She hesitates, her whisper catching. "Do you think it's true?"

What I think to be true and know to be true are two very different things. And the many rumors of the Republic, even what the citizens of it themselves say, are varying stories, all at odds with one another. "I've heard as much. Reds, Silvers, whatever the others are. All together, equal." I hesitate as I say it. Somehow, I don't want to mislead her, or give her hope she shouldn't have. "But I don't believe everything I hear. I get it wrong half the time."

"Well, that's where I'm going." Her voice sharpens with resolve. "At least, that's where I'm trying to go."

That explains the money, her coin counting. Saving payment for another long journey. "After the Gates."

"I planned to try and get passage up the Ark, but there's too much traffic. Scarlet Guard, Prairie armies, raiders. And if the Silver alliance in the east decides to attack Montfort directly, that's the route they'll take." Lyrisa traces each step on the wood grain of the rail, and I see it in my mind, familiar as my charts. "So I'll hire a boat in Mizostium. Cross the Sea of Tirax. And find another boat to take me upriver, along the Rion Granda. Into the mountains. And freedom."

I puff out a breath. "That is a long way." *Obviously, idiot.*

She doesn't move. "It's worth the cost."

Money, she has to spare. But her life? I want to tell her what danger she'll be in, and not just from a Lakelander prince. The triarchs, the raiders—and then when she reaches the Republic itself. Why would they take in a Silver princess?

"You've been planning this for a long time" is all I say instead, feeling like a coward.

She shrugs. The moonlight bounces off the water below, rippling on her face. The dark freckles across her cheeks stand out, highlight the upturned angle of her eyes. She seems made of stone, not flesh.

"Not really. I knew I wanted to run, but that was it. Until Montfort revealed themselves in their attack on Norta, I had no plan. I just knew I had to run." Her face is still but her hands are nervous, fingers twitching over one another. "Now there's an opportunity for something different."

"A land where you're equal to any Red standing next to you."

She turns to me sharply. Her gaze is electric, charged with something I don't understand. "I heard the Disputed Lands were like that too."

"We call ourselves the Freelands. And I wish that were true. Just like in the Crownlands, a divide exists. We might not live at the mercy of Silvers here, but we certainly live apart, our worlds separate even on the river." I suspect the Republic is secretly the same. Divided and weak. "I have to say, I don't think I've ever met a Silver willing to give up so much over a bad marriage."

Her eyes narrow to slits and I feel like I've misstepped. My skin crawls. *Idiot.*

"Red or Silver, men always have trouble comprehending the lives of women."

All I can do is bob my head, nodding. Anything else feels like another mistake. "My mother would agree with you," I finally say, hoping to turn the conversation. I don't want it to end. If nothing else, it's helping pass the terror of this night. "She lives in Mizostium, near the East Gate."

Lyrisa knows what I'm doing but allows it anyway. She looks back to the river. "Is that a . . . good part of the city?"

"Better than most." It's the truth. East Gate is comfortable, a strong community with deep roots. Red streets, Silver streets. Lovely gardens and fountains. I don't know why, but I picture myself showing it to Lyrisa. If only from the deck of the keel. I shake off the thought as suddenly as it comes. I'm leaving her behind as soon as I can. "The city governs itself, and some parts are truly without law."

"The Freelands certainly live up to their name," she offers, sounding diplomatic. More like a Silver than before. It's a stark reminder of who she is and who I am. The very clear divide between us, in more ways than one. "I'm excited to see more."

"And you will," I answer quickly, without thinking.

Her lips twitch, curling into a bitter smile. "It's good at least one of us believes that."

"Lyrisa—"

She waves me off easily. This time, it doesn't feel so dismissive. "If it comes to it, if Orrian gets the upper hand, if whatever happens tips past what you and the crew can scratch your way out of . . ." She falters, searching for the words. "Let me know. And I'll end this."

Under the moon, I realize we look the same. Her blood and mine could be the same color. I watch her as she stares, waiting for me to give her my permission. To surrender, and be taken away. I should do it. For Riette's life, Gill's, Big Ean's, and mine.

"Nah," I drawl, turning back to the river with a shrug.

Her eyes widen in a flash, pupils blown in the dim light. Her nostrils flare in frustration. "I beg your pardon?" she says, almost too loud.

Winking, I push off the rail. "Something Reds share no matter what—we live to piss you people off. And I'm not giving some drunk prince the satisfaction. He's got enough in this world." Before I can stop myself, my hand grazes her arm. It sends an electric shock trailing from my fingers all the way down my spine. "He doesn't get you."

I leave her sputtering behind me, all my focus on keeping my back straight and my steps quiet. My cheeks flare with heat. I'm glad for the darkness as I pass Gill.

Ashe, why are you like this?

"Smitten," I think he hisses under his breath.

If not for the Lakelander prince pursuing us, I would push him into the river.

Instead I gesture for him to lean close.

And I whisper the plan formulating in my head.

SIX
Ashe

Sometimes I wonder if the differences are more than I realize between Silver and Red. I've never known a Silver, or cared to know one before. There is the blood, of course: the color and what it gives. Abilities I cannot understand or comprehend. Great speed, control over water or fire or metal, animals, weather, or superior strength like Lyrisa's. But beyond that, is there more? Are they born different from us, more rigid and cruel and violent, or do they become that way? I used to think the former. Now I'm not so sure.

I've spent many a sleepless night on the river. I'm used to the exhaustion. Either Lyrisa is too, or she's talented at hiding weakness. I guess both.

The sun rises on familiar banks and growing signs of civilization along the widening river. The confluence is a major point of crossing, and docks start to peek out among the roots and rushes of the Freeland banks. To the north, the Lakelands are still mostly fields, though the road is coming. It winds down from Sanctum farther north, to dead-end at the point where the Ohius and the Great River meet. Here Lakelanders can enter the Freelands if they so dare.

I wonder where the prince and his cackling hunters might be. *Are they watching us now? Are they close? I hope you're enjoying this, jackass.*

Other boats, big and small, joined us as the night lifted, giving way to dawn. Some are barely more than rafts poled by children, a pastime I knew well once. They swarm near the keels, hoping for castoffs. I toss a few apples, the familiar ritual bringing comfort.

In his scurry, Big Ean waves to a few, calling them over. He's doing as we planned, passing on news of a Lakelander prince nearby, a fine prize for any who might think to rob or ransom him. The wet and tanned kids spread the word eagerly, paddling back to their docks or farther into the boat traffic.

Lyrisa isn't a pale, porcelain-skinned Silver, the kind who might be spotted from yards away. Her skin is darker, like cold copper, but she still takes precautions. I don't know where she found a hat, but she tucks her hair up and away. Despite the ill-fitting uniform, she could pass for keel crew and not a princess. As she finishes the transformation, I nod at her, and even Riette offers a bob of approval.

The sun is hot already and I can feel the humid press of the day. I can only imagine what a long summer we're in for.

I shade my eyes and look for the telltale sign of the confluence—a strip of brown water against the horizon, the muddy churn of the Great River meeting the gray blue of the Ohius. While my normal route would take me farther out into the middle of the river, where the current is strong and fast, I keep the keel as close as I can to the Freeland banks. It slows us down but keeps us at least half a mile from the Lakelands, and out of the kind of deep water a nymph could turn against me. Should the worst happen, at least we have a chance of making it to shore.

There's a bustling market town just south of where the rivers join, part of it built out over the water. If I can get us there before Orrian strikes again, put in at the docks . . . *Will I leave her?* It seemed like an easy decision last night.

I clench my teeth. I'll cross that bridge if it comes. For now I focus on the water right in front of us, and what to do if Orrian appears before we reach the market. The crew is in on the plan, with everything in place. Lyrisa too, though she only knows a piece.

The pistol never leaves my side, and we're careful to place our rifles at the rails, hidden just out of sight. For once, I wish I were gunrunning too, with a vast store of ammunition at our disposal. As is, our supplies are terribly finite.

The confluence gets closer by the second, and my heart races with the current driving us forward. It takes all my restraint not to maneuver farther out into the river, away from the bank traffic, where I can open up the motor and fly. I don't know how much more of this my nerves can take. An hour? A minute? It's excruciating.

I nearly jump out of my skin when a fellow keel captain shouts hello, his own boat turning out into the river.

Lyrisa abandons her post at the stern to stand next to me again, this time the rifle tucked close under an arm. Her eyes dart along the bank, taking in the docks and the meager settlements set away from the water. I doubt she's seen anything like it.

"You remember the plan?" I ask.

Her nod is curt, focused. And almost insulted. "Of course."

"We're putting word out about Orrian, and I told Hallow to do the same ahead of us." The river rushes on, quicker by the second. "News travels fast in places like this."

It comforts her, if only a little. "Good. Let's hope we're lucky."

"I'm not a fan of either."

"Hope and luck?" She grins a true smile. "Me neither."

I think it's her smile that sets him off.

The river explodes around us with a roar like a thunderclap, sending walls of water ripping up into the clear blue sky, caging us in for a split second of terror. It's as if a giant hand has slapped the surface of the river, disturbing the current all around us. The water falls as quickly as it rose, smashing down in a scream that drenches us to the bone. Gill's pole snaps in his hand and Riette throws hers to the deck, replacing it with her rifle. Big Ean already has his sights trained on the Lakelander banks, so far to the north. Too far for any gun we possess.

Lyrisa knows better.

"In the Freelands!" she shouts, pointing to the bank, so close I could almost reach out and touch it.

I whirl and my body goes cold.

I count eight of them, seven Silver nobles ringing the unmistakable Lakelander prince standing in the shallows. One of the Silvers—a woman—has dogs, two drooling hounds, their noses pointed at the boat and Lyrisa.

Orrian Cygnet is skeleton thin and pole tall, limbed like a nightmare. His skin is pale and sallow, his dark hair wet and slicked back against his skull in a tight braid that pulls at his face. I can't see the color of his eyes but I can see his smile, wicked and sharp. His clothing is dark blue, a river color. *I've never feared the color blue before,* I think wildly.

He's armed with a gun and a sword, just like his companions, though his greatest weapon is all around us.

"Come now, Lyrisa, you've had your fun," he crows, his attention only on the princess.

She doesn't condescend to answer, keeping her head high. Even as the keel halts on the current, impossibly still on a moving river.

Around us, the boats and rafts scuttle like insects, pushed away by the ripples of Orrian's power. White-faced and slack-jawed Rivermen watch in terror or turn their crafts to flee, all of them knowing the telltale signs of a nymph with a temper. On the shore, the few Freelanders traveling on foot slink into the trees, disappearing.

My hand strays to my hip, and I loose my pistol as slowly and quietly as I can. The Silvers don't seem to notice. Orrian's friends laugh coldly among themselves, passing a bottle of something back and forth. One of them twirls a dagger in his hand. If we moved fast enough, we might be able to shoot dead three or four of them. But the rest would fall on us like falcons on a rabbit and tear us apart.

For the first time, Orrian shifts his focus to the crew, lowering himself to look at Reds. He sneers across my boat before his eyes land on me.

"By the gods, you smugglers get younger every year," he laughs.

Like Lyrisa, I say nothing. It incenses him.

He takes a step into the water. No, not into. *Onto.* He climbs the river like stairs, a new burst of current rising to meet him as he ascends to stand right in front of me. Eye to eye.

"I'm speaking to you, boy," he sneers, slapping me across the face without much strength. It isn't meant to hurt me, but humiliate me. I know that. My cheeks burn.

Behind me, I can hear the crew jostle and move, reaching for their weapons. Orrian's pack does the same, moving farther into the water. Just as Lyrisa guessed, he's the only nymph in the bunch.

At the rail, Lyrisa tightens. "Orrian," she warns.

It only feeds his anger, as well as his amusement. He slaps me again.

"Since when do you care about Red rats, Lyri?" The horrible prince sneers at her. "Such a stupid girl, thinking you could outrun me. Outrun Kirsa and her bitches," he adds, laughing toward the hounds on the bank. The Silver woman ejects something between a giggle and a bark, her hounds reacting in kind.

Then Orrian raises his hand for a third time and Lyrisa moves, lightning fast, her hand grabbing his wrist. The threat is plain as day. She could tear his entire arm off if she wanted. "Pick on someone your own size," she spits in disgust.

Orrian sneers but doesn't move. He could subdue her with the river, but not before inflicting terrible pain on himself. I was right. He's a coward through and through.

They stare at each other with such hatred I fear it might set the boat aflame.

Good.

"Now that we're all acquainted . . . ," I sigh, raising my pistol. In the shallows, Orrian's nobles tense, ready to spring. Until I put the gun to Lyrisa's temple, cold metal against skin. "Let's get down to bargaining, shall we?"

For a moment, all is still. Lyrisa's face drains of color; her eyes flash to mine, wide and afraid, her lips moving without sound. And Orrian brays a laugh, drenching us both with spittle. Lyrisa doesn't loosen her grip, but she slackens in shock, staring at me with such pain and accusation I nearly falter.

"Ha-ha!" the prince howls, still standing upon his watery step. "What a show this has been. Oh, bravo, rat—bravo!" Then he looks over his shoulder, to his friends cackling and laughing as loudly as he is. "Did you hear that? Lyri probably *paid* this rat too, and now he's trying to sell her back to me! You're a smart one, I'll give you that," he adds, swinging back to me with a wagging finger.

"I'm a survivor," I tell him, and he laughs again.

"Then tell me, survivor," he sneers, "why don't I just take her right now, flood your wretched excuse for a boat, and leave you drowning behind me?"

I blink at him like the answer is so obvious. "Because I'll kill her. There are no magnetrons with you, and a bullet moves pretty quickly at this range." Then I glance at his wrist and Lyrisa's fingers still tight on his skin. "Pretty sure she might take your hand with her too."

He bares his teeth, an animal denied an easy kill. With a will, he steps up and over the rail, wet boots slamming against my deck. Lyrisa is forced to step back, me moving with her, her back square against my chest. But she never loosens her grip.

"Let me go, Lyri," he hisses into her face.

Her grip only tightens, and a sheen of sweat coats his brow. She's hurting him, just enough to remind him of what a precipice he stands upon. Behind him, his nobles move farther into the water, crawling up the sides of the keel to jump onto the deck. They outnumber us almost two to one, odds no Silver needs against Reds. Riette and Gill keep their gun sights on two, but they're terrified, barrels trembling.

Lyrisa doesn't break, even with Orrian standing over her and my gun jammed against her skull. She's caught and caged, and still refusing to yield.

Behind me, the crew moves as we discussed. Toward the cargo hold, the trapdoor below propped ajar by Big Ean's boot.

"Lyrisa," Orrian says, his voice changing so quickly it shocks me. Now his words are honeyed, and he says her name with loving reverence. Like the princess, he slips behind a mask too easily. It frightens me. "Let's put this behind us, my dear. It's natural to be afraid before a wedding, to fear a new country and a new life. I'm willing to forget this, or, better yet, thank you for it!" He gestures to his friends with his free hand, his grin manic. "We haven't had such fun in ages. So let me go, give the man what's left of the coin in your belt, and let's get off this stinking boat. Hmm?"

"So few of you," she replies, her eyes darting over the noble faces leering at her. I suppose she knows them all. "And weaklings too. Barely worth the blood in their veins. Drunks and imbeciles. I'm surprised this is the best you could do, Orrian. I thought you a prince?"

"You strongarm bi—!"

With a growl, she twists her hand and snaps his wrist, the sound of bones breaking somehow louder than his resulting scream. He falls to his knees, clutching a hand now hanging off the joint, kept in place only by skin. The sight nearly makes me vomit, but I keep my bearings, moving the pistol from Lyrisa's head to Orrian's.

His nobles are already lunging, their weapons and abilities ready. Behind me, Big Ean flicks his lighter open, the clink of metal as warming as my mother's voice.

I squeeze, blasting off a round.

But the gun jams.

"Shit," I whisper.

Orrian's eyes are like a hurricane at the Gates, ready to rip me apart. The river rises behind him, born of all his fury, a wall eager to crush me.

I'm sailing through the air before I can register what's happening, hurtling for the deeper water off the bank. Then I realize: Lyrisa tossed me as easily as a doll. I barely have time to heave a breath before I crash into the water, narrowly missing a child's raft. I learned to swim when I learned to walk, and I fight back to the surface easily, breaking through in time to see Big Ean, Riette, and Gill leap from the side of my keel, their bodies silhouetted against the spread of flame.

And I'm left to hope Lyrisa did the same, jumping into the water as the cargo hold filled with spilled oil and alcohol caught fire. She knew the plan. Well, almost all of it. I had to improvise a bit. I hope she'll forgive me for holding a gun to her head.

The wave falls in on itself as the keel burns, signaling the end of Prince Orrian. Burned or torn apart by a strongarm or both. Screams rise with the smoke, impossible to decipher. I swim as fast as I can, legs kicking, arms pumping, to close distance.

On the river, other boats stop to watch, and one of the river kids is good enough to slow her raft next to me, letting me grab hold. She steers the small motor with one hand, lazy and at ease despite the pillar of smoke up ahead.

When I get close to the bank, the crew are already fighting out of the shallows, torn between triumph and defeat. We lost the keel, but we lived. Exhausted, I let the river girl pull me up to them, and Big Ean offers a hand, half dragging me to my feet.

We look back together at the now-crumbling hulk of my boat. It exploded quickly, faster than I anticipated. Anyone aboard would surely have been incinerated. A few yards away, one of the hounds bales mournfully, before the pair runs off together.

My chest tightens, a sharp pain springing to my eyes.

"Did she . . . ?" Gill murmurs, but Riette waves him off.

Together, we wait for one of the Silvers to fight their way out of the river. An enemy or a friend, we don't know. I hope for Lyrisa, hope her luck was as good as mine. But the boat sinks and no one comes.

I wish I could have shown her the Gates.

SEVEN
Lyrisa

The river washes clean most of the blood. If not for the water, I would be soaked in it. Orrian's, mostly. That tends to happen when you remove a head.

It doesn't wash away the memory. I doubt anything ever will.

The river fumed behind him, rising like the wings of a predatory bird. On either side, his friends lunged at me, slowed by their drunken state. The worst of them was Helena, but she was at the far end. A strongarm like me, she would have been difficult to kill.

But I could only look at Orrian, screaming beneath me, trying to rise from his knees. There was fire in his eyes. No, that was the ship, the cargo hold catching alight, exploding from either end.

"You will be mine," he hissed, even as my hands closed on either side of his head. In that moment, I saw my life as it could have been, as so many had lived before me. Resigned to a crown, unhappy and spreading that unhappiness. Miserable in my strength and power. Inflicting my pain on everyone around me, and my children after me.

I would not have that life for myself, not even if the alternative was to die.

I felt the spray of the river as it trembled over us, claws reaching for my throat. I grabbed and pulled. I don't know what I expected to happen. For him to die, certainly. Perhaps for his skull to break before his spine. Instead his neck tore clean, like I was removing the top from a jar. I didn't know a body could do that.

I didn't know there could still be so much blood, a heart still beating even without a head.

Strange, his water saved me. It crashed as soon as he died, falling upon us both even as the ship burned. I dove as fast as I could, my wet clothes reluctant to catch fire. Even so, I felt the searing pain of the flames behind me, consuming everything and everyone still left on the ship.

I feel them now, hot and angry. They'll need tending, but I doubt I'll find a skin healer at the confluence. In Memphia, maybe. For now I'll have to make do with what I can cobble together from the market town.

It was the right thing to do. Keep low in the water, watch the bank. Wait for Ashe and his crew to move on. Let them think I died with Orrian. Let no whisper of me travel down this river. Let no one else follow my trail.

It's the only way to get away properly. Leave no trace.

I'll have to be more judicious with my coin. Luckily, the pouch on my belt survived the explosion and the river. It should be enough, if I spend it wisely.

First things first, I manage to trade my Lakelander uniform, soaked as it is, for better-fitting clothes. The coveralls stink, but they'll do, and I'm eager to get out of a dead woman's clothes. The market town is larger than I anticipated, with hundreds of stalls spread out across dirt streets and the docks. Keels, ferries, and even larger boats crowd the riverbank, loading and unloading cargo and passengers. It won't be difficult to book passage to the Gates. It won't be hard to leave this world behind, as I have so many others.

The ground beneath my feet shifts from earth to wooden plank to earth again, this part of the river junction crossed by smaller canals and shifting streams. I keep my head down, my ears open, and my hair loose to hide my face. I catch snippets of conversation here and there, some of it about the "commotion" at the confluence. The rest is jarringly normal. Traders exchanging news, boatmen reuniting with friends, gamblers advertising games, merchants their wares. I pass it all quickly, aiming for the main docks where the larger boats wait.

Until one voice above the rest gives me pause.

A sly voice, familiar, with a confident smirk behind it.

I turn to find a small crowd gathered, ringing a table with two chairs, one of them occupied by a kindly, smiling ox of a person. He offers a hand to another large man as he gets up from the table, rubbing his arm with a grimace.

"No hard feelings?" Ean says, still smiling in his gentle way.

The Red opponent turns without another word, cursing under his breath. He leaves coins on the table as he stomps off, his footsteps shaking the planks beneath my feet.

Ashe is quick to scoop the coins into his jacket pocket, still drying beneath the afternoon sun. He claps Ean on the back.

"Well done, Ean," he says with a grin, before turning back to the market crowd of travelers and traders. "Come on now, anyone else want to try Big Ean? Strongest arm this side of the Freelands! All or nothing, first arm to touch the table wins the coin!"

I shouldn't stop. I should keep walking. Pay my way onto a boat and go.

Instead I find myself parting the people in front of me, my coin purse in hand.

I smirk as I sit, laying my money out slowly. Then I put my arm out, elbow to the tabletop, hand open and ready.

Big Ean balks, but I only have eyes for Ashe.

He stares at me, his face impassive for a second. Then his lips curve into a grin.

"I'll take that bet," I tell them both.

TIMELINE

290–300:

- The Scarlet Guard is formed in the Lakelands. Gradually, its influence and power will grow throughout the kingdom and bleed across its borders to Norta.

SUMMER 296:

- Tiberias VI is crowned King of Norta following the passing of his father, Tiberias V.

FALL 300:

- Crown Prince Tiberias is born to Tiberias VI and his wife, Coriane, of House Jacos. He is nicknamed Cal.

LATE FALL 302:

- Mare Barrow is born in the Stilts to Daniel and Ruth Barrow.

FALL 301:

- After the death of his first wife, King Tiberias VI marries Elara of House Merandus.

WINTER 302:

- Prince Maven Calore is born to King Tiberias VI and Queen Elara.

SUMMER 320:

- Queenstrial is held. While working as a servant, the Red girl Mare Barrow displays an impossible Silverlike ability. She is disguised in the court as a Silver woman to hide this new power.

LATE SUMMER 320:

- After weeks of aggression, the Scarlet Guard attempts to seize Whitefire Palace in Archeon, but fails. Betrayed by Maven, Mare is exposed as a Scarlet Guard operative and Cal is forced to kill his own father. Mare and the crown prince are arrested and sentenced to death. They narrowly escape with the help of the Scarlet Guard.
- With his brother in exile, Maven is crowned King of Norta.

FALL 320:

- Mare and the Scarlet Guard travel throughout Norta, looking for more Reds with Silver abilities to join their army. They are called newbloods.

LATE FALL 320:

- After their team is cornered, Mare trades herself to King Maven in exchange for their lives. She is imprisoned in Whitefire Palace.

WINTER–SPRING 321:

- King Maven undertakes a coronation tour of Norta and negotiates an end to the Lakelander War. He breaks his betrothal to Evangeline of House Samos to cement the peace treaty with a marriage to Princess Iris of the Lakelands.
- The Scarlet Guard pushes the fortress city Corvium into riots and chaos. Led by the exiled Cal, they conquer the city.

SPRING 321:

- After months as Maven's prisoner and political puppet, Mare escapes with the help of Evangeline during a Scarlet Guard uprising at Maven's wedding.

- The Kingdom of the Rift is formed by House Samos.
- The democratic Free Republic of Montfort allies with the Scarlet Guard, hoping to remake the Silver kingdoms of the east into blood-equal democracies. They forge a shaky alliance with Piedmont, based on blackmail, but have many resources and troops.

EARLY SUMMER 321:

- Together with the Lakelands, Maven attempts to win back Corvium, but his army is defeated by an alliance of the Scarlet Guard, Montfort, the Rift, and rebelling Silver houses led by Tiberias VI's mother, Anabel Lerolan.
- The king of the Lakelands is killed in the attempt on Corvium.
- After the battle, the Red and Silver alliance proclaims Cal as Tiberias VII, the true King of Norta.

SUMMER 321:

- The alliance of Tiberias VII, the Scarlet Guard, and the Rift petition and win aid from Montfort's government.
- Acting on behalf of her husband, Queen Iris of Norta removes the leverage Montfort has over Prince Bracken of Piedmont. The Silvers overtake the Montfort base in Piedmont.

LATE SUMMER 321:

- The Red and Silver alliance strikes the tech slum New Town and Harbor Bay at the same time, winning both from King Maven. The two sides agree to a parley.

- Queen Iris turns on her husband and trades him over to the alliance in exchange for the man who killed her father.
- Maven is stripped of his crown and sentenced to execution by his brother. The war for the throne is won, and the undisputed king refuses to step down. The Scarlet Guard and Montfort dissolve their alliance with Norta, and kidnap Maven before he can be killed.
- The Lakelands return in full force to assault the weakened Norta, striking the capital at Archeon. Evangeline and Ptolemus of House Samos flee the city, forsaking their royal house. Their father, King Volo Samos, dies in the battle. The Nortan forces are almost overrun, until the Scarlet Guard and Montfort infiltrate the city with Maven's guidance. When he tries to escape in the battle, Mare Barrow is forced to kill the fallen king.
- King Tiberias VII abdicates his throne in favor of a new Norta and reconstruction into the Nortan States begins.

Montfort archivists have been hard at work, as have I, to best record and comprehend the events of the last year or so, including the Nortan Civil War. Naturally our own historians have been somewhat lacking, both in point of view and in the ability to write while weathering a change in government. Obviously, the documentation I have found in Norta is quite biased toward the Silver viewpoint and not worthy of inclusion just now. That said, I found it fascinating to look back on events through another lens, and you might find it useful as well, if not simply interesting.

—JJ

safe passage for Ardents in hostile nations. The Monfortan government and military undertook a joint operation to identify, warn, and relocate Ardents within Prairie, Piedmont, Norta, the Lakelands, and the Disputed Lands. The need for secrecy complicated our efforts, but thousands of these individuals and their families were removed from these lands in the years leading up to the Nortan Civil War.

The first Ardent to be publicly identified outside Montfort was Mare Barrow, a young woman from the Capital Valley of Norta. At seventeen years old, while working as a servant to the Royal Family of Norta, she was caught on a Nortan broadcast using her electricon ability. While the Nortan government and monarchy quickly covered up her blood status by labeling her a Silver noblewoman, it was clear to anyone with knowledge of Ardents what she truly was. Barrow was betrothed to the second prince of Norta, Maven Calore, and used as a vital tool in Queen Elara Merandus's plot to usurp her husband and place her son on the throne of Norta. While living as a Silver noble, Barrow was contacted by the Scarlet Guard, a rebel group, and oathed herself to their cause. She gathered intelligence and aided the Guard in its efforts to destabilize the Nortan government. Barrow was integral to organizing the Sun Shooting, one of the Scarlet Guard's first open acts of violence in Norta. During a failed Scarlet Guard coup, Queen Elara arranged the murder of King Tiberias VI. Barrow and his heir, Prince Tiberias, were framed for the deed and sentenced to execution. They escaped with the aid of the Scarlet Guard. (*For more information on the Scarlet Guard, see subsection 12.*)

Following the exposure of Mare Barrow, Montfort dispatched more operatives to Norta and the Lakelands. Most were assigned to observing and eventually making contact with the Scarlet Guard, while several were charged with tracking down Barrow for purposes of alliance. The latter did not succeed. After rendezvousing with the Scarlet Guard at one of the group's bases, she left with a small detachment including Prince Tiberias, a Scarlet Guard captain, and her brother, another Ardent. (*For more information on Ardent inheritance, see subsection 3.*) Montfort intelligence postulates that Barrow was forced to flee the Guard base, fearing persecution of herself and the Nortan prince. On the Nortan mainland, her team, much like our own, sought out other Ardents (now widely recognized and called *newbloods* in Norta) to protect them from the Silver government.

Now king, Maven Calore was seeking newbloods as well. Barrow was operating off a list utilizing Red blood mapping, a Nortan innovation. Later on, Montfort would use similar tactics to expand its objective of finding, protecting, and sometimes relocating Ardents in danger. On the outskirts of the radiated lands of the Wash, in the once-abandoned Corros Prison, Queen Elara was collecting the Ardents her son found. She was believed to be examining them and using her whisper ability to control them. Barrow and her group stormed Corros, and Queen Elara died at Barrow's hands. King Maven tripled his efforts to find Barrow, and she was eventually forced to turn herself over to the Silver king. It's clear the young monarch became obsessed with the Ardent following her time in the Nortan court.

King Maven was quick to use Barrow to his advantage, putting out broadcasts of her to the Nortan nation. On camera, she rebuked the Scarlet Guard and praised King Maven, calling for Ardents like her to join him. Paired with King Maven's decrees lifting harsh measures on the Red population, it increased his popularity within the kingdom considerably. Many Ardents answered Barrow's call, joining the king's army to be trained and wielded as his weapons. The first vestiges of fracture appeared during an attempted assassination of King Maven, when three Silver houses declared open rebellion against their king. They supported the return of Prince Tiberias. During King Maven's coronation tour of Norta, the Scarlet Guard and the exiled prince captured the fortress city of Corvium, weakening Norta's northern defenses. Feeling the strain, King Maven signed a treaty with the Lakelands, effectively ending the Lakelander War, which had lasted more than a century. He was forced to break his betrothal to a Samos noblewoman to marry Princess Iris of the Lakelands instead. Now the Silvers of both Norta and the Lakelands were free to turn all their military might on the Scarlet Guard, which was still growing in size, notoriety, and danger.

The Scarlet Guard struck again, attacking Archeon during the royal wedding of King Maven to the Lakelander princess. This was the first joint effort between the Scarlet Guard and Montfort, following weeks of careful contact and planning. During the attack, the combined forces rescued Barrow and dozens of Ardents, and raided the Nortan treasury to further fund the rebel efforts. Unbeknownst to the Nortans, Montfort had facilitated a deal with the neighboring nation of Piedmont, and the assaulting force returned to a military base in the south. The Kingdom of Norta splintered further when Lord Volo Samos declared himself King of the Rift, and his region seceded from Norta. This is generally considered a watershed in the Nortan Civil War.

King Maven moved to retaliate against the Red rebellion. Some weeks later, he and an allying force from the Lakelands marched on rebel-occupied Corvium. Together, the Scarlet Guard and Montfortan troops led by Premier Dane Davidson were able to throw back the Nortan and Lakelander assault. They were aided by Samos troops from the Rift as well as other rebelling Silver houses led by Anabel Lerolan, a former queen of Norta and grandmother to Prince Tiberias. Facing defeat, King Maven was forced to flee with his army, and King Orrec of the Lakelands was dead, killed at the hands of a lord acting on behalf of King Volo. Following their victory at the Battle of Corvium, the Scarlet Guard, Montfort, the Rift, and Lerolan turned their coalition into an unprecedented Red and Silver alliance against King Maven.

Unable to maintain Corvium and the Piedmont base, while still manning the war effort in Norta, the coalition elected to destroy the fortress city. Prince Tiberias named himself the true King of Norta, backed by the Red and Silver alliance, which pledged to put him back on the Nortan throne. He was betrothed to Princess Evangeline of the Rift, to cement a much-needed alliance. Still needing more troops, King Tiberias VII, Queen Anabel, Princess Evangeline, Mare Barrow, and General Farley of the Scarlet Guard accompanied Premier Davidson to Montfort. Together, they petitioned the People's Assembly and were given more troops to overthrow Maven. During this time, the Montfort arrangement with Piedmont fell apart, and King Maven's forces took over their base in the south. King Tiberias struck back in a double-pronged attack, directing the bulk of his forces to Harbor Bay, a vital city to the Nortan war effort and economy. Barrow, Scarlet Guard troops, Montfort Ardents, and Premier Davidson himself took over a Red tech slum nearby. Even though Lakelanders, including the ruling Queen Cenra herself, arrived with a fleet to protect Harbor Bay, Tiberias's forces were victorious. After nearly dying to win the city, King Tiberias organized a parley between his coalition and Maven's alliance. No agreement was reached until Queen Anabel offered up a trade—the killer of King Orrec for Maven. Both Queen Cenra and Princess Iris agreed, and they turned on King Maven Calore. He was brought back to Harbor Bay in chains. With Maven defeated, the Scarlet Guard and the Premier of Montfort offered King Tiberias a choice: step down from the throne, or lose their alliance against the still-hostile Lakelands. Tiberias chose his crown, and the Scarlet Guard, Barrow, and Davidson returned to Montfort with a kidnapped Maven.

In Norta, King Tiberias struggled to hold together the pieces of a country falling apart, with many Silvers remaining loyal to his brother. The Lakelands moved to strike the capital, meaning to conquer all of remaining Norta in a single swoop. Together, Montfort and the Scarlet Guard interceded, using Maven's guidance to infiltrate the city. King Tiberias and his army were surrounded until he was once again given the choice to step down. He pledged to abdicate, and the joint troops pushed back the Lakelander force. King Volo Samos died in the battle, while his son and daughter went missing. Mare Barrow killed Maven Calore when he attempted to escape the city. Queen Cenra's fleet was forced to retreat when Scarlet Guard submersives appeared in the river and torpedoed the Lakelander ships. They escaped to the sea and then to their homeland, their navy severely hobbled by the Battle of Archeon.

In the following weeks, the Ardent Mare Barrow returned to Montfort while her adoptive country, the Scarlet Guard, and the shattered Norta attempted to rebuild.

Below are my attempts at the flags of the new alliance. The Nortan States, the Scarlet Guard, and Montfort.

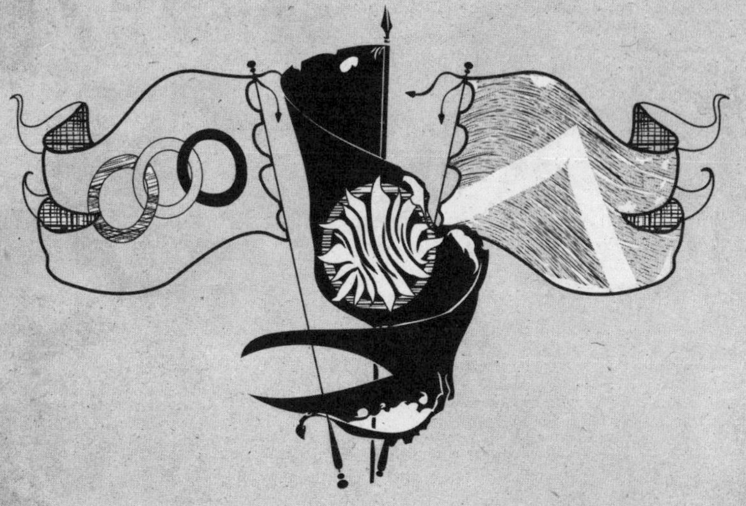

And the flags of our direct adversaries—Piedmont, the Silver Secession of Norta, and the Lakelands.

IRON HEART

ONE
Evangeline

Despite the autumn chill, the sun is bright overhead, and I squint behind my shaded glasses. The garden is empty, albeit still green and thriving. The mountain cold holds no sway over Carmadon's domain. There are flowers, a vegetable patch, fruit trees, even a meticulous square of corn growing in half a dozen rows. The premier's husband tends to this corner of the city estate like a pet, visiting every morning and every evening. He's a greenwarden, and he doesn't need much time to take care of it, but he lingers anyway. Still, he can't spend all day here, and that leaves the afternoon blissfully quiet.

It's a good place to hide.

Not that I'll ever admit to doing such a thing.

I pluck another mint leaf and crush it into my drink, spinning the cubes of ice with a rattle. The sharp bite of sweet whiskey and sugar floods me with warmth. I lie back in the sunlight, content to be still on the blanket I took from our suite of rooms upstairs. It's soft wool, not meant for grass or dirt, but that's what servants are for.

It should only be another hour or two. I could sleep the minutes away if I wanted. But that feels like something a coward would do. Remove herself from the equation entirely. And I still have some pride left. Not much, but some.

Elane is busy. By design. She knows I want to spend this afternoon alone, without an audience. I might revel in her attention most days, but not right now. No one else needs to see Evangeline Samos running from her duty one more time.

I reach the bottom of my glass too quickly, draining the last drops of alcohol. If I didn't want to be found, I might call for a servant and order another. I settle for turning the glass over in my hand instead, holding it up to the sky. The sun sparkles on the many facets of the crystal cup, reminding me of the way Elane can make light dance and split. She fits here better than I do. Not perfectly, of course. The Free Republic of Montfort is as different from our home as can be possible. Silvers, Reds, and newbloods, living together as equals. Beneath a *democracy*, of all things. It's still a shock. I should get used to it, though. This is my place now, and Montfort is what the Nortan States are going to become, if all goes to plan.

I don't put much faith in plans these days, not when I know first-hand how easily they can change.

Another reason I like the garden—there isn't much metal here. I don't have to feel anything I don't bring with me. And these days, I bring very little. In my old life, I used to wear dresses formed from sheets of chrome, or pants laced with steel. Iron-toed boots. Armored jackets. Platinum crowns. Even my most beautiful gowns were bullet-proof. My clothes were a message as much as an artistry, displaying the strength and power we Silvers held so dear in Norta. And everything

I wore came in varying shades of black and silver, the colors of House Samos. A family that no longer exists, or at least is of no importance anymore.

Cousins of iron, kings of steel. The refrain rings in my head, an echo and a ghost. I would forget those words if I could, and the ill-fated ambitions that birthed them.

Though I have no cause to fear attack in Montfort, I'm not an idiot, and I don't go anywhere without some metal. It's just jewelry today. A necklace, a bracelet, several rings, all winking around the edges of my soft sweater. Enough to defend myself if needed, but easy to forget it's even there. I wonder if this is what everyone else feels. Nothing but themselves. The cold breeze, the scratch of drying grass, the sun dipping steadily toward the distant mountains. I like the emptiness, vulnerable as it leaves me. I sit back, enjoying the sensation, and look upward. I can see the peaks even over the walls of the garden, their heights crowned in deepening snow. Mare went up there once, trying to outrun something. I understand the urge. Now she's somewhere even farther north, still recuperating. Still mourning. Still *running*, even if she's finally standing still.

Suddenly the edge of my perception sings. The lack of metal on my person also makes it easy to sense intruders. This one has no weapons, no guns that I can feel, but his steps are sure and quick, closing the distance from the far side of the garden. I clench a fist, reluctant to move and break the silent spell of afternoon. I know who the visitor is. I can feel the wedding band on his finger. Gold and silver both, braided into a circle.

"I promise, I'm not disturbing the plants," I mutter, drawing up my knees as Carmadon approaches.

He surveys me with a keen eye, smirking in his usual way. His gaze snags on my empty glass. "That mint wasn't ready."

"It tasted ready," I lie, the air cold in my mouth.

The premier's husband chuckles, showing even, white teeth. He doesn't mind the temperature like I do; he's used to the shifting weather of the mountains. This is his home, and he has watched it change more than I can fathom. Sometimes I forget his blood is as silver as my own, despite the cool undertones to his dark skin. He's married to a newblood, and he certainly acts like one.

He folds his arms, settling into a firm stance. Carmadon is a handsome man, and he cuts a striking figure against the autumn sun. As always, he wears white, fresh as fallen snow. "I know that locks aren't an obstacle to you, Evangeline, but they should at least be a suggestion." With a tick of his thumb, he gestures across the garden, in the direction of a gate now hanging off its hinges.

"My lord Carmadon," I reply, pretending to bask. Donning a winning smile forged in a lost court, I push the shaded glasses up onto my head. "I'm simply enjoying your fine work. Isn't that the point of this place?" I wave a hand at the garden still in bloom. "To show off?"

Of all the Montfortans, I think Carmadon tolerates me most. So it rankles when he shakes his head. "Sometimes I forget how much you have to learn."

I sneer, feeling the familiar prickle of annoyance. I'm not a child and I'm not stupid. I will not be condescended to.

"I suppose this is a good place to think," he says, gesturing to the meticulously arranged garden. "You know, there are clerks in the city who specialize in job placement. Perhaps I can arrange an appointment for you?"

I roll my eyes. The careful prodding toward finding a profession, a *life*, here in Montfort never ceases to annoy. Even if my time living off the Republic's government is coming to an end soon, I don't want to think about it. Not today.

"Whatever job I choose will be lucky to have me. I don't need *placement.*" And I don't need to be reminded of the clock steadily ticking against me, against Elane, against Tolly and Wren.

Carmadon knows it too. But it doesn't stop him from pressing on. "You're a talented young woman, yes, but you'll fare much better if you line up a job *before* my husband's government stops paying your way."

Quickly I push to my feet, slinging the blanket over my shoulder. A flush rises on my cheeks, hot with blood. I don't need to listen to this. Not today.

"If your intent was to drive me out of your little vegetable patch, then well done. You've succeeded," I mutter.

"Oh please, don't leave on my account. I don't mind you visiting my garden. But eventually your brother is going to come stomping through and crush something he shouldn't." His easy, joking manner returns as quickly as it disappeared. "That, I would like to avoid."

Mention of my older sibling puts me on edge. My fingers curl tighter around the blanket, and suddenly I wish for something large and metallic to shred. "Ptolemus doesn't know I'm here."

Carmadon tips his head, letting the afternoon light gleam against his naked scalp. "You think he isn't going to search every inch of this place until he finds you?"

"He doesn't have the time."

"That jet won't leave until he wants it to," he scoffs. "You can't wait him out."

At that I laugh out loud. The sound echoes through the empty garden, a bark more than a demure laugh. Sneering, I lay the blanket back down with a flourishing wave, before sprawling out against the fabric.

Feeling petty, I even slide my shaded glasses back into place. "Watch me, Carm."

Only his eyes flicker in response. Coal black, but flecked with deep, emerald green. I shriek when something wriggles beneath me, a snake or a—

Vine.

A dozen of them, swift and taking me by surprise. I lash out with my bracelet, weaving it into a razorlike whip, but the vines twist and dodge, pushing me back to my feet in a graceless heap. One even flicks the blanket over me, covering my head.

"Excuse me," I snap, ripping the blanket away. My faces flushes again and I can feel my hair falling out of its braid. If I didn't look like a mess before, I certainly do now. "That was quite rude."

Carmadon drops into an exaggerated, insulting bow. "I beg your pardon, Princess."

The title lands the way it should. Like a kick in the gut. The rings on my fingers sharpen, growing spikes as my insides twist. For a second I stare at the grass, trying to collect my thoughts and swirling feelings. But they dance beyond my grasp, too far to reach.

Princess Evangeline. Lady of House Samos. Daughter of Volo and Larentia.

I am none of those things anymore. Not after today. I should be glad—I should be relieved to be rid of the name and the life my parents gave me. And parts of me are. But the rest of me can't help but be reminded of what I traded away to live as who I am now. What I betrayed. What I killed. What I lost forever.

"Will you miss it?" Carmadon asks softly, taking a step forward. I shift as he moves, keeping my distance.

My eyes crack back to his, blazing and furious. A challenge and a shield. "Titles and crowns mean nothing here. There won't be anything to miss."

But I feel the absence like a hole in me. I've felt it every day for weeks, since I set foot on that underground train, put Archeon behind me, and abandoned my parents to whatever fate waited for them. My blood runs cold. I know what happened. I wasn't there, but I know. And the thought of my father, terrible as he was, walking off the bridge, his body broken and smashed apart below . . . I can't stand it. I hate it. I wish I never knew.

"You should be going with Ptolemus." Carmadon is undeterred by my emotional storm, ignoring it as kindly as he can. "It's the best way to end this."

Behind me, his vines slither back over the grass, curling over one another. I turn with my old skill, loosing the necklace from my throat. It slices the thickest vine in two with a satisfying hiss before wrapping around my neck again.

"Are you going to make me?" I ask, doing all I can to keep my voice in check. *I've already made my decision. Will no one honor that?* "Will the premier?"

"No, Evangeline," he says quickly. "But you know I'm right. Your brother is abdicating his crown, and you should be with him when he does."

My lip curls. "He can speak without me holding his hand."

"I know that. But I mean, when he abdicates, the Kingdom of the Rift passes to you."

Even a Silver child knows that. It's painfully obvious. Everyone knows the laws of succession in my old country, or at least what they were. Men first, and when none are left, the crown passes to a daughter. A person born to be a pawn becomes the ruler of the board.

I would be a liar if I said I had not thought about it. In the dark, in the quiet moments, in the space between lying awake and falling asleep. No one could stop a ruling queen from living how she wished, with whoever she liked.

A queen of a Silver kingdom, and all that entails. The thought pricks at me, drawing a blossom of shame. Once, the sensation was unfamiliar. Now I feel it most days. It's difficult not to, in a country like this, compared to the country I came from, the country I would have maintained.

"That's what the letter is for," I mutter. Just a few sentences, enough to cut me out of the life I was meant to live.

"That's hardly the same. It won't carry the weight your voice will." This isn't the first time I've heard this argument. From Carmadon or from Premier Davidson. Even Ptolemus hinted that my presence would be helpful. And Elane did as well. She has a mind for these kinds of things. "It must be difficult, to give up—"

I cut him off, tired of this conversation. "I don't want that place," I almost shout, my voice too forceful, too loud. "I don't want any of it anymore."

Not weighed against what I have now. It's not worth the trade. But still—I was raised to that place. To Ridge House, to the scarring valleys of the Rift. Shadow and tree and river. Quarries of iron, coal mines. A beautiful home I will never forget. And no matter how much I love Elane, how much I value being who I am, it's a difficult life to forget.

"I'm not going back."

"Fine," he replies, teeth clenched. "Then you can tell Ptolemus that in person. You can stand and watch him leave. Have some spine, Evangeline," he adds, looking me up and down with a withering glance. In spite of myself and my pride, I feel exposed beneath his judgment.

Carmadon is like me, and deep down, I value his opinion. "You can live your own life here, so live it proudly."

Rage quickly replaces any embarrassment in me. It licks up like flame, feeding my dogged resolve. I almost sit back down again, petulant as a child.

But he's right.

"Thank you for your advice, my lord Carmadon," I hiss, dropping into a curtsy even lower than his bow. When I rise, my fingers dance, sending a ring sailing through the trees. It returns in a blink, bringing a small, red apple directly to my palm.

Carmadon doesn't move. "That isn't ripe," he says, his voice tinged with amusement.

I take the largest bite I can as I walk away, ignoring the bitter taste.

TWO
Elane

Was it wrong to send Carmadon after her?

I can't say. Evangeline wanted this time to herself, to wait out the clock on Ptolemus and Wren, but she'll regret it later. If she can't find the stomach to go with them, she'll wish she was there to see him off at least. There are few people she values more than her brother, and I know firsthand what an effect we have on her emotions. Evangeline thinks I don't notice how easily swayed she is by the rest of us. The smallest word, a wrong-sided glance. It unsettles her, any risk to our bonds and relationships. Even the slightest possibility of unraveling our circle. After all, we're the only thing she has left.

And she is the same to me.

I do what I can in the time I have. Packing up her clothes without magnetron help can be an arduous affair, but I do my best. In Norta and the Rift, we both favored our house colors, which made for a very monotone color palette in our closets. Black, silver. Some white. Montfort is different. House colors have no meaning, and I sort through a rainbow of shades to choose outfits suitable for an abdication. Most of Evangeline's gowns are too heavy for me to move without aid, so I stick to silk when I can. The chrome chain mail is less cumbersome, but still a chore to drag off its hook.

After an hour I'm sweating slightly, but I have two cases stuffed with any specific items we might need. Dresses, shirts, pants, jackets. Not to mention my own clothing. Just in case Evangeline changes her mind.

I leave the cases in the closet, shutting the door behind me to hide them from sight.

Our suite of rooms here is less grand than at Ridge House, naturally, but it is still splendid enough as our status demands. For the time being.

Though we slept in the same place back in the Rift, I always had my own chambers somewhere else, to keep up appearances. It's both strange and exhilarating to know the space is ours to share, and no one else's. Davidson's estate has a very specific flair, and my own tastes don't match with exposed wood or forest green. I haven't bothered decorating, though. We will not be here much longer.

The windows face west, at Evangeline's request. She prefers waking with the dawn, but she knows I don't. It was a kind gesture, though it does require some finesse in the afternoon, when the sun seems to be directly at eye level. As usual, I spin my hand as if turning a doorknob, and the light beaming in dims to a golden glow. *Much better.*

I have little true cause to use the full extent of my shadow ability here. Montfort has no royal court to speak of. There is no queen to eavesdrop on, no young prince to follow unseen. Still, that doesn't mean I don't do my fair share of listening where I can. Mostly on the street, exploring the city of Ascendant without worry. After all, I'm a Nortan noble, a Silver born to rule, and once I was the future queen of the Rift. Though I am safe here, I am not often welcome outside the estate. Reds and newbloods who recognize me look on me with scorn, Silvers with pity or jealousy. Sometimes I go out with Evangeline, shielding us both behind a veil of my ability, though it makes navigating the crowds more difficult. Not that Evangeline has ever minded stepping on toes.

Premier Davidson's meetings are too well guarded, even for me. He retains his council behind locked doors with newblood guards on his heels. One can detect abilities; the other has elevated senses that allow her to smell or hear even an invisible intrusion. The latter reminds me of Evangeline's mother, a woman never caught off guard. She always had too many eyes to see through, too many noses, too many beasts at her command.

If everything carries on as it should, I might be spending a lot more time with the newblood guards, and Davidson especially.

It's been at least two hours since Evangeline disappeared. She ate breakfast in unusual silence, devouring whatever the servant put in front of her. I didn't push. It's a difficult day for all of us, most of all her. When she told me she wanted to be alone for a while, I was ready to give her the space she so desperately wanted.

She gave me a copy of the letter she wrote, the one Ptolemus is supposed to read during his broadcast tomorrow. She isn't the type to want input or even support, but there are no secrets between us these days. She wanted to give me the choice.

I haven't read it.

It sits on the coffee table in our salon, taunting me even from the next room. I'm not a fool. I've lived in Silver courts as long as Evangeline has, and I've probably overheard more than she will in her lifetime. It's a shadow's way to watch and listen. Sending a letter, instead of going to the Rift herself—it's risking disaster. And no matter how many times I tell her this, Evangeline refuses to listen. She's always been stubborn, always quick to dig her heels in. I thought this place might cure her of that. She could be different here. But very little about her has changed. She's still proud, still venomous, still terrified of losing the few people she holds dear.

I avoid the salon and the letter's temptation, busying myself with the already-made bed instead. We don't have personal servants, but there are maids who clean our rooms daily, ready to provide anything we might ask for.

Not for much longer.

I huff out a breath, blowing a lock of hair out of my face. I don't have the faintest idea how to clean most of my clothing properly. Especially not the lacy pieces Evangeline likes best. I made sure to tuck a few of those in the cases. She deserves a reward if she changes her mind.

On the abdication, and other things as well.

Sighing, I lie back against the cool coverlet of our bed. The blankets are dark green, the same color as the Montfort flag, and I imagine I'm sprawled against a forest floor. My scarlet hair looks striking against the fabric, bright as a wound. I debate ringing for the maid and asking her to draw me a hot bath, when someone enters the salon from the hall. There's only one person who wouldn't bother to knock, and I steel myself for the inevitable disagreement over today.

Evangeline moves with grace. Not like a cat, but a wolf, always on the hunt. Usually I like when she's hunting me, but I'm not her prey right now. She doesn't meet my gaze when she enters the room, even though I'm silhouetted quite nicely against the windows. The light shifts over me, dappling my pale skin and red dress in a pretty haze. I like wearing red. It matches my hair. It makes me feel alive. Evangeline wears her house colors today even though she doesn't need to anymore. Black leather, gray wool. She seems dull in comparison to her usual self.

She drops something on the floor, and I catch sight of a half-eaten apple as it rolls under a chair. The former princess doesn't seem to notice or care. I wrinkle my nose.

"You better clean that up, Eve," I say, speaking before she can scold me for sending Carmadon after her. Throw the wolf off the scent.

She barely shrugs, letting the softened light catch in her silver hair. It dances and refracts. For an instant she wears a crown only I can see. "I think I'll enjoy our last few hours of maid service."

So dramatic, I think, fighting the urge to roll my eyes. "I doubt they'll cut us off so quickly."

"You know Davidson so well, do you?" She angles a knifelike smirk in my direction. I feel the sting of a familiar accusation and brush it off with a wave.

"I'm not having this argument again. We have more important matters to discuss."

She paces to the foot of the bed, stopping to lean forward on her hands. Her gaze meets mine, storm-cloud eyes against my sky blue. I see desperation in her, and anger. "Your future profession is important to me."

"It can wait," I tell her, and not for the first time. Whatever role I decide to play in Montfort—that choice is mine. "You should be there," I murmur softly, sitting up so I can touch her.

But she moves quickly, her cheek evading my fingers. With a huff, she flops down against the blankets, arms crossed over herself. Her hair splays, close enough to mingle with mine. Red and silver, the two colors that rule this world.

"Why send Carmadon to tell me that if you're just going to parrot the same argument? Seems a bit circular, my dear."

"Very well," I mutter. As usual, my blood heats with her lying so close. "Should I try another tactic?"

Evangeline glances at me, pressing her cheek against the bed. I move slowly, deliberately, swinging one leg over her waist until I'm firmly settled above her.

Her smile doesn't reach her eyes. "Please do," she whispers, one hand finding my hip. The other remains still.

I lean down, speaking so my breath ghosts along her neck. She shivers beneath me. "There are already two factions within the Silvers of the Rift. One favors reorganization." I press a kiss to the vein in her neck. "Joining the Nortan States. Living beneath the laws of that new government. Blood equality, a restructured society. They would prefer losing their status to shedding any more blood in another war."

Her throat jumps as she swallows hard, keeping her focus. But the hand on my hip strays, trailing up my ribs. Over my dress, I feel her touch keenly, like she's dragging her nails across bare flesh.

"Smart," she says. Evangeline is far from stupid. She'll let me play my game, but she'll play her own as well. One of her fingers hooks into the ties at the back of my dress, toying with them. If she wanted, she could cut me out of my gown without blinking. "We Silvers always know how to save our own skins."

I lean down again, putting a hand to her throat. At the edge of my vision, the light around us spots. Dark and light, bleeding between each. It pulses with my heartbeat. "And the other—"

Her voice is sharp. "I don't care."

I press on, undeterred. "The other is backed by your remaining cousins," I say, pulling the collar of her sweater to the side, exposing the pale skin beneath.

She pretends to laugh. A hollow attempt. "I didn't know they were still around."

A lie, Evangeline. My Samos princess knows every piece of her family still breathing.

"Even the low members of your house have a vested interest in keeping a Samos on the throne."

Her grip tightens on me, both hands at my waist now. Holding me in place. Keeping me still. "There won't be a throne—"

"Your brother is doing what he must to make that clear," I snap, sitting up to put some distance between us.

She only glares, retreating into bitter silence.

Once, I might have left her to this. Let her drive me away only to call me back when *she* was ready. But that isn't fair. And I won't live that way anymore. I don't have to. "Eve—"

"It doesn't matter who supports me." She shuts her eyes, speaking through clenched teeth. "I'm never going back. I'm not staking a claim. I'll never be a queen or a princess or whatever they want."

"That's not the point." I cover her hands with my own. Her fingers are cold. "Your cousins will be supporting a queen in exile. They could say you're imprisoned, enslaved—anything to justify maintaining their laws and their superiority. There will be a regent, whoever the highest-ranking Samos is left. Speaking in your name, ruling in your name. All while you *hide* here—"

Her eyes flash open, bright with anger. She shifts beneath me, sitting up so I have to clamber away.

"Are *we* hiding, Elane?" Angry, Evangeline gets off the bed and begins to pace. She combs a hand through her hair, tangling and smoothing the silver locks in succession. "Or are *you* hiding? It is what you're good at, isn't it?"

Everything in me tightens. I am not quick to anger, not like Evangeline. I've never had a temper like hers. But I am not a stranger to rage. Slowly, I slip a bracelet from my wrist, grateful I'm wearing no other metal for her to sense as I let it drop to the floor.

And I disappear.

"Elane," she sighs, not in apology, but exasperation. As if I am some burden or embarrassment.

It only incenses me further.

I am well practiced in the art of silence. Every shadow is. She keeps her eyes on the bed long after I've left it, unable to see me as I cross the room.

"Apologize," I hiss in her ear. Evangeline jumps as if electrocuted, whirling to face my voice.

I release my grip on the light, unwinding the manipulation keeping me invisible. But I don't let go entirely. Shadows gather along my edges, open wounds for her to see. After all, Evangeline is always twisting her iron and steel with every passing emotion. She might as well see how much she affects me too.

Her focus lingers on the shadows, tracing them. For a second she reaches out to touch one, but thinks better of it. "I'm sorry," she says, deflating before my eyes. I hear regret in her voice, enough to take the edge off. "That wasn't fair of me."

"No it was not," I reply. My shadows ripple in response, ebbing and flowing in a tide. It's my turn to hunt, and I circle Evangeline. "If anyone is hiding, it is you, Evangeline Samos. You never leave the estate. You barely speak to anyone outside our circle. You won't even say good-bye to Ptolemus, let alone go with him. Or tell anyone—anyone from before—what *you* are."

What we *are*. But even now, I'll never admit it, not to her, not out loud. She's sacrificed a life for me—and still, somehow, I want more. I need more. Her love, her dedication. A promise given in sunlight instead of shadow. It feels wrong and selfish. But I can't deny it either.

She must read disappointment all over my face, and venom overtakes her. "Oh, and you've sent letters all over, haven't you? Given a broadcast detailing every piece of your romantic inclinations?" I half expect her to shred something, a doorknob or one of her gowns, maybe. Instead she stands still, moving only to point a shaking finger. "If I'm hiding, so are you."

"My father knows. My house knows. Every person in this building knows who I spend my nights with and why." I hear my voice tremble, but I have no issue holding my ground. I've faced far worse in the courts of Norta and the Rift. "I am doing what I can to build a life here for us."

Evangeline just sneers, and I see the disdain in her. Not for me, but for herself. It hurts more than anything she can say. "You think blending in isn't hiding, Elane? Invisible or simply in shadow—either way you avoid being seen."

Suddenly the dark edges around me flare, blinding for a moment.

"What is so very wrong with wanting to belong here?" I thunder, waving my hands at the timber-and-stone walls. "Evangeline, I know how difficult it is to unlearn the lessons we were taught. By my colors, I know." The old motto of our country spills out on instinct. It already feels like a relic. "I would be lying if I said I didn't dream of going back. Ruling a kingdom next to you. But that world, as we are, is impossible. This place might be harder. This might feel against nature. Reds and Silvers, the newbloods—I'm still getting used to it. But they let us live as we want. It's worth the trade."

Only when I'm finished do I realize I'm holding her hands, and specks of light circle around our joined fingers. Evangeline is still, her face carved from stone.

"I believe that's why *I* brought us here in the first place," she says softly. "I wanted our freedom. And I wanted you safe."

I blink away tears of frustration. She's so good at turning arguments back on her opponents. I'm just usually not one of them. "Evangeline, I won't be in danger. I've told you that so many times."

"If you're going to keep telling me to attend the abdication, then I'm going to keep telling you to decline Davidson's offer." Despite her combative tone, her thumb grazes the back of my hand. Such is Evangeline's way. To push me aside while pulling me closer.

"These things are not the same, not by a long shot," I tell her. "And you don't see me trying to persuade you away from patrol service."

She tips her head back and laughs. "Because I'm much better at fighting than you are."

I try to match her laugh. It comes out hollow, a mockery. And I speak without thinking. "Some of the best warriors in the world end up in early graves."

Her fingers rip from mine and she recoils as if burned. Evangeline turns so quickly I almost miss the tears springing to her eyes. Naturally, I try to follow, but she waves me back, palm up and shaking. Her rings, bracelet, and necklace quiver and dance, spinning around her. Mirroring her pain.

"I'm sorry," I blurt out, feeling like a prize fool.

Her father, Elane, she's remembering him. A great warrior in an early grave. Even though Volo Samos kept her trapped, he made her what she is. So strong, so fierce. And she loved him, no matter what anyone else thought. She loved him and she let him die. I know she blames herself.

She still has nightmares about it. Escaping her cage, and paying for it with a man's life.

All thoughts of the abdication and my future profession melt away. Without hesitation, I wrap my arms around her, laying my cheek against her back. The wool sweater scratches, caught between my face and her shoulder blade.

"Eve, I'm so sorry," I whisper. "I didn't mean to remind you."

"It's fine," she clips back. "Every door hinge reminds me."

Every earring. Every lock. Every lamp. Every knife. Every gun. Every piece of metal within her perception. He taught her as much, made her into the weapon she is now. *No wonder she always runs to the garden. She escaped him, but never his memory.*

At least she's letting me hold her. That's a start. And an opportunity. A responsibility.

"I know you like to pretend to be made of iron," I murmur, tightening my grip. She leans into me, her shoulders rising and falling. "Even in your heart, my love. I know better, and you don't have to hide with me."

The letter in the salon seems to burn a hole in my brain. *She must abdicate with Ptolemus. It's the best way to end this, the safest way. It might not save us any more bloodshed, but it will save her any more guilt. I don't know how much more of this she can stand.*

"I know why you won't go back to the Rift," I murmur against her. She stiffens but doesn't run. A good sign. "You're afraid your mother will be there."

Evangeline breaks my hold on her so easily, I almost don't notice she's gone.

The door slams behind her, and I am left alone.

THREE
Evangeline

I'm on the other side of the premier's estate before I feel like I can catch my breath. Once, I might have blamed the altitude, but I'm long since accustomed to the thin air. No, the tightness in my chest is from inconvenient, idiotic *feelings.* Not to mention the usual shame.

Elane is no stranger to my tears. That doesn't mean I enjoy crying in front of her, or showing weakness of any kind. To anyone. For as brutal as the Nortan court was, I understood it. It was a game I played well, shielded by my jewels and armor and family, all as fearsome as any other. Not anymore.

I wasn't there; I didn't see him die. But I heard enough of the whispers to know the ending he met, and I dream of it anyway. Almost every night, I wake up with that image in my head. Volo Samos, striding across the battlefield, stepping onto the bridge. His dark eyes are glazed and faraway. Julian Jacos sang to him, and sent him walking to his death. I still wonder if he knew. If he was trapped inside his own head, watching as the edge came closer and closer.

Every time, I see my father's body smashed against a Lakelander ship. His skull cracked open. Fingers still twitching. Silver blood running freely from a dozen wounds. The picture changes sometimes. Spine broken. Legs twisted. Guts spilling. Armor shattered. Sometimes he explodes into dust and ashes. I always wake up before the Lakelander queens reach him, or the river swallows him whole.

We think the Lakelanders kept his corpse. He wasn't in the river when our own nymphs dredged the water looking for survivors. Cenra and Iris kept his body for reasons I cannot fathom, speeding away to their distant kingdom with my father rotting between them.

"Nymph bitch," I mutter under my breath, echoing the words of a long-dead king. It helps a little, even if my anger is misplaced. Iris Cygnet didn't kill my father. I don't even think I could blame Julian for it. Only one person still living carries that burden.

I knew it was coming, and I did nothing.

My fingers comb through my hair, pulling the roots. The familiar sting clears my mind a little, chasing off the deeper pain.

Shaking my head, I try to take stock of my surroundings. Davidson's palatial compound isn't as large as Whitefire Palace, but the estate is more winding, and it's still easy to get lost. *Good.* Like the rest of the rooms, this distant hall has polished wood floors, river-stone accents, and dark green walls. A nearby bank of windows looks out on thick pine forest standing sentinel above Ascendant. The sun dips lower with every passing second. I feel so much as hear the clock ticking on a small table nearby. Certainly Ptolemus will go before sunset. No pilot wants to take off from the mountains in darkness.

Since I've been effectively chased from Carmadon's garden, and now from my own chambers, I'm faced with a choice and two very different forms of distraction. Namely, the kitchens or the gymnasium. My heart tugs toward food. Carmadon might be a busybody, but he's a splendid cook, and his kitchen staff are just as talented as he is. Unfortunately, the kitchens will be busy with servants and probably Carmadon himself, overseeing his next interrogation disguised as a dinner party.

I shudder at the thought. There's supposed to be some kind of gala soon, a celebration, though the war in the east is far from done. What we could be celebrating I'm not sure, but it will certainly be a spectacle. Davidson's doing, I know. He'll invite delegates from the Nortan States, both Red and Silver, as well as members of his own government and the Scarlet Guard representatives who can be spared from their positions. Some have already been back and forth, but I wager he'll try to get as much of the alliance in one room as he can. He does love the false image of a united front. Red, Silver, newblood, alike in goals and allegiance.

Maybe in a decade, I scoff to myself. There is much still to be done, to make Davidson's dream come true. The Lakelands stand directly in the way, alongside Piedmont, Prairie, and too many other obstacles to name.

I wonder if I'll have a part in it. If I *want* to have a part in it.

Enough, Evangeline.

That settles it. I need the gymnasium. My brain is too much of a mess to do anything but hit something big and heavy.

The training arenas of Norta were sterile places. White walls, glass enclosures, padded obstacle courses. Rigid and perfect, with healers on hand to tend even the smallest of injuries. The training arena in the Ridge was similar, though ours at least had a view of the surrounding landscape. I spent hours in those places, drilling myself to military perfection. It isn't difficult to fall back into an old routine.

Montfort favors the outdoors and fresh air. They probably think it makes them hardier, training in the dirt and snow. The training compound on the estate is near the armory, made of a collection of small buildings surrounding a circular track, itself a makeshift arena for sparring.

After changing into my lightweight gear, I start with a warm-up run. Pine trees cast long shadows across the empty track.

When I first came here, it was harder than I realized it would be to push through a run. The altitude gets to everyone, and I spent a good week gulping water whenever I could, trying to stave off dehydration. Eventually we adjusted, though Elane took a bit longer. She's still generous with moisturizers and balms to combat the dry air.

Now I barely feel the strain. *This place makes you stronger, in more ways than one.*

After thirty minutes, with my pulse surging in my ears, I slow to a walk, sweat cooling my skin. It makes me shiver.

I whirl at the distant feel of copper, adrenaline surging through my veins. In spite of my pride, I almost take off running.

"Ptolemus," I mutter.

My brother picks his way across the compound, that same copper disc tucked away in his belt. A beacon, an anchor. A piece of metal that means we will never lose sight of each other on the battlefield. He wore it today, not because we're going to war together, but because he wants me to feel him approaching. He wants to give me a chance to run away.

I grit my teeth and set my feet.

I owe him this much.

Technically, my brother is a king now. The second my father's skull smashed on a ship deck, Tolly became King Ptolemus of the Rift, though none of us will ever acknowledge it. He looks like a shadow today, his silver hair plastered back, his body clad entirely in black. Not court clothing, or even something suitable for travel. As he gets closer, I realize he's wearing a training suit like mine. Black leather, silver detailing. Enough stretch to move, but firm enough to blunt a blow. He's ready to fight.

"Afternoon, Eve," he says, his voice neither soft nor hard.

I can't help but sigh, exasperated. At this point, I think I should just carry around a sign with *I'M NOT GOING* written on it.

"Is everyone following me? Are you all taking turns? Well, okay, Tolly, here's your chance."

The corner of his lips twitches, betraying the urge to smile. He glances at the trees. "You saw Wren already?"

"Wren?" I scoff. My stomach twists at the thought of facing down yet *another* person trying to sway me from my decision. Tolly's girlfriend won't press as much as the others, at least. "No, I haven't seen her *yet.* But I've already gone through Elane and Carmadon. I think they rehearsed."

"Elane maybe. Carmadon definitely." Tolly chuckles, putting his hands on his hips. His stance broadens, highlighting the width of his shoulders. It makes him look like Cal. Just another soldier in the grand scheme of our mess. "I take it they didn't have much luck."

I raise my chin, defiant. "They did not. You won't either."

He doesn't seem deterred. "I'm not here to try."

"You're not?"

Tolly shrugs, as if bored or uninterested. "No." I look for the lie, but I can't find it.

"Then . . . ?" I hesitate and glance around at the quiet training circle. Now that I think about it, this area shouldn't be deserted. Not at this hour. We're alone, left to do as we please. I suspect Davidson has something to do with it. Clearing the way for me wherever I go, giving my family an opportunity to try to change my path. *They won't,* I tell myself. *Stand your ground.*

My brother isn't bothered by my silence. He starts stretching instead, twisting his body to flex his arms. "I thought I'd get one last training session in before I go," he says. "Care to join me?"

"You know I sort of invented this tactic." My mind flashes to Mare Barrow and the training gym back at Ridge House. I sparred with her while Cal watched, and we beat each other into bloody pulps. Both to nudge Calore and Barrow closer to each other, but also to get Barrow's head out of her own damn ass. I suspect my brother thinks he can do the same.

"What tactic?" he asks, widening his eyes in mock innocence. I don't miss the way his fingers twitch. Tolly and I have sparred enough in our lives for him to know I strike hard, fast, and usually without warning.

Grinning, I start to circle him. He shifts to match my motions, never letting me get behind him or out of his eye line. "If you can't convince them, beat them."

"So you're finally admitting I can beat you," he says, puffing out his chest.

Buying time, I feel for any metal in the area. There isn't much, and my meager jewelry won't be sufficient to subdue someone like Ptolemus. "I did no such thing."

He watches me with the Samos smile, a wolfish knife of a thing. I'm sure he knows I'm searching for weapons and coming up empty-handed. "Certainly sounded like it, Eve," he says, spreading his hands wide. I notice as much as feel the six rings spread across his fingers.

Each one is tungsten, a heavy, brutish metal. His punches will hurt.

If he can land them.

Tolly expects me to make the first move, so I wait instead, continuing to circle. It puts him on edge. My steps quicken a little and I'm careful to keep my ring hand between us, ready to shield whatever he tosses my way. He does the same, smiling. His weapons far outnumber mine.

Or so he thinks.

Magnetrons can't control dirt.

Lightning quick, I scrape and kick, sending up a cloud of earth to blind him. He flinches, shutting his eyes and whirling to avoid the worst of it. I don't waste time, leaping toward him as the bracelet and ring on my hand melt into a blunt-edged knife. If I can get behind him, it's over. Put the dagger to his throat or his ribs, jab so he feels it, and claim victory. Over him and anyone else who might try to tell me what to do.

I catch him around the chest, meaning to swing myself around him with my momentum. But he recovers quickly, planting a firm hand to my shoulder and tossing me to the ground. I hit hard and roll, missing a sure-footed kick by inches. I dodge; he chases. He dodges; I chase. We go back and forth, twisting around each other in almost mirror images. We have the same ability, the same training. I know his moves and he knows mine. He meets my knife with a circular shield; I parry with a thread-thin whip of steel. He just lets it close around his fist and squeezes, forming a glove of spikes over his hands. He knows I'm quick enough to dodge again, and I do, the needle-sharp glove whistling by my ear. I respond with a swipe to his ankle and a corresponding tug on his heavy rings, using them to drag him backward. His ability wars with mine, the two of us ripping at each other. I manage to loose two tungsten circles and draw them to my side. Both flatten and stretch into thin but strong staffs, easy for me to wield.

Ptolemus only grins at me. He doesn't form a weapon of his own, leaving the remaining rings on his fingers. The dance begins again, both of us evenly matched and equally prepared. His strength is beyond my own, but I'm faster, and it balances us out. Sparring with Ptolemus is like fighting with my own shadow, or my own ghost. Every time we do it, I hear my father's voice, or Lord Arven's, or even my mother's. The people who made us into the warriors we are now, hard and unforgiving as the steel we control.

We carry on like this for long, exhilarating, exhausting minutes. We tire at the same pace, both breathing hard and sweating. I have a cut above my eye, shallow but bleeding freely. Tolly spits blood when he gets the chance, maybe down a tooth or two. His face is flushed and mine must be too, but neither of us is the type to surrender or even ask for a break. We'll push each other hard, until someone gains the upper hand. Usually me.

I slide again, my knees skidding through the dirt training ring with a satisfying hiss. With crossed arms, I deflect another blow and gather myself to retaliate. But as I get my legs beneath me, Ptolemus lunges too, arms outstretched, as if to hug me.

Instead his hands, his *rings*, find either side of my face, striking both my temples in tandem. It's like being hit by a train. I see stars immediately and slump, though every instinct tells me to stay upright. The dirt is cool beneath my cheek when I blink my eyes open again. It was only a second, nothing to fret over. Ptolemus hasn't even had time to look concerned yet.

The world spins for a few seconds, and he gives me enough room to get my bearings. I stay down longer than I need to, wishing away the dull pain on either side of my skull.

"I'll call for Wren," he says, but I wave him off.

"It's just a dizzy spell." Gritting my teeth, I get to my feet, careful not to stumble and give Tolly an excuse to get a healer. I don't need anyone else nannying me. I almost hiss at my brother when he tries to help me up. "See, I'm fine. No harm done."

He doesn't need to know I feel like I've just taken a hammer to the head. Certainly bruises are springing up already.

"Good move," I add, if only to distract Tolly. And myself. The dirt training ring whirls around me still. Tungsten is nothing to sneer at, especially in the hands of a skilled magnetron.

Tolly examines his rings with a strange expression, his lips pursed. One of the rings is thicker than the other, and heavier too. He spins it around his finger, and a blush colors the top of his cheeks with bright silver. My brother isn't exactly a talkative sort. Neither of us was taught how to handle our emotions, only to hide them. He didn't learn that lesson as well as I did.

"Father taught you how to do that, didn't he?" I mutter, turning away. The sudden motion makes my head spin. The memories come too fast. Tolly was my father's heir. Naturally, he got different treatment than I did. Lessons with our father, mostly. Training, statecraft. He prepared Ptolemus to lead our house, and our kingdom too.

"He did."

Those two words hold so much meaning. Their relationship was different from ours. Closer. Better. Ptolemus was everything my father wanted him to be. A son, a strong warrior, dutiful and loyal to our blood. No *flaws* like mine. No wonder he loved him more. And my brother loved him in return, no matter what happened back in Archeon.

I absolutely refuse to cry for the second time today. So I focus on the splitting pain in my skull instead of the pain in my heart. "I'm—"

He cuts me off quickly, forcing me to turn around and look at him. "If you apologize for what happened to him, I'll muzzle you." We have the same eyes, storm-cloud eyes. Tolly's threaten to explode.

I bite my lip. "Good luck with that."

The tired jibe does nothing to calm him. In fact he draws me closer, putting his hands on my shoulders so I can't look away. "We all did what we had to, Eve. They forced our hands." *They. Our.* We've been in this together for so long, and Tolly never lets me forget. "They always wanted to make us survivors, and they succeeded."

We survived them.

House Samos is not known for the ability to display affection, and Tolly and I are no exception. I remember watching Mare Barrow hug her family good-bye the last time she left Montfort. They were all arms and movement, clinging so tightly, making such a fuss in front of an audience. Not exactly my taste. But when I hug Tolly, I think of her, and I squeeze him just a bit longer than usual. He responds in kind, giving me an awkward pat on the back that nearly knocks the air from my lungs.

Still, I can't help but feel a now-familiar burst of warmth. It is an odd thing, to be loved and know you are loved as well.

"Do you have your speech prepared?" I ask, pulling back to see his face. If he's going to lie about the abdication speech, I'll know it.

To his credit, he doesn't dodge the question. Tolly offers a crooked smirk. "That's what the flight is for."

All I can do is roll my eyes. "You never could finish your schoolwork on time, no matter the punishment."

"I seem to remember you cheating on many of your own assignments, Lady Samos."

"But did anyone ever catch me?" I fire back, an eyebrow raised.

Tolly just shakes his head and lets me go, refusing to give me the satisfaction. He heads for one of the nearby buildings, where both of us can clean off.

"That's what I thought, Ptolemus!" I shout, eager to catch up with him.

When we reach the building, he holds open the door, letting me enter first. The changing room inside is narrow but tall, with airy skylights open to the pine boughs. Ptolemus bangs open one of the nearby closets and paws through a medical kit, looking for a bandage. I grab a towel from a neat pile and toss it over to him. He wipes off his face, staining the plush cotton with dirt, sweat, and a little bit of blood from his mouth.

I do the same, taking a seat to towel off the sweat at the base of my neck.

"I would have made a poor king," he says suddenly, and with such a casual manner. As if it's a foregone conclusion, the end of an easy equation. He continues hunting for something to bandage up his cut. "I think Father always knew that crown was going to die with him. No matter how much he talked about legacy and family. He was too smart to think the Kingdom of the Rift could exist without Volo Samos." He pauses, thoughtful. "Or Evangeline."

The bandage hunt is pointless. Wren Skonos can regrow hands. She'll have no issue mending a tiny cut. He just needs something to do, another distraction now that we're not trading blows.

"You think Father wanted us to rule together." I try to keep my voice as calm as his. My court training does me well. Even Tolly wouldn't know that the idea, the lost possibility of such a future, unwinds in front of me. Ruling with my brother, Elane between, a queen to us both. Subject to nothing and no one. Not even our parents when the time came. I could live as I wished, in all the splendor and strength I was born to. But no, that can't be true. Ptolemus was always the heir, and I was always the pawn. My parents were ready to bargain me away for another inch of power. It's a useless thing to think of, a rotten future that will never come to pass.

"Even then, who knows," Tolly sighs. His eyes focus on the medical kit, still searching. I count no less than three bandages that I can see, but he ignores them all. "The war would have come for us eventually."

"It still is coming for us." The fear that always follows, the kind so small I can usually ignore it, bubbles to the surface. Despite the sweat and our training exertions, my flesh goes cold. The Archeon battle is still a close memory. And though it drove back the Lakelanders, the Scarlet Guard victory hardly ended the struggle still ripping through Norta.

It won't be long before it reaches us here. The raiders on the border are getting bolder, their attacks coming more frequently down on the plain. Nothing in Ascendant yet, but it's only a matter of time until they try the heights of the mountains.

Ptolemus seems to read my mind. "Elane mentioned you're thinking about patrol."

"It's what I'm good at." I shrug, tossing away the dirty towel. "That's how you choose a job, right? Find something you're good at and get paid for it."

"I suppose professional insult thrower was already taken."

"No, they're holding the position until Barrow gets back from staring at mountains."

I laugh at the thought. Mare Barrow greeting everyone who arrives in Montfort with a snappy observation or cutting remark. She'd certainly be good at it. Ptolemus laughs with me, forcing the sound. His discomfort is obvious. He doesn't like it when I mention Mare, or the Barrows. He killed one of them, after all, and there's no amount of penance he can do to make up for it. Even if Ptolemus Samos became the most stalwart champion of Red equality, even if he saved a boatload of newborn Red babies, it still wouldn't balance the scales.

I must admit, they worry me still. The Barrows and General Farley. We owe them a life, and while Mare promised never to collect on the debt, I wonder if the others might one day try.

Not that they could. Ptolemus is a soldier as much as the rest of us. And he certainly looks it in his training uniform. He's better suited to armor and weapons, not crowns and finery. This life suits him. I hope.

"What about you?" I prod.

He gives up on the medical kit quickly, happy for a change in subject. After the abdication, we're all in the same boat. The premier and his government have no reason to keep us fed and housed if we aren't dignitaries anymore.

"I wouldn't mind patrol," he says. My heart leaps at the prospect of serving next to him, but I can tell he hasn't given it much thought. "I don't have to decide too quickly."

"Why?" I wrinkle my nose. "Do former kings get better treatment than princesses?"

The lost title doesn't bother him as much as it bothers me. He lets it glance off and fixes me with an impish look. Mischievous, even. "Wren is a healer. She's lined up for a job already. I can take my time."

"Ptolemus Samos, house husband," I crow. He only grins, a flush spreading over his cheeks. "You are going to marry her, aren't you?"

The flush spreads. Not because he's embarrassed. My brother could almost be described as *giddy*. "Springtime, I think," he says, toying with one of his rings. "When the snows melt. She'll like that."

"She would." *Well, now we certainly have something to look forward to.*

His smile ebbs a bit, softening with his voice. "And you?" he asks. "You can do that here."

My heart skips in my chest, and I have to clear my throat. "Yes, I can," I say simply, and to my great relief, Ptolemus doesn't push the subject. No matter how much I think about Elane, how much I would enjoy marrying her one day, this is hardly the time. We're too young, in a new country, our lives barely formed. Our paths far from chosen. *Refuse Davidson's offer, Elane,* I plead in my head. *Tell him no.*

"What's that look for?" Tolly says sharply, reading my face.

I exhale slowly. It isn't the job that bothers me, not really. "Elane says I'm hiding."

"Well, she's not wrong, is she?"

"I wear metal spikes most of the time; I'm a bit difficult to miss," I snap. For emphasis, I gesture to the still-bleeding cut over his eye. My brother is far from deterred, fixing me with a weary stare that makes me fumble for words. "It isn't—I shouldn't have to stand there and tell the world what I am. I should just *be.*"

Because Ptolemus has no skill in hiding emotion, or even in expressing it, sometimes he can be too simple. Too blunt. He makes too much sense. "Maybe in a century that will be true. People like you *will* just be. But now?" he says, shaking his head. "I don't know."

"I do, I think." This is Montfort, an impossible country. A place I could have never dreamed of a few years ago, so different from Norta, the Rift, and any other reality I believed in before. Reds stand up with the rest of us. The premier has no reason to hide who he loves. "I'm different, but I'm not wrong."

Tolly tips his head. "You sound like you're talking about blood."

"Maybe it's the same," I murmur. Once again, there's that familiar curl of shame. For my cowardice now, for my stupidity before. When I refused to see how wrong the old world was. "Does it still bother you?"

"You?" my brother scoffs. "Eve, if anything about you bothered me, I would have said something by now."

"That's not what I meant," I mutter, swatting him on the shoulder.

He dodges the blow with ease. "No, Montfort doesn't bother me so much anymore. It isn't easy, to relearn how things just *are*," he says. "And I'm trying. I check my words. I keep quiet in mixed company so I don't say the wrong thing. But sometimes I do. Without even knowing it."

I nod, understanding what he means. We're all doing the same, fighting against old habits and old prejudices as much as we can. "Well, keep trying."

"You too, Eve."

"I am."

"Try to be happy, I mean," he says, his voice sharp. "Try to believe this is all real."

It would be easy to agree, to nod along and let the conversation end. Instead I hesitate, a thousand words caught on my lips. A thousand scenarios playing out in my head.

"For how long?" I whisper. "How long will this be real?"

He knows what I'm saying. How long before the Scarlet Guard loses ground and the Nortan States implode? How long until the Lakelanders decide to stop licking their wounds and return to fight? How long can these days last?

Patrol service is adjacent to joining the Montfort military. You get a uniform, a rank, a unit. You drill; you march; you make your rounds. And when the time comes, when the call goes out, you fight to defend the Republic. You risk dying to keep this country safe.

And Elane never asked me to consider anything else when I thought about joining patrol. She won't push me away from it.

Slowly, I turn the re-formed bracelet on my wrist, shifting the metal to catch the light. I could make a dozen bullets from it easily. "Would you fight for this place, Ptolemus?" *For Montfort, and for our new place in the world.*

"I'd fight for you. I always have and I always will." His reply is quick, without thought.

So is mine.

"I need to give you my letter."

FOUR
Elane

The bath takes longer to fill here. Either because the water has to be piped up from the lake below in the city, or because I still haven't mastered the art of doing it alone. It feels silly to call for servants these days, especially for something I should be able to do without help. And I must admit, knowing I am able to perform the task myself—it's a satisfaction I've never had before.

I sit in the water long after it's gone cold and the soapy bubbles have melted away. There's no reason to rush. Eve will be back soon, trying to hide her regret, already wishing she'd gone with her brother instead of remaining here. I heave a breath, gathering the energy I'll need to calm her down and soothe her enough to sleep. For someone so accustomed to physical pain, she has absolutely no idea how to grapple with emotional turmoil. No matter how much I tell her to lean on me, she always resists, and it maddens me to no end.

Shifting, I tip my head back, letting my hair splay out in the magnificent bathtub. It's smooth, rippled with stones like a riverbed, and the water looks dark in the waning light. I doubt we'll be able to afford something so grand once our time in the palace runs out. I should enjoy it while I can.

But before I can reach for the faucet to pour more scalding water into the cold, I hear movement in my chambers. A door bangs open in the salon, then the bedroom. Evangeline—and a companion.

Annoying.

She's harder to deal with in front of an audience. Too proud to show her cracks.

The air is colder than the water, and I shiver as I step out onto the tile floor, almost flailing for my robe. I tie the fur-and-silk garment around myself, wondering if Davidson will let me keep it. I have a weakness for fine things, particularly ones in this emerald shade of green.

The voices in our bedchamber are familiar. Eve, obviously, and my own former husband, Ptolemus Samos. His deep timbre is difficult to mistake, and I relax a little. We shared something, he and I. Something neither of us wanted. A marriage of convenience, yes, but a marriage against our hearts as well. We did what we could to make it easy for each other, and for that I'm grateful. My father could have given me to someone so much worse, and I have never forgotten how lucky I was.

Lucky, my mind echoes, a taunting sound. Another might find no luck at all in the life I've led, in being forced against my nature, cast out of my family, fleeing to a strange place with nothing but the clothes on my back and a noble name from another country. But I survived it all and, what's more, so did Evangeline. I'm lucky to have her with me, lucky to have escaped the future we were doomed to.

When I emerge, I brace myself for their bickering. Ptolemus isn't one to raise his voice, not with his sister, but he might for this. He knows she should be abdicating with him as much as I do.

"Tolly," I say, greeting him with a wary smile. He nods in return.

Both of them look unkempt, with new bruises blooming over their exposed skin. "Sparring?" I muse, running a finger over the purple spotting at Evangeline's temple. "Who won?"

"Not important," Evangeline says too quickly.

I smile in my soft way, squeezing her shoulder. "Congratulations, Tolly."

Ptolemus doesn't gloat. "She's just eager for a rematch."

"Always," Evangeline huffs. She takes a seat on the edge of our bed and strips off her boots, leaving them discarded and dirty on the lovely carpet. I bite my tongue and refrain from scolding her about cleanliness again.

"And what exactly did you win?" I ask, looking between the two siblings. Both of them know exactly what I'm asking, no matter how much I dance around it.

Silence settles over us, thick as one of Carmadon's huckleberry pies.

"Pride," Ptolemus finally says, as if realizing that Evangeline isn't going to speak. Or admit what she cannot face. "I should be going. I'm late as it is." Even he can't keep his voice from cracking with disappointment. "I'll need the letter, Eve."

Still quiet, Evangeline nods her head toward the salon. And the envelope still waiting, a white square on polished wood. I haven't touched it yet. I don't think I ever will.

"Right, thanks," Ptolemus mumbles. I half expect him to mutter his annoyance under his breath as he strides into the next room, wishing Evangeline would follow.

I watch her instead of him. In spite of all the glamour and shine of the Nortan court, Evangeline is more beautiful in Montfort. Without her painted makeup, her needle gowns, gems ablaze on every inch of her skin. She's easier to see. The sharp nose, the familiar lips, cheekbones to die for. And everything she keeps locked inside, the anger and the want and the pain. She has no armor here.

So I recognize the shadow passing over her features, the darkness being chased. It isn't resistance anymore. It is surrender. And relief.

"Eve—there are two." Ptolemus returns quickly, the open envelope in one hand. Two pieces of paper in the other. His eyes dart between us in confusion. "Two letters."

She keeps her eyes on her bare feet, as if counting her toes. "Because I wrote two. It's not a complicated scenario." Her haughty tone sends me spiraling through time, and suddenly I'm sitting at a gala luncheon, watching her shred some poor suitor to pieces. But she smiles at her brother in a way she would never smile at another man. "I like to be prepared for multiple outcomes."

One of the letters is obvious. Her own abdication, to read before her country after Ptolemus refuses the throne of the Rift. But the other? I can't say.

"Go ahead," she urges. "Read it."

Brow furrowed, Ptolemus does as she asks. He raises the second letter, covered in fluid handwriting, and opens his mouth to recite her words.

"'Dear Iris.'"

My mouth falls open in shock, and Ptolemus hesitates, just as taken aback as I am. "You're writing to Iris Cygnet? To the Lakelands?" he hisses, his voice suddenly dropping in volume. "Are you insane?"

"Eve, they're our enemies. Montfort is funding and fighting a war against them *right* now. You could—you could jeopardize everything we have here." I find myself sitting on the bed next to her, already clutching her hands in mine. "They'll throw us out, send us into Prairie. Or worse, Evangeline, this could be seen as *treason*." And I know what Montfort does with traitors. What any country would do. "Please, my love—"

"Read it," she says again, her teeth clenched.

This time, her voice takes me to a different memory. A worse one. My marriage to Ptolemus, small and private as it was. Quieter than a union of the High Houses should have been. Probably because my parents knew I would spend the entire ceremony crying, and that Ptolemus would refuse to spend the night with me. Evangeline stood by my side through it all, as required. Sister to the groom, friend to the bride. *We can bear it*, she said then, her words coiling with desperation. As they are now.

Ptolemus glances at the windows, and even the door, as if expecting to see one of Davidson's spies listening in. To satisfy him, I flare up, filling the room with blinding light for a second. Illuminating every corner and shadow.

"There's no one here, Tolly," I say. "Do as she asks."

"Very well," he whispers. I can tell he isn't convinced, and probably thinks we're both lunatics.

Dear Iris,

I will not bore you with the overdone greeting as befitting your rank. I'm a commoner now, and I'm allowed to take such liberties. I'm writing to you not as a friend or an enemy. Not even as one former princess to another. Though I hope my expertise on this subject, as well as my experience with the loss of kingdoms, can be of use to you if you haven't burned this letter already. Or would you drown it? Who's to say, really.

Our paths crossed before, and I promise you, as they stand now, our paths will cross again. If your mother keeps up her campaign, if she holds to this war still ripping between your country and my own, I swear to you, we will meet again. Either on the battlefield or across the negotiating table. If you survive long enough to see it. Norta fell to the Scarlet Guard, to Montfort, to the Red tide now sweeping across your own borders. Even you will not be able to weather it, no matter how strong you are. The Nortan States might seem ripe for the taking, but you will find no greater opposition than Tiberias Calore, the Scarlet Guard, and the delegation government now in place.

The pieces on this board we share are already in place, and it isn't difficult to guess the game. Piedmont has been your proxy with the raiders of Prairie, to keep Montfort preoccupied with their own borders and give the Lakelands time to regroup. After all, you were sorely beaten at Archeon, and I imagine your own nobles have been at your mother's throat over the entire affair. You've found opposition in the Rift, not because the Silver nobles are against you, but because they feared and respected my father. He ended up dead on your ship, did he not? What a terrible misunderstanding. Rumors really can get away from us, can't they? And your own country, the pious, proud, bountiful Lakelands—you are steadily moving into winter. Your harvest is soon. And I suspect there are a great deal of Red workers missing, aren't there? Who can blame them, when they can simply cross the border to seek a better life for their children?

You are a nymph, Iris. You can read the tides; you can change currents. But this current, this swift course, cannot be changed. Well

I know metal, Princess. And I know that any steel that does not bend is fated to break.

If you value your throne, your crown, and your lives, you will consider what can be done to protect all three. Blood equality, new laws, as fast as you can write them, are the only way you survive this—and survive it with some power still in your grasp.

Evangeline Samos of Montfort

While Ptolemus stares, wide-eyed, at his sister's bold strategy, the world goes hazy around me. A buzzing sounds in my ears, drowning him out as he rereads select pieces of her advice to the Lakelander princess. *Evangeline Samos of Montfort.* I knew she wouldn't have the titles any longer, but to hear it, to see that name written so plainly. *Of Montfort.* She truly has let go of what she was, and—she's embracing what we can be.

Tears prick my eyes, and her hand tightens in my own.

Evangeline Samos of Montfort.

Elane Haven of Montfort.

"And the abdication letter?" I say thickly, trying to keep the tears at bay.

Her jaw tightens, but she dips her head in acknowledgment. "I'll read it myself."

All the tension of the last few days unwinds, and a pressing weight lifts from my shoulders. I almost sigh in relief. Instead I jump to my feet, my robe swirling around me as I head for the closet.

"I guess it's a good thing I've already packed."

It's sunset, red and cold, by the time we reach the airfield cut into the slopes of Ascendant. The pines seem to lean in, watching as the four of us clamber out of our transport and onto the tarmac. We are very much behind schedule, but no one seems to mind. Not Ptolemus, not our Montfort pilots and escort, not even Carmadon and Premier Davidson, who have come to see us off. They stand out sharply from their crowd of retainers—Carmadon in his white suit, and the premier with his familiar, inscrutable smile. Neither looks surprised by Evangeline's presence, as if they knew she would change her mind.

Though Ptolemus will be the first to abdicate and is still the heir to the Rift, he walks behind Evangeline, letting her set our pace. She walks quickly, eager to be done with this already. Though she certainly looks the part of a princess. Her battered training suit has been discarded for black leather leggings, a matching jacket, and a silver cape that ripples like liquid mercury. It could be, for all I know. The rest of us are equally dressed. Ptolemus is in a uniform, with a cape to match Evangeline's, while Wren wears a gown patterned in red and silver, the colors of House Skonos. I don't favor my house colors tonight. Instead of black, my dress is pale blue and gold, like clouds at dawn. It sets off my eyes.

Evangeline likes it, and she isn't trying to hide the sentiment. She glances back at me as we walk, running her eyes over my outfit with eager satisfaction.

Our escort of Montfort guards and diplomats wastes no time boarding the waiting jet, barely acknowledging the premier before disappearing up the steps. Evangeline tries to do the same, sidestepping Carmadon's outstretched hand, but the premier is a difficult man to ignore. He doesn't block her path and gives her the chance to avoid him.

She is wise enough not to.

Good, I think, watching as she clasps his arm. She begrudges the action but allows it just the same. The premier is the best ally we have here, and she needs to be civil. Even with his offer of employment hanging over my head.

They mutter to each other, dropping their voices so as not to be heard. I hope she tells him about her message to Iris. Not to get his permission, but to show her intentions. I have no doubt the letter will be intercepted and read, and I'd rather the premier know what Eve is up to beforehand.

Ptolemus and Wren are brief with Carmadon. He's too talkative for their taste, but I quite enjoy his company. I grin when he takes my hands, surveying my brightly colored clothing with a genuine smile.

"You look like a winter sunrise, Lady Haven," he says, kissing me on one cheek.

"Well, one of us had to bring a little color," I reply, glancing at his white suit.

He wags a dark-skinned finger at me in jest. "You must be certain to visit us, after all this is done and you're settled in the city."

"Of course. At the premier's pleasure," I add, sweeping into the curtsy I've performed since I could walk.

"Aren't we all," he mutters under his breath. He even winks, up to his old tricks. But there's something beneath his usual jest. A deeper acknowledgment.

I wonder if he feels the same kinship I do. I'm a child compared to him—Carmadon is easily three decades older than me—but we were both born to different worlds from the one we live in now. And we both love people the old world told us we couldn't. Great people, who cast long shadows. We're both content, if not happy, to stand in their darkness.

That's what Evangeline is. Greatness. Strong, proud—ruthless, even. And undeniably great. Not just on the battlefield, where she is formidable, to say the least. The letter is proof of that. Even in her weakest moments, I see it. The ability to push forward and through where most would admit defeat. Not for the first time today, I find myself staring at her, still locked in whispered conversation with the premier. Carmadon follows my gaze, but his eyes flicker to his husband quickly. We watch them both, staring down a winding path with no end in sight.

Where will these people lead us?

It doesn't matter.

I'll always go.

The premier merely takes my hand when I pass him. We exchange nods of greeting, but little more.

"We'll talk soon," he says quietly, and his meaning is clear.

The offer of work.

Evangeline doesn't miss it, though she's already climbing the stairs into the jet. She freezes momentarily, her back stiffening. Her metallic cape ripples like the surface of a disturbed pond.

"Soon," I echo to the premier, if only to be polite.

Truthfully, I wish I could shove him for being so blatant.

The last thing I need is any more tension with Evangeline. This is going to be difficult enough.

FIVE
Evangeline

I should sleep.

The flight to the Rift is several hours long, over the flat, empty fields of Prairie and then the winding borders of the Disputed Lands. It's too dark to see anything out the jet window, and even the stars seem distant and dull. I won't be able to tell when we cross into my father's former kingdom, the land I grew up in. It's been months since I last set foot in Ridge House, my family's ancestral home. Before my father died, before Archeon fell. Before I was free to love who I chose and go where I wanted. The Ridge was beautiful, a sanctuary away from the razor-edged life of court, but it was a prison too.

Elane dozes on my shoulder, her cheek pressed against the soft leather of my coat. When she's asleep, her abilities disappear, leaving her bare of her usual glow. I don't mind. She looks lovely either way. And I like being able to glimpse behind her shield of soft light and perfect complexion. She's vulnerable in those moments, and it means she feels safe.

That's why I'm doing this, more than any other reason. To keep her safe.

And to bargain.

We'll talk soon.

The premier's words still echo.

I should focus on my speech, the broadcast, and denying my blood tomorrow, but I can't get rid of Davidson's words.

When Elane told me about his offer, I thought about packing our things. We wouldn't need much. Fine gowns and pretty clothing have no use in the wilderness. All I needed was a good stockpile of metals, some training gear. Rations, of course. I still think about it sometimes, ticking off the list of what to bring if we have to run. A force of habit, I think, after the months of war and risk. It isn't in me to trust anyone outside my small circle. Not yet, at least.

"Please don't," I asked her, holding her hands in mine. The sun was bright through the windows in our salon, but I remember feeling cold.

"It's just a job, Eve," she said, almost scolding me. "He wants me to be an aide. To accompany him like those newbloods. Watch his back, keep my ears open. He knows I have experience in Silver courts—I'll be good at dealing with the Silvers here in Montfort. I know what they come from, how they think. It's not like I haven't done the same before."

For you. I hear it in the spaces between her words. Yes, she's spied for me in the past. Yes, she's risked her life for mine, to help me and my family push pieces along. She spied on Maven more than once, and that was certainly a death sentence if she was caught.

"It's not the same, Elane." *He doesn't value your life the way I do.* "You'll sit in the corner at first, quiet and invisible. Then he'll ask you to go places he can't, or won't. To watch, report back. You'll spy on his political opponents, his military generals, his allies—and maybe his enemies too. Each assignment more dangerous than the last." I tightened my grip on her, already feeling her slip away. Already I could picture Davidson convincing her to *check up* on a raider camp or the court of a Prairie warlord. "You're a shadow, my love. Just think of what he'll use you for."

Her fingers ripped from mine. "Some of us are more than just our ability, Samos."

I remember the sting of her voice, so sharp and so final. I expected her to march down to the premier's office and accept the position on the spot. But she didn't then, and she hasn't yet. It's been a long month since he offered her a place in Montfort, a permanent one. No matter how much she wants to fit in the mountains, she still waits.

For you.

I tip my head back, leaning against the wall of the jet. It isn't fair, to hold her back. We will both need to pull our weight soon, and she's right: she's done this before. In more dangerous places, with worse consequences. *Surely the premier will protect her?*

Don't be so naive, Evangeline.

Montfort isn't Norta, but Montfort isn't without its dangers either.

"You should rest," Ptolemus whispers across the aisle, pulling me out of my thoughts. He doesn't look up from the papers in front of him, scraps covered in his untidy scrawl. Our speeches won't be long by any account, but he agonizes over his anyway. His tiny lamp illuminates the otherwise dark interior of the jet, punctuated only by the low lights along the ceiling and in the cockpit.

The Montfort delegates are all dozing, clustered at the back of the craft to give us space.

I shake my head, unwilling to speak and disturb Elane. Wren is out cold too, sprawled across the seats facing Ptolemus, curled beneath a fur-lined blanket, her face buried against the cool air.

My brother glances at me sideways, his eyes catching the weak light. He looks me over for too long, but I have nowhere to run. I can only let him look.

I wonder if the Ridge is still standing. With my father dead, I can only imagine what disarray our home has fallen into. Silver nobles fighting to fill the hole he left. Reds rising up to join the Guard, or the Nortan States, or carve out their own place. Part of me hopes the sprawling estate has been burned to the ground. The rest aches to see those rooms of steel and glass, looking out on marching hills and valleys.

My chest tightens as my mind dances around the inevitable question. I try to avoid it, edging the center of a whirlpool. It never fails to pull me under.

"Do you think she'll be there?" I rasp, and Elane shifts, but doesn't wake.

Ptolemus's gaze sharpens, one eyebrow raised.

The words almost stick in my mouth. "Our mother?"

He doesn't answer.

He doesn't know.

I expect shame. Regret. Relief. Fear. But when I set foot on the airfield tarmac and breathe my first gasp of Rift air, the only thing I can think of is teeth. Wolf's teeth. Pressing into my neck, not breaking skin but holding me down, pinning me in place.

I only made it a few feet.

For a split second, I'm on the floor again, my cheek pressed against cold tile. My parents loom over me, their faces pulled in matching scowls of disgust. I betrayed them. I attacked my father. I tried to run.

I didn't get far. My mother's wolves made sure of that. She could have made them tear me apart if she'd wanted. Larentia Viper is no woman to trifle with, though I certainly tried.

Ptolemus is the only reason she didn't drag me home by my ankles, wolves snapping at me all the way. If not for his interference—if he hadn't knocked my father out cold, and killed the wolf holding me in place—I don't want to imagine where I'd be now.

Back here, I think, looking at the hills rising around the airfield.

Autumn has come to the Rift as well, dappling the green forests with orange and red. A breeze shudders the leaves, making the morning sunlight dance across the treetops. In the distance, I can just make out Ridge House sprawled across the crest of a hill. It looks small and unimportant, a dark smudge against brighter color.

Elane steps down from the jet after me, following my gaze. She heaves a heavy sigh and nudges me toward the waiting transports, her hand a gentle guide. Ptolemus and Wren are already there, clambering into the first vehicle. The rest of the Montfort delegates and guards head for the second transport, allowing us time alone. I expected at least one of them to follow, if only to observe. After all, we are the heirs to this kingdom, the surviving children of Volo Samos. For all they know, we could be planning to take up our birthright before the eyes of a continent.

It's almost insulting, that no one sees us as threats anymore.

Wren is still yawning when I climb up and into the transport, sliding onto the seat across from her. Her Skonos colors look darker this morning, her gown a bloodred scarlet and iron gray. She's ready to stand and watch, resolute in her support of Tolly's choice to abdicate. Elane will do the same with me. She favored the lovely blue-and-gold dress yesterday, and now she wears a gown beaded with rose and blush pearls. Her own message is clear. The old house ways, the colors, the alliances and stratifications of nobility, are no more to her. House Haven is not her family or her future.

The same cannot be said of me, or Ptolemus. House Samos abdicates a throne in an hour, and we must look like House Samos to do so. Our armored clothing is polished mirror and chrome, matching our silver hair and storm-cloud eyes. I clatter every time I move, disturbing the many rings, bracelets, earrings, and necklaces dangling off my body. I was raised to such pageantry, and this might be my very last parade.

"Will you rehearse?" I ask my brother, raising my chin. He finished the speech on the flight but never read it aloud.

Ptolemus nearly rolls his eyes. With his hair slicked back, he still looks like a prince. Or a king. "Will you?"

Smirking, I settle back in my seat, hands folded neatly in my lap. My sharp rings click together as the transport roars over the tarmac. "I'm glad I get to go second. You're an easy act to follow."

"Is that a challenge?" he replies.

I shrug, enjoying our game. Anything to distract from the familiar land speeding by in the window. "Just an observation."

Wren puts a hand to Tolly's shoulder, letting her long fingers drape against his armor. She brushes away an invisible piece of dust.

"It won't take very long," she says. Her eyes tick over my brother, looking for any sign of imperfection or flaw. Her touch is soft and familiar when she turns his face, running both thumbs over the gray circles under his eyes. Her black skin is dark against his as she wipes away any physical sign of exhaustion. The circles disappear beneath her ability. Suddenly he looks as if he spent the night in a palace instead of a cramped jet. "Especially since the others won't be speaking."

"Others?" My jaw tightens, as does my chest. Next to me, Elane draws in a sharp breath, and her eyes dart to mine. She looks as confused as I feel. "Tolly, I don't like surprises. Especially today."

He doesn't look away from Wren. "Don't worry—it's no one you haven't fought before."

"That doesn't exactly narrow it down," I mutter. My brain spins through the possibilities.

Mare comes to mind first, but she is far away, still recuperating in a Montfort valley where no one can reach her. When she returns to civilization, the entire country will know it.

Before I can possibly begin to list the many, many people I've sparred with, fought, and maimed, the answer quite literally flies by. Two air transports buzz us as we begin the climb up the hills, drowning out all conversation for a moment. I press my forehead to the window, feeling the heavy drone in my teeth as well as with my ability. The aircraft aren't carrying any heavy weaponry that I can sense.

"Scarlet Guard," I breathe, noting the torn crimson sun stamped on the side of the lead craft. The other might as well be dripping fresh paint. Its tail is marked with a new emblem. Three circles linked together—one red, one silver, one white. For each kind of blood. Woven as equals. "And the Nortan States."

I know exactly who will be waiting for us at Ridge House, standing in the shell of my old life.

Normally the drive from the airfield to the estate is too long, but today I wish it wouldn't end. We summit the rolling hills in what feels like a few seconds, with the familiar gates of the old palace looming through the trees. I lower my eyes as we pass through, unable to glance at the imposing façade of glass and steel.

I could shut my eyes if I wanted, and navigate the halls without any difficulty. It would be easy to walk to the throne room without even looking up. A coward would do it.

Instead I barely blink, and let everyone see me as I step down into the wide, leafy courtyard. A stream runs through, winding beneath fluid iron bridges as it tumbles from the spring near the center of Ridge House. The flowers and trees are the same as I remember, unchanged but for the brush of autumn's fire. I glimpse familiar walls through the plant life, and instinctively remember the rooms looking down on the receiving courtyard. Guest chambers, the servant halls, galleries, guardrooms, a statuary. Nothing looks amiss. War has not reached the Ridge. It seems we have stepped back in time.

But that isn't true. Before my father died, there were only Silvers flanking the doors. Warriors loyal to House Samos. Now there is only Scarlet Guard. Their crimson and cardinal scarves hang proudly, impossible to ignore. They watch, hard-eyed, as we approach.

The Montfort delegates are first to enter Ridge House, leading us all in their white or forest-green clothing. Their own guards are meant for us as well, and they are attentive as we walk. Some are Reds; some are newbloods; some are Silvers. All are armed in their own way, ready to fight should the need arise. I pity anyone who decides to attack Ptolemus and me here, in a place we know so well. There is no sense in fighting a magnetron in a palace made of steel. Even my Samos cousins would not try. They might be stupid enough to attempt a coup in my name, but they aren't suicidal.

The air inside Ridge House tastes stale and old, shocking me from my ruminations. While the Ridge itself is intact, I immediately see the decay all around us. Even in a few months' time so much has changed. Dust coats the usually pristine walls. Most of the rooms branching off the entrance hall are dark. My home, or this part of it, is abandoned.

Elane grips my hand tightly, her touch cool against mine. I'm suddenly aware of the flush crawling beneath my skin, making me sweat. I squeeze back, grateful for her presence.

Cords of wire almost blend into the stonework beneath our feet, winding through the shadows at the base of the wall to my left. It leads to the throne room, already prepared for what we must do and what we must say. The Sunset Stretch was our receiving hall once, before my father decided to call himself a king. It still holds our thrones now, along with a great deal else. I can feel the machinery from here. Cameras, broadcasting equipment, lightning. Aluminum, iron, edged with absences that can only be plastic or glass.

I don't hesitate, as much as I want to. There are too many eyes, Montfort and Scarlet Guard. Too much risk in appearing weak. And the pressure of an audience has always made me a better performer.

Unlike the rest of the Ridge, my father's throne room is pristine. The windows have been cleaned, offering a clear view over the valley and the Allegiant River. Everything gleams beneath the too-bright lights the broadcast crew has assembled, now pointed at the raised platform where my family once sat. Whoever cleaned was very thorough, scouring everything from floor to ceiling. I assume it was the Scarlet Guard. Reds have more practice with such things.

The Nortan States didn't send much of a delegation. I only count two of them. They don't have uniforms, not like Montfort or the Guard. But it's easy to tell who represents the new country to the east, still rebuilding itself from the ashes of the old. And these two are even easier to recognize. While the Guard busies themselves arranging cameras and perfecting their lightning, the two Nortans hang back. Not to avoid the work, but to avoid getting in the way.

I don't blame them. Julian Jacos and Tiberias Calore are useless here, reduced to spectators. They look even more out of place than the armed Reds scuffing up my mother's floors.

I haven't seen Cal since his last visit to Montfort. And that was brief, only a few days. Barely enough time to shake hands with the premier and exchange pleasantries at one of Carmadon's dinners. He's been busy shoring up alliances and relationships, acting as a go-between for the Silver nobles of his former kingdom and the new government taking shape. Not an easy job, by any means. He's exhausted—anyone can see that—his burning eyes ringed by dark shadows. Sometimes I wonder if he'd rather be at the head of an army instead of the negotiating table.

He catches my eye and the corner of his mouth twitches, the best smile he can muster.

I do the same, ducking my head.

How far the two of us have come from Queenstrial.

Cal isn't my future anymore, and for that I am eternally grateful.

It's the uncle who worries me, making my stomach swoop.

Jacos stands as he always does, looking small at Cal's shoulder. The singer stares at the floor, unwilling to meet my gaze or my brother's. I can't tell if it's guilt or pity guiding him. After all, he killed our father. Sometimes Jacos is in my nightmares, his teeth fanged, his tongue like a snake. So different from the bookish, unassuming reality.

When we approach, Julian is good enough to excuse himself, head still bowed. Only Wren gives him a smile as we pass, small as it is. One of her cousins is his companion, and even with the Nortan court in ruins, the bonds of the old nobility still hold tight.

Ptolemus reaches Cal first, clasping his hand firmly as he offers the warmest smile he can muster. No mean feat for my brother. Cal responds in kind, lowering his chin.

"Thank you for doing this, Ptolemus," he says, one abdicated king to another. Cal looks odd in his plain jacket, without a uniform dripping with medals. Especially in comparison to my brother, all dressed up in his colors and armor.

Tolly releases his grip. "And thank *you* for coming. It wasn't necessary."

"Of course it is," Cal replies, his tone light. "It's an exclusive club you're joining. I have to be on hand to welcome you into the Abdicators."

My lip curls. All the same, I take Cal's arm, pulling him into a stiff but quick embrace. "Please don't start calling us that," I growl.

"I think it has a nice ring to it," Elane interjects. She tips her head, finding the light. Everyone else looks skeletal or garish beneath the harsh fluorescent of the lighting gear, but of course she doesn't. "Good to see you, Cal."

"And you, Elane. All of you," he adds, his eyes sweeping over me to Wren. They keep moving, searching the room. Hunting for someone else.

But Mare Barrow isn't here.

"Are you all the States sent to witness?" I ask, and he looks glad for the question. Happy to change the subject, happy for a distraction.

"No, the other representatives are with General Farley," he replies. "Two Red organizers, the newblood Ada Wallace, and one of the former governor Rhambos's children." With a twist of his fingers, he points to the far side of the throne room. I don't bother to turn. I'll see them in a moment. And truthfully, I don't want to look and find Diana Farley staring daggers at Ptolemus. My stomach twists the way it usually does whenever I'm near the Red general. *Stop it,* I tell myself. I'm already afraid of the cameras. I don't have the energy to be afraid of her too.

"Wren said you wouldn't be speaking . . . ?" I say, my voice trailing off.

"Correct." Cal crosses his arms over his chest and settles into a stance I know well. He's battle ready. "We won't be on the broadcast either. Sends the wrong message."

His logic isn't difficult to follow. "Ah. You want the country to see us do this of our own volition. No sword hanging over our heads." I wince as soon as the words are out of my mouth, and so does Cal. I imagine he's thinking of the moment a sword cut through his father's neck. "Sorry, bad turn of phrase."

He waves me off, though his face pales. "We're just here for support, mostly," Cal mutters.

I blink at him, brow furrowed. "For us?" I scoff.

He shakes his head. "For them." His eyes dart across the throne room, toward the far end, still empty of equipment. A small crowd waits by the windows, packed tightly together like a flock of brightly colored birds. Suddenly I feel like I might vomit, and I search for a familiar silhouette, a panther on her heels. But my mother isn't with the Silver nobles.

Elane is not so lucky. She draws in a shaking breath when she spots her father.

Jerald Haven speaks quietly with the nobles of the Rift, and a few of old Norta too. None of House Samos that I can see, but I recognize Lord General Laris, an ally of my father's and the former commander of the Nortan Air Fleet. None of them will look at us. They refuse. They don't approve of what we're doing, but they certainly can't stop us either.

Elane looks away first, her face clear. No blush, no paling cheeks. As far as I know, she hasn't seen her father in months. They've spoken only in a few letters, and those were short, terse, and on Jerald's end downright insulting. He wanted her to come home, and she always refused. Eventually he stopped asking, and stopped writing.

The sight of him incenses me, knowing how much pain he caused her. As usual, Cal is woefully bad at reading women, and he mistakes my anger. The former king nudges my arm.

"It's all right. Don't let them scare you. The same was done to me, when I abdicated," he says, his voice low and thick. "My grandmother couldn't speak to me for days."

I resist the very familiar urge to roll my eyes at Tiberias Calore.

Wren raises an eyebrow. "But she came around?" The hope in her voice is small, and ill advised. I know enough of Anabel Lerolan to understand that.

Cal almost laughs. "Not really, no. She accepts it, though. She doesn't have a choice. The Burning Crown dies with me, and there will be no other to rebuild the throne I broke."

Not while you live, I want to say. For such a brilliant military strategist, Cal can be terribly shortsighted. *Pretenders will come. They'll do it here, and they'll do it in Norta. This won't be over until long after we are dead.*

Someone else might despair of such a notion. But somehow I find comfort in it. I'm choosing to step away because I can. And if someone else comes to claim the crown I throw away, so be it. That isn't on my shoulders. I've done all I can to make sure of that.

"Our people need to see we're united in this," Cal murmurs. He still watches the Silvers, eyes alight as if he can burn them away. "That we're ready to let go of the old world. Together."

As simple as his platitudes are, I certainly can't argue with them. Or deny the surge of emotion deep in my chest.

My smile is true and wide. "Yes, we are."

SIX
Evangeline

I don't move as my brother gives his speech, which is a little rushed but otherwise perfect, in short, decisive words. He looks straight ahead, unblinking, sitting at a plain desk drawn up before our old steel thrones. I remain at his side, the two of us alone before the broadcast. The rest of the throne room is deathly quiet, watching history unfold before them.

"My name is Ptolemus Escarian Samos, King of the Rift and Lord of House Samos. Son of the late King Volo Samos of the Rift, and Queen Larentia of House Viper. I hereby abdicate the throne of the Kingdom of Rift and renounce any claim I, or my descendants, might have on this country or land. It is my solemn wish that the Kingdom of the Rift be dissolved, as it was created by illegal secession from the former Kingdom of Norta, and be absorbed back into the boundaries of the Nortan States. I hope I live to see this land thrive beneath a free government and an equality of all blood."

Though he is throwing away his crown, Ptolemus has never looked or sounded more like a king. He stares down the whirring camera for a long moment. Letting the broadcast spread across our country, into video screens in all our cities, so that everyone—Red and Silver and newblood—might know. It won't stay within the borders of our country for long. The Lakelands will know within minutes, and Piedmont too. The Nortan States are already rumbling with abdication after Cal stepped down. Another broken throne could spark celebrations or riots.

Elane stays as close to me as she can, just out of the camera's line of sight. I don't look at her directly, but her red hair, glowing in the morning light, is difficult to mistake at the edge of my vision. Her father and his Silver supporters are more obvious. They position themselves directly in my eye line, clustered behind the camera in the middle of the long throne room. I stare through them, the way my mother taught me.

The Scarlet Guard brass keep to the sidelines, some leaning against the wall. General Farley looks rigid and tense, her eyes on her feet. She either can't or won't watch my brother speak, and for that I am grateful. The less attention she gives him, the safer he'll be.

Ptolemus doesn't flinch when he bends his head, raising the pen to sign the official declaration of abdication. His signature is sparse and sharp, impossible to miss. He leaves space below his name, enough for me to write my own.

I am queen now, for a few strange, stretching seconds. I feel different, and also the same. In between, hovering at the threshold of two very different doors. In an instant, I see inside both and what they hold for me. What heartaches and triumphs there could be, in the lives of a commoner or a queen. I tremble as I look at Elane, letting myself find refuge in her. The choice is crystal clear.

When Ptolemus stands up from his chair, the Silver supporters' attention shifts as one, and every eye lands on me. I feel each of them, a needle in my skin. I don't need to be a whisper to know what they're begging me to do.

Refuse to kneel.

I find Cal, half obscured by the sunlight pouring in from the windows. He leans up against the glass, arms crossed over his jacket. I feel a pull of kinship to him, a weight we both know and share. Slowly, he dips his chin an inch. As if I need his encouragement.

I sit slowly, gracefully, my face schooled into a cold mask of content. My mercurial cape drapes over one shoulder, pooling at my feet.

"My name is Evangeline Artemia Samos, Queen of the Rift." In spite of all my courtly training, I can't keep the tremor from my voice when I say those words. *Queen. Without a king, without a father, without a master. Without any rules but the ones I would make for myself.*

A fantasy. A lie. There are always rules and always consequences. I want no part of this. No crown is worth the price I would pay. I steady myself with thoughts of Elane, and the flash of red in the corner of my eye.

"Lady of House Samos. Daughter of the late King Volo Samos of the Rift, and Queen Larentia of House Viper. I hereby abdicate the throne of the Kingdom of Rift and renounce any claim I, or my descendants, might have on this country or land."

In the end, our speeches had to be nearly identical. Very little can be left to chance or interpretation here. Neither of us can allow any room for misunderstanding, willful or otherwise.

"It is my solemn wish that the Kingdom of the Rift be dissolved, as it was created by illegal secession from the former Kingdom of Norta, and absorbed back into the boundaries of the Nortan States. I hope I live to see this land thrive beneath a free government and an equality of all blood."

Slowly, I take up the pen, still warm from my brother's grip. The page on the desk is crisp, a sheet of white printed with the same words we just spoke. The colors of House Samos, black and silver, are stamped at the bottom. I stare at it, feeling unfinished. Then I look up again, finding the eye of the camera, one of thousands of eyes now watching me.

Something flutters in the window, catching my attention for a split second.

The moth is small, its wings gleaming between green and black like a pool of oil. It shouldn't be out in daylight. Moths are nocturnal creatures, better accustomed to islands of light amid darkness. They also have remarkable hearing. All this passes through my mind in an instant, and the pieces click together neatly.

My mother is watching.

The wolf is at my throat again, its teeth sharp and digging. It threatens to rip me in two. Only the camera, the audience, the eyes of so many keep me rooted to the spot. The familiar fear and shame claw up my spine, poisoning my insides, but I cannot let them see. I cannot let her stop me now. There is still more to say and more of her dreams for me to ruin.

Under the desk, my hand curls into a fist. For once it isn't rage driving me, but resolve.

I have only ever thought the words I speak next. Never even whispered them. Let alone spoken them to an audience, of ten or ten thousand. Let alone said them to my mother. That woman is always listening, and perhaps now she will finally hear me.

"Hereafter, I shall be known as Evangeline Samos of Montfort, and

I swear my allegiance to the Free Republic, where I can live and love freely. I renounce my citizenship in the Rift, in Norta, and in any country where people are caged for the circumstances of birth."

The pen scratches across the page, nearly ripping it in two with the force of my flourishing signature. Heat bleeds over my cheeks, but my makeup is thick enough to hide any flush that might betray my thundering heart. A buzzing sound rises around me, drowning out the whir of machines. I keep steady and do as I was told. Hold eye contact. Stare. Wait for the signal. The lens of the camera seems to swallow the world; the edges of my vision go soft.

One of the Red technicians fusses with the camera, flicking switches while motioning for Ptolemus and me to remain still. I feel the vibrations of the machine cease as the broadcast ends, cutting to black everywhere but here. The Red lowers his finger and we are released, exhaling in unison.

It's over and done with.

With a burst of concentration, I shred the steel chair behind me, letting my throne collapse into a pile of needles. It doesn't take much energy—steel is familiar to me—but I feel exhausted afterward and lean forward on my elbows.

The Reds and the Scarlet Guard shrink back a little, wary of the outburst. The Silver nobles look only disgusted, though none would dare say so to our faces. With a sneer, Jerald makes for his daughter, but Elane avoids him neatly.

She is quick to take my shoulder, and her hand trembles against my skin, quivering.

"Thank you," she breathes, so only I can hear. "Thank you, my love. My iron heart."

The lights of the room seem to collect in her skin. She is dazzling, glowing, a beacon calling me home.

It wasn't just for you, I want to say, but my mouth won't open. *It was for me.*

In the window, the moth is gone.

And for her.

Like the rest of the estate, the sculpture garden is abandoned, and somewhat overgrown without a greenwarden's touch. Carmadon could do wonderful things here. One side offers a commanding view of the valley, down to the Allegiant. Every statue seems bigger and more foreboding than I remember, frozen in arcs of steel and chrome, resolute iron, proud copper, even polished silver and gold. I draw my fingers along them as I walk, rippling each one. Some dance at my command, re-forming into swooping curves or spindles thin as thread. Using my ability for artistry is cathartic, a release of tension that I can usually only find in the training arena. I spend long minutes alone, molding everything to my liking. I need to relax as much as I can, if the next obstacle is to be hurdled.

I must face her alone. Without any crutch. Not Elane, not Ptolemus. It would be too tempting to let them fight this battle for me. And that is not a habit I want to make.

She is waiting for me in a place I love. To taint it. To hurt me. She looks small without her usual creatures, almost hidden in the shadows of a steel arch. No panther, no wolf. Not even the moth. She wants to face me alone. Even her clothes seem dull, an echo compared to the jewels, silks, and furs I remember. Now her dress is simple, a fine dark green, and I glimpse leggings beneath her skirts. Larentia Viper is on the move. I imagine she's allied with Jerald and the other Silvers, opposing us in sentiment but unable to do so openly.

The wind rustles through her black hair, and I glimpse streaks of gray I've never seen before.

"You knew what they were going to do to him."

The accusation hits like a sledgehammer. I keep my distance.

"You knew that woman, and that weakling, that coward of a librarian, were going to kill your father." Her teeth gleam, a predator's snarl. Without her animals to control, my mother is quite vulnerable. Powerless against me, in a garden brimming with my own weapons. It doesn't deter her in the slightest. She moves swiftly, almost hissing as she stops inches from my face. "Do you have anything to say for yourself, Evangeline?"

My voice rasps. "I gave you both a chance."

It's the truth. I told them I was leaving. Told them I wanted no part of their schemes anymore. That my life was my own and no one else's. And my own mother sent a pair of wolves to hunt me down. My own father sneered at my heartache. No matter how much I loved them both, or how much they loved me, it wasn't enough.

My mother's lips quiver and her eyes dart. She searches me down to the bone. "I hope the shame follows you into your grave."

It will, I think. *It always will.*

"But that grave will be far away," I whisper. I'm taller than she is, but she still makes me feel small. "On a mountaintop you will never see. With Elane right beside me."

Her green eyes snap with fury. "And your brother too."

"His choices are his own."

For a moment, her voice breaks. "You couldn't even leave me my son." I wish I couldn't hear her, or see into her eyes so clearly. There's so much anger, so much pain. And realization too. My mother is alone in the world now, cut off from the pack. Forever. Despite all she's done and all the hurt she has caused me, I can't help but feel pity.

"One day, I hope you might see things differently." My offer is shaky at best. Without any guarantee. "And there will be a place for you." I couldn't imagine her in Montfort if I tried.

She finds the notion just as preposterous as I do. "Not in that cursed place you call home," she sneers, turning away. Her shoulders rise with tension, bony and sharp beneath her gown. "Not the way you are, without pride or honor or even your name. Living so *openly.* Where is your *shame*?"

I've lost count of how many times my mother has mourned my *flaw.* The person I was born as, the inclinations I cannot change and will never deny again. Still, hearing her disappointment never gets easier. To know she sees what I am as a failure—it is so difficult to bear.

I swallow around the lump in my throat, unable to speak for fear of crying. I won't do that in front of her. She doesn't deserve my tears or my pity or my love, small as it may be.

Larentia raises her head, her back still turned. Her body shudders as she heaves a delicate breath. "This is the last time you will ever see me." Never have I heard a voice so empty. "I wash my hands of you both. My children are dead."

In my hand, my bracelet twists and trembles, running lazy ripples over my pale skin. The distraction helps me think straight. "Then stop chasing ghosts," I murmur. And turn away.

I don't sleep again until I'm home, in the mountains, in Montfort, with Elane's arms around me and the red light of sunset washing over my face. Thoughts of war and of our future drift and pass me by. They can wait. We'll tackle them together, Elane and I. Find the middle ground and compromise.

For now I can rest, and heal my iron heart.

FIRE LIGHT

ONE
Mare

I had my pick of days, but in the end, the snow made the decision for me.

All the better. The choice was out of my hands. How long to stay, when to return to the Montfort capital—those questions disappeared when the weather turned. It was only six inches, barely a dusting for a place like the Paradise Valley, but more would follow. I'd been told the winters here were much harsher than those I was used to, worse even than the one we weathered at the Notch. Here the snowdrifts pile up ten feet deep; rivers freeze solid; blizzards last for days on end. Too perilous for transports or dropjets. Of course, we could stay for the season if we wanted. Davidson made it clear in his last communication that the cabin outpost was at our disposal as long as we needed, but I didn't even broach the subject with the rest of my family. None of us, myself included, have any desire to spend the winter buried in snow with only the geysers and the bison for company.

Outside the cabin, Bree makes a show of digging out the front door while our father supervises, leaning on his shovel. They spent all morning clearing a path through the snow to the dropjet landing field, and their faces are red beneath their scarves and hats. Tramy helps Mom pack for the flight south, following her from room to room. She tosses clothes and he catches, folding them on the run. Gisa and I watch from the stone-walled kitchen, our things already packed away. We wear matching knobbly sweaters and curl around hot mugs for warmth. Gisa's cup has cocoa thick as pudding and just as sweet. Though it smells divine, I stick to tea and honey. I'm getting over a cold, and I don't want to return to Montfort with a scratchy throat.

Certainly I'll have to make the rounds of speech and conversation once we arrive. While I'm happy to go back to Ascendant, the capital, it means returning in time for the growing chaos of a gala with the alliance. And I'd rather do it at full strength.

Especially if Cal is there, I think, taking another boiling sip. The heat makes me shiver down to my toes.

Gisa watches me shrewdly over her mug and stirs the cocoa with a spoon. Her lips curve into a smirk. "Counting down the seconds?" she asks, her voice low enough to not be overheard by the whirlwind in the next room.

"Yes," I reply bluntly. "I'm already mourning the loss of some peace and quiet."

She licks the spoon clean and somehow gets a fleck of cocoa over her eyebrow. "Oh please, you're going insane up here. Don't think I didn't notice the little bit of lightning swirling around with the snowstorm yesterday."

Insane. I wince. I've known very few people to whom that word could be properly applied, and one in particular still unsettles me to my core.

The tea seems to freeze in my stomach.

When we first came here, I told myself it was so we could heal and mourn together. And so I could forget. Put aside all the things Maven did to me and I did to him. Instead, barely a day goes by without me agonizing over him and his fate. Whether he deserved it or not. If I made the right choice. If he could have been saved.

I still remember the small dagger in his hand, the pressure of him holding me down. *It was you or him*, I tell myself for the thousandth time this morning. No matter what, it always feels like a lie. *You or him*.

My sister reads my silence with a keen eye. She's good at deciphering my emotions, as much as I try to keep them hidden. She knows when to push me on them. And when to let me be. Today must be the latter.

"Are you finished?" she says, gesturing to my mug.

I nod and drain the rest of the liquid. It scalds its way down my throat. "Thanks."

She bustles to the deep sink and sets to scrubbing the last of our dishes. After a second, I follow, putting away the dried plates from breakfast. I wonder if anyone else will come up here in the next few months, or if we're the last faces the cabin will see until spring. It must be lovely up here in winter, albeit difficult to get to. And difficult to leave.

"Has anyone seen my socks?" Bree howls from the sitting room, ignoring the chorus of protest from Mom and Tramy. He must be trailing snow all over the floor.

Gisa giggles into the soapy sink. "I burned them!" she yells back. "For the good of mankind!"

My laughter is silent these days, little more than a gasp of air and a tight smile that pulls at my scars. Still, my stomach tenses as I laugh quietly, almost doubling over with good ache. We were right to come here. To rebuild ourselves, to figure out who we are now, in spite of our missing pieces.

Shade might be buried a thousand miles away, but I feel him here with us. And for once, it doesn't make me entirely sad.

There wasn't much to pack. The furnishings, rations, everything down to the soap in the bathrooms, stays at the cabin. We only have our clothes and other personal items to worry about. Gisa easily has the most *stuff.* Her art supplies and sewing kit are probably the heaviest thing loaded into the dropjet waiting at the edge of the clearing. She worries over them like a nervous mother, keeping a close watch as the Montfort pilot tucks them in with the rest of our baggage. I'm surprised she didn't insist they travel in her lap. Mom and the boys are already inside, strapping themselves in away from the cold.

Dad stands back a little from the craft with me. He scrutinizes the frosty ground beneath us. I think he half expects a geyser to explode beneath our feet and blow the jet sky-high. It isn't an entirely ridiculous notion. Many of the clearings and basins throughout the Paradise Valley are pocked with geysers and hot springs, steaming even beneath the snow.

Our breath clouds in the air, a testament to the cold. I wonder if Ascendant will feel this frozen already. *It's only October.*

"Are you ready?" Dad says, his voice a low rumble barely audible over the jet engines as they spool up. On top of the drop, massive propellers whirl around at a quickening pace.

I want to tell him yes. I'm ready to go back. Ready to be Mare Barrow again, where all the world can see. Ready to return to the fight. Our work is far from over, and I can't spend the rest of my life surrounded by nothing but trees. It's a waste of my talent, my strength, and my influence. There's more that I can do, and more that I want from myself.

But that doesn't make me ready. Not by a long shot.

The pilot waves for us before I can speak, sparing me the pain of lying to my father.

It doesn't really matter. Dad knows the truth of it anyway. I feel it in the way he supports me as we walk, even though he's the one with a regrown leg.

Each step feels heavier than the last, the safety belt like a chain across my lap. And then we're flying, the ground disappearing beneath a bank of gray cloud as everything goes bright and empty.

I let my chin fall forward onto my chest, and I pretend to sleep. Even with my eyes shut, I can feel them all looking at me. Gauging my mental and physical state by the set of my shoulders or my jaw. I still have problems talking about the worries prancing around my head, so my family has to improvise. It's made for some very idiotic questions from Bree, who is without any kind of emotional sense. But the others have found ways, Gisa and my father especially.

The roar of the dropjet makes speaking difficult, and I only catch snippets of their conversations. Most are innocuous. Will we be staying in the same apartments at the premier's estate before moving to the new house? Is Gisa going to bring that shopgirl around to meet everyone? She doesn't want to talk about her, and Tramy is good enough to provide a change in subject. Instead, he needles our sister about wanting a new jacket for the upcoming gala. She huffs but agrees to make him one. Something embroidered with the wildflowers that dotted the Paradise Valley—purple and yellow, green too.

The gala. I haven't even begun to think about the specifics of the celebration. Needless to say, I'm not the only one returning to the capital this week. Part of me almost wonders if Davidson dispatched a storm up here to drive me back to the city. I wouldn't be upset if he did. It gave me a good excuse to return right now, in time for a gathering of so many.

The snow made the choice, not me.

Not the party.

And certainly not the lure of a young man with bronze eyes and a broken throne.

Kilorn is waiting when we land at Ascendant, to the surprise of exactly no one. I don't know if it's possible, but he looks taller than when I saw him last, only two months ago. He said he would visit us up north, but he never got the chance between his duties in Montfort and building his own life here. Cameron might have something to do with it too. She's acting as a go-between, with her father, bouncing between the Scarlet Guard, Montfort, and her home in the Nortan States, speaking up for the Red men and women of their tech town. They've been invaluable to the reconstruction effort in the States and smoothing over relations with the Republic. Kilorn waits alone, so Cameron must not be here yet, if she's coming at all. As much as I'd like to see her and hear of everything going on back east, I'm happy to get Kilorn to myself for a little bit.

He grins widely when he sees us, a tall figure on the landing ground. The jet propellers cast a furious wind, whipping Kilorn's tawny hair back and forth. I try not to rush to him and inflate his ego any more than it already is, but I can't help it. I'm eager to see him. And eager to get out of the cramped metal box we've been stuck in for three hours.

He embraces my mother first, always a gentleman with her. She's more of a mother to Kilorn than the woman who abandoned him years ago.

"You haven't been missing meals," Mom jokes, patting him on the stomach. Kilorn grins and flushes. Indeed he looks broader too, filled out by Montfort food and a less-than-lethal lifestyle. While I still kept to my running schedule up at the cabin, I don't think he can say the same. He looks healthy, normal—settled.

"You shouldn't call him fat, Mom," Gisa says teasingly, poking him in the side with a grin. "Even if it's true." Whatever schoolgirl crush she had on him, born of proximity, jealousy, or good old-fashioned *want*, is completely gone.

Mom swats her away, scolding. "Gisa! The boy finally looks like he's had a decent meal."

Not to be outdone, Kilorn musses Gisa's hair, sending red locks spilling from her perfect bun. "Hey, I thought you were the polite one in the family, Gee," he shoots back.

Bree hoists his pack up onto his shoulder. Then he elbows Gisa for good measure. "Try living in an isolated cabin with her for months. You'll lose all your illusions of the little madam."

Our sister doesn't bother shoving him back. Bree is nearly twice her size. Instead she folds her arms and turns up her nose as she stalks away. "You know," she calls over her shoulder, "I *was* going to make you a party jacket as well. But I guess I shouldn't bother!"

Bree is after her like a shot, already whining, while Tramy follows with a grin. He won't dare jeopardize his own outfit, so he keeps quiet. Mom and Dad follow along with shrugs of their own, content to watch everyone else scurry ahead, leaving me behind with Kilorn.

Thankfully, no one points out that *I've* somehow become the proper one in the family, what with my court training, my time spent masquerading as a princess, and my new affinity for silence. Such a change from the Stilts thief always covered in mud, sweat, and a foul temper. And Kilorn knows it. He eyes me thoughtfully, glancing over my clothes, my hair, my face. I look healthier than I did when I left, just like him.

"Well?" I hold out my arms and spin on the flat tarmac. My sweater, jacket, pants, and boots are all shades of gray or green, muted colors. I don't intend to attract more attention than I need to. "Are you done with your examination?"

"Yep."

"And what's the verdict?"

He waves for me to walk next to him. "Still look like a pain in the ass," he says as I match his pace.

I can't help the burst of warmth in my chest. "Excellent."

The Stilts was not a good place to grow up, but that doesn't mean there weren't good pieces. And I'm lucky enough to say those are still with me. Walking side by side with Kilorn, picking our way toward the city and the premier's estate, I'm reminded of days long ago, the little things that made them bearable.

Our path takes us above most of Ascendant, the city already shadowed by the shortening days. Lights pinprick the mountainside below, some moving back and forth, marking the major roads. The lake at the base of the city reflects it all like another sky, deep blue with yellow and red stars. We move slowly, letting my parents and siblings go ahead. I catch them staring at the surroundings as I am. We forgot how beautiful it was here, in an impossible city in an impossible country.

As much as I want to stop and take it all in, I have to focus more on my breathing than anything else. The electricity pulsing through the city is more than I've felt in months, even when we were caught beneath a passing thunderstorm. It taps at my senses, begging to be let in. Instead of shutting out the sensation, I let it flow through me, down to my toes. This is something the electricons taught me, months ago in another country, in what feels like another life. It's easier to flow than fight.

Kilorn watches me the entire time, green eyes dancing. I don't feel scrutinized, though. He isn't watching to make sure I keep control. He knows I don't need him to do that, or anyone else. I'm my own.

"So what am I walking into?" I mutter, noting the lights in the city. Some are transports, weaving among the streets. Others are windows, lamps, lanterns, flickering on as the afternoon gives way to purple dusk. How many belong to government officials or soldiers or diplomats? Visitors?

The premier's estate is above, the same as I remember. *Is he there already?*

"Things are buzzing up at the premier's," Kilorn replies, following my gaze. "And in the People's Assembly. I don't live up that way anymore, got a little place down the hill in the city, but it's hard not to notice the constant traffic going up the mountain. Representatives, mostly, their staff, some military filtering in. The Scarlet Guard mouthpieces arrived yesterday."

What about him?

Instead a different name falls off my tongue. It tastes like relief.

"Farley."

She's the closest thing I have to an older sister. I immediately wonder if she'll be up at the estate with us, or housed somewhere in the city. I hope the former, for my own sake as well as my mother's. Mom has been dying to see baby Clara and will probably end up sleeping wherever her grandchild is.

"Yep. Farley's already here, and already bossing everyone around. I'd take you to see her, but she's in meetings right now."

With the baby in her lap, no doubt, I think, remembering how Farley carted my niece into war councils. "And what's going on over in the Lakelands? There's still a war happening." *Here, there, everywhere.* It's impossible to ignore the threat still looming over all of us.

"On hold, more like." Kilorn glances at me and notes my confusion. "Didn't you read the reports Davidson sent you?"

I grit my teeth. I remember the packets, pages of typed information that arrived at the cabin every week. Dad spent more time with them than I did. Mostly I scanned for familiar names. "Some."

He smirks at me, shaking his head. "You haven't changed at all," he says with some pride.

Yes I have, I want to reply. I cannot even begin to list all the ways I have changed, but I let it go. I've only just arrived. I can give Kilorn a little time before I inundate him with my problems.

He doesn't allow me a chance to wallow.

"Basically, yes, we're still at odds." He holds out a hand, ticking off names on his fingers. "Lakelands and Piedmont against the Republic, the Guard, and the new Nortan States. But we're in a standoff for the moment. The Lakelands are still regrouping after Archeon, Piedmont isn't willing to strike alone, and the Nortan States aren't in any position to pursue or go on the offensive for now. We're all on the defensive, waiting for the other side to make a move."

I picture a map of the continent as we walk, with pieces upon it set in motion. Lines of division clearly drawn, armies waiting to march. *Waiting, waiting, waiting.* Somehow, up at the cabin, I could pretend that the rest of the world was moving on too. Recovering from the violence as I was. If I ignored the reports, avoided news from the south and east—it might just all come together without me. A sliver of me thought the war would end beyond my reach. But the war was hiding too, catching its breath as I was. *The bitch was waiting for me.*

"Lovely," I mutter, drawing out the word. The paved pathway is dotted with frost beneath the shadow of the pines, still clinging where the sun cannot reach. "So no progress made."

Kilorn shakes his head, laughing. "I didn't say that."

"It's fine." I shrug my shoulders with exaggerated motion. "I don't expect you to know anything of importance."

He gasps and puts a hand to his chest, the picture of wounded pride. His jaw drops open to hide a grin. "Excuse me, I am incredibly important to the cause. Who do you think helps Carmadon catch fish for his dinners?"

Who organizes charity drives for refugees in the Nortan States? Who petitions the Montfort government to aid war orphans scattered across the battlefields we made? Who all but sleeps in Representative Radis's office, working with officials both Silver and Red? Kilorn, of course, though he isn't the type to brag about such things, admirable as they may be. Strange, the most worthy people are often the least likely to say so.

"And at these dinners, do you ever find yourself in . . . female company?"

A scarlet flush swipes up his neck and onto his cheeks, but he doesn't dodge. Kilorn doesn't have to do that with me. "Cam isn't keen on parties," he mutters.

I don't blame you, Cameron.

"So you're . . . ?"

"We're spending time together when we can, that's all. She's got much bigger and more important priorities than me. But we write letters. She's better at it than I am." His tone is matter-of-fact, without a hint of jealousy or even annoyance over her time spent elsewhere. He knows Cameron has her hands more than full with the Nortan reconstruction. "And neither of us is a soldier. There's no pressure to rush into anything we aren't ready for."

He doesn't mean it as a rebuke. Still, it's impossible not to draw parallels to my own life. Every romance I've ever been involved in had a sword hanging over it. Sometimes quite literally. Cal kissed me when I was his brother's betrothed, before he was sent off to war. When I was a deadly secret hiding in plain sight. Maven loved me as he could beneath terrible circumstances, where death threatened me, and where Maven himself was the greatest threat of all. In truth, I don't know what it's like to be in love without a storm cloud overhead, ready to erupt. The closest I can think of is my time at the Piedmont base, days spent training with Cal. Training for war, of course, but at least we weren't afraid of dying in our sleep.

I snort at the thought. My definition of normal is incredibly screwed up.

The path curves downward, breaking into steps that wind through the high meadows above the city. The premier's estate is just ahead, awash in golden sunlight. The pines seem to bend over the palatial compound, taller even than the highest tower.

The windows are shut fast against the chilly autumn air, each one polished to a high sheen. We're too far away to see inside, but I squint anyway, searching the dozens of glass panes for a familiar face.

"Are you going to ask about him or keep dancing around the subject until I break?" Kilorn finally huffs.

I don't miss a step. "It seems you have broken."

He huffs again.

"Cal's supposed to be in tomorrow morning at the latest." He gestures vaguely at the estate. *Tomorrow morning.* My heart thuds wildly in my chest. "With Julian and his granny in tow, as well as other members of the Nortan delegation. Reds, Silvers, newbloods. An even spread."

Members of the former High Houses, lords and ladies who would rather skewer a Red than sit beside them. *If not for Cal, if not for Montfort.* I can't imagine what the delegation looks like, or how rife with chaos and conflict it must be.

With Cal at the center of it all, no longer a king. Little more than a bystander, a soldier, another voice in a crowd of many. I can't imagine him like that either.

"I guess you'll want to talk to him."

I feel slightly sick. Of course I do. Of course I'm dreading it. "Yes."

The last time I saw Cal, we stood in the cold shadow of a jet, saying good-bye to each other. We were angry and exhausted and heartbroken, in mourning and in pain. Or at least I was. I needed to leave. *I won't ask you to wait for me,* I told him. In the moment, it felt like the right thing to do. The fair thing. But the look on his face was so horrible when I said it. As if I'd killed his brother all over again. He kissed me, and I could feel how deeply the hurt ran in us both.

"Any idea what you're going to say?" Kilorn glances at me sidelong and I still my face, trying to hide the torment beneath. My mind whirls, a hurricane of every thought I've had over the past months. Everything I've wanted to say to him.

I missed you. I'm glad I went away. It was a mistake to go. It was the right thing to do. I'm sorry I killed him. I'd do it again if I had to. I need you now. I want more time. I love you. I love you.

"Not sure," I finally mutter, forcing the words out.

Kilorn makes a clucking sound, a scolding teacher. Annoyed. "Are you clamming up because you really don't know or you just don't want to tell me?"

"I can barely talk it through in my own head, let alone out loud," I reply quickly, before I lose my nerve. "I don't know what I'm going to say, because I still don't know . . . what I want."

"Oh." He pauses, thoughtful. Always an odd look on Kilorn Warren. "Well, that's a perfectly fine way to feel."

Something so simple shouldn't bring me such relief, but it does. I put my hand on his arm, just for a moment, and squeeze. He nudges me back.

"Thanks, I needed that," I whisper.

"I know," he whispers in return.

"The gala isn't until the end of the week." I count off the hours in my head. *Tonight, all of tomorrow, the day after* . . . "Do the Nortans really need that much time to get ready for a party?"

Or do they want more time here? Did *someone* want to be here early? And will he stay for very long after? *Get a grip, Mare Barrow.* Just one mention of Cal, a few hours separating me from him, and I'm already going crazy. And for what reason? It's only been two months since I saw him last. That isn't very long, at all.

Was it even enough? For us to heal, to forget, to mourn?

Or was it too much? Has he moved on? Did he wait? Have I?

Both possibilities fill me with icy dread.

"If you bothered to read your reports, you might have figured out that the gala is pretty much just cover," Kilorn says, his voice bringing me back. "An excuse to get all the key players in the alliance in one spot without causing too much concern. There have been delegation meetings before, but we've never been able to get everyone together at the same time until now. The States, the Guard, the

Republic. The whole gang."

I narrow my eyes at Kilorn. "The Lakelands aren't stupid. They're watching our movements. They probably have spies in our ranks. Iris and Cenra will know we aren't just drinking and dancing all week."

"Like you said, I don't know anything of importance," he says brightly. I have to roll my eyes as he keeps talking. "Farley mentioned something about deniability. If we convene for war councils and make our intentions clear, the Lakelands and Piedmont have no choice but to move first. It's escalation."

The logic isn't entirely sound, but when has that stopped any of us?

"So the gala buys time," I mutter.

"And some drinking and dancing never hurt anyone." Kilorn spins for effect, his boots sliding over the pavement.

In my experience, balls, parties, and gala events aren't cause for celebration, but it isn't in me to ruin his fun. I can tell Kilorn is excited, and I suppose my family might be too. Back home, the best we ever got were a few fiddles in the market square or a barn hall. They've never seen what the other half is capable of in their delights.

Sneering, I brush some nonexistent dirt from the shoulder of his jacket. It's too small for him, though it used to fit a few months ago. "I hope you have a suit handy."

He flicks my fingers away. "I figured Gisa could help."

In the distance, I can hear Bree still needling our sister, probably begging for the exact same thing. I grin at the thought of her being in such high demand. She'll certainly enjoy turning the boys away, or forcing them into increasingly more extravagant costumes.

I wonder what she has in store for me. Again, my heart thuds. I haven't had much cause for beauty in the last few months. I suppose I should make an effort for such an important gathering, and look the part of the hero everyone thinks I am.

And if it makes Cal blush, all the better.

"Gisa will help, right?" Kilorn mutters apprehensively glancing in my sister's direction.

"You should get in line."

TWO
Cal

It's just past sunset in the mountains; the snowy peaks are still painted blood red. A fitting color for this place. I watch through the jet window as we fly in, weaving toward the now-familiar valley outside Ascendant. As one of the representatives going between the Nortan States and the Republic, I feel like I've done this a thousand times. There's always a great deal of movement within the alliance, and Montfort is always at its center. I've been back and forth so much by now, enough to know what to expect from approach. The craft rattles, hitting pockets of turbulence over the peaks. It hardly registers. The updrafts of mountain air make the landing bumpy, and I jostle against my buckles when we touch down onto the runway.

Even though we land safely, my heart rate climbs and my hands tremble as I unfasten myself. It takes more willpower than it should not to sprint from the jet.

Nanabel certainly takes her time getting off the craft. She plays up the charade of an old woman, leaning on the seat backs for support as she walks down the aisle. "Can't imagine how you do this so much, Cal," she grumbles to me. Her voice is louder than it needs to be, even over the drone of the airjet. "I'm stiff all over."

I roll my eyes behind her back. It's all an act—I know firsthand how spry she is. My grandmother is no wilting flower. She just wants to slow me down, keep me from looking overeager. *Like a puppy hoping for a treat*, she hissed to me when I volunteered to go to the Samos abdication. Not to see Evangeline or Ptolemus, not even really to show my support to royal Silvers making the same choice I did. She knew I thought Mare might be there. And just the chance was enough for me.

But she never showed, to my disappointment.

Don't be unfair, I tell myself. She had no reason to go to the Rift. She's had more than her fill of Silvers struggling to give up their crowns.

Uncle Julian is good enough to take Nanabel by the arm, helping her along at a quicker step. She offers a bloodless smile in thanks, clutching at him with strong, lethal hands. He pales under her grasp, knowing exactly how deadly the hands of an oblivion can be.

Thank you, I mouth to him, and he nods in reply.

Julian is excited to be here too, albeit for very different reasons. He enjoys the Republic as only a scholar can, and my uncle is eager to show the country to Sara. She walks in front of him, setting a good pace in quiet determination. Like me, Julian and Sara have ceased wearing house colors. I'm still not used to seeing my uncle in anything but faded gold, or Sara in colors that aren't red and silver.

Nanabel, of course, keeps to the old tradition. I don't think she owns anything that isn't red, orange, or black. Her long silk coat trails as she walks down the jet, displaying explosive red brocade set with chips of black stone. No one would ever know we aren't royal anymore if they looked in her closet.

And she isn't the only one to still dress like the old days. Today, the Nortan States delegation has four other Silvers in it, two of them from the High Houses. One is from House Laris, a representative for us as well as the now-returned Rift. Her yellow clothing seems garish in wartime. The other, Cyrus Welle, is a former governor and an old man, run ragged and thin by war. His green robes are clean, but they seem faded. His medallion, a jeweled tree, barely reflects the lights inside the jet as he walks. He catches my glance and offers a smile weaker than his chin. *At least he's here,* I remind myself.

The other two Silvers aren't nobles at all, but selected from the many merchants, craftsmen, career soldiers, and other professionals who volunteered from the lower houses. Naturally, they're less opposed to restructuring than any noble would be.

The rest of the Nortan States delegation files off the jet with us, some of them already stamping their feet against the chill. It isn't quite this cold at home, and most of the delegation, the Reds especially, have never been to such high altitude.

Ada Wallace weaves among them, speaking in a low voice. Probably explaining exactly how high we are, why the air is so thin, and what that does to the human body. She keeps telling them to drink more water, with an encouraging smile. Though I've only known her a year, Ada feels like an old friend, and a relic of a different life. Like Mare, she's a newblood, one of the many we recruited so many months ago. She's more valuable than ever now, perhaps the most valuable member of the States' reconstruction effort. And a real comfort. Someone who knows me as more than an abdicated king.

Not like the Silvers. Though I'm glad to have some nobles of the High Houses working with us, I never let my guard down around them.

Not Welle, not Laris, not Rhambos or any of the others. Not even my cousins of House Lerolan. I'd be stupid to think they're here because they believe in blood equality, and not because they know they'll lose any effort to return Norta to her former self. Not because this is the only way to keep their heads above water.

The same cannot be said of the Secession, the Silvers of both Norta and the Rift refusing reconstruction. A familiar ache twists behind my eyes when I think of them, so many powerful nobles lined up against us. They might not be well organized yet or have a numbers advantage, but they're strong, they have resources, and they have the Lakelands to back them up. Their danger can only grow, and I know it certainly will if they unite properly.

This war is far from over, and my job is far from done.

The hard truth exhausts me, even after my nap on the flight. Despite the chance of seeing Mare again, I suddenly want nothing more than to collapse in whatever room they give me and sleep until morning. Not that I'll even be able to do that.

I don't sleep well, and haven't since my father died. *Died.* I still have to remind myself to say *he died* instead of *I killed him.* It was Elara, not me. I know that, but it doesn't change what I see in my head at night. There's no cure for what ails me. I'm not like Mare. Having another person in the room doesn't settle me down. It doesn't matter who's in my bed—the nightmares still come.

This was the last place I saw her, my mind whispers. I try not to remember. Mare said good-bye to me here on this runway. She told me not to wait, told me she needed time. And while I understand what she meant, it still cuts me up to think about.

Luckily, the welcoming party from the Republic approaches, giving me an easy distraction from the haunting memories.

One glance tells me the premier isn't here at the airfield to greet us. I'm not surprised. The Scarlet Guard representatives are already in the city, and he'll be deep in council with whoever they sent. Farley is certainly one of them. I don't expect she'd miss all the action over the next few days. She fights with words as well as guns these days.

Instead of Davidson, Representative Radis, one of the Silver Montfortans, waits by the transports ready to take us into the city. He's accompanied by a half dozen others from the People's Assembly, both Red and Silver and probably newblood too.

He greets me with a firm handshake, and I'm reminded of his sharp nails. As one of the former lords of Montfort, before their own monarchies were overthrown to create the Republic, his influence holds great sway over the Silvers from my own country. I'm careful to introduce him around, and let him charm the others. *Let them see the future is not as bleak as they think.*

It's been this way for months now. Forcing smiles and pleasantries, coaxing men and women who would rather die than feel inferior into some kind of understanding. Somehow, the posturing is more tiresome than battle. I used to spar to stay sharp, stay focused and in shape. Now I do it as a relief, and a rare one these days. Stupid as it may be, I find myself almost wishing everything would boil over and go back to outright battle. I understand war, at least.

I should be good at diplomacy. I was raised to be a ruler. I was a king. But most of this is simply beyond my grasp or desire.

As the introductions go around, Julian must notice my eyes glazing over and my energy waning. He puts a hand to my shoulder, taking over to give me a break. And permission to check out.

I hang back, listening occasionally, smiling when needed. When my stomach growls, seemingly as loud as a jet engine, we trade easy, forced chuckles. Even the Reds, still understandably wary around us, crack smiles.

"I'm afraid you've missed Carmadon's dinner parade for the evening," Radis says. His wispy, white-blond hair gleams beneath the lights of the airfield.

The thought of Carmadon's cooking reminds me of exactly how famished I am. I don't get to eat as much as I like, not because of rations, but because there simply seems to be no time. "I'm no stranger to raiding kitchens, sir," I answer with a false smile.

Radis dips his head and gestures toward the waiting transports. "Then shall we? I'm sure you're all eager to settle in." He looks over my shoulder, speaking to the others. "Tomorrow morning, we've arranged a tour of the city for those of you interested, followed by council . . ."

I tune him out. This part of the performance isn't for me. *A tour.* Like Radis himself, a tour is another convincing argument to make, especially to the Silvers. The Montfortans want to show what reconstruction can look like. What beauty can come out of a few difficult years.

As for me, tomorrow I get to look forward to meetings, meetings, lunch during another meeting, meetings, dinner, and passing out. The Scarlet Guard, the Republic, the Nortan States. Premier Davidson and the People's Assembly, Farley and her officers. Presentations and pleas from all, myself included. I'm imagining my previous visits, where we lived on coffee and furtive glances across an oak table. Argued over everything from refugee aid to newblood training. *Now multiply that by how many dozens are here now. And add Mare to the equation.*

A headache explodes in full force as my stomach drops.

Food first, Calore. One step at a time.

* * *

It's fully dark by the time our transports reach the estate, having taken a circuitous route to the premier's home above Ascendant. I'm sure Radis and the transport staff were instructed to show off the city as night fell—the lights, the lake, the mountains cutting high against brilliant stars. Compared to Norta, with its cities ringed by tech towns smothered in pollution, Silver estates separated from the world, and dirt-poor Red villages, this must look like a dream. The Red delegates in particular are wide-eyed as the transports come to a halt in the estate courtyard, looking up at the palace of columns and white stone. Even the noble Silvers look impressed, though Nanabel keeps her eyes firmly in her lap. She's doing her best to behave.

When I step out, the cold air is a welcome slap to the senses. It keeps me from grabbing the first person I see to ask about a certain electricon who may or may not be inside. This time I take Nanabel by the arm, not to speed her up, but to slow myself down.

She pats my hand softly. For all I've done, all the disappointment I've brought, she still loves me. "Let's feed you," she says under her breath. "And let's get me a drink."

"Yes to both," I mutter back.

The receiving hall of the estate buzzes with activity, and it's no wonder. The premier's home will be full to the rafters housing the delegations from the Scarlet Guard, the States, and everyone in between. I assume some will have to be housed in the city as well. The estate isn't as large as Whitefire Palace, and even that couldn't house the full Nortan court if necessary.

The sudden memory of my former home stings, but not as badly as it used to. At least now I'm doing something more important than maintaining a monarchy.

Another representative from the People's Assembly joins Radis in the center of the hall, her suit so deep green it could be black. Her hair is bone white, her skin is dark brown, and her blood is red, judging by the warm flush beneath her cheeks. While she introduces herself as Representative Shiren, and apologizes for the premier's late meeting, I try to remember the quickest way to Carmadon's kitchen.

Servants begin showing our delegation to their rooms, leading them away in very specific groups. I frown when I realize the Reds and Silvers are being separated, and obviously so. A foolish maneuver, in my opinion. If reconstruction is to work, if blood equality is going to stick in Norta, we have to do everything we can to make it the norm among ourselves. Perhaps the Montfortans think this separation will be less jarring to my nobles, but I couldn't disagree more. I swallow the urge to object. It's been too long a day. I'll find someone to argue with later.

"Officer Calore, ma'am." One of the servants nods at my grandmother and me. The title, new as it is, doesn't bother me at all. I've been called far worse. *Tiberias, for example.* And it has a nice ring to it. It suits me better than Your Majesty ever did.

I nod in acknowledgment to the servant. He responds in kind. "I'd be happy to show you to your rooms."

I duck my head to the older man in his neat gray-green uniform. "If you tell me where, I can manage. I was hoping to find something to eat—"

"That won't be necessary," he says, smoothly cutting me off in a way that is skillfully polite. "The premier and his husband have arranged for dinner to be brought up when you're settled. Mr. Carmadon isn't one to let his fine meals go to waste."

"Ah, of course." *Of course they don't want any of us snooping around. Even me.*

Nanabel stiffens next to me, raising her chin. I half expect her to refuse. No one orders around a queen, former or otherwise. Instead she presses her lips together into a grim, lined smile. "Thank you. Lead on, then."

The servant nods his thanks and gestures for us to follow, looping Julian and Sara along. I expect my uncle to protest as I did, wanting to visit the vast library instead of the kitchens. To my surprise, he hesitates only a second before following in step with the rest of us, Sara's arm tucked into his own. Her eyes dart, taking in the vast mansion around her. This is her first visit, and she keeps her opinions to herself, perhaps to share with Julian later. Long years of silence are a hard habit to break.

Though my grandmother and I are no longer royals of another nation, and I'm barely more than a soldier, the premier houses us all in the main structure of the estate, in a proud suite of green-and-gold rooms branching off a private salon. I expect he means to charm Nanabel with finery, and keep her happy over the next few days. Like me, she's integral to maintaining a relationship with the Silver nobles tentatively helping the reconstruction. If a nice view and silk-upholstered couches help her along, so be it.

Truthfully, I'd rather be housed down in the barracks, tucked into a bunk with a mess hall nearby. But I won't say no to a feather bed either.

"Dinner will be served in a few minutes' time," the servant says before shutting the door behind him, leaving us to our own devices.

I cross to the window and draw aside the curtains to find that we face out over a terrace and up the mountainside, into the pitch-black forest of pine trees. The roar of transports whines in my ears as the memory of climbing up and over the peak rushes through me.

Nanabel looks approvingly at the decor, and especially at the neat, well-stocked bar set along the far wall beneath a gilt-framed mirror.

Wasting no time, she sets to pouring herself a heavy dram of caramel-colored whiskey. She takes a drink before preparing three more glasses.

"I'm surprised your friend wasn't here to greet us," she says, handing the first glass to Sara and the next to Julian. Her gaze lingers on the latter. "You two exchanged so many letters, I thought he'd at least take the time to say hello."

My uncle is difficult to bait, and he just smiles into his drink. He takes a seat on the long sofa, folding himself in next to Sara. "Premier Davidson is a busy man. Besides, there will be plenty of time for scholar talk after the gala."

I turn from the window, brow furrowed. My stomach swoops at the prospect of leaving Julian behind, even for a short while. I reach for the last drink on the bar and sip carefully. It tastes like liquid smoke.

"How long do you intend to stay on here afterward?" I ask, drumming a finger on the crystal glass.

Next to him, Sara shifts and sips her liquor. She's had her fair share of domineering Silver queens, and doesn't tremble beneath my grandmother's imperious stare. "We haven't decided," she replies.

Nanabel sniffs, wrinkling her nose. "It's an odd time to be taking a vacation."

"I believe the term is *honeymoon*," Julian says. With a deliberate motion, he reaches for Sara's free hand, and their fingers intertwine. "We'd like to be married here, quietly and soon. If that suits everyone."

If that suits everyone. At first my grandmother scoffs, and then her lips spread into a true smile.

As for me, I feel like my face might split in two. It almost *hurts* to smile like this, so broadly and without abandon. Happiness hasn't been familiar to me in the last few months, but it courses through me now. Quickly, I cross the room and hug them both, nearly spilling all our drinks.

"It's about time," I snicker in Julian's ear.

"I agree," Sara murmurs, her eyes shining.

When dinner comes, it is unsurprisingly marvelous, and another display of the bountiful Free Republic. There's bison steak, of course, as well as fresh trout, salmon, fried potatoes, three kinds of greens, a cheesy soup, and fresh-baked bread, followed by huckleberries and cream for dessert and a honeysuckle tea. The food must have been brought in from every corner of the Republic, from here in Ascendant to the northwest coast strewn with mountains and a foreign ocean. Everything is perfectly prepared. Certainly the rest of the Nortan delegation have received the same treatment in their rooms, especially the Silver nobles. On the flight they openly complained about the state of their kitchens at home now, what with Reds being free to pursue work where they please, as well as the war shortages. A few good meals in the Republic might be just the kind of convincing they need.

Between the whiskey and the hearty meal, Julian, Sara, and Nanabel are quick to retire to their bedrooms, leaving me to stare over the table that's now in disarray. It's a battlefield of empty plates, bread crumbs, and drained teacups, with knives and forks stained with sauce like swords in blood. It makes my hair stand on end. Though a servant will certainly clear away the scraps sometime in the night, I can't stop myself from gathering it all together into some form of order. I try to be quiet as I stack plates and cups, and it makes the process slow going.

It gives my hands something to do, my mind something to focus on that isn't *her.*

Julian wants to get married here because everyone he values is here. Me, the premier, and Mare. Certainly he knows she'll be back for the gala, if she isn't already. Davidson must have mentioned it in his letters, between long-winded ruminations on the Montfort archives in Vale or Horn Mountain. *And by the way, your former student will be back in town. Best catch her before she traipses off into the wilderness again.*

The last plate clatters as I drop it an inch, but it doesn't break.

I should go to sleep. I'm weary in my bones, and I need to be sharp for the days ahead. But instead of heading for my own bedchamber, I find myself standing on the terrace, watching my breath cloud in the cold. I naturally run hot, and my breath almost looks like steam.

If Davidson really wants to impress the nobles, he should just tell them to look up.

Indeed, the stars above the mountains are like nothing I've ever seen in my country or any other. Even with the light pollution from the city below, they are magnificent, brilliant, and vast. Leaning on the terrace balustrade, I crane my neck to see out and over the trees. The light from the estate doesn't reach far into the forest, illuminating only the first few rows of pines before their branches blend into darkness. The sky looks even more striking against the peak, bald of vegetation, the early snows glowing beneath the starlight.

I understand why people want to stay here. Despite contributing so much to the war effort in the east, Montfort still looks untouched by any of the ravages I've seen. A paradise compared to the hell I came from. *But a paradise bought with another war, with equal bloodshed, and more effort than I can comprehend.* The Free Republic was not always so, and is still rife with its own flaws, hidden as they may seem.

If I were a Lakelander, it might be comforting to ask some distant god for guidance now, for a blessing, for the power to make everyone see what we can accomplish if given the will and the chance. But I believe in no gods, and I pray to nothing.

My bare hands start to go numb; the cold has that effect even on someone like me. I don't bother clicking my bracelets to draw forth flame. I'll go inside in a second and chase some sleep. I just need one more bracing gasp of cold air, and one more glance at the stars overhead, infinite as the future.

Two floors down and maybe twenty yards away, someone else has the same idea.

The door creaks slightly on old hinges as she steps out into the chilly air, already shivering. She's careful to shut it softly behind her so as not to wake anyone. Her terrace is bigger than mine, wrapping around the corner to face down into the city. She keeps to the darker edges, staring into the trees as she tightens a blanket around her shoulders. Her frame is small and lean, her motions smooth with lethal grace. More warrior than dancer. The dim lights of a sleeping mansion aren't enough to illuminate her face. I don't need them to. Despite the distance and the darkness, I know.

Even without her lightning, Mare Barrow still manages to strike me through.

She raises her chin to the sky, and I see her as she was when we found her in that disgusting room, surrounded by blood, both silver and red. There was Silent Stone all around them. She was sprawled, her hair matted and wet, her eyes shut against the gloom. Next to her, Maven's eyes were open. So blue, so wide. So empty. He was dead and I thought her gone too. I thought I'd lost them both, lost them to each other one last time. My brother would have liked that. He took her once before and he would have taken her forever if he could have.

I'm ashamed to say I reached for him first. His wrist, his neck, searching for a pulse that wasn't there. He already felt cold.

She was alive, her breathing shallow, the rattle of it softer by the second.

I can tell that her breath is even now, clouding like my own in tiny, rhythmic puffs. I squint, hoping to see more of her. Is she well? Is she different? Is she *ready*?

The act is futile. She's too far away, and the lights of the palace are too dim to do much more than outline her bundled figure. It isn't too far to shout, and I don't care about waking up half the estate. Still, my voice dies in my throat, my tongue weighted down. I keep silent.

Two months ago, she told me not to wait. Her voice broke when she said it, broke like my heart when I heard it. I wouldn't have minded her leaving if she'd done it without telling me that. *Don't wait.* The implication was clear. *Move on, if you want. To someone else, if you want.* It stung then as it stings now. I could never fathom saying such a thing to a person I loved and needed. Not to her.

The balustrade warms beneath my hands, now clenched tightly and flooding with heat.

Before I can do something foolish, I spin and wrench open the door, only to close it softly behind me, making no noise at all.

I leave her to the stars.

THREE
Mare

Before I open my eyes, I forget myself for a moment. Where we are, what we're doing here. But it comes back to me. The people around us—and the person who wouldn't speak to me last night. *He saw me; I know he did. He was out on the balcony just like me, looking at the stars and the mountains.*

And he didn't say a word.

The ache hits me like a hammer to the chest. So many possibilities blur through my head, too fast for my waking mind to fathom. And they all come back to his silhouette, a shadow against the night sky as he walked away. *He didn't say a word.*

And neither did I.

I force my eyes open, yawning and stretching for show. My sister worries about me enough. She doesn't need my heartache added to her list of concerns. We still share a room, at my request. I haven't tried sleeping alone in months and don't intend to start now.

For once, she's not fussing over me. Instead Gisa is standing over her sewing supplies, contemplating them with a stern glare.

"Has the thread offended you somehow?" I say around a true yawn.

She turns the glare on me. It scares the worry right out of me.

"I'm getting a head start," she says. "The gala will take up most of my time, what with Bree and Tramy and Kilorn and you and Farley and half the people I've ever met begging for something to wear."

In spite of myself, I grin. I knew she wouldn't really leave Bree out in the cold. Gisa is all bark, no bite.

"Fine, tell me how to help," I say, swinging my feet out of bed. The wood floor is cold beneath my toes, and I immediately set to hunting down the socks buried in my blankets.

We aren't moving to our permanent home for another week or so, but Gisa already insists on packing. Or rather, on rearranging the meager amount of what's already packed.

Gisa hums as she shakes her head. "You're not exactly known for your skills in organization."

I sputter, but Gisa doesn't bother to argue. She simply points to my mismatched socks. One is green and threadbare; the other is thick black wool. My mouth shuts with a click of teeth.

"Besides," she says, still smirking at my feet. I wiggle a toe in her direction. "You have your own things to worry about, and a much busier schedule than I do. I don't envy you your meetings," she adds, nodding to the messy pile of papers at my bedside.

I fell asleep reading the overview of the delegation arrangements and agenda, my head spinning with details on Montfort trade, Scarlet Guard movements, the Nortan reconstruction, and the inner workings of the alliance. I try not to think about it now. I don't need a headache this early in the day, though I'll certainly have one by the end of the first meeting this morning.

"Leave the clothing and moving arrangements to the rest of us." Gisa gestures to the apartment at large. Her message is clear. The Barrows will take care of everything they can here and give me the space I need to get through the next few days unscathed.

Little does she know the worst has already begun.

With a sweater half over my head, I pull my sister into a tight hug. She fights it weakly, grinning.

"Can we trade?" I whine. "I'll make shirts and you suffer through hours of debate?"

"Absolutely not," she snaps, pushing away from me. "Now try and dress yourself properly. Farley's waiting for you out in the sitting room, by the way. She's got a uniform on and everything."

"Fat chance of that." I pull on a pair of dark pants instead, not even bothering to hunt for whatever uniform might be buried in our closet. My memories of tight, stiff red fabric are punishment enough. Not to mention, I think I looked downright stupid in it. Hardly what I want to be wearing when I come face to face with Cal again. *If he even wants to see me at all.*

Gisa isn't a mind reader, but my thoughts aren't difficult to discern. She looks me over with an eyebrow raised, then waves me forward. "No, no, no. The premier left you some clothes precisely so you wouldn't go back to looking like a river rat."

I bark a laugh, knowing exactly what a river rat *actually* looks like. I am far from that girl now. "Gisa, this sweater doesn't even have any holes in it!"

She doesn't bat an eye, pulling garments from our shared closet with swirling motion. To my relief, the outfits are plainer than I expected, and there are no dresses in sight. While I'm excited to dress up for a gala, spending all day in meetings while squeezed into a ball gown certainly isn't something I care to suffer.

Gisa peruses the clothing with a seamstress's eye, looking over ensembles in dark shades of red, green, blue, purple, and gray. When she chooses for me, I wonder if my sister wouldn't also be suited to politics.

"Purple is neutral," she says, handing over the corresponding outfit. "Shows you're allied to everyone, and you belong to none."

It's the perfect selection. Though I'm still oathed to the Scarlet Guard, I have cause to support both Montfort and the Nortan States. My new home and the old.

Pride for my sister swells in my chest. I run a finger over the soft velvet of the long purple jacket edged in gold. "I have a history with this color," I mumble, remembering Mareena Titanos and the mask of a Silver house.

Gisa nods, her eyes darting between me and the clothes. "Well, it's a good thing it suits you."

My sister works quickly, helping me into the tailored velvet pants, boots, and high-collared shirt before slipping the jacket onto my arms. She tsks at the length of the sleeves, a bit too long for my frame, but otherwise finds no other flaw. Finally, she brushes out and braids my hair into a long plait that fades from brown to purple and gray.

When she licks her thumbs and smooths my eyebrows, I have to jump back.

"Okay, I think you've done all you can do, Gisa," I tell her, putting a hand between us. Gisa isn't as bad as what the Nortan court used to demand, but she isn't pleasant either. Especially when I feel like I might vibrate out of my skin with nerves and fear.

She pouts, holding out a palette of colored powders. "No makeup?"

"Is Farley wearing any?" I sigh, crossing my arms in defense.

Gisa doesn't miss a beat. "Does Farley need any?"

"No—" I start, remembering how pretty she is, until the implication hits me. "Hey!"

Gisa doesn't flinch and simply points to the bedroom door. She must be eager to get me out of her hair. "Fine, get moving. You're already late."

"Well, I wouldn't be if you allowed me to dress myself," I snipe, darting around her.

She leers after me. "What kind of sister would I be if I let you face down an abdicated king looking like Stilts alley trash?"

With a hand on the doorknob, I feel a familiar tug in my stomach. "Our lives would be very different if he didn't secretly like Stilts alley trash," I shoot back without thinking.

But he didn't say a word.

My face falls. Luckily Gisa misses it, too busy smothering her laughter.

In the sitting room, Farley jumps to her feet, one hand tugging her uniform into place. She still hates it, favoring body armor over tight collars.

"We're late," she clips, her first words to me since we went north. She's written plenty of letters, but this is our first time seeing each other since we left. To my delight, her cold manner doesn't reach her eyes, which crinkle with a hidden smile. "Or are you trying to skip out on what will prove to be a riveting and relaxing day?"

I cross to her in a few short strides and she stretches her arms out to embrace me. Her grip is firm and strong, a comfort as much as anything in this world. I lean into her a little, drawing resolve from her dogged strength.

"Is skipping an option?" I ask when I pull back, running my eyes over the young general. She looks the same as I remember, beautiful and fierce. Maybe even more determined than usual.

"I'm sure you could beg off if you wanted," she replies, calling my bluff. "But I doubt you do."

I flush. She's right, of course. A wild bison couldn't keep me from the delegation meetings.

Her hair is long enough now for a single braid that runs tight across her scalp, like a crown. It makes her look softer, but no less intimidating. As Gisa said, she doesn't bother with makeup, nor does she need to. Diana Farley cuts a striking figure, on the battlefield and in my sitting room.

"No Clara today?" I ask, looking around her for my niece. My heart sinks a little when I see neither hide nor hair of the little girl.

"I would have carted her to the meetings, but I doubt even I'll stay awake through them, let alone a baby. Besides, your parents would gut me if I didn't hand her off. They took her down to the gardens after breakfast."

"Good." My body floods with warmth at the thought of my parents playing with Shade's daughter. Leading her through the autumn trees, letting her rip up Carmadon's meticulous flower beds.

"The Colonel is with them too, I think," Farley adds, her voice quiet. But also firm. That is as much as she's willing to say.

And it isn't my place to push. Her relationship with her father is not my business until she wants it to be. He must be making a monumental effort, that much is clear, if he's choosing time with his granddaughter over the delegation meetings.

"Should we go?" I breathe, gesturing for the door. Already I feel the familiar burst of nerves, my stomach fluttering at the prospect of this day.

Farley is good enough to lead. She doesn't know how to do anything else. "We should."

The first meeting is the largest, and can hardly be called a meeting at all. It's more like a circus.

The assembly of delegates from every corner of the alliance takes place in the grand library of the premier's estate, the only room large enough to hold us all comfortably. Besides the People's Gallery, of course, but Premier Davidson didn't like the optics of using his government's representative hall for this sort of meeting. I think he also didn't want to intimidate the Silvers of the Nortan States. They're a skittish bunch, according to the few reports I read. We have to be careful with the nobles, lest we drive them away and into the waiting arms of the Lakelands and the Silver Secession.

Indeed, I assume that will be the most pressing topic for the next few days—the precarious position of the Nortan States and the always looming threat of the nymph leaders Iris and Cenra. I didn't think of them much at the cabin. It was easy to put those two, and their kingdom, out of my head while isolated in the wilderness. But not here. I can almost feel those women hanging over me, waiting for the chance to strike.

The library unsettles me as I enter. It's only half full. We might be late, but so is everyone else. One glance tells me the delegation from the States isn't here yet. *Good.* I want to be settled and ready when Cal arrives, my face schooled to neutral perfection. Right now, dozens of eyes rove over my skin, and whispers seem to follow me. I don't bother trying to tune them out. Most are harmless, words I'm used to. *Mare Barrow, the lightning girl, she's back.* The gallery ringing the floor above us is empty, unlike last time, when it brimmed with Scarlet

Guard officers. Three months ago, the premier and the Command of the Guard planned our attack and defense of Archeon here.

They interrogated Maven in this room. It was one of the last times I saw him alive. I shiver as I walk over the spot on the carpet where he stood, spitting venom even under interrogation. I can still hear him in my head. *You think I can't lie through pain,* he said when Tyton got too close. *You think I haven't done it a thousand times?*

He meant the torture his mother inflicted on him. I knew that then and it haunts me now. Whatever his mother did to him whenever she entered his mind—it was torture. It was pain. And it twisted him beyond repair.

I think. Still, I wonder. If more could have been done for him. If I—if Cal—if *someone* could have saved him from the monster she made. Like always, the thought burns and leaves a bitter taste in my mouth. I clench my jaw. I refuse to vomit in front of so many people. With a will, I empty my face of expression and raise my eyes.

Across the room, one of the Montfortan officers is silent in his chair, his back to the window. His white hair glows in the morning light.

Tyton never takes his eyes off me as I pass, and I dip my head in greeting. The other electricons aren't as high ranking as he is and won't be here. I doubt Ella could even sit still through ten minutes of pleasantries, let alone an hour of stilted debate. I make a note to ask after them later. We have catching up to do, both in conversation and in training. No matter how much I exercised up at the cabin, I've certainly gone soft during my time away.

The library is set with three long tables, each angled to face the others in something like a triangle. Premier Davidson is already seated at his own, flanked by Montfortan officers and government officials. More arrive by the minute, fluttering into the library in groups of two or three. I get the feeling some have no real use, but are just curious to see the proceedings. Their numbers certainly make for an impressive sight, all aligned in their green military uniforms or politician's robes. Aides and assistants speed through their ranks, handing out papers and packets of information. Most of the pages pile up in front of the premier, who arranges them carefully with a thin-lipped smile.

Representative Radis is close on Davidson's right, whispering to him behind one long-fingered hand. I catch the premier's eye as I pass him, and we exchange nods. He seems more serene than the last time I saw him, despite the chaos bubbling around us. I get the feeling that all-out war is not his field of expertise, despite his newblood ability. He likes to fight with a pen rather than gunpowder.

I won't be sitting with the Montfort delegation, at least not today. Even though my family lives here, and I'll probably become a citizen eventually, I'm Scarlet Guard first. I said my oath to Farley before I even knew Montfort existed, and I'm proud to take a seat next to her at the Guard table. Behind us, various officers and diplomats fill in, from all corners of the eastern continent. Four Command generals, Farley included, hold the center of the table, alike in uniform and stern bearing. They make for an intimidating sight.

With a swoop of unease, I wish I had just worn the damn red uniform.

A cold shiver runs through me at the sight of Evangeline Samos, sitting quietly in the second row, peacefully resigned to her place. I didn't notice her at first. Even with the silver hair, she somehow manages to blend in with the rest of the Montfort delegation. Her clothes don't glint or shine like they used to. Instead her uniform is dark green and unremarkable, with no medals or insignia. Her brother is the same, close at her side with his head bowed.

She watches me, her lethal hands folded in her lap.

I almost smile at the sight of her fingers.

While her clothes are rather plain, her hands are laden with rings of all kinds, in every metal, sharp and ready to bend to her will. Knowing Evangeline, she has other metals hidden all over her body. Even here, in a meeting of diplomats, she's prepared to cut throats if she has to.

I meet her charcoal eyes and she smirks, never bowing her head. Once, that look might have filled me with dread. Now I feel only assurance. Evangeline is a mighty ally, no matter what we started as. Though she will never return the gesture, I bend my neck toward her and nod. Ptolemus is good enough to keep his head bowed, eyes averted from me. I want nothing to do with my brother's killer, even as he repents for that sin and so many others.

As I watch, Radis turns in his seat, looking over his shoulder to whisper something to Evangeline and Ptolemus. Their whispers hiss, the words inaudible. The three Silvers remain in close confidence, and it doesn't bother the premier at all. Their alliance has been cemented—even I received word of the Samos abdication and Evangeline's pledge to Montfort.

I'm still looking at them when the last delegation enters the library, all of them organized and moving as one. Ada Wallace leads, her eyes on the room. She glances back and forth, noting every face and committing it to her perfect memory. She looks the same as I remember. Skin like deep gold, dark brown hair, eyes too kind for all she has seen and all she remembers. As one of the States' representatives, she wears a neat black uniform and a pin at her collar. The three interlocking rings are easy to decipher—red for Reds, white for newbloods, silver for Silvers. I can think of no one better to serve the Nortan States and their campaign. My hands close on the edge of the table, keeping me in place. If we were anywhere else, I would hug her.

Julian Jacos follows on her heels, his clothing spare but fine. The sight of him releases some tension in my chest. He looks odd without his colors, wearing black instead of his usual yellow. For once, he seems quite dashing, and younger somehow. Unburdened. Happy, even. It looks good on him.

The so-called common Silvers wear the suited uniform too, delineated from Reds and newbloods only by the cold undertone of their skin. To my pleasant surprise, they walk closely with their red-blooded counterparts. As merchants, tradesmen, soldiers, and craftsmen, the common Silvers are not as separate from Reds as the nobles are.

Of course, the nobles from the Nortan States are hardly so modern in their clothing, though they also wear the pin. I know their faces as well as their colors—green for Welle, yellow for Laris. Knowledge of their houses was drilled into me long ago, and I wonder what I've forgotten in order to remember such idiocy.

Their house colors are symbol enough. The nobles will not go quietly, or easily. They'll hold on to their power—and pride—as much as they can.

Anabel Lerolan most of all. She must have cracked open her jewel box for this occasion. Her throat, wrists, and fingers gleam with flame-colored gems, each brighter than the last, easily overshadowing her States pin. I half expect to see a crown on her gray head. But her boldness only goes so far. Instead she clutches the closest thing to a crown she has left.

She walks with Cal on her arm, her elbow hooked in his.

Like Julian, his new appearance suits him. No cape, no crown, no riot of medals or insignia. Just the black uniform, the circle pin, and a red square on his collar to mark him as an officer. His black hair is close-cropped again, in the military style he likes best, and he must have shaved this morning. I can see a fresh cut on his neck, peeking out just over his collar. It's barely scabbed over, still spotted with silver blood.

There are dark circles around his eyes. He's exhausted, overworked, and, like Julian, somehow looks happy. I feel the jealous, impulsive urge to ask why.

He isn't looking at me. *And he didn't say a word.*

Under the table, Farley squeezes my wrist in a show of comfort.

I jump at the contact, almost sparking her in the process.

"Easy," she says without moving her lips.

I mumble an apology, my words lost in the hubbub as the final delegation settles in.

Like me, Cal takes a seat at the table, in the center next to Ada. He always liked being on the front lines.

His grandmother and uncle are no different. The rest of the delegation is evenly split, a mix of Reds and Silvers, nobles I recognize and commoners I don't. The latter gape at the room. The nobles are less easily impressed, and doing their best to show it.

The premier doesn't mind either response.

He simply claps his hands together, a signal to us all.

"Shall we begin?"

FOUR
Cal

Don't look at her, don't look at her, don't look at her. Focus, focus, focus.

I'm so wound up I nearly set fire to my chair. Even my grandmother, more fireproof than most, leans away, lest I singe some of her precious silk. It's not like she'll be able to procure more, at least not the way she used to as a queen.

If the rest of my delegation notice my unease over Mare, they're good enough not to say anything. Ada carries on without hesitation, laying her papers out in front of her. They're covered in neat, meticulous notes ranging from troop numbers to distances between cities. Not that she needs any of it. The information is all in her head already. I get the feeling she just doesn't want to unsettle anyone. After all, her ability is rare, even among newbloods, and largely unstudied.

There was some grumbling from the nobles, but she was the obvious choice to represent us at the first meeting. Ada Wallace has seen this war from many angles and perfectly understands the rest, not to mention the history of any revolution and reconstruction she could get her hands on. Most, she said, were flawed, if not outright failures. I shudder to think what might come to pass if we are the same.

"Welcome to the honored delegations of the Nortan States and the Scarlet Guard," the premier says, bowing his head to both our tables. He folds his hands in front of him, his posture open and inviting. Everything about that man is a calculation. "The Montfort delegation and my government thank you for making the journey to be here with us."

"The *long* journey," one of the Nortan nobles mutters, only to be politely ignored by the chamber. I resist the very royal urge to send him from the room. But I don't have the power to do that anymore. We're all equals here, even the ones who don't deserve it. Even the ones who deserve to be more than the rest.

I clench my jaw. It's still an undertaking not to look at her. I manage a glance toward her hands, hidden beneath the table. Farley is safer territory. She sits resolutely at Mare's side, her attention and iron focus on the premier. She's buttoned into that uniform she hates. Mare isn't, having forgone the stiff, scarlet uniform for purple velvet. It's the color she wore as Mareena Titanos. Her sister must have chosen her clothes for her, since Mare doesn't have much taste or talent for fashion. If not for the circumstances, I would laugh at the thought of Gisa scolding Mare into dressing appropriately, and forcing her into the jacket.

I blush at the thought of getting her out of it.

Focus, my mind screams, and heat flares around me.

"Could you not?" Julian mutters through clenched teeth. The corner of his mouth twitches, betraying amusement.

"Sorry," I mutter back.

One of the Scarlet Guard Command generals speaks up for her delegation, responding to Davidson. "Of course, Premier," she says, her voice carrying. I recognize her as General Swan. The Scarlet Guard still insists on code names, even now. "And we're grateful to your country for hosting us."

Not that there was really another option, I think to myself. *The Scarlet Guard has territory but no central government of their own, and the Nortan States are still rebuilding. And of course, holding meetings on democracy in a king's former palace might send the wrong message. Trading one king for another, and all that.*

"The delegation of the Nortan States concurs," Ada says, raising her chin to the premier.

Uncle Julian leans in next to her, speaking to the room. "We're happy to be here, and to see firsthand what a former Silver kingdom can look like."

My grandmother has little taste for pleasantries. She purses her lips next to me but holds her tongue. I can't say I disagree with her impatience. We should be getting down to business, not blowing smoke at one another.

Premier Davidson pushes on at a glacial pace. He gestures to the papers in front of him, with matching sets all over the room. "You should all have your agendas, as agreed upon in our prior communications."

I nearly roll my eyes. Who could forget the *prior communications,* a largely useless back-and-forth of posturing within the alliance? There were arguments about everything from timing to seating arrangements. In fact, the only position they could all agree upon was a need to summarize progress across their delegations. And even in that, the Scarlet Guard was less than happy to oblige. They play things too close to the chest for my taste. Though I can't blame them for their hesitation. I know what Silver betrayal looks like up close. But their obfuscating certainly makes everything all the more complicated.

"Would the delegation for the Scarlet Guard like to go first?" Davidson says, extending a hand toward their table. His lips curve into his inscrutable smile. "What can you say regarding your progress in the east?"

Farley leans forward, her face tight. She's annoyed too. "Progress is being made," she says, speaking for the Guard. The other generals look on, satisfied.

The rest of us wait expectantly for a real explanation, but she settles back into her chair, her mouth pursed shut. Next to her, Mare bites her lip, eyes downcast. She's fighting the urge to laugh.

I grit my teeth. *Farley* . . .

Davidson merely blinks, unfazed. "Would you care to elaborate, General?"

She doesn't miss a beat. "Not in an open forum."

"This is hardly an open forum," my grandmother says, bracing her hands on the table. She half stands, ready to fight. Just in case, I put a hand out, grabbing the edge of her silk clothing beneath the table. She's an old woman, yes, but I'll pull her back if I need to. On my other side, Julian stiffens, his posture going rigid.

Nanabel pushes on, her voice even. "How can we hope to accomplish anything if you refuse to share any information whatsoever? Our delegations are handpicked, each one of us dedicated to this alliance and our nations."

Across the floor, the Scarlet Guard remain resolute and in solidarity. General Swan and the others don't flinch beneath the glare of a former queen and powerful oblivion. Farley even manages to respond without speaking. Her eyes flicker, just for a moment, to the other Silver nobles at our table. They turn to stone beneath her gaze, eagerly meeting her challenge. And I wonder if it isn't just Nanabel I should worry about. Breaking up a fight between Diana Farley and a former Silver lord is not high on my list of things to accomplish today.

Farley's meaning is crystal clear. She doubts the Silvers in our delegation, the nobles who would have executed her only a few months ago if given the chance. Some of them look like they still might; their gazes are that sharp.

To my surprise, Ada is the one to move first. She slides a single page out from her stack of papers, her eyes scanning it thoroughly. "A progress report from the Scarlet Guard is not needed. We have more than enough information to go on."

At her table, Mare's mouth falls open in confusion. "Ada . . . ?"

Ada merely speaks over her, the words coming out rapid-fire.

"Based on fluctuations in shipping and unscheduled troop movements in the Lakelands, you've been fighting along the Ohius River border. And if the recent trade patterns of the rivermen smugglers are any indication, you've been using them to ferry resources and personnel in and out of Sanctum. That's a good amount of Guard traffic, much more than usual in other cities. It's matched only by the patterns I observed at the Piedmont base you once held. I believe you took the Lakelander city approximately three weeks ago, and are using it as a base of operations in the southeastern Lakelands, allowing for easy cooperation with the rivermen of the Disputed Lands. Not to mention the news out of Citadel of the Rivers."

The silence that follows is deafening. Ada merely flips another page, the movement of paper soft as the beating of a bird's wing.

"The Lakelander fortress sits at the confluence of the Ohius and the Great River, with quick access to the Tanasian into Piedmont. It's a very important military installation servicing both the Lakelander river navy and their land army. Or at least, it was until you occupied it—two days ago, perhaps? That's what I gathered from the sudden flood of Lakelander soldiers fleeing upriver, as well as the cessation of Lakelander communications to the Citadel."

The warmth that bleeds through me is born of pride, not anger.

I could hug Ada. I really could. Of course this was all in our reports, sourced from Montfort's shared intelligence, our own operatives in the region, and even simple news from citizens living on the border. But only she could connect the dots so thoroughly and perfectly. She's truly brilliant. If I still believed in royalty, she'd make a fearsome queen.

And though this is not a royal court, I do my best to gauge the library the way I would a throne room. The Guard generals remain still, but their aides exchange worried looks and even whispers. I force myself to look at Mare, at the mask she maintains so well. Her face doesn't move, but she glances sidelong at Farley. Clearly she has no idea if anything Ada says is true. I'm guessing she didn't spend much of her time away poring over war reports. *Typical.* I almost laugh to myself.

The young general is much easier to read. Farley's eyes narrow and her brow draws down into a familiar arrow of irritation. Ada avoids the stern look deftly, though a blush rises high on her cheeks. It's taken a lot for her to say such things. It probably even feels like a small betrayal.

"We didn't occupy it," Farley says coolly. "We destroyed it."

Another Silver fortress burning flashes in my head. The flames are my own, all-consuming, leaving ash in their wake. I return Farley's gaze. I know what it's like to destroy a city piece by piece. "Same as Corvium," I breathe.

"Less for us to defend, less for them to win back." Her words are knives thrown in every direction "And fewer Silver monuments to Red death."

Farley has always been the Scarlet Guard attack dog, and she plays her role well today. The Reds of my delegation look on her with pride. The Silver nobles would leave the room in protest if they could.

"May I remind you there are Silvers in the Montfort delegation?" Again, my grandmother rises to Farley's bait, eager to bicker. She flicks one wrinkled hand toward the premier's table and the two steel-haired siblings sitting in the rows behind him.

Evangeline and Ptolemus look as they did on the day of the abdication, hiding their nerves behind a performance of cold detachment. Both wear green banded with metal—iron for Evangeline, chrome for her brother.

In front of them, Representative Radis shifts to shield the scions of House Samos from view. He drums his long fingers on the table. One corner of his mouth rises in a feral smile, showing a glint of teeth.

"And we've proven our loyalty to our Republic, Anabel," he says in a low voice. This man was a royal too, years ago. He threw his crown away like so many here. "You're all currently doing the same."

Under the table, I clench a fist, digging my nails into my palms. I've had more than enough of this posturing from every corner of the room. It's nothing more than a useless waste of time and energy.

"Forgive me," I blurt out, half rising in my seat. Cutting off Radis and my grandmother before they can really start splitting hairs on Silver sacrifice is the least I can do. "I know I'm going off agenda here, but we only have so much time this week, and I think we need to focus on the matter at hand."

Radis turns his sneer on me. It's nothing compared to what I'm used to. "And what do you think that is, Officer Calore?"

If the title is meant to sting, he has certainly failed. *Better than Your Majesty.*

I straighten under his scrutiny, now standing fully. I'm more use on the battlefield or in the training ring, but I'm no stranger to speaking in front of a crowded room. "Montfort is well defended; the Scarlet Guard are mobile and military ready. As it stands, the Nortan States are the weakest link in this alliance. The soft underbelly. We're trying to rebuild as fast as we can, but even under the best of circumstances, it will take years. You know that," I say, gesturing to the Montfort delegation with a gentle hand. "You've done it before, and done it well."

The premier nods. "There are always improvements to be made, but yes, we've done what we can to build the Republic."

Davidson is a reasonable man and Julian's friend. If anyone will understand our plight, it must be him.

"We're trying to do it all with an ax hanging over our heads," I bite out. Even here, in a stoic library, I feel the threat of another war looming. It breathes down my neck like a ghost. "The Lakelands are regrouping, the nymph queens will return, and when they do, they're going to find a country barely able to feed itself, let alone fight through the winter."

Without looking, Davidson shuffles through his papers and pulls out a page I can't read from this distance. He doesn't seem surprised. "Do you have a suggestion?"

I have too many. The list rattles off in my head, quick as gunfire. "We need a quick stabilization of our economy, our national treasury—"

Radis folds his arms. "Whose national treasury, exactly? Your brother's?"

I do all I can to temper a reaction, keeping my face still and empty. Inside, my heart still bleeds for the brother I lost. Across the room, Mare shifts in her seat, her eyes faraway.

"My country's," I reply, stone-voiced. Whatever court Radis grew up in was not as married to etiquette as my own. "Anything still sitting in the vaults of Archeon belongs to our people now."

From the Scarlet Guard, the Command general Drummer laughs unkindly. His portly face flushes crimson with the effort. "So you've been distributing it fairly among the Reds, how lovely."

I clench my jaw. "We've been using it to rebuild—"

"*Silver* cities," Drummer mutters under his breath, even as I keep talking.

"—bolster wages, improve conditions for Red soldiers, improve the tech cities, maintain the harvest—"

General Swan looks at me over steepled hands. Her smile is tight. "Then it sounds like you're doing quite well."

It takes all my restraint not to laugh in her face.

"We're going to institute price controls throughout the States, to avoid price gouging of food and other resources—"

I know the next voice in my bones. She's thunder in broad daylight.

"From the Reds now in full control of what they produce. Farmers. Factory workers."

Mare crosses her arms tightly, almost painfully so, in an effort to shield herself from the scrutiny of the room. She doesn't enjoy things like this. Never has. Even if she's good at it, never backing down. I stare back at her across the floor. The yards feel like a canyon and an inch, too far and too close.

For her, I have no quick response; the words die in my throat.

On my left, one of the Silvers speaks in my place. Welle, a former governor, has a voice like honey, too sweet and sticky. "Someone else owns the tools they're using, Miss Barrow," he says with punchable smugness.

Mare doesn't hesitate. "They are welcome to use them," she snaps.

This man used to rule the village she lived in, and all the land she'd ever known. "What else?" she adds, her eyes flying back to challenge me.

It almost feels like sparring with her again. I admit, it thrills me.

"The Silver wealth of the noble families—"

"Should be used to even the field," she snaps again, but I hardly mind. I'd take it all, just to speak with her. With a burst of warmth, I realize this is our first conversation in months. Even if I can barely get a word in. "That money was earned on the backs of Red workers for generations. Tens of generations."

You're not wrong, I want to say. *But what you're asking can't be done.*

Still in his seat, Julian puts a hand on my arm, motioning for the floor. "You need the Silver nobles placated," he says. Mare and the Scarlet Guard turn their fiery resolve on him, each of them like a lit ember. "We need them with us. If any attempt is made to seize their assets now, I fear the bottom falls out, and the Nortan States die before they've even begun to live."

Farley flicks her wrist like she's batting away a pesky insect. "Because a few Silver lords and ladies lose their jewels? Please."

"We share borders with Piedmont and the Lakelands, General," I reply, doing my best not to sound condescending.

"Surrounded by Silver enemies, what a foreign concept," Farley snaps back.

I sigh in exasperation. "I can hardly control geography of the *world*, Farley," I reply, to a low hiss of amused whispers.

My uncle's grip tightens on my arm. "Even now, defecting to the southern princes or the Lakelander queen is still an option for many noble families," Julian says, his voice taking on an apologetic tone. "Some of them did in the war, some never returned, and others are waiting for the excuse to do so again. We can't give them that."

"There will be adjusted rates of taxation," I add quickly. "We've agreed. Nobles will be paying their fair share."

Farley's response is acid. "Sounds like *everything* is their fair share."

Again, I wish I could agree. I wish what Reds deserve from us were within the realm of possibility.

To my surprise, Radis comes to my defense. "The Nortan delegation isn't wrong." He adjusts the already immaculate collar of his green-and-white suit. While Davidson is all stillness, impossible to read, Radis likes the spotlight and basks in it. Both are performers, charmers, intent on winning hearts—and votes. No king ever had to be so deft or charismatic with so many. "Allowances must be made. We did the same here, all those years ago."

"Inches for miles," Davidson agrees, finally breaking his silence. He turns to face the Scarlet Guard, explaining for their benefit. "With the formation of the Free Republic, all Silvers who oathed themselves to the new government were pardoned for their crimes against the Red and newblood populace. Those who did not were exiled, their assets seized. I'd suggest the same, but the Nortan States are nearly at war again, and they need every soldier at their disposal. Both to protect their fledgling nation, and to ensure that the Scarlet Guard do not spill their own blood needlessly."

The Scarlet Guard hardly likes the sound of that. The generals and officers both react as if being asked to drink poison. I expected as much. Even though this is only the first of many meetings, the entire week already feels like a failure.

Put it on the list, Calore.

"If you help us get back on our feet, give us the room we need to do so . . . ," I say, almost pleading to the other delegations. I understand why they won't budge, but they *must* be made to see. *This is how we win, the only way we win.* "It's better for all of us in the grand scheme of things."

Mare's lips twist into a scowl. Her glare cuts with a lovely blade, and it feels like she and I are the only people left in the room. "Ends justifying means has been used to defend many, many atrocities, Cal."

Cal. She refused to call me that for so long; it still shivers me when she does it. Even though we stand at odds, both of us seemingly at opposite ends of the earth again, I want to reach out and touch her so badly my knees almost buckle. The hairs on my arms rise, as if responding to some electric current.

"You have my word this won't be one," I say thickly, my tongue feeling too big for my mouth.

Something softens in her eyes, or perhaps it's just a trick of the strange mountain light. It's still early, the windows full of gold. She looks lovely in it.

Evangeline is very noisy about standing up, letting her chair scrape and her rings clink together. She all but rolls her eyes between us.

"*I* have some progress to report," she drawls.

FIVE
Mare

"Officer Samos?"

One of Davidson's many aides turns in his seat, craning to look at Evangeline.

Officer.

The title was strange on Cal, who I've only ever known as a prince and a king, but for *Evangeline,* it seems against nature. It's impossible to picture her as subordinate to anyone, let alone acting as a soldier. I wonder what poor Montfortan captain has to deal with giving her orders. Or if she even bothers to turn up on time to whatever she's doing. If I weren't sitting in the front of my delegation, I wouldn't think twice about checking the information packet just to find out. There's a list of delegates, with photos and summaries of each person here. I certainly pity whoever has to deal with her.

Evangeline is regal as ever, with or without a crown. She even pauses long enough to ensure the undisputed attention of the room.

She flicks her single braid over her shoulder, the silver hair glinting beneath the light of the library windows.

After a moment, she speaks, ringed hands clasped in front of her.

"My correspondence with Princess Iris of the Lakelands has been most informative," she says simply, a smirk tugging at her lips as the room explodes into noisy chaos. She lets it wash over her, enjoying every second.

The Scarlet Guard buzzes around me, not bothering to disguise their whispers. I only catch fragments, most of them some form of the word *betrayal*.

Farley leans in close to me, her voice rough and movements jerky. "Did you know—" she begins before my glare stops her short.

"How could I?" I growl back. "We're not exactly pen pals." I can't even begin to comprehend what Evangeline is getting at, or what she might accomplish communicating with Iris. I want to assume the best of her—she did it for the cause—but my intuition tells me to prepare for the worst.

At the Nortan table, Cal's delegation is just as confused as we are. Heads bend together and whispers fly. Julian and Cal turn to each other, and my old mentor's lips move furiously, saying something no one but Cal can hear. Ada shifts, adding her own assumptions to Julian's. They listen intently, eyes alight. Anabel jumps to her feet again. Apparently losing her crown has turned her into a rabbit.

"Evangeline, what is the meaning of this?" she snaps, almost scolding. "Premier?"

The premier doesn't react, stoic as ever. I have to assume he already knew—nothing happens in the Republic without his knowledge. Nor is Evangeline foolish enough to jeopardize her place here, or the safety of the people she loves.

The Montfort delegation is more reactive, whispering like the rest of us. An aide whispers to Ptolemus, who waves him off.

Dread pools in my stomach. I grit my teeth.

Evangeline raises her chin, weathering the low buzz of speculation with ease. "We've been exchanging letters for some weeks now. She's been very responsive."

Ugh, she's enjoying this too much.

"To *what*?" I blurt out.

She smirks at me, one silver eyebrow raised, "You of all people must know what wonderful advice I give," she says coyly, before turning back to the room. I feel the very familiar urge to spit at her. Forgetting myself, I glance at Cal, only to find him already looking at me. He seems just as exasperated as I am. Despite our traded barbs a moment ago, we share a sigh of frustration.

"I spoke to her as one princess to another," Evangeline tells the chamber. "I've seen my kingdom rise and fall, born of war and ended by war. My father refused to adapt our country, and would have never taken the pains Officer Calore is taking now with his former kingdom."

"A kingdom he already lost before he ever agreed to our terms," Farley all but snarls.

At his seat, Cal tightens his jaw, his eyes on the papers in front of him.

Under the table, I put a hand on her wrist. "Easy," I mutter under my breath. Cal's got enough on his plate. There's no use in smacking him around more than we already have.

But Evangeline acquiesces to Farley, extending a hand. "Exactly. He wasn't able to adapt either, and lost his crown for it. I told Iris that she can avoid the same fate."

General Swan, cool as ever, surveys the former princess with narrowed eyes. "You have no right, no power to promise her anything. Premier, get your people in order."

I expect Evangeline to cut the general for speaking so sharply. To my surprise, Evangeline shrugs her off. The mountains have been good for her. "I did nothing of the sort."

"You told her to bend instead of break," Cal muses.

Her daggered smile takes on a cold, bitter edge. "Yes, I did."

The thoughts come as fast as I can speak them, puzzling out Evangeline's plan. "Make Reds equal to Silvers, all the same subjects to the Lakelander crown," I murmur, seeing the logic alongside the danger—and the defeat.

"With some representation in government thrown in for good measure," she says, nodding at me. "I can't speak for her mother, but Iris seems receptive. She's seen what's happening in the Nortan States. If the Lakelands must change, she'd rather do it in a slow slide rather than a plummet."

Cal shakes his head, his dark brow deeply furrowed. "Why would she even entertain the idea? The Lakelands are strong, far stronger than the States."

"Yes, but they aren't stronger than *this* alliance, or at least they know it will be a hell of a fight." She looks around the room, as if to marvel at our number. Our strength and power. "They certainly aren't stronger than their own Reds, millions of them. If that fuse is ever truly lit, they'll lose their country too." Her eyes land on the Scarlet Guard. The generals stare back, and I try to picture what Evangeline sees. Terrorists to one, freedom fighters to another. Rebels and revolutionaries with a real chance at victory. Desperate people willing to do whatever the cause requires. "It's a risk to keep fighting us, a real risk. Iris is clear-sighted enough to see that."

"Or she's simply stringing you along." Farley keeps herself in check this time, her voice measured and even. Beneath the table, her fingers curl. "Lulling us into a false sense of security before another attack. Our soldiers have been fighting tooth and nail along the river borders and in the north. If their princess has any hesitation, they certainly don't show it."

"I don't expect you to trust Silvers, General," Evangeline says slowly, and for once, her familiar bite is gone. "I assume you never will. But you can at least trust our talent for survival. It's something most of us do very well."

And just like that, the bite returns, whether she knows it or not. I feel it deeply, as if jaws have closed around my throat. *Most of us.* Many Silvers have died since all this began. Her father, Cal's father—and Maven too.

One glance at Cal tells me I'm not alone.

He's trying to forget just as I am.

And failing just as I am.

Is that why he never said a word?

I am many things, many people. And I am also the killer of Maven Calore. Is that what rises to the surface when he looks at me? Does he see his brother, dying with his eyes open? Does he see me with silver blood all over my hands?

There's only one way to know.

No matter how much it frightens me, no matter the pain it may cause, I have to speak to him. And soon.

Thanks to Cal veering us so quickly off course, the delegations abandon the agenda entirely and spend the next two hours bickering back and forth over every point that comes our way. I should have expected he would want to dive in as soon as possible, and rile everyone up in the meantime. We find ourselves drifting from subject to subject, each one branching into another. *If the Nortan military needs to be fed, who will be rationed? How are the farmers paid? What can be traded through the rivermen? What can be bought? Why are the transport fees so high?* Most of the people I know in the room are warriors only, with little talent for economics or supply. Julian and Ada do most of the talking for the Nortan States, while Davidson, Radis, and a few of his government ministers serve for Montfort. General Drummer, who coordinates with the Whistle network for the Guard, has almost too much to say about shipping routes and old smuggler trails still in use. Farley hunches into an uncomfortable position for the duration, if only to keep herself from falling asleep. She interjects when she can, as does Anabel. The latter, I think, is doing her best to placate the Nortan Silvers. They look jumpy at best, liable to run from the room and the alliance at the first sign of instability. I keep silent, for the most part. My expertise is far from here.

The clock ticks, signaling two hours gone, and I exhale a long breath. This was just the *overview*. It was supposed to be the easy part. I can only imagine what the more specific and smaller meetings might turn into.

Everyone else seems to mirror my exhaustion, eager to get out of the room and on to the rest of their schedules. I barely have the energy to think about the trade meeting I'm supposed to attend next, where I will be of no use to anyone. Chairs scrape all over the library, and the delegations mix together. Some gather for comfort and safety—the Nortan Silvers are quick to keep to their own. Others approach each other to talk even more. Julian reaches Davidson with some effort, and the two shake hands for a long moment. I can't imagine wanting to speak at all after this, but they both carry on without thought.

Cal remains sitting through it all, quietly arranging his papers into a neat pile. Anabel hovers over him, a nanny and a shield. She puts a hand on his arm and whispers something to coax him out of his seat.

I'm still in mine, unable to move. Rooted to the spot despite the swirl of people around me. He doesn't look my way. Doesn't take a single step in my direction. But his body angles, shoulders open to me for a long second. Until he turns his back and lets his grandmother lead him from the room, the rest of his delegation moving in his wake.

It's impossible, but I think he might be more handsome than I remember.

Farley moves in a blur of blond hair and red uniform, catching Ada by the elbow as she goes. The newblood offers a weak smile until Farley pulls her into a warm embrace. The two share a grin of familiarity, a kinship we all gained those weeks at the Notch. Even if Ada is working directly with the States now, and not us, that doesn't matter.

Still, I can't move. It feels better to watch. Easier, somehow. My brain might be overloaded after two long hours of not-so-polite argument.

And there's only one way I know to clear my head.

Well, two, a voice whispers, *but he seems busy.*

I jolt out of my seat before that voice can betray me and send me scouring the halls in search of a fallen fire king.

Tyton hasn't left the library yet, allowing some Scarlet Guard officer to talk at him while he stares at the ceiling. I manage to catch his eye as I walk, gesturing for the door. Thankfully, he catches my meaning and politely detangles himself from the chatty Guardsman.

"Thank you," he murmurs, falling into step beside me. We do our best to navigate the surging crowd of delegates, and I'm careful to keep my face down.

"Think you can get Ella and Rafe down to the training yard?" I reply. Quickly, I decide the trade meeting can survive without me.

He cracks a grin. "*We* can't train in the yard, Barrow."

I smile in return, remembering our weeks at the Piedmont base. Electricons require a lot more room to spar and train, our abilities too destructive when let loose. We trained there at a place called Storm Hill, set away from the sparring circles, with enough open land for even Ella to push herself. I wonder what we must resort to here.

There's some commotion in the hall—more delegates stopping to talk or whisper. Promises offered, deals proposed. Too much politics for me. The narrower space makes it all the more difficult to move, and I wish I could spark up, just a little, to get through quicker.

"Excuse me," I grumble sharply, trying to elbow my way around a willow-thin and slow-moving Montfortan representative. She takes no notice of me, locked in conversation with a Red delegate from the Nortan States.

Tyton puts a hand on my back to guide me through. And probably to keep me from shocking anyone. It has a calming effect, his electricity barely brushing against mine.

I relax a little, only to tense up again when a wall of warmth washes over me. My body knows what that means, even if my head doesn't.

I almost knock right into his shoulder, my forehead inches from him. "Sorry—" I begin, my mouth moving faster than my brain.

He turns, face blank, looking down on me from a familiar height. Everything about him is familiar and inviting. The warmth, the smell, the shadow of stubble along his chin and cheeks, the flickering bronze of his eyes. Every piece of him threatens to draw me in. So I resist, doing my best to ignore how much he affects me. I square my shoulders, clench my jaw, and give him my most polite nod. It must combine into something frightening, because he pulls back, the beginnings of a smile dying on his lips.

"Good to see you, Cal," I say, courteous as any noble he's ever known. It seems to amuse him.

Cal nearly bows, but thinks better of it. "And you, Mare. Hello, Tyton," he adds, reaching around me to shake hands with my companion. "No Kilorn today?"

This is far from the ideal place to speak, let alone have a conversation of any importance. I grit my teeth. Half of me wants to bolt and half of me wants to latch on to him with no intention of letting go.

"He's prepping for the refugee meeting, as Radis's aide," I reply, eager for the easy topic. Anything to distract from the very large elephant in the very narrow hallway.

Cal's eyebrows rise a little. Like the rest of us, Kilorn has certainly changed. "I suppose I'll see him in my next meeting, then."

I can only bob my head, swallowing around the lump in my throat. "Good."

"Good," he echoes, almost too fast. His eyes never leave my face. "I'll see you . . . around?"

"Yes, I'm around."

How is it possible to sound so stupid in so few words?

Unable to stand there any longer, I give Cal one last nod and seize the opportunity to push through the crowded hallway, leaving him in my wake. He doesn't protest or try to follow. Tyton says something behind me, probably a proper good-bye, but I keep walking. He can catch up.

When he finally does, I've escaped to one of the wider halls with fewer people and more room to breathe. Tyton all but snickers as he approaches, hands shoved in his pockets.

"Do you two need help speaking or something?" he murmurs as he falls into step beside me.

I snap back at him, lashing out. "As if you can lecture anyone on the ability to talk."

He only stares at me in silence, a lock of white hair falling over his eyes. "Point made."

Tyton isn't the only one to have followed me, apparently. I whirl around at the grating sound of metal boot heels, clinking with every step.

"Can I help you, Evangeline?" I growl.

She doesn't break stride, moving with her lethal grace and lazy detachment. Montfort has given a cold glow to her skin and a new, mischievous light in her eyes. I don't like it one bit.

"Oh, darling," she purrs, "I hardly require anything from you. But I agree with this one—you certainly need help where Cal is concerned. As you know, I'm always happy to oblige."

It wouldn't be the first time. My heart squeezes at the memory of Ocean Hill and its secret passages. The choices Cal and I couldn't make there—and the choice we made later, after Archeon. The choice I'm still trying to understand.

Evangeline just leers at me, waiting.

"I'm not here to entertain you," I mutter, turning my back on her. Certainly she can find other ways to fill her time.

She isn't thrown off in the slightest, even when Tyton levels a glare at her that would send most running off. "And I'm not here to pester you," she says. "Much."

I keep walking, the other two matching my pace. "Isn't that your primary function?"

"In case you haven't noticed, I've had to find a profession." Evangeline pulls a face and gestures to her drab uniform. Well, drab for her. Up close, I can see she's worked bits and pieces of iron through the green, sharpening the joints and seams. There's iron in her hair too, tiny bits of it woven into her braid like shrapnel. "After abdicating and becoming a citizen here, I enlisted in the Montfortan military. I've been assigned to guard duty, specifically in the premier's residence."

The thought of Evangeline Samos standing at doorways and following Red dignitaries around is particularly delicious. A smirk spreads across my face. "Do you want me to feel sorry for you?"

"Feel sorry for yourself, Barrow—I'm your bodyguard."

I almost choke on nothing. Next to me, Tyton forces out a scoff. "I beg your pardon?" I sputter.

She merely brushes her braid over one shoulder, gesturing for us to walk on.

"I'm so good at saving your life, I might as well get paid for it."

Three hours later, the sun begins its early descent in the mountains, fading fast over the western range. The sweat cools on my skin, sending a shiver over me as I towel off, walking back down toward the premier's palace. Evangeline casts annoyed looks over her shoulder, willing me to hurry up. She didn't care for the electricon sparring session. She knows what it's like to fight one of us—seeing the combined might of four was probably a shock for her. Rafe and Tyton follow me at a slower pace, talking to each other. Their voices echo down the mountainside, away from the electricon sparring ground upslope. Ella keeps close to my side, a towel over her shoulder and a grin on her lips. Overhead, an electric storm turns and whirls, weakening with every passing second. Soon it will be just a whisper, a shadow against the pale pink sky.

"When do you move out of the estate?" Ella asks, her blue hair vibrant against the sunlight. Her dye is fresh. Mine, not so much. The purple ends of my hair have gone dull, with bits of gray fading through.

"After the gala," I reply. The excitement in my voice is real. "It'll be good to finally get our own space." After nearly a year of barracks and borrowed rooms, I know my family is eager to have a home once more.

Ella smiles kindly. "You living lakeside or slopeside?"

I curl a piece of hair around my finger, enjoying the feeling of soreness after good workout. My muscles ache and my blood sings. "Slope. The lake town house they offered was beautiful, but I like being up high."

Where I can see, where no one can sneak up on me.

She nods, thoughtful. "How is the family adjusting?"

"Better than expected. They like it here. And what's the alternative?" *The Stilts?* I almost laugh. None of us would return to that trash heap, not for anything short of Shade's return. The odd thought sobers me, and any delight from the training session fades away.

Ella notes my sudden change in mood. Her excitable air fades with my happiness, and we both lapse into easy silence.

In spite of the memories always threatening to surface, I like being here too. With my family, with newbloods like me. With people who believe the world can change, because they've done it already. It makes the future look less daunting.

At the rear gates to the palace, the other electricons break off. Rafe waves first, his brown skin taking on a golden edge in the sunshine. "Same time tomorrow?"

"If our schedule allows," Tyton mutters.

Ella elbows him in the ribs, trying to draw a smile from the taciturn man. "Of course, Ty, how could we forget? You with your important meetings all week, whispering and dealing—"

"Wining and dining!" Rafe crows, blowing Tyton a kiss. Like Ella's, his green hair is freshly dyed. "Tomorrow, loves!"

"Tomorrow," I echo, watching them go. I swear I'll make time tomorrow. I don't think I'll keep sane otherwise.

Evangeline taps her foot loudly, impatient as ever. She inspects her nails, for once free of metal claws. "You Reds are always so sentimental."

"You should try it." I roll my eyes, pushing past her and into the still-lush grounds of the palace. Carmadon hasn't neglected an inch of his husband's government home. Guards nod at us as we go, looking impressive in their dark green coats and polished boots. Evangeline even nods back to a few, both Red and Silver. I wonder if she's starting to make friends in her new home—if she's even capable of making friends.

"Well, do you feel better, at least?" she asks, her breath fogging in the crisp air. Leaves crunch beneath our feet.

"Are you my bodyguard or my mother?" I grumble, meeting only her twisted smirk. "Yes, I feel better."

"Good. It's easier to protect people with a clear head." She taps her hands together, her rings clinging together like bells. "So it's been a while."

"Two months," I echo, not knowing what else to say.

"You certainly seemed like you needed the time away."

Her eyes rove over me, as if she can see through my clothes all the way to my bones. Evangeline remembers what I looked like before, the last time I saw her. She had been in Montfort only a few days, having fled Archeon and the iron grip of her father. I thought she was passing through, just another refugee of the war making her way west. Never did I think she'd stay in a place like this, a country where she was equal to any Red. Equal to me.

I suppose Elane was worth the price. Love was worth the price.

When I saw her, she had crossed half the world to be here, on foot, by boat, and finally by jet. Somehow I looked so much worse. Hollow, in shock, unable to sit still or slow down. We passed each other in Carmadon's garden, and even she knew to give me space. For once, Evangeline Samos had no snide remarks for me, and let me walk alone.

Perhaps this is the cost for such kindness. Having her trail me everywhere.

"I'm ready to be back," I admit. Somehow, it's an easier thing to say to her than to Gisa or Farley or Kilorn. She's seen me at my worst, at my darkest, when I thought the rest of my life would be Silent Stone and a cruel king's love.

Usually, Evangeline reserves her pride for herself. Today she spares some for me. "I don't like you," she replies, and it sounds like another admission. An acceptance. A step toward friendship.

My response is automatic. "I don't like you either." It draws a rare, true smile from her. "So, what's next on my schedule? I know I skipped out on the trade meeting, but is there something else I have to be at before sunset?"

She blinks at me like I've grown a second head. "How should I know?"

I almost laugh. "The last time I had a bodyguard, he kept me to a schedule." *Strange. He was a Samos too.*

Evangeline sighs, following my train of thought. "Lucas wasn't all bad. He didn't deserve to die." Her eyes cloud a bit, darkening with memory. "And he was a better bodyguard than me. I don't have any idea where you're supposed to be right now."

"Brilliant."

The mischievous glint returns, brighter than ever. She grins, showing teeth. "I do know where *someone* is, though."

My stomach flips. "*Why* do you keep nudging us at each other?"

"Well, before, it was to make sure he didn't marry me. I mean, could you imagine? No thank you," she says, pretending to retch. I purse my lips as we step into the palace. "Fine, to each her own."

The change from crisp, cold air to the warm halls inside falls around my shoulders like a blanket. The scent doesn't change, though. Inside and out, the palace smells like the fresh tang of pine.

"Why do you keep nudging *now*?" I drop my voice. Several meetings are still in session, and too many people roam the palace for my taste.

Evangeline does no such thing. "There aren't many who deserve to be happy. I'm certainly not one of them, but here I am." She leads me around a corner, winding us toward the entrance hall. "I think you might deserve it, Barrow."

I gape at her. That's one of the kindest things another person has ever said to me—and somehow it's coming from Evangeline Samos.

Again, it feels easy to talk to her. Maybe because we aren't friends or family. She doesn't have the same expectations of me, or the same fears for my well-being. There's no risk to her.

"He saw me the other night." The words fight their way out of my mouth. "He wouldn't speak to me."

It feels shameful to say, shameful to even care about. I was the one who left, after all. I told him to move on if he wanted to. *I won't ask you to wait for me.*

And yet he didn't say a word.

When I look at her, I expect judgment. There is nothing but Evangeline's usual detached sneer.

"Are you physically incapable of talking to him first?" she drawls.

"No," I mutter, sullen.

Evangeline flounces off again, a bit of a spring in her step. Her rings jingle again as she snaps her fingers, gesturing for me to follow.

"I think you need a drink, Mare Barrow."

This sector of Ascendant is lively beneath the sunset, looking out over the lake waters from a man-made cliff. Lanterns cross over the pedestrian streets, glowing brightly already. Many bars and restaurants spill out onto the sidewalks, their chairs and tables filled with patrons returning from work. Laughter and music wash over me, both foreign sounds. Part of me wants to turn around and go back to some quiet corner of the palace. The noise is almost too much, grating on my nerves. Every happy shout could be a scream, and the smash of a glass somewhere makes my entire body jump.

Evangeline puts a cool hand to my arm, grounding me. This isn't a battlefield. It isn't a Silver palace either.

It reminds me of Summerton, of Archeon, of Silver cities where places like this would never allow Reds to enter, let alone serve us. But both kinds of blood are here, evident in their varying shades of skin. Cold bronze, warm ivory, icy porcelain, vibrant copper. Many still have their military uniforms, either coming off shift or enjoying break time. I recognize the white and green of politicians too, seeking refuge from the delegations.

One of the bars is quieter than the rest, and dimmer, full of alcoves clustered around a main bar. More like a tavern than a cosmopolitan meeting place. Those, I remember. Those, we had at home. It's where I met the prince of Norta, though I didn't know it at the time.

And, of course, that's where Cal is sitting, his back to the street, half a drink in hand. I'd know his broad silhouette anywhere.

I glance at myself, my velvet clothing discarded for a training suit.

There's dried sweat on my body, and my hair is probably still on end from all the static electricity.

"You look fine," Evangeline says.

I huff at her. "Usually you're a good liar."

She raises a fist and fakes a yawn. "Watching over you is very taxing."

"Well, you've certainly earned a break," I say, gesturing to one of the tables at another bar. "I can handle myself for an hour or so."

Thankfully, she doesn't argue and sets off toward the loudest, shiniest, and most boisterous bar on the street. A flash of scarlet ripples at a seemingly empty table on the curb, and suddenly Elane is sitting there, a glass of wine in hand. Evangeline doesn't look back as she waves me on. I scoff to myself—that meddling magnetron probably had her shadow girlfriend keep tabs on Cal so she could shove me at him when he was alone.

Suddenly I wish I had more time. To think of something to say, to rehearse. To figure out what the hell I want. I could barely speak to him this morning, and the sight of him last night left me haunted. What will this do to both of us?

Only one way to find out.

The seat next to him is empty, and high up. As I climb into it, I thank my body for remembering its agility. If I fall out in front of him, I really might die of embarrassment. But I stay level, and before he can even turn to look at me, I have his glass in my hand. I don't care what it holds. I just drink, steadying my nerves. My heart hammers in my chest.

The liquid is slightly sour, but cold and refreshing, with an edge of cinnamon. It tastes like winter.

Cal stares at me like he's seeing a ghost, his bronze eyes wide. I watch as his pupils dilate, eating up all the color. His uniform jacket is unbuttoned, hanging open to the fresh air. He doesn't need a scarf or coat to keep him warm right now, just his own ability. I feel it at my edges, ready to wash over me.

"Thief," he says simply, his voice deep.

I look back at him over the rim of his glass, finishing the drink. "Obviously."

The familiar words hang between us, meaning more than they should. They feel like an ending, and a beginning. To what, I can't say.

"Is the great Tiberias Calore skipping out on his delegation?"

I reach, putting the glass back in place in front of him. He doesn't move, forcing my arm to graze across his. The simple touch explodes through me, down to my toes.

The bartender passes by, and Cal motions with two fingers, silently ordering for both of us. "I'm not a king anymore. I can do as I like," he says. "Sometimes. Besides, it's another trade debate right now. I'm no use."

"Me neither."

It's a relief to know that, for now, no one else is relying on me. Not to speak, stand, or be someone else's flag bearer. When the bartender puts a full glass down in front of me, I drink half of it in one gulp.

Cal watches my every move, a soldier surveying a battlefield. Or an enemy. "I see your brothers taught you drinking."

I grin, shrugging. "Had to do something to pass the time up north."

Cal sips more politely and wipes the foam from his lips. "How was it?"

The Paradise Valley beckons, even now. The empty wilderness, the mountains, the quiet of falling snow beneath a full moon. It is a good place to forget yourself, to be lost. But I can't do that anymore. "It was good for me. I needed . . ." I bite my lip. "I needed to be away."

He furrows his brow, watching every tick of my face. "And how are you?"

"Better." Not perfect. Not whole. I'll never be whole again. His eyes darken, and I know he sees that in me. He feels it in himself. "I still don't sleep properly."

"Neither do I," he replies quickly, forcing another sip of beer. I remember his nightmares, some quiet, some thrashing. About his father dying at his own hand. I still can't imagine what that must feel like. And now I bet he dreams about Maven. The body he found, my wound in his belly. I dream about him too.

"I try not to think about him," I whisper, wrapping my arms around myself. A sudden chill blows over me. From Cal or the mountain, I can't say. "It doesn't work."

Another gulp of his drink. He breaks first, looking away from me, his gaze like embers. "I know." After a long moment, his eyes sweep back to me. The sorrow clears from his face. "So what's next?"

I'm not sure what he's asking, so I answer the easiest interpretation of the question.

"Proper resettlement. Gisa is supervising a move from the palace to a town house of our own, up the slope." I point over his shoulder, gesturing in the general direction of our new home. "She said it has a beautiful view, and I guess it's close to where we electricons can train."

One side of his mouth draws up in a grin. "I figured that storm up the mountain wasn't natural."

I return the smile and gesture to my ragged appearance, sweat and all. "In case you couldn't tell."

"You look beautiful. You always do." He says it so nonchalantly, then takes another sip of his drink without blinking or breaking his gaze.

Cold air whistles past my teeth as I suck in a breath, a last gasp before the plunge. My grip tightens on the glass in my hand, until I'm afraid it might shatter. "You saw me last night," I whisper, my voice almost lost in the tavern.

An emotion I can't name shadows his face. "Yeah."

I hoped for some clue in his voice or expression, but I'm left to stumble in the dark for understanding. "Why didn't you say anything?" I ask, trying not to sound desperate. I can't tell if it works.

He forces his trademark grin, lopsided and easy. "You wanted me to wake up half the palace, including your dad?"

"That's not why." At least I know how to see through his charm by now.

A blush blooms over his cheeks. I unsettle him as much as he unsettles me. Frowning, he takes another drink of his beer. A long one, as if he can just wait me out. *Fat chance, Calore.*

I don't waver, staring until he can't avoid the question anymore.

"I figured you needed every second you could get," he admits, biting out the words. As if there is shame in them. "I didn't want to rush you."

His warmth ripples over me, tentative and searching. "Into what?"

"Into making up your mind, Mare," Cal huffs, throwing up one hand in exasperation. Like this is the most obvious thing in the world.

I swallow around the tightness in my throat, biting my lip. He notes every movement in me, watching my face like a battlefield. Looking for an advantage, looking for opportunity. "I did a lot of thinking up at Paradise," I say. I feel like I'm balancing on a cliff, ready to tip in either direction, with no idea how far the drop might be.

He didn't say a word. I won't ask you to wait for me. The thoughts are haunting.

"I would certainly hope so," he says, laughing darkly. He even shakes his head, then takes another gulp. His frustration doesn't last long, quickly melting into apprehension. I shiver as his eyes dart over me, his lips parted. "And?" he adds quietly, as if holding his breath.

"And I don't know. I still don't know." Before he can react, my head bows and I look at my hands twisting in my lap. If anyone at the tavern is listening or even looks our way, I don't notice. Again, the world has narrowed to him and only him. At first I clench my teeth, to hold back the words rattling in my throat. *No,* I think. *You don't have to do that with him.* "I missed you terribly," I whisper. "I was so afraid to speak to you this morning."

The heat grows, cocooning me from the cold air of the mountain. "I was afraid last night," he murmurs.

My head snaps up to find him leaning closer. The edge of my vision swims. "And now?" I ask, feeling breathless.

He doesn't flinch, his face stone, his eyes fire. "Terrified."

I'm all lightning, my nerves crackling beneath my skin. "Me too."

"Where does this leave us?" One of his hands brushes mine on the bar top, but doesn't linger.

I can only shake my head. *I don't know.*

"Let me simplify." He licks his lips, and his voice takes on a warrior edge, resolute and unyielding. "In a perfect world, without war, without the reconstruction, without the Lakelands or the Guard or any other obstacle you can think of, what would you do? What would you *want* for us?"

I sigh, waving him off. "It doesn't work like that, Cal."

He never wavers, only leaning farther into my space, until our noses are just inches apart. "Humor me," he says neatly, as if carving every letter.

My chest tightens. "I suppose I would ask you to stay here."

His eyes flash. "Okay."

"And I would hope that, in a perfect world, every time you looked at me, you wouldn't see your brother's corpse." The last word comes out hoarsely, broken apart. I lower my gaze, looking anywhere but his face. I settle on his fingers as they twitch, betraying his own pain. "And every time I looked at you, I wouldn't see him, and what he could have been. If I could have . . . done more."

Suddenly his hand is beneath my chin, forcing me to meet his eyes. His touch is flame, almost too hot to bear. "In a perfect world, who would you have chosen?" he rasps.

I know what he's asking. Who I would have chosen between Cal and Maven, long ago, before we knew what his brother was, and how far he had fallen. It seems like an impossible question. Balancing two people who don't actually exist.

"I can't answer that," I mutter, slowly removing his hand from my face. But I keep hold of him. "Not because I don't want to, but because I simply can't. It isn't something I can ever solve."

His grip tightens on me. "I don't see him every time I look at you," he says. "Do you really see him every time you look at me?"

Sometimes, yes.

Every time? Now?

I search him, my eyes weaving back and forth over every inch of skin I can find. Sure, callused hands. The veins of his exposed neck. A shadow of stubble already spreading over his cheeks. Strong brows, straight nose, the forever crooked smile. Eyes that were never Maven's.

"No," I tell him, and I mean it. "Did you wait, Cal?"

His fingers weave through mine as he grins. "I'm still waiting."

This must be what it feels like for a gravitron to fly. Somehow my stomach drops and leaps at the same time. Despite the warmth of him all around me, I begin to shiver. "I can't make promises," I sputter hastily, already trying to get ahead of the admission we've both made. "We don't know where the world is going. My family is here, and you have so much to do back east—"

"I do," he says, nodding. "I am also very good at flying jets."

I can't help but laugh. "You and I both know you can't just commandeer a jet when you want to see me." Though the thought does make my heart skip a beat.

"You and I both know you aren't going to stay put here either," he retorts, and his free hand goes to my chin again. I don't push it away. "The future won't let you. And I don't think you can let yourself sit still much longer."

The words continue to spill out, as quickly as they pop into my head. Obstacles in our way, problems to be solved. "That doesn't mean I'll be anywhere close to the States, if and when I do decide to get involved with all this again."

Cal just grins wider. For a moment he is a second sun, beaming warmth all over me. It breaks and re-forms my heart. "If geography is really the only thing standing in our way, then I consider this settled."

Sighing, I allow just a bit of the tension in me to release. I relax into his hand, angling my head. *Can it really be this easy?* "Do you forgive me?"

His eyes darken and his smile seems to fade. "Have you forgiven yourself?"

Again he looks me over, hunting for an answer. Ready for me to lie. It takes all my strength not to.

"No," I whisper, expecting him to pull back. To turn away. "I don't know if I can."

He has his own demons, as many as me. I wouldn't blame him if he didn't want to shoulder the burden of mine too. But he only tightens his grip, until I can't tell where my fingers end and his begin.

"That's okay," he says simply, like it's just so obvious. "We have time."

I blink as I feel myself fall from the cliff, the balance finally tipped. "We have time," I echo.

My heartbeat thumps, a steady rhythm. The electricity in the walls, in the lights, responds to my call, humming with energy. And then I simply shut it all off, plunging the tavern and the street into embracing darkness. It's as easy as breathing. Voices around us rise in alarm, but I ignore them, focused on Cal instead. No one can see us now.

His lips meet mine slowly, a steady invitation. He always lets me set the pace, always gives me a chance to step back. I have no intention of slowing down, or stopping. The sounds of the tavern fade away around me and my eyes slide shut, until the only sensation is the feel of him. And the crackle of electricity beneath my skin, begging to release again.

If I could hold it back forever, I would.

When the lights return, buzzing back to life, I pull away first.

He lingers, reluctant, then smirks as he reaches for his money. But I've already left some on the countertop, my hands quicker than his ever will be. We grin at each other. I wish I still had the coin he gave me, that night when I stood in the shadows and waited for someone to see me for who I was.

I take his hand and lead him back up the mountainside. To his room, to mine, to the forest. To fire or lightning. It doesn't matter.

I am almost nineteen. I have nothing but time. To choose, to heal. To live.

SIX
Cal

By the time the gala catches us, I would rather sleep through the evening. And it really does feel like a predator, crouching at the end of the week, waiting to pounce. I've had more than my fair share of balls, parties, and overblown celebrations in my lifetime. I know how this goes, and I know how boring, exhausting, and otherwise nauseating this night will be. After our days filled with meetings and debates, small talk with the delegates will be salt in an open, oozing wound.

At least I'm not alone here. Mare hates this as much as I do, but when I suggested we both conveniently come down with sickness, she set my hair on end. We spend enough time together. People would believe it.

But she's right. We owe it to the alliance, to our delegations, and to ourselves to make a show of this. In the end it's just a party, and maybe we can hunt down a little fun in the midst of it all. Not to mention, Carmadon has had the kitchens working all week. At the least, I'll leave tonight very well fed. Besides, I'd rather not risk Nanabel's wrath or Julian's gentle disappointment. Both have worked too hard this week, especially Nanabel. She settled after our first meeting, doing her best to bridge the gap between the Silvers of Norta and the rest of the alliance. Without her work, and Radis's too, we might have another rebellion on our hands, with more nobles ready to join the Secession. Instead, we have allies.

Tonight she intends to bask in her small victories, bedecking herself in the old jewels she once wore as a queen. As we wait for Julian and Sara, she inspects herself in the mirrors of our salon, turning back and forth to let her fire-colored gemstones catch the light. Her long, flowing orange gown seems to dance as she whirls. Anabel is no fool, and she was careful to avoid wearing a crown, even if she does still dress like a queen.

"Julian tells me you're going to be staying on a few days after his wedding," she says to her reflection, though the words are meant for me.

I've been ready for half an hour and I'm almost asleep on the couch when she speaks. Her voice jolts me back, and I sit up, sharp as ever in my plain black suit. Only the badge on my collar, the joined circles in red, white, and silver, adorns my clothing.

"Yes," I reply after gathering myself. Her eyes follow me in the mirror. "A few weeks, I think. Then I'll head back to Archeon and return to work."

My body tightens, bracing for a scathing remark or scolding refusal. Instead Nanabel just fixes her hair, smoothing her gray locks back behind her ears. She draws out her response, making me wait.

"Good," she finally says, and I nearly fall out of my seat. "You've earned a break."

"I—I suppose so, yeah," I sputter, surprised. She knows who I'm staying with, and why. Mare Barrow isn't exactly her favorite person in the world. "Thanks."

"Of course," she says. My grandmother grins as she turns around, amused by my shock. "You might not think it, but I'm proud of you, Cal. What you've done, what you continue to do. You're a young man, and you've accomplished so much with your time." Her footsteps are soft, muffled by the rich carpets of the salon. The couch sinks as she sits next to me, one lined hand taking mine. "You're strong, my dear boy. Too strong. You deserve the happy moments when you find them. And all I want, beyond anything else, a crown or a country, is for you to *live*."

My throat threatens to close, and I have to look away from her, if only to hide the sharp sting of tears. She clenches her jaw, just as uncomfortable with emotion.

"Thank you," I force out, focusing on a spot in the carpet. As much as I've wanted those words from her, they aren't easy to hear or accept.

Her grip on my fingers tightens, forcing me to look at her. We have the same eyes, she and I. Burning bronze. "I've lived through the rule of four kings. I know greatness—and sacrifice—when I see it," she says. "Your father would be proud of you. In the end."

When Julian and Sara finally emerge, they are good enough to ignore my red-rimmed eyes.

With the delegations out of their uniforms and in finery, it's easy to pretend this is just a party. Not simply another meeting veiled by silk, liquor, and roving plates of stupidly tiny foods. At least Montfort isn't as rigid as old Norta or its court. I don't have to wait to be announced, and I descend into the grand ballroom with the rest of the delegates, all of us moving like a school of jewel-colored fish.

The chamber can't compare to Whitefire, or even the Hall of the Sun. Royals have the edge when it comes to splendor, but I hardly mind. Instead of white molding and gilt frames, the long ballroom has polished timber arches and brilliant cut-glass windows looking out on the valley as night falls. The fire of sunset sparkles off mirrors that make the space seem grander and bigger. Overhead, cast-iron hoops are set with a thousand candles, flickering with golden flame. No less than six fireplaces, all of them rough stone, throw off pleasant heat to warm the expansive room. I feel each one at the edge of my perception, and I look across the floor, searching for familiar faces.

Mare's brothers and Kilorn would be easiest to spot, tall as they are. They aren't here yet, so likely she isn't either. The premier is, of course, greeting delegates as they filter into the room. Carmadon stands proudly at his side, waving over servants as they pass. I watch as he nearly force-feeds one of the Nortan nobles a tiny portion of salmon.

Evangeline must have the night off from her bodyguard duties. She has Elane hanging on her arm, the two of them hovering near the string band that's still warming up. When the violinist raises his instrument, the pair of them begin to dance in perfect rhythm. As always, Evangeline manages to sparkle in the most threatening way. Her gown is beaten bronze, sculpted to her form but somehow fluid. The color looks good on her, warming up her otherwise cold appearance. Elane, on the other hand, seems to be playing the part of a winter queen. Her red hair flames as always, made even more bright by her pale skin, a light blue suit, and silver lipstick. Ptolemus stands nearby, not so loudly dressed, with Wren Skonos on his arm. Both of them favor dark green, an emblem of their new allegiance to Montfort.

If anything is proof of the new world, the new possibility we could have, the Samos siblings are. First Evangeline, once meant to be my queen and my burden, then a princess of a hostile kingdom—now a soldier of an equal nation, with the woman she loves at her side. And her brother, heir to a throne as much as I was, nearly crushed by the expectations of a similar father—Ptolemus is here too, oathed to defend all he was raised to destroy. Both have so many sins behind them; both have no right to forgiveness or a second chance. But they found it, and the world is better for having them.

Like Mare, I can't help but think of Shade when I see them. He was my friend and I miss him, but I can't hate Ptolemus for what he did. After all, I've done the same. Taken siblings and loved ones, killed for what I was told to believe. How can I condemn him without condemning myself?

Behind me, Julian and Sara keep watch, already halfway through their first drinks. "Just doing our duty," Sara quips, catching my eye.

"Thanks," I reply, grinning.

The pair of them pledged to keep any delegates away from me as long as I wanted, to give me time to breathe. Today was the worst of all: I spent most of it policing a shouting match between a Scarlet Guard general and one of Montfort's transport ministers.

Nanabel needs no such reprieve and is already working her way through the room, angling into the circle of diplomats around the premier. By party's end, they'll either never speak to each other again or be close friends. I'm not sure which is more frightening.

"Behind you, Cal," Julian says and points his chin back up the stairs. From our spot on the floor, we have an excellent view of the crowd as it descends, and it doesn't take me long to pick them out.

Gisa really outdid herself with the whole family, even Mare's father. Daniel doesn't look particularly comfortable in the dark green dress suit, but there's a distinct pride to him as he walks unaided down the steps. Mare's mother, Ruth, looks regal next to him, her graying hair swept up into a complicated braid set with green clips to match her dragonfly-patterned gown. Tramy's suit jacket is particularly bright, embroidered with flowers and vines over yellow silk. Bree is his broader counterpart, though his jacket is pale orange. Kilorn completes the trio, grinning broadly over his blue and gold-vined coat. Even Farley received a Gisa Barrow original outfit: she's clad head to toe in red-and-white silk offset with gold detailing and flower embroidery. She doesn't have Clara with her, the party being too late for the infant. I wonder what the young general will abandon first—her gleaming jacket or the party.

Gisa follows at a distance, looking as smug as a cat with a caught mouse. She has a girl I don't recognize at her side, their elbows joined, both their dresses pale pink with intricate lacing.

She chose purple for Mare again, sheer silk overlaid with gold branches and silver blossoms. The meaning isn't difficult to figure out. All the Barrows and Farley too wear some sort of plant in bloom—roses, lilies, magnolias, fresh leaves. Though winter looms, they are spring. Reborn.

Mare smiles just for me as she walks, careful to keep the hem of her skirt in check on the stairs. The many candles dance above her, making her glow. I wait patiently, letting the rest of the crowd break around me in a river. If someone tries to speak to me, I don't notice. My focus is on one person in the room.

A flush colors the tops of her cheeks, the perfect complement to the berry color of her lips. And the curl of freshly dyed hair, purple at the ends. I can't help but smile like an idiot, especially when she tucks a lock of hair behind her ear. The stones glimmer there, for her brothers, for Kilorn, and for me. The scarlet gem winks across the room, a star I would follow anywhere.

When she reaches the floor, I don't move, letting her maneuver carefully around her mess of brothers. They spot me and offer curt nods, better than I deserve. Mare's mother is more polite, offering a smile, while her father pointedly looks at the ceiling. I don't mind. I have time with them. I have time with her.

"I have to say, I expect more from you," Mare says, stepping up to me. She runs a hand down the lapel of my suit, letting her fingers trace the buttons before finding the badge on my collar. Her touch, even through the clothes, makes me shiver. "You look like you're dressed for a quiet night in."

"I wish," I mutter, closing my hand over hers.

She squeezes my fingers. "I wager we make it thirty minutes or so."

As much as I enjoy the thought of stealing away with her, my stomach growls in disagreement. We could have food brought up to my room, but that just seems rude, and certainly Carmadon will see that we're sent the worst of the kitchen scraps.

"And miss dinner?" I balk. "No thanks. If I'm going to suffer, I'm going to at least get something out of it."

She pulls a face but nods in compliance. "Good point. But if he runs out of steak again, I'm leaving."

I laugh quietly, wanting to pull her closer, regardless of propriety. But tongues are already wagging about us, and the last thing we need is a gossip circle about our *status.* Not that we can even agree on that. No promises, as Mare said. We're simply taking things as they come, with our priorities and boundaries starkly drawn.

"Are you all ready for next week? Does Anabel mind?" Mare looks at me, her teeth gritted, prepared for the worst. She searches for any hesitation in my answer, knowing all my tells.

I smile wider. "Believe it or not, she gave me her blessing."

"To go up to the cabin when the weather breaks?" She blanches, her eyes darting to pick out my grandmother in the crowd. "I'm impressed."

"I haven't told her about Paradise, but I doubt she'll care either way. It's not exactly easy for me to get frostbite."

"Unless you piss me off and I lock you out in the cold."

Before I can laugh her off, Bree and Tramy appear on either side of us, almost leering. "Don't think she won't," Bree warns, his brow furrowed.

Tramy bobs his head in agreement. "I almost lost a toe."

"And you would have deserved it," Mare snaps, shooing both of them off with an exasperated grin. "So, are you going to make me dance?"

Elsewhere, the string band is in full swing, serenading a floor teeming with dancing couples of various skill. I glance at them, remembering the last time I did this. Mare was there, on Maven's arm, dancing steps I taught her.

She feels the memory as I do, both of us lost to watching the floor. Her smile fades, as does mine, and we weather the storm of loss and regret together. It's the only way through it.

"No," we say in unison, and turn away.

We don't stay glued. That's not her way, or mine. She goes where she wishes through the gala, as do I. As much as I hate it, I make the rounds I must, thanking members of the delegations for their time and expertise. Julian does it with me, at least, his smile unfailing. Once or twice, I wonder if he might have to use his singing ability to disentangle us from a particularly loathsome or chatty delegate, but he always manages to spin the conversation without it. Despite all my training for battle, the runs with Mare every morning, and my rigorous workouts, I flag long before she does.

"Unless you're particularly invested in dessert, I think you can call it a night," my uncle mutters, his grip gentle on my shoulder. "You look ready to drop."

"I certainly feel it," I whisper back. As with training, the ache in me, the exhaustion, is the good kind. This pain accomplished something. "Where's Mare?"

"I believe she's scolding one of her brothers for ripping his dress jacket. Unlike you, she has some stamina left."

She always does.

"Should I get her for you?" he adds, looking over me with concern. "I can let her know you went up early—"

I wave him off. "No, it's fine, I can wait her out. Bree certainly deserves it, after all the work Gisa put in."

Julian and I have the same smile, a crooked slash across our faces. He looks at me fully, eyes searching mine. Now I realize how much he looks like my mother, and for a moment, my heart breaks with the need to know her.

"It's good to see you like this," Julian says, putting both his hands on my shoulders, forcing me square to him. "I knew you'd find your way back to Mare, but I did have my fears for a while."

I glance down at my feet, sighing. "Me too," I say, chewing my lip. "And what about you? Why did you wait so long with Sara?"

Julian blinks. He is rarely caught off guard or unprepared for a question. "We planned to marry," he says, searching for an answer. "Before my father—"

"I know that. It was in the diary pages. I mean after." My voice catches and Julian pales. "After what Elara did."

His lips thin into a grim line. When he speaks, his eyes lose focus, and he descends into memory. "I wanted to. I would have. But Sara wouldn't let me tie my fate to hers so fully. She didn't know what Elara would do, if she might decide to finish the job. Have her executed. She couldn't bear the idea of me dying with her." His eyes water, and I look away, giving him time to recover as best he can. When I look back, he forces an empty smile. "And now, well, we had a war on, didn't we?"

I try to give him a smile of my own but fail. "There's time for everything, isn't there?"

"Yes. But we always have the choice. To let things get in the way, or to pursue what we really want," he says quickly, with fervor. "I'm glad you read the diary. I know it could not have been easy."

To that, I have nothing I can say. Reading the copy of my mother's diary felt like ripping my flesh apart and sewing it back together. I almost couldn't do it. But to have even a glimpse of her, no matter how painful—I owed her that much.

Julian's grip on me lessens and he steps back, fading into the kindly uncle I know—and not the haunted man he is. "I have more to give you, of course. Not from your mother, but other writings, collections, what I can get together from the Royal Archives. Things to help you understand what you came from, both the good and the evil."

Part of me quails at the thought of the pile Julian might force on me, but I take it in stride. "Thanks, I appreciate it."

"Cal, it is a rare man who is willing to look at himself and see what truly stands. A rare man indeed." I try and fail not to blush furiously, heat smoldering in my cheeks. Julian ignores my embarrassment, or he simply doesn't care. "You would have made a good king, but never great. Not like you are now. A great man who needs no crown."

My insides twist. *How can he know who I am? What I might be in the future? Who I could become?*

It is a worry, I suppose, we all carry. Me, Mare, even my uncle. We are chosen to some kind of greatness, and cursed to it.

"Thank you, Julian," I force out, overcome again.

He claps me on the shoulder, voice dropping. "This isn't over, but you know that, don't you? It won't be for years. Decades, maybe."

"I know," I reply, feeling the truth of it in my gut. The Lakelands, the Silver Secession. No matter how strong this alliance is, there will always be someone to challenge it—and the world we're fighting to build.

"History will remember you, mark my words," Julian says, now steering me toward the terrace. Outside, Mare has Bree by the scruff of his collar, forcing him to bend down so she can shout at him.

"Make sure it remembers you well."

FARE WELL

Maven

I would turn this horrid little room to ash if I could, but the Silent Stone is a poison and an anchor. I feel it working in me, spreading beneath my skin like black rot. My limbs ache, weighted down by the sensation. Everything feels wrong in me, my very nature denied. The flame is extinguished, or at least it is far beyond my reach.

This is what I did to her. It's only fair they do it to me. She was kept in a different room, but I feel her here just the same. I almost smile at the thought of just punishment, of balancing my sins. But that would be impossible. There is no penance I can make to wash me clean. I am stained forever, impossible to redeem or cure. And it makes things easier. I can do what must be done to survive, without thought, without restraint. To make it all worth what I've done. Nothing is beyond possibility.

The two chairs in my lavish excuse for a cell are drawn together near the windows, facing each other as if prepared for a meeting. I sneer at them and lie flat on the long couch instead, enjoying the cool feel of golden silk beneath my skin. The salon is fine enough, a forgotten sitting room instead of the dungeon I deserve. Foolish Cal, trying to show me mercy—or show the rest of them how merciful he is, how different he is from me. He is as predictable as a sunrise.

I focus on the feel of the smooth fabric instead of the dead weight of Silent Stone, pressing down with every breath I take. The ceiling above me is molded plaster, sculpted into intricate shapes of wreathed flame. This part of the Ocean Hill palace is foreign to me. It was a favorite of Cal's mother's, and my father didn't bring the court here much.

I wonder if I'll live long enough to return to Whitefire. My fists clench at the thought of my brother invading my room there. Not because it's mine by right, but because he'll see too much of me in it. The smallness of my bedchamber, the emptiness of the one place I was ever alone. It feels like exposing a weakness to him—and Cal is just so good at taking advantage of weakness once he finds it. Usually it takes him quite a long time to do so, but I've made it easy for him. Maybe he'll finally know what abyss there is in me, what a cliff I stand upon and throw myself off.

Or maybe he won't see at all. Cal has always had a blind spot where I am concerned, for better or worse. He could just be the same shortsighted, bullheaded, honor-bound and over-proud dullard he's always been. There's a chance this war has not changed him or his ability to see me for what I am. A good chance.

I comfort myself with such thoughts—my idiot brother, the golden son blinded by his own light. It isn't his fault, really. The Calores are warrior kings, the heirs raised to battle and blood. Not exactly a breeding ground for intelligence or intuition. And he didn't have a mother watching over him to balance what our father wanted of a son. Not like me. Mother made sure I learned to fight beyond the battlefield, on a throne as well as in a sparring circle.

And look where you are now, at the end of it. Look where he is.

Snarling to myself, I sit up and seize the closest thing to me, then hurl it against the wall. Glass, water, and flowers smash, a momentary balm to the sting inside. *No wonder Mare did this so much,* I think, remembering how many times she threw her meals at the walls of her own cell. I throw the other decorative vase in the room for good measure, this time against the window. The glass pane doesn't even crack, but I feel a bit better.

The relief doesn't last. It never does. First I think of her, of Mother. Like always, her voice comes to me in silent moments, a whisper and a ghost. I've long since learned not to try to block her out, because it doesn't work. In fact, that only makes her worse.

Lash for lash, she says to me, an echo of words spoken before her death. *Cut for cut.* If they're going to hurt me, I must hurt them too. I must do *worse.*

If only she had better advice. I'm truly stuck, imprisoned by a brother with no choice but to execute me. And I see no way out of that fate. If it were just Cal's decision, then yes, I would survive. I wouldn't worry at all. Even now, he doesn't have the spine to kill me. But he has the crown again, and a kingdom to convince. He can't show weakness, especially with me. What's more, I don't deserve his mercy. But I shall do as my mother says. I'll hurt him as much as I can, as deeply as possible, before my time is ended. It will be some small consolation to know he bleeds as I bleed.

And Mare too. There are still wounds in her, wounds I made, that can always be cut open. They say animals are most dangerous at their end, fiercer and more violent. I will be the same, if I manage to see her before my sentence is carried out. I desperately hope I do.

Iris didn't speak about her gods often, and I didn't ask. But I did some research of my own. She believes in a place beyond death, somewhere we go in the afterward. At first, I wanted to believe it too. It would mean seeing my mother again—and seeing Thomas. But Iris's afterlife is split in two, separated into paradise and punishment. Certainly I have earned the latter.

And Thomas, my dear Thomas, certainly did not.

If there is something after death, it will not be for both of us.

I return to what I've always known, the burden I've carried with me, the end always waiting. I will never see him again. Not even in my dreams.

My mother gave me so much, but she took in return. In an attempt to rid me of my nightmares, she took my dreams. Sometimes, I prefer it. But right now, in this room, I wish I could sleep and escape, and see his face one more time. Feel what I felt with him one more time. Instead of this corrupted anger, a tangle of pain and rage that threatens to split me open every time I think of him and his body, burned beyond recognition, burned by my own damned fingers.

I wonder if I mourn him so much because I do not know what could have been, what he could have made me. Or is it because my mother never corrupted what I felt for him? Not while he lived, at least. She certainly tried later, when his memory destroyed my days. She did the same with Mare, pulling at every new burst of feeling like a gardener ripping out weeds at the root.

But even Mare doesn't tear me apart like he still does. Even she doesn't make me bleed like this.

Only one person living still can. And I'll have to face him soon.

I lie back down again, hissing out a breath. I'll make him bleed as I bleed.

* * *

I'm still lying down, an arm over my eyes, when the door opens and shuts, accompanied by heavy footfalls. I don't need to look to know who it is. His breathing, ragged and so boorishly loud, is enough.

"If you're looking for absolution, I think Iris has a silly little shrine somewhere in her rooms. Bother her gods instead of me," I grumble.

I don't look at him, keeping my eyes resolutely shut. Looking at him makes me burn with rage and jealousy. And anguish too, for what he was, the brother I no longer have the ability to love. I would incinerate my clothes if not for the Silent Stone. What's more, he is a betrayer as much as I am, but no one seems to mind. It isn't *fair.*

"Absolution?" Cal scoffs from somewhere above me. I don't hear him sit. "It's you who needs it, Maven. Not me."

Sneering, I draw the arm away from my eyes and sit up to look at him fully. My brother recoils under my gaze, taking a step backward across the floor. He looks kingly, even without a crown. More kingly than I ever could. Envy ripples through me again.

"You and I both know you don't believe that," I snap. "Do you, Brother? Do you truly think you are without any blame?"

Cal drops his eyes, his resolve wavering for a second. Then he grits his teeth, all fire again. "It was your mother, Maven. Not me," he forces out. I get the sense he's told himself this more than once. "I didn't kill him."

I wave a hand through the air, dismissive. "Oh, I hardly care about what happened to Father. Though I'm certain you'll be haunted by that for the rest of your life, however short."

Again, he looks away. *You are so easy to read it's almost infuriating,* I think.

"I'm talking about me," I growl, setting the pieces in motion. Confusion steals across his face, and I almost roll my eyes. Cal has to be led to the point like a dumb mule to water.

Cut for cut, Mother whispers.

"I wasn't always this way, was I?" I continue, pushing myself to my feet. He's taller than me, always has been, and it stings. Still, I take a step toward him, eagerly moving into his shadow. I'm used to it there. "You remember better than I do. When I was a boy, your little brother. Always trailing at your heels, eager to spend every moment I could with you. I used to ask to sleep in your room, didn't I?"

Cal narrows his eyes. "You were afraid of the dark."

"And then I wasn't. Just like that." I snap my fingers, expecting him to flinch. He does not. "Her doing, of course. She couldn't be the mother to a whimpering, weakling son afraid of shadows." I begin to pace, circling him. Cal doesn't give me the satisfaction of movement, staying rooted to the spot. He doesn't fear a physical attack from me. Even without his flame, he would have no issue subduing me. I'm little more than a moth fluttering around light. Or at least, that's how he sees me. It's an advantage I've used so many times. "You never noticed when she took things from me, small pieces. You didn't see the change."

As I pass behind him, his shoulders curl, riddled with tension. "That isn't my fault, Maven," he whispers, his voice ragged. He doesn't believe it. *So* fucking *easy to read.* I almost laugh. It isn't difficult to make him bleed.

"So when she cut you out entirely, took my love for you, twisted everything—you didn't notice. You didn't care." I pause in my steps, leaving us side by side. He has to turn his head to look at me, to watch as I school my face into careful blankness. "I've always wondered why."

Cal has no answer, or can't find the strength to speak. I'm better at pain than he is. I always have been.

"It doesn't matter now, of course," I say. "My mother wasn't the only one who took from me—you took something from me too."

Even the hint of her makes him bristle.

"I didn't take Mare," he snarls, rounding on me. I shift before he can grab my arm, his fingers barely brushing the sleeve of my jacket.

I grin up at him, speaking gently, my voice soft and taunting. "It didn't surprise me. You were used to it, having whatever you wanted. Seeing only what you wanted to see. In the end, I realized you knew what was happening to me, what Mother was doing. It was in pieces, in slow shifts, but you still saw it—and you did nothing to stop her." Tsk-ing like a scolding teacher, I shake my head. "Long before you knew what a monster I was, you did monstrous things too."

Cal stares at me, eyes full of accusation. And longing. This time he takes me by surprise when he steps closer, and I fall back on my heels. "Did your mother destroy you entirely? Is there anything left of you?" he asks, searching my face. "Anything that isn't hers?"

He won't tell me what he's looking for, but I know. Despite the walls my mother built around me, Cal always manages to weasel through. His hunting eyes fill me with sorrow. Even now, he thinks there's something in me left to save—and to mourn. There is no escaping our fate, not for either of us. He must sentence me to die. And I must accept death. But Cal wants to know if he's killing his brother along with the monster—or if the brother died long ago.

Cut for cut, my mother whispers, louder now, taunting. The words slice like a razor.

It would hurt him deeply, wound him forever, if I let him glimpse what little is left of me. That I'm still here, in some forgotten corner, just waiting to be found. I could ruin him with one glance, one echo of the brother he remembers. Or I could free him of me. Make the choice for him. Give my brother one last proof of the love I can no longer feel, even if he never knows it.

I weigh the choice in my heart, each side heavy and impossible. For one terrifying moment, I don't know what to do.

Despite all my mother's fine work, I can't find it in myself to land that final blow.

I drop my gaze, forcing a detached smirk to my lips.

"I would do it all again, Cal," I tell him, lying with such grace. It feels easy, after so many years behind a mask. "If given the choice to go back, I would let her change me. I would watch you kill him. I'd send you to the arena. And I'd get it right. I'd give you what you deserve. I'd kill you now if I could. I'd do it a thousand times."

My brother is simple, easy to manipulate. He sees only what lies in front of him, only what he can understand. The lie does its job well. His eyes harden, that undying ember in him almost extinguished entirely. One hand twitches, wanting to form a fist. But the Silent Stone affects him too, and even if he had the strength to make me burn, he could not.

"Good-bye, Maven," Cal says, his voice broken. He isn't really speaking to me.

The farewell is for another boy, lost years ago, before he became what I am now. Cal lets go of him, the Maven I was. The Maven I still am, somewhere inside, unable or unwilling to step into the light.

This will be the last time we speak to each other alone. I can feel that in my marrow. If I see him again, it will be before the throne, or beneath the cold steel of the executioner's blade.

"I look forward to the sentencing," I drawl in reply, watching him flee the room. The door slams behind him, shaking paintings in their frames.

Despite all the difference between us, we have this in common. We use our pain to destroy.

"Good-bye, Cal," I say to no one.

Weakness, my mother answers.

Cal

Julian says I don't have to start this with "dear diary" or anything official. Still, this feels stupid. And a waste of time. My days aren't exactly empty.

Not to mention this whole thing is a security risk.

But Julian certainly knows how to nag.

He knows I'm not talking enough about, well, anything. Not with him, not with Mare. She isn't exactly forthcoming either, but at least she has her sister, her family, Farley, Kilorn, and whoever else she needs when she does decide to say <u>something</u>. I'm nowhere near as lucky. All I have is her and Julian, and I guess Nanabel. Not that I really want to talk to my grandmother about my mental state, or my girlfriend, or the trauma of the past year.

My mother had a diary too. It didn't stop Elara from doing . . . what she did. But it seemed to ground her, in the beginning. Maybe it will help me too.

I'm not exactly good at writing. I certainly read a lot, but it hasn't rubbed off. And I really don't want another liability for the Nortan States. Things are precarious enough.

Or am I just being vain, thinking that anything I scribble down could somehow threaten the reconstruction? Probably.

How does anyone do this? Journals are impossible. I feel idiotic.

Mare wasn't kidding about the Paradise Valley. It's gorgeous and dangerous. We had to wait for a storm to clear out before we could get up here. Had to burn a hole in a snowdrift just to get to the cabin door. And we heard wolves all night long. I wonder if I can lure any to the cabin with dinner scraps?

Do not lure wolves with dinner scraps.

The States and the Scarlet Guard are cooperating well even without me running between them. I was expecting Nanabel to drag me out of the cabin after twenty-four hours, but it looks like we'll get the full time away. And we got to celebrate my birthday properly, despite the bison interruption. They are very noisy.

Third day cooped up inside the cabin. Normally wouldn't mind, but Mare insists on doing puzzles, and I think they're all missing pieces. Seems rudely symbolic.

Fell in a geyser. Very happy to be heatproof. My clothes, not so much. Gave a bison a real show on the jog back to the cabin.

Another snowstorm last night. Mare couldn't help but get involved. Thunder snow is incredible. And she's a show-off.

Convinced the supply-drop pilots to take us on a quick tour around the valley. The whole of Paradise is on top of a caldera and a dormant volcano. Bit unsettling. Even for me.

No bad dreams for the last two weeks. Usually I'd blame exhaustion, but we're not doing much more than lying around and hiking nearby. I think something about the wilderness is settling me. The question is, am I healing—or is this just stasis? Will the nightmares come back when we leave? Will they be worse?

Worse.

And always the same thing.

Maven, alone on that island, standing just out of reach no matter how hard I try to move.

She doesn't want to come with me. And I'd rather she didn't.

I need to do this alone.

Cal

The fog lifts slowly. I wish it wouldn't. I wish visibility would be too poor for a landing, and I'd have to turn back to the mainland.

I could always lie and turn back anyway. No one would question it. No one would care if I made it to Tuck or not. No one would even know.

No one but me.

And him.

The island is gray this time of year, as the autumn days bleed toward winter. It barely stands out in the steel-colored ocean, little more than a smudge against the rising sun. I buzz the northern cliffs, maneuvering my small dropjet with a few easy movements of the controls. It looks the same as it did last year. I try not to think, to remember. I peer down at the landscape, focusing on that instead. Few trees, the dunes, slopes of yellowing grass, the docks of the small harbor, the abandoned base—it unfurls below me in a second. The runway bisects the island and makes for an easy target. I try not to look at the squat barracks as I wheel the dropjet into position, its propellers whipping up a cloud of sand and dune grass. This place holds enough bad memories—I can only handle so many at a time.

Before I can change my mind, I drop altitude. The landing is rougher than it should be, the craft jarring as it touches down. But I'm eager to be finished, and my hands shake, even as I flip the necessary switches and levers. The roar of the propellers lessens as they slow but don't stop. I won't be here long. I can't bear it.

Julian offered to come, as did Nanabel. I refused both.

The island is without any sound but the wind in the grass and the seabirds calling out over the water. I'm tempted to whistle, just to make some human noise. It's odd, knowing I'm the only living person on the island. Especially with the remains of barracks and such human memories all around.

Tuck has been without people since the Scarlet Guard evacuated, fearing a raid after Mare's capture. They still haven't come back. While the base has been worn by wind and the changing seasons, the rest of the island looks content to be left alone.

My feet follow the path from the runway, winding into the tall grass and up the gentle hills. Soon the trail fades, gravel giving way to sandy soil. There are no markers to lead the way—only people who know what they're looking for will find him.

Shade is on the other side of the island, his grave overlooking the dawn. That was Mare's request, when the time came. To make sure he was as far away from her brother as the island allowed.

There was talk of burying him elsewhere. He asked to be buried with his mother, but he did not specify a place. Elara was on Tuck, in a shallow grave. Despite the state of decay, she would have been easy to dig up and move to the mainland. Of course, there was opposition to the idea. Not only because of the gruesome nature, but because, as Julian quietly pointed out, he didn't want Maven's grave to be well known or easily accessible. It could become a rallying point or a monument, giving strength to anyone who might take up his cause.

In the end, we decided Tuck was best. An island in the middle of the ocean, so isolated that even Maven might find peace.

The loose ground shifts beneath me, sucking at my boots. The steps become more difficult, and not only because of the terrain. I force the last few yards and crest the rise beneath the gray light of autumn. I can smell rain, but the storm hasn't hit yet.

The field is empty. Even the birds don't come here.

At first glimpse of the stones, I drop my eyes, focusing on my feet. I don't trust myself to keep walking if I have to watch it get closer. The dream rattles in my head, haunting me. I count off the last few feet, looking up only when I must.

There is no silhouette, no impossible shadow of a lost boy waiting to be found.

Elara's headstone is unmarked, a single gray slab already worn smooth by the wind. There will be no record of her here. Not her name, not her house. Not a word of who she was in life. She doesn't deserve a memory. She stole so many others'.

I refused to give Maven the same treatment. He deserves something at least.

His stone is milky white, with rounded edges. The letters are cut deep, some already filled with dirt or dead grass. I clean them out with a few swipes of my fingers, shivering as I touch the cold, damp stone.

MAVEN CALORE

Beloved son, beloved brother.

Let no one follow.

He is without his title, with little more than his name. But every word on the stone is the truth. We loved him—and he strayed down a path no one else should pursue.

Even though I'm the only person on the island, the only one for miles and miles, I can't find the strength to speak. My voice dies; my throat tightens. I couldn't say good-bye to him if my own life depended on it. The words simply won't come.

My chest tightens as I bend a knee, bowing over his grave. I keep one hand to the stone, letting it flood me with sickly cold. I expected fear—I'm standing over two corpses. Instead there is only grief.

I'm sorry races through my head, a hundred times, a thousand times. Memories of him flash just as quickly, from when he was a young boy to the last time I saw him, and sentenced him to die. *I should have found another way.* I curse myself, and not for the first time this morning. *I could have kept him alive somehow. There was a chance.* Even in Archeon, during the siege. Something could have been done. There must have been a way—and I just couldn't find it.

Some days, Mare tells me to move past it. Not to forget, but to accept what has been done. Some days, she bleeds with me, retreating to blame herself as I do the same. And some days, I can only blame him, blame Elara, blame my father. I was just a boy too. *What was I supposed to do?*

The wind turns icy, a sudden gust howling through my jacket. I tighten against the cold, letting heat flood my chest.

Maybe I should have burned him. Given his body to flame, and let the rest of him go where it willed, carried on the wind.

But like always, I could not let him go. Even now, I cannot let Maven go.

I never will.

My face is already wet when the rain comes.

While the Nortan Civil War officially ended with the abdication of King Tiberias VII, dissolving the Kingdom of Norta as it was known, the cessation of hostilities did not occur until several years after. The conflict that followed was known as the Dancing War, as each side stepped when the other did, matching move for move in a stilted, halting fashion.

Only through the efforts of Montfort and the Scarlet Guard did the fledgling Nortan States manage to hold off invasion attempts from both the Lakelands and Piedmont. It was outwardly a defensive war, with the Nortan States maintaining their borders. However, the Scarlet Guard and General Diana Farley in particular were often accused of infiltration and interference within sovereign nations, attempting to encourage Red and newblood uprisings against Silver governments. The War of Red Thunder two decades later would bring those efforts to fruition.

Diplomatic maneuvers were also integral to maintaining a shaky peace in the eastern nations. The once Queen of the Rift, Evangeline Samos, was ultimately able to intervene on behalf of Montfort and the Nortan States. She treated with Queen Cenra and her successor, Queen Tiora, several times over the course of the Dancing War. Together with the former King of Norta, Tiberias Calore, she was also able to negotiate peace among the former Silver houses still chafing under reconstruction. Premier Leonide Radis, a Montfortan Silver who was elected to the office after Premier Dane Davidson, was a stalwart ally to the Silvers of

Norta who gave up their titles.

By the time of Red Thunder, the Nortan States were largely settled, and therefore escaped much of the turmoil that gripped the Lakelands, Piedmont, and the territories of several Prairie warlords. Most notable in Red Thunder was obviously the Storm of the Citadel, an electricon mission to destroy the Lakelands' largest military installation. In an assault led by Mare Barrow and Tyton Jesper, the fortress was torn apart by lightning.

The Nortan States were not without their own troubles before and during Red Thunder. There were several Silver-led efforts to return a Calore to the throne of Norta, largely in support of Tiberias Calore's two children as they grew up. Both Shade Calore and Coriane Calore broadcasted their own abdication, renunciation of rights, and citizen pledges to Montfort several times, hoping to quell any conflicts of succession to the former Nortan kingdom. Ironically, Tiberias Calore was a general in Red Thunder, as was Mare Barrow, and both defeated the forces that were hoping to elevate their children to the old Calore throne. At present, the States are governed by a mixed council of elected representatives and military officials. Unlike Montfort, the Nortan States also utilize blood speakers—one individual elected from each of the three blood groups to represent their own. They are currently Jemma Harner of Delphie, Cameron Cole of Harbor Bay, and Julian Jacos of Archeon, representing Reds, newbloods, and Silvers, respectively.

Research into Silver and newblood abilities continues to this day in facilities across the continent, with Montfort leading the charge. The current premier, Nortan-born Kilorn Warren, prioritizes education, and thereby history and science. The Montfort efforts of discovery are the best funded among the organized nations. Most integral have been human subjects, specifically second-generation newbloods who have volunteered for blood testing. Clara Farley-Barrow is a name well known to scientists, as she is a half-newblood, half-Red observed nearly since birth. Her ability to teleport presented in her teens, which is considered a common age of discovery for newbloods.

Many breakthroughs have been made in the past decade. It is now a largely accepted belief that radiation from the Calamities caused many humans to mutate, with most dying off. Those who survived developed abilities over the course of generations and became the Silvers we know today. Scientists are also circling the general hypothesis of competitive evolution. They now believe that Reds were constantly evolving alongside Silvers, and the presence of Silver abilities forced some Reds to adapt abilities of their own for survival.

At present, the Nortan States, the Union of the Lakes, and the Piedmont Federation stand in alliance with the Free Republic of Montfort. All have democratic governments with equality of blood at their cores, unlike the Silver-led nations of Tiraxes and Ciron and many fiefdoms of Prairie. Some detractors accuse Montfort of empire building, as it appears to hold sway over the other governments. The balance of power has certainly shifted, and the remaining Silver nations strive to maintain peace with the Equal

Alliance. Some are making strides toward their own transformations. Tiraxes, for example, is introducing equality laws and representation for its Red citizens, while the Warlady of Fourskulls in Prairie recently married a Red.

Who can say where the paths lead, or how the scales may balance in another decade? I suppose I can, but that is my curse. To watch, to see, until the ending of all things. We destroy. We rebuild. We destroy again. It is the constant of our kind. We are all a god's chosen, and we are all a god's cursed.

—JON

ACKNOWLEDGMENTS

I'm not known for short acknowledgments, but I'll do my best. These were written on a plane during holiday travel, so they were done under great duress.

Thank you to the greatest hits, the people who constantly make this possible. Mom, Dad, Andy, Morgan, Tori, Jenny, Indy. Okay, the last one is a dog, but she's earned it. Thank you so much to all my extended family and friends who have supported me through all my excellent nonsense. I have a job and a life where it would be very easy to lose myself, and you make sure I don't.

To my warrior team—Suzie, Pouya, Veronica, Mia, Cassie, Hilary, Jo, and all of New Leaf Literary. To Steve Younger, guiding me through contracts and an increasingly adult life. To Alice Jerman, Kristen Pettit, Erica Sussman, Jen Klonsky, Kari Sutherland, and Kate Morgan Jackson, who ferried the Red Queen series from overwritten submission manuscript to a short story collection wrapping up an entire franchise. The HarperTeen family for their support, love, and genius. Sarah Kaufman, again, for covers that will never be beat. Gina Rizzo, Ro Romanello, and the entire squadron making sure the world gets to see what we see. This would never exist without any of you.

I also need to note my dear friends within publishing, constantly teaching, encouraging, and checking my dumb ass when I desperately need it. Thank you for your grace and tolerance as I plan distant writing retreats—Alex, Susan, Leigh, Soman, Brendan, Ally, Jenny, Morgan, Adam, Renee, Veronica, Sarah Enni, Maurene, and my dear Emma. To Sabaa, a constant since this started, we're all lucky to have you and your talent. I'm so happy we're in this together. And to any author who has ever tolerated me on a panel, I owe you a drink.

Special thanks to my agents, editors, and publishers across the world. There are literally too many of you to list, which sounds rude, but it's true. I never dreamed I'd write something published across the world; thank you so much for making that a reality. I've been fortunate to get to tour internationally, and the teams in the UK, Canada, Germany, Poland, Brazil, the Philippines, and Australia have been consistently incredible. Love to Andrew, JB, Alex, Lauren, Ulrike, Ewa, Ashley, and Diana. You are all brilliant and so accommodating.

To my creative inspirations and constants: George Lucas, Steven Spielberg, Kathleen Kennedy, Peter Jackson, Fran Walsh, Philippa Boyens, J. R. R. Tolkien, J. K. Rowling, C. S. Lewis, Mindy Kaling, George R. R. Martin, and Suzanne Collins. Wouldn't have made it without you.

I must, of course, wrap this up by thanking the readers who have come this far with me. I'm astounded that people read anything I write, let alone in the capacity required for a short story collection. There are no words for my level of gratitude. I have no way to express what you've done for me, or more important, what you've done for the maladjusted, ill-tempered, terrified, daydreaming thirteen-year-old I was. That girl had no idea what was in store. I write for her and I write for you.

Go break some thrones.

Help us make the next generation of readers

We – both author and publisher – hope you enjoyed this book. We believe that you can become a reader at any time in your life, but we'd love your help to give the next generation a head start.

Did you know that 9 per cent of children don't have a book of their own in their home, rising to 13 per cent in disadvantaged families*? We'd like to try to change that by asking you to consider the role you could play in helping to build readers of the future.

We'd love you to think of sharing, borrowing, reading, buying or talking about a book with a child in your life and spreading the love of reading. We want to make sure the next generation continue to have access to books, wherever they come from.

And if you would like to consider donating to charities that help fund literacy projects, find out more at **www.literacytrust.org.uk** and **www.booktrust.org.uk.**

THANK YOU

*As reported by the National Literacy Trust

Don't miss a moment of Mare's story . . .

Discover the entire internationally bestselling *Red Queen* series